From Senenmut and Yahmose
to the First Exodus

From Senenmut and Yahmose to the First Exodus

E. WILLIAM PETTER

The Shortest Journey is a Detour Series

RESOURCE *Publications* · Eugene, Oregon

FROM SENENMUT AND YAHMOSE TO THE FIRST EXODUS

The Shortest Journey is a Detour Series

Resource Publications
An Imprint of Wipf and Stock Publishers
199 W. 8th Ave., Suite 3
Eugene, OR 97401

www.wipfandstock.com

PAPERBACK ISBN: 978-1-6667-5182-6
HARDCOVER ISBN: 978-1-6667-5183-3
EBOOK ISBN: 978-1-6667-5184-0

07/26/22

To the St. Cuthbert Church, Houston, Men's Group

Who used my first novel, *From Havram to Abraham*,
in their study group, and whose enthusiastic
support inspired me to write this novel.

Recapitulation

The Shortest Journey is a Detour is an eight book series. In the first novel, 'From Havram to Abraham,' Abraham travels to Stonehenge, England, for confirmation to their priesthood. It was the world's only fact-based religion, relying on its authority to predict eclipses. There were two requirements: the first was to invent. His team invented the chariot and its short-length compound bow. The second was to discern something new about their religion. Abraham discerned that:

1. God is spirit, existing is a separate spirit world

2. God created this matter world at a specific time in the past

3. God is a God of love

4. God asks us to be His stewards for this world

Upon graduation, the Council exiled him to Hebron in today's Palestinian Levant. When Egypt deciphered the code for eclipse prediction, the Stonehenge religion was eradicated, leaving only Abraham. Through his faithfulness, using ingenuity in warfare strategy and tactics, and the power of England's longbow, his thirty men defeated the Babylonian rebels' thousand-man army and rescued his King and nephew. He became the founder of Judaism.

Prequel

RAMOSE'S OFFICE, EGYPTIAN MILITARY ACADEMY, INEBU-HEDJ

May 1484 BC

Senenmut paused in the door to the Dean's Office, Egypt's Military Academy. The Dean sat at his table, reading. Noticing Senenmut's presence, uplifted eyebrows preceded the Dean's lifted head.

Senenmut answered the eyebrow's question, "Father, I need to book passage to Waset for an interview for tutor to the princess."

Ramose's body tensed, his face hardening, his voice demanding, "No! Don't go."

Senenmut, impassive, stepped forward, handing a papyrus sheet across the table.

Amose Pen-Nekhebet, the tutor to Princess Neferure, is on his deathbed. Queen Hapshepsut requests Senenmut's presence to interview for his replacement.

Ramose first noticed that the Queen's counselor signed the note. Digesting the two sentences, his lips pursed, then exhaled in surrender, "You're right. This is a command, not an invitation." He held up his finger, forcing his son's attention. "I know I've said this before. Now that it is not hypothetical, it bears repeating. There is a reason the Academy is in Inebu-Hedj, five hundred miles from the capital. You are going to the Pharaoh's court in Waset, Egypt's political bulls-eye. There are only two reasons to go there: money and power. Money is the root of all evil and absolute power corrupts absolutely. Fifty aristocrats with varying degrees of familial ties to the

Pharaoh are continuously vying for power. The court is cutthroat. You have no political training or experience. If you stay in Neferure's nursery, you will not mix with the court's movers and shakers. You should be safe. Beware going beyond that."

Senenmut's shoulders raised, "But, Father, it's my chance to make a name for myself."

Ramose cocked his head. "What will a name bring you? Enemies more powerful than you are. When you were eleven, those three older students spent months harassing you. Eventually, they pushed you down and kicked you. I ejected all three that day.

"The three fathers stormed into my office demanding I reinstate their sons. I showed them the Academy rules prohibiting their behavior. The penalty was ejection. They did not care. Their sons were aristocrats, and you were a commoner. That excused their son's behavior. I refused. They went to the Pharaoh to demand he dismiss me. One was the Libyan Army Commanding General. Pharaoh backed me, dismissing the General from his post on the spot. It was only because I had Pharaoh's backing that I survived. Without that, I would have been dog meat.

"Let this be a lesson. Egyptians think we are ordinary commoner technocrats. That protects us. Aristocrats do not allow any breach into their closed society. They inherit position and power, and they zealously control it as a god-ordained right.

"But this assignment isn't hereditary."

"That won't matter. We are Hebrews; Egypt is not our home. We are sojourners; strangers in a strange land. As technocrats, we are safe. Aristocrats earn their glory by hiring superior technocrats. We do the work; aristocrats get the glory. The second you get glory, you put a target on your chest. If you get glory, you are buzzard meat. The aristocrat who should have gotten that glory will cut your heart out."

"But I can earn titles and wealth."

"How would a fat purse compensate for your life? No, son. Go with my blessing. However, go with wisdom and caution. Keep your head down. Don't become noticed at court."

Senenmut left his father's office shaking his head.

QUEEN'S AUDIENCE CHAMBER, WASET

June 1484 BC

Queen Hatshepsut stationed herself on her throne. Her svelte body displayed a twenty-three-year-old woman's physique in beauty's prime. She was five-three; but tall women had been common in Pharaoh Ahmose's bloodline for four generations. Her coiffured black hair glistened from reflected window-light, her poised manner displaying assurance and control.

A guard ushered Senenmut into Her Majesty's presence. At five-feet eleven, he towered over the guard. His upper body revealed the muscular chest and arms of professional soldiers. A one-inch vertical lilac-colored stripe sewn to the edge of his wrinkle-free shendyt kilt was his sole affectation. Approaching the dais, he bowed. "Senenmut, your Royal Majesty."

Hatshepsut, looking past his physique, unconsciously blurted, "Where did you get red hair?" Recovered her regal tone, she continued, "Sorry, people have probably asked that a hundred times. I have never seen someone with red hair before." Only after recovering composure did she realize he had blue eyes.

"It is all right, Majesty. I am used to it. However, I do not know where our red hair comes from. Red hair appears in our family every few generations."

"Thank you, Senenmut. I'd like to ask some questions to discover your breadth of knowledge." She switched to Western Semitic. "Are you ready?"

He answered in kind, "Yes, Your Majesty, I'm ready."

She switched to Eastern Semitic. "Have you been on any diplomatic missions?"

He answered in Eastern Semitic, "Yes, Your Majesty, I accompanied your father and mine in Nubia."

She switched to Nubian, "So you were there when the army razed Kerma?"

He answered in kind, "Yes, Your Majesty, I was Captain of Archers for that battle."

She reverted to Egyptian, "You speak our principal ally's and enemy's languages. Do you speak others?"

He continued in Egyptian, "Yes, Your Majesty, I also speak Algerian and Mittanian. It is necessary to know your enemy's language so you may question their captured officers."

"My daughter Neferure will become Queen and God's Wife of Amun. The next pharaoh will marry her. What does that mean?"

"Your Majesty, to explain its meaning, I will need to give you the long answer. Before writing, a time so long ago legend has lost the details, our people lived in a Sahara filled with lakes and streams. Women, not men, led us. Each leader was both Pharaoh and High Priest. The gods blessed these women with divinity and gave them the land of Egypt. Succession of leadership and the land went from mother to daughter. The legend says you always knew the mother, but could not be certain of the father. That is why only the women's children inherit divinity. If a divine father wants his son to be divine, he must marry a divine woman.

"But duties of both Pharaoh and High Priest proved taxing, so one pharaoh transferred control of the secular state to her brother, keeping her religious duties. Your Majesty, you are God's Wife of Amun; the most important person in Egypt. More important than pharaoh. Your daughter Neferure will be God's Wife of Amun after you. He who would be pharaoh must marry God's Wife of Amun. Egypt belongs to her, not him. That is its meaning."

Hatshepsut kept a straight face. She had not heard of this legend. *Did it reflect reality? I must check with the priests. From his matter-of-fact tone, he believes I already know. If true, I should know, but do not. How does this commoner know more about history and religion than I do? He is a soldier, not a priest.*

Hatshepsut continued, "One last question. What is the difference between men and women?"

"Your Majesty, this is a question better asked of Amun. However, I will give you my limited understanding. From a boy to an old man, a man never changes. Yes, a boy cannot father children; that happens only at puberty when his voice deepens and he grows a beard. If you castrate a man, he will revert to being a boy. A man is simply an older boy. A woman is different. When a girl grows breasts, she can bear children. Remove her breasts and she can still bear children. She can never revert to being a girl. When she lays with a man, she changes again. She changes when she bears her first child. Her last change is losing the ability to bear children. Thus, she goes through five stages, and she can never revert to an earlier stage. She never loses the girl within her, but she can never revert to being that girl. This is the difference."

Who is this man? He is intriguing. My question had many answers precisely because I wanted to discover his depth of knowledge. However, he did not give an answer from knowledge; he answered from wisdom. I have never met so young a man with this depth of wisdom. Many regard him as one of the three wisest men in Egypt. One question remains: can he teach a young girl or can he only talk to adults?

"Let's visit my daughter, Neferure."

Hatshepsut's Captain of the Guard interrupted, "Your Majesty, do you want him to carry his throwing knives into the nursery?"

"Throwing knives?" she asked.

"Yes, Your Majesty," the Captain replied, "He always carries a knife on each hip, and he consistently scores in the top five in the army in throwing competitions. We can always monitor him in your presence, but he will often be unguarded with your daughter."

Without asking, Senenmut reached for the hilts at each side, withdrew the knives from under his kilt and offered them to Hatshepsut.

Hatshepsut waved her hand. "No. He is not a security risk. Allow him to keep them. At worst, he will offer added protection for Neferure."

Hatshepsut led Senenmut and her guards to the children's nursery. Opening a door, there was a girl of perhaps six or seven—she had both front teeth—on the floor playing dolls with one of her nurses. She looked up, her face beaming. "Mommy." She jumped up and ran into Hatshepsut's arms.

After a hug, Hatshepsut took her hand, and they turned to Senenmut. "Honey, I'd like you to meet Senenmut."

He dropped to one knee, so he looked level with her eyes. "I'm glad to meet you. I have heard so much about you. May I ask you a question?"

She nodded.

"Your mother is thinking about adopting me. Would you like an adopted uncle?" He raised his eyebrows into a question.

"I never had an uncle. I only had a cousin, Amenmose. He died."

"I could be your uncle in his place, but only if you want one. Would you like an adopted uncle?"

"I think I would. You are much nicer than the son of my cousin is. He's mean and nasty." She turned her head, looking at her mother, "Mommy, could we adopt Uncle Senenmut?"

Hatshepsut had been following the conversation. She noticed Senenmut go to one knee. This meant he was not looking down at her, softening any imposing feelings for a child who does not know you. Next, he asked her what she wanted; he did not tell her what she would get. That gave her a feeling of power and removed any residual anxiety the child might have felt. Yes, if he could gain her daughter's trust in their first minutes, her last questions dissolved. "Yes, honey, we can adopt him." Turning to look at Senenmut, she asked, "You're now her adopted uncle. When can you start?"

"Well, I'm a bachelor and I brought my belongings." He nodded his head at Neferure, "and I think I've already started."

He turned to Neferure. "If I'm your favorite adopted uncle, you need to know my nickname." He leaned over, put his hand beside his mouth and whispered, "Kyky."

Her eyebrows shot up in amazement. "Your nickname is 'monkey?'"

"Yes," and he reached up to grab a lock of his hair, "It's because of my red hair."

"Is it real?" she asked.

"Yes, would you like to feel it?"

She nodded, tentatively touching it, running her fingers through his hair.

He waited a few seconds. "Now, if you're going to adopt me, I'll need to know your nickname."

She puffed out her chest, "Mine's Tahemet."

'Queeny,' fitting nickname for a princess, he thought. "I think that's a great nickname."

"Would you like to play with me?"

"I would love it," he replied. Turning to look at Hatshepsut, he asked, "Do you mind?"

Hatshepsut smiled. "No, it pleases me. Come see me when you get a break. We have to talk about what I'd like her to learn." She nodded to one of her guards. "Stay with him and lead him back."

The guard answered, "Yes, Majesty," and moved beside the door.

Tahemet took Kyky's hand and led him to her dolls. Both sat cross-legged on the floor.

As the door closed behind Hatshepsut, she heard Senenmut say, "Now, you need to introduce me to your dolls. What are their names?"

Hatshepsut thought, *He is one of the most intriguing men I have ever met.* She carried a smile on her face to her audience chamber.

Three hours later, Neferure, Senenmut and her nurses had finished lunch, and it was time for Neferure's nap. The guard was escorting Senenmut to see the Queen. Senenmut was thinking, *I am accepted. I am important. I have broken into the royal coterie. I have created my destiny. I will get a title. I have arrived.*

BOOK 1

Senenmut

Chapter 1

Office of the Director, Smithsonian Museum

Present

Doctor David Scortun, the Director for the Smithsonian, called up a photo on his computer screen of the first six rows of signet ring impressions on the Ephod tablet, the new artifact they had recently put on display. He centered the eleventh in the first row and enlarged it, checking it against an email from the translator. It was the sole hieroglyphic impression. The translated name was Senenmut.

Senenmut, thought David. *I know that name. Where did I hear that name?*

He entered "Senenmut" into Google. The first entry began: "Senenmut claimed to be the chief architect of Hatshepsut's works at Deir el-Bahri. Senenmut's masterpiece building project was the Mortuary Temple of Hatshepsut."

Remembrance flooded into memory. *I studied that temple in archae-ology class thirty years ago. Probably the most famous Egyptian mortuary temple and most beautiful. The man whose very existence was erased from Egyptian memory and only recovered recently. Wait, something is missing. I seem to remember that he began his court duty with some other task.*

David reached for the Egyptian archaeology textbook from college days, and located Senenmut's entry. Yes, he had begun in the court as tutor to Neferure, Queen Hatshepsut's daughter. The famous black block statue with Neferure's head protruding from the top of the block, with Senenmut behind her. The oddity was multiple granite copies. No one had discovered why there were multiple copies or who made them.

This makes no sense, he thought. He opened Senenmut's first dozen Google entries. *Every entry portrays Senenmut as Egyptian. There is no hint of Senenmut being Hebrew. Senenmut's name on the tablet is in hieroglyphic, also suggesting he is Egyptian. Not cuneiform, signaling Hebrew. What is going on here?*

Then the critical issue became apparent and his thoughts slammed into a brick wall. The computer entries universally portrayed Senenmut as a bachelor. Yet his name appeared in the unbroken line of Abraham's ancestry. *A bachelor is a dead end in an ancestry tree. How does an unbroken genealogical line of succession insert a dead end?*

David switched back to the Ephod screen and scanned Irving's translations of the cuneiform names. The tenth ring impression was indisputably a Hebrew name, but the twelfth was unusual for another reason. *Yes, his name was in cuneiform. However, the name was not Hebrew. Yahmose was half-Hebrew and half-Egyptian. 'Yah' was an archaic form of 'Yahweh,' used as part of a name–but 'mose' was Egyptian for 'son of.' What was a half-Egyptian, half-Hebrew name doing in Abraham's lineage?*

David felt another headache approaching and reached for his bottle of aspirin. *Ever since we received this Ephod artifact, I have felt like I am trying to fund Bayer aspirin production.*

After swallowing two pills, he thought about an indisputable Egyptian in Abraham's line of descent. *This investigation needs informed decisions on which knowledge fields need involvement. Therefore, I need more than my current passing knowledge of Egyptian culture, politics, and religion.*

Well. Time to wear out some shoe leather. I need to see some ancient Egyptian experts. Who? For backgrounding, I will probably need some symbolic anthropology, probably Professor Clifford Geartz. For understanding culture and politics, the best social anthropologist would be Professor Alex P. James. Last would be a philosophical perspective of Egyptian religion, say Professor Robert Rinter.

I need to set meetings so I can assign the proper tasks to the research team.

COURTLY INTRIGUE

Pharaoh's Court–Egypt's "African Savanna"

The African savanna's mantra: "Eat or be eaten."

On the African savanna, when carnivores are hungry, they select and kill an herbivore and consume its flesh.

In Pharaoh's court, the food for the ambitious is power. The court defines power by access to the Pharaoh, and Pharaoh is the supreme power. The ambitious in Pharaoh's court are uncontrollably ravenous–and they consume everyone blocking their path.

When carnivores on the African savanna have eaten their fill, they leave the balance of the kill for scavengers.

In Pharaoh's court, the hunger for power is never satiated. Small successes lead to becoming more ravenous.

On the African savanna, everyone knows which animals are carnivores and herbivores.

In the court, no one can be sure–an herbivore one day can morph into a carnivore the next. The gazelle can turn and eat the lion.

On the African savanna, herbivores form herds to survive.

To survive in the court, people must form 'alliances.' However, alliances are fictitious; only interests are genuine. Today's interests are subject to today's friend becoming tomorrow's enemy.

The African savanna is a dangerous place for an herbivore.
Pharaoh's court is a dangerous place for everyone.

Pharaoh's court mantra: "Eat or be eaten."
Pharaoh's court *is* Egypt's savanna.

COUNCIL ROOM OF THE GREAT TEN OF UPPER AND LOWER EGYPT, WASET

June 1484 BC

For a Council room, at thirty by seventy feet, it was not excessively large. Its purpose determined its odd shape. The dais was not along the thirty-foot wall, but the seventy-foot. Its gentle curve allowed everyone on the dais a clear view of the petitioner before it. Twenty-one chairs spaced at three-foot intervals. The entrance and exit doors sat in the center of the long wall.

Chair Nefer-Weben opened the meeting. The Great Ten of Upper and Lower Egypt sat on the dais; ten each from Upper and Lower Egypt. The plaintiff, Amunemhet, stood before them with his sister-wife Ast, wearing their best white linen. At five-three, his sister-wife Ast topped his five-two. To achieve every iota of height, Amunemhet always stood ramrod straight.

"Amunemhet, you are petitioning the Council to depose Pharaoh Thutmose the Younger and for Egypt to install yourself as pharaoh in his stead. You cite as evidence the succession sequence for pharaoh:

- First, a doubly divine blood man, married to the God's Wife of Amun.
- Second, a doubly divine blood man, married to a divine wife.
- Third, a divine man married to the God's Wife of Amun.
- Fourth, a divine man married to a divine wife.
- Fifth, a noble blood man married to the God's Wife of Amun.
- Sixth, a noble blood man married to a divine wife.
- Seventh, lacking an available divine wife, a noble blood man married to noble blood women.

"Last, you state you could not make a petition earlier because you were serving on a diplomatic mission to the Minoans on Crete. Is there anything else?"

"No, your eminence, I have nothing more to add."

"The Council has examined the evidence. We have found the following facts:

- First, both you and your wife are doubly divine, Amenmose and Neferibity, both divine, being your parents.
- Second, because Neferibity died before her mother Ahmose, she did not inherit the title of God's Wife of Amun, and thus did not inherit the land of Egypt.
- This combination makes you second in line of succession.
- Third, Hatshepsut has divine blood and is the current God's Wife of Amun, inheriting the title and land of Egypt from her mother, Ahmose.
- Fourth, Thutmose the Younger has no divine blood. Mutnofret, a concubine commoner, was his mother. However, he has noble blood, since Thutmose the Elder was his father.
- Last, Thutmose the Younger is husband to Hatshepsut, the current God's Wife of Amun.

- This combination makes Thutmose fifth in line of succession.

"These facts mean, if you had made your petition when Thutmose the Elder died, you would have the better claim. However, no one raised a petition."

Amunemhet broke in, "But I was on a diplomatic mission to Minoan Crete. I just returned recently. I wasn't here to . . ."

Nefer-Weben held up his hand to stop Amunemhet, who fell silent.

Nefer-Weben continued, "If you had made your petition before Thutmose the Younger's yearlong coronation ceremony completed, the Great Ten would have ruled in your favor. You would be pharaoh."

Amunemhet broke in again, "But I wasn't here . . ."

Again, Nefer-Weben held up his hand.

"But you did not. The Council understands you were not in Egypt. However, you had alternatives. You could have made your petition in writing from Crete. However, you did not. It is also noteworthy that no one believed selecting you as pharaoh was worth petitioning on your behalf. Last, the Council questions why the long delay; Thutmose has been Pharaoh for almost ten years.

"The Council questioned your motivation in waiting a decade to take action. However, that is now irrelevant. The coronation ceremony is complete. Amun has blessed Thutmose the Younger as Pharaoh, and Hatshepsut is God's Wife of Amun. Therefore, the Great Ten denies your petition."

Amunemhet's nose went into the air. He might have lost this petition, but he would not surrender. This battle was a minor setback; he would still win the war. Losing was unacceptable. He would inevitably win. His pride was at stake. The fact remained; he was the rightful heir to the throne of Egypt. He might face difficulties, but he defied defeat. He would become Pharaoh. Whatever it took.

Ast hung her head and dragged herself out of the Council Room.

ANTEROOM OF THE GREAT TEN OF UPPER AND LOWER EGYPT, WASET

June 1484 BC

Grandfather paused outside the doors to the Council of the Great Ten. *Like Amunemhet, the Council long ago unjustly deprived me of being the rightful pharaoh.*

However, Egypt's gods are righteous. They need me to clear their earthly path for their heavenly will to prevail. I may wait for my time to come. However, come it will.

How? Manipulation without realization. Never command; use gentle suggestion. Nudge here; pause there. The result? They believe they created the result. They block one another, knocking one another off the playing field. That clears my path.

STUDY, HOUSE OF USERHAT, WASET

June 1484 BC

As Nebetka entered the room, his voice, at a quick pace and high pitch, portrayed excitement, "I made it! I made it! I am a Sau Priest. Today they took us graduates through the Amun Temple library. It is more extensive than imagined. It has tens of thousands of spell scrolls."

His two older brothers, Userhat and Meriptah, had been discussing nothing in particular in Userhat's study. Userhat responded, "Finally, we're all in place. I'm on the Counselor's Staff for the Pharaoh."

Meriptah added, "I'm the Djat's assistant."

Nebetka finished, "And I have access to the kingdom's black magic spells."

Userhat concluded, "All the pieces are in place; we're ready. Thutmose, you do not know it, but you are dead."

Userhat paused, reflecting, then said, "Gentlemen, it's time," He stood up and stretched out his arm with his hand down, and chanted, "Pharaoh." The other two men rose. Mariptah put his arm, hand down, into Userhat's fist at the halfway point between Mariptah's elbow and hand, after which Userhat closed his fist on Meriptah's arm. Then Mariptah chanted, "Djat." Nebetka inserted his arm into Mariptah's fist at the halfway point between Nebetka's elbow and hand, and Mariptah closed his fist on Nebetka's arm. Last, Nebetka closed his fist on Userhat's arm and the triangle was complete. Nebetka chanted, "High Priest." Userhat continued the sequence, "All for one." Mariptah and Nebetka echoed, "One for all." They broke the chain of hands.

Anticipation in the air was thick enough to cut. If their smiles were any wider, it would dislodge their ears.

Userhat pointed out, "With Thutmose out of the way, there's only Marytatum and Amunemhet ahead of us in the sequence of order for pharaoh."

Meriptah added, "Marytatum is too old for the Council of Ten to approve him."

Nebetka observed, "And Amunemhet just enraged the Council with his arrogance."

Userhat concluded, "That means we are actually first in line. Our decade of preparation is ready for the payoff. Nebetka, go find that spell. We need to kill Thutmose."

ROYAL COMMUNAL TOMB, WASET

June 1484 BC

Khuenre held his body as stiff as a weathered oak and face hard as carved granite, resolve implacable. He watched as the priests carried his father, Weshptah's mummy, into the Ahmose extended royal family's communal tomb. Plain white linen wrapped the body. His father's meager income did not allow for his own tomb, nor even any grave goods beyond his simple embalming, his canopic jars and six ushabti. The priests laid his mummy beside that of his wife. Side-by-side in life, they would remain side-by-side in death. He knew they would survive the lake of fire and the scales of Maat, and would make the journey to Aaru. Eventually, they would reunite with their bodies at their resurrection and remain together in everlasting life.

During the long weeks of embalming, he had made peace with his grief. Man's fate was to die. Knowing they would return to everlasting life did not remove the sorrow, but knowing made the sorrow bearable.

However, the dishonor his father had suffered at the hand of Thutmose the Elder he could not and would never accept. Weshptah had served the army faithfully for twenty-five years. Finally, he commanded the Egyptian Army for the Nubian Campaign, only, on the day before the battle, to have Thutmose the Elder demote him and make Ramose the Army General. He reduced his father to the Infantry General for the battle. Demotion equaled exile and death. Afterward, his father's body had lived on, but his soul had died. He spent his remaining years as a broken man.

Ramose was not responsible for this outrage. He was a brilliant man, his strategy a stroke of genius. However, he was not of noble blood. Custom demanded his father be general and Ramose his adviser.

The battle's result? They slaughtered the Nubian army, but Thutmose allowed it to flee. Then Thutmose forbade the pillage of Kerma. Everyone knows a soldier earns a paltry salary; his wealth comes from pillaging the enemy's goods after conquest. First, Thutmose forbade pillaging. Then he gave no bonus or compensation for losing pillaging rights. Therefore, his father died almost penniless.

Khuenre remained riveted in place while the priests sealed the tomb door.

His steely face reflected the resolve underlying it. His emotions and thoughts roiled inside him. *Justice demands revenge. Thutmose the Elder, I should have inflicted revenge on you, but you died before I became of age. No matter. Your son, Thutmose the Younger, is Pharaoh, and by custom, he inherits your sins. He will pay for my father's disgrace and humiliation. Thutmose, you might be my distant cousin, but you are also my enemy.*

As he left, his mind promised his father. *By the gods, I will not rest until I have vindicated your humiliation.*

SANTORINI ISLAND

June 1484 BC

The Minoans gave the place two names: Thera was the volcano's name; Santorini, the name of the mountain ringing the volcano's sunken caldera. Santorini sported plaster-white buildings clinging to its summit and sides. Its mid-Aegean Sea location was the linchpin of their east–west and north–south trade routes. Its huge central harbor provided a haven from storms and raging seas, accessible only through two narrow, easily defended passages. As a strategic asset, it could house their entire fleet.

Its second name caused the concern. Thera was more than just land; it was also a volcano. Its central cone had exploded seventy thousand years earlier, leaving its collapsed caldera below the harbor. This remnant kept the fissures that build the original volcano. When the cone sank, the harbor water's weight had closed those openings.

After a rest spanning centuries, Thera yawned, awakening. Thera's blood–a fresh surge of lava from deep below–forced its collapsed veins to reopen. The water resisted the upward and outward pressure. In the fisticuffs between volcano and sea, the volcano always wins the first round. However, the boxing match never lasts fifteen rounds. It never results in a draw.

As the molten rock welled up through the volcano's ancient central conduits, it slowly cracked the brittle walls apart, forcing them open. Seawater slowly seeped through the conduit's cracks, softening the surrounding rock. Each time seawater met magma, it flashed to vapor. It was a terrible relationship. It starts steamy, becomes volatile and destructive, and slowly cools–the land's cohesive forces always degrading. As pressure rose and the lava climbed, fumaroles erupted in the harbor, signaling its torrid tempera-tures below. A few fissures emerged on land to allow their sulfurous content to drift into the houses.

As the fissures approached the surface, minor tremors, at first too faint to feel, intensified. The quaking ground sounded its alarm. In the central harbor, an island approached the water's surface. Santorini's inhabitants did not know what was happening, but they knew Thera was telling them to leave. They gathered their valuables and fled.

This was the first of four phases of Thera's eruption.

Chapter 2

Princeton University, Princeton, NJ

Present

Princeton University professors' offices lack the maze of some universities. Doctor David Scortun did not need the nameplate beside the opened door to know this was Professor Clifford Geartz's office. He recognized the man behind the desk from his trademark full beard with shaved cheeks, a tweed jacket, small checkerboard-style tie and suspenders.

David began, "Good morning, Clifford. Been a few years. Glad to see you. You ready for lunch?"

"More than ready." Clifford donned his jacket, and the two left for Misral, a local fine dining restaurant.

Clifford was familiar with the menu. "I recommend the burrata with basil and pesto."

"No, thanks," David replied. "If I'm coming to New Jersey or Maryland, I'm getting the crab cakes–with soft-shell blue crabs. You can't get good crab cakes in Washington." David sighed and explained his comment, "A few years ago, I went to the annual Society for Applied Anthropology Convention in Salt Lake City and made the mistake of ordering halibut. They do not know how to cook saltwater fish in Utah; it tasted like more like hell-ibut. Today, I intend to enjoy my meal."

After the server had taken their order, Clifford pushed back his chair and crossed one leg atop a knee. "OK, how can I help?"

David explained the Ephod artifact and its history. One-hundred eighty-seven signet ring impressions in the hardened clay tablet recording Abraham's lineage, spanning almost four millennia.

Clifford's eyebrows rose. "I saw the initial news release, but this additional information wasn't included–and it wasn't called an Ephod. You have successfully both revealed it openly and kept some evidence secret. You realize, of course, when you finally release this added data, it'll be a nuclear bomb in archaeology?"

"Precisely. That is why we are being careful with the research. I am an archaeologist, not an anthropologist. You could write what I know about anthropology on a postage stamp backside in large font. That is why I need your help. No one realized this degree of religious sophistication existed in 1750 BCE. Is this real?"

Clifford put his hand under his chin and thought, "Let me sketch what we used to believe." He reached into his jacket pen-pocket, pulled out a small tablet, and thought better. "No." He returned it and reached for a larger pad from his jacket's side pocket.

"Sorry, I'm a doodler." and paused as he wrote:

hunter-gatherer → pastoral → agricultural

Clifford continued, "We used to think that society developed from the simple to the complex as it developed from a simple hunter-gatherer lifestyle to pastoral to agricultural. As agriculture developed and the population grew, we knew that society's political and social control grew more complex." He sketched the next development path.

independent settlements → villages and hamlets → cities → city-states → countries

"We believed that formal societal control, and therefore political control and enforcement, didn't become necessary until you got to city-states. Until then, social pressure and informal control by clan leaders sufficed. We assumed that religion, which can also be a way of societal control, grew alongside increasing political control, not becoming formal until city-states," and he underlined:

independent settlements → villages and hamlets → cities → _city-states_ → _countries_

"We were wrong. In 1963, the discovery of Gobekli Tepe upended our world. It's a collection of multiple independent, yet related sites in one complex. Each site obviously had a distinct role. However, archaeologists can't agree with what each was. Another 6500 years passed before writing, and we lost its memory. Radiocarbon dating suggests the builders erected its various sites over a thousand years, from roughly 10,000 to 9,000 BCE."

His doodling done, Clifford leaned back. "Each Gobekli Tepe site contains stone pillars featuring carvings of humans and predatory animals. Some weigh nearly twenty tons. That scale immediately evokes images of Stonehenge in England. However, more time elapsed between building

Gobekli Tepe and Stonehenge than between Stonehenge and today. How did they quarry enormous pieces of stone, and cut them to size and shape with no metal tools? Each site's purpose appears to be religious. This is despite happening before we believed organized religion began. Put this into perspective: The builders erected Gobekli Tepe before domestic animals, agriculture, permanent buildings, written language, the wheel, and pottery. The only tools available were of rudimentary stone and bone."

Clifford let the weight of what he had just said sink in. "To conclude, anthropologists agree with archaeologists that Gobekli Tepe has changed our understanding of prehistory. Now compare this with Stonehenge Phase I and Phase II. The time is 3000 BCE and 2400 BCE, respectively. Although England had domestic animals, agriculture, and permanent buildings, it is still the Stone Age. The Mediterranean region had primitive pottery and the wheel. However, these may not have reached England in Phase I. In Phase II, most lived in hamlets of a half-dozen buildings. No unified government and no police force existed. Leadership was by local leaders, who had consent of the governed and enforcement by local civic norms. Despite this, the Sarsen stone building Phase II only lasted forty to a hundred years. From excavations on the plain beside Stonehenge, archaeologists estimate hundreds of people congregated every year to erect Stonehenge's mammoth Sarcen stones. The work was voluntary. Yet people throughout England and as far as the northern Scotland isles regularly took part. What they shared was a common culture and religion. The result? In any year, perhaps 10 percent of the population worked at Stonehenge for one to three months. They gave life to their common religion, heritage and beliefs."

David began, "Then that means?"

Clifford interrupted, "The take-home is religion did not begin as a means of population control, rather from a shared sense of community. It reflected who they were and what they believed. Further, it began with hunter-gatherers. It is too early for proof, but religion might have launched civilization, rather than civilization begetting religion."

Clifford leaned forward for emphasis. "For an overall summary of your data? Believe it unless proven otherwise. It's likely an accurate reflection of reality."

LOUNGE IN THE HOUSE OF AMUNEMHET AND AST, WASET

June 1484 BC

That night in their home, Ast sat on a divan, legs folded beside her. She could not climb out of her emotional apathy to perform her usual nålebinding.

Amunemhet paced the floor, arms flailing, furious. He ranted, "I'm the rightful heir to Egypt's throne; the Council contains a collection of idiots. I am going to Siwa to the Oracle of Amun-Ra. We'll see if Amun wanted that blithering idiot as pharaoh."

Ast remained silent. *My husband is wrong. The Council members are not idiots; they have some of Egypt's best minds. Nor is Thutmose an idiot. Yes, every farmer knows that, if you want a prize heifer, you mate the cow with a prize bull. If you want a dumb dog, mate the female with a Dalmatian male. Yes, Thutmose the younger is the product of two consecutive matings with commoner women. Strong on beauty, weak on brains. Yes, it diluted the royal bloodline. Yes, Pharaoh Thutmose has merely average intelligence–perhaps slightly lower. However, he is not an idiot.*

However, when her brother was blustering, he would not listen to reason. She would not even try.

QUEEN'S AUDIENCE CHAMBER, WASET

July 1484 BC

Pawah, the High Priest of Amun, entered Her Majesty's council chamber. "Yes, Your Majesty, you asked for me. I regret not coming sooner, but I was in Inebu-hedj."

Hatshepsut motioned for Pawah to sit with her on the dais. "Pawah, I need to know if what I heard was accurate, historic information. I asked Senenmut why it would be necessary for the next pharaoh to marry Neferure.

"He gave me what he called the long answer. He said a legend relates the Sahara used to be a land of many lakes. Women, not men, led our people as both Pharaoh and High Priest. The gods blessed these women with divinity and gave them the land of Egypt. Succession of leadership went from mother to daughter, and only the mother passed on their divinity. However, the duties of both Pharaoh and High Priest were too taxing, so one pharaoh turned over control of the secular state to her brother, keeping her more important religious duties. Is this true?"

Pawah paused, collecting his thoughts. "Your Majesty, he is correct as far as he went. I will give you additional information. Let us examine the topic for each of his responses. First was the legend of our people living in the Sahara at Siwa. That is true. Waset's original homeland was the oasis of the Oracle of Amun-Ra, close to the Libyan border. Why? You cannot worship the gods anywhere. They choose where to set up links between heaven and earth. You must go to a god's link to pray and worship. Pray or worship anywhere else and the god will not see or hear you. When it became time to move to the Nile valley, Amun chose Waset to set up his new home; that is why we live here. Other gods chose different places up and down the Nile. Their worshippers set up towns there."

Hatshepsut's eyebrows went up, "So that may explain why each of our major cities has its own city god. That god is the one they worshipped in the Sahara before they moved to the Nile?"

"Exactly. His next topic was the women leading our people. That is true. Because a woman led the people, the gods blessed her with divinity and the land. Only mothers pass on divinity to their children. The pharaoh must marry God's Wife of Amun; because Egypt belongs to her, not him."

Hatshepsut broke in, "I knew that. That's why my brother had to marry me to become Pharaoh."

Pawah nodded, continuing, "The next topic is the woman turning over political leadership to her brother. The legend says a leader–we have lost her name–surrendered her secular leadership. The title pharaoh did not yet exist. What Senenmut did not tell you is, when circumstances demand, Pharaoh is actually her title. Not his. When needed, she may reclaim it. In our history, women have repossessed both the title and power of pharaoh for Egypt's sake. Examples are Merneith, Niticris, and Sobekneferu. Note: every time a woman reclaimed the title, it was a crisis. However, there is a consequence to reclaiming the crown: If she does, she can no longer surrender it; she must be Pharaoh for life."

Hatshepsut's face registered surprise. "I didn't know that."

Pawah was silent for a second, and continued, "His last answer was only partially right. Senenmut said the woman kept her religious duties. However, she also surrendered most religious duties to the priests. Why? Like political duties, it was burdensome, but for a different reason. The background is that Amun cannot look into your heart; he can only hear your words and see your actions. So he does not know what you intended, he only knows the result. The gods demand hundreds of rituals. Each needs its unique set of words and actions. For example, for the morning offering, after we clean and dress Amun's statue, the priest carrying the offering enters the temple door. Where should he stop? At a particular spot? After a set number of steps? When he presents the offering, should he hold it waist-high, chest-high, shoulder-high, or eye-high? Are these heights different for a five-foot tall man than for a six-foot tall man? These are an example of myriad details a priest must learn and perform exactly every time. Amun wants us to perform his rituals without error or he will withhold his bless-ings. His attitude: if you do not care enough to perform the ritual properly, why should he care about you?"

Hatshepsut broke in, "So if Amun can't look into my heart, he doesn't know why I do something. It could be a mistake or intentional, and he can't tell the difference?"

"Exactly, Majesty. That is why performing the rituals without error is so important. As you can see, no one man can learn all the details for every ceremony. It takes ten years to learn the rituals each priest performs. There is no room for error; it is demanding and stressful. That's one reason for the large number of priests."

Hatshepsut shook her head, but said nothing.

"As you can see, Your Majesty, it is no small task to be High Priest of Egypt. That is why the leader assigned most religious duties to priests. There remain a few duties only God's Wife of Amun can perform. You cannot delegate these. Similar to a crisis where the woman may reclaim the title of Pharaoh, you may also reclaim the title of High Priest. However, your High-ness, as you can see, that is not practical for most God's Wives. Preparing Egypt's next generation of rulers needs most of your time. You depend on your priests to placate the gods."

Hatshepsut nodded understanding, but remained silent. She would need some time to assimilate what she had just learned.

Pawah concluded, "That's a more comprehensive answer. Does that satisfy your need, or should I go into more depth?"

"No, Pawah. You are correct. I have the answer I needed."

"However, Your Majesty, the question you asked brings up another is-sue. Senenmut, from everything I hear, is a knowledgeable and competent teacher on myriads of secular topics, and choosing him as Neferure's tutor is undoubtedly a wise decision. I am concerned, however, about his knowl-edge of the religious fundamentals Neferure will need to know and become skilled when performing her duties as the next God's Wife of Amun. There-fore, with your permission, I will conduct an examination to select the best priest to prepare her to succeed you as God's Wife of Amun. Would that meet with your approval?"

"I hadn't thought that far ahead. Thank you, Pawah, please do that."

Pawah rose, bowed, and departed.

Pawah had no sooner entered the grounds of the Temple of Amun than he asked a guard to fetch Khusebek.

When Khusebek came into the audience chamber, Pawah dismissed everyone else. When they had left, he said, "This is for us alone. The Queen has asked us to train her daughter in the rites and duties of God's Wife of Amun. Effective immediately, that task is your assignment. Begin an exhaustive study of the scrolls to ensure you understand and memorize every detail. Remember, she is only six years old. She will learn best by performing the rites in a playacting role. She is not old enough to understand the mysteries behind the acts; that will come later.

"However, training Neferure isn't your primary task. Your primary task is to be my spy in Pharaoh's Court. The Queen has selected Senenmut as Neferure's tutor, replacing Amose Pem-Nakheret. I have heard that he is a brilliant military tactician and an exceptional teacher, but I do not know this man. As a six-year-old, Neferure will ask him religious questions and secular ones. The Queen has already related how much he knows about what should be religious knowledge, and he knows more than we want him to teach. I have no quarrel about him teaching her any secular topic. However, he may not be knowledgeable about religious ones. We have to control what Neferure learns. If Senenmut intrudes beyond secular subjects, I want to know about it immediately."

"I understand, my lord."

The following day, Hatshepsut had just introduced Khusebek to her daughter and left the nursery. Senenmut asked Khusebek to go with him to the corridor.

Once outside the hearing of Neferure, Senenmut said, "I am glad to see you. I have been afraid Neferure would ask me a religious question. I have some religious knowledge, but I don't even know what I don't know."

Khusebek did a double take. Then he realized. *An interesting turn of phrase. Senenmut is saying he has limited religious knowledge, but cannot identify the boundary between what he knows and what he only thinks he knows. Sounds like a way of speaking only soldiers would use.*

Senenmut continued without pausing, "Without proper religious knowledge myself, I shouldn't even try to answer religious questions, since I could cause more harm than good. Is it proper to refer all religious questions to you?"

Khusebek's anxiety level evaporated. Khusebek did not have to win Senenmut over to his view; Senenmut was already there.

However, without Khusebek understanding what was happening, *Senenmut* was convincing *Khusebek* to be *his* ally.

LOUNGE IN THE HOUSE OF AMUNEMHET AND AST, WASET

August 1484 BC

Amunemhet flopped on the divan, his clothing sweat-stained, his face set in stone, his gaze sword-sharp.

Ast knew her brother and husband well. He had progressed through furious to cold cunning. She stopped her nålebinding. She recognized he needed to talk through his experience.

"Next time," he stated, his face sporting a wry look, "remind me that oracles never give straight answers. I asked an unambiguous yes-no question so I would have Amun's oracle to overturn the Council's rejection. Care to guess Amun's answer?"

Since he intended it as a lead-in and not a question, he did not wait for her answer, "'Thutmose is Pharaoh for as long as he lives.' Now, how to interpret that? First, I cannot use it to overturn the Council's decision. It is ambiguous. However, on to the real question. What guidance *are* the gods giving?"

He gave it ten seconds to sink in. "I've thought about it during my return. For two solid weeks, I have ruminated. Amun obviously knows I want to be Pharaoh. He knows the Council rejected my appeal. Further, by Amun's phrasing, all legal alternatives will prove fruitless. That leaves the illegal. However, which illegal option do the gods want? From his phrasing, I believe he intends for me to aid Thutmose the Younger in his transition to immortality sooner rather than later."

Now, Ast rose in her seat, her eyes widening. Her husband was talking about assassination.

Amunemhet continued, "I realized that if Thutmose were to die first, that would not make me Pharaoh. Marytatum has a closer lineage to Amose-Maritamon. In hierarchy, he would be first; I would be next. If Hatshepsut remained alive, Marytatum could marry her and be Pharaoh. If she died first, then Neferure would be God's Wife of Amun. Marytatum could marry her and I still would not become Pharaoh. No, there is only one option to guarantee becoming Pharaoh; I must encourage all three to achieve early immortality. The two women must make the journey first. That would make you God's Wife of Amun, and we're already married."

Now Ast was panicking. *All three? Nothing like this has happened in Egypt for hundreds of years. Is Amun asking her brother to wipe out half the royal house of Ahmose?*

LATER THAT EVENING

"Ast, I've rethought my priority. Before I commit to any illegal actions, I need to talk with Grandfather."

"I don't know why you always call him that. He's not your grandfather."

"I know. Everyone calls him Grandfather because he is the man you wish your grandfather had been. Do you know of a more knowledgeable man?"

"No, he's the wisest man in Egypt. The next two are Ramose and Senenmut, and you certainly could not ask them. However, that is exactly why I am worried. Grandfather is smart enough to detect your actual purposes from the fragments or nuances of what you say. And, as Djat, he has the power to act on his suspicions. Are you sure you can disguise what you're thinking?"

"No, I'm not sure. He might suspect my goals, but I am smart enough to avoid giving him anything to confirm his suspicions. I will say nothing that would be admissible as evidence."

"I would still advise against going. He is too wily. Remember, he might not deduce your plans, but if you make a future mistake, he can use this visit to confirm your motives."

"Ast, he already knows my motives. Remember, we share a misfortune of history. He's just like me; he would be Pharaoh if he had started life at a more opportune time."

Ast shrugged her shoulders.

Amunemhet knew that was her signal of surrender.

MARYTATUM'S HOUSE, WASET

August 1484 BC

"Thank you for meeting me, Grandfather," Amunemhet began. "I'd like to ask for your advice. As you know, I petitioned the Great Ten of Upper and Lower Egypt to remove Thutmose and install me as Pharaoh instead. I will not ask how you voted. Nefer-Weben admitted that, if I had been in Egypt at the time Thutmose the Elder died, the Council would have voted to have me installed, since I had the better claim. That decision did not convince me. It appeared to be man's decision rather than Amun's will. Therefore, I went to the Oracle of Amun-Ra and asked if he had intended to make Thutmose the Younger Pharaoh rather than me. If he had said yes, then I could accept it. However, Amun did not give me a yes or no answer. In hindsight, I should have expected that, since gods notoriously never give yes or no answers, even when asked a yes or no question. The answer he gave was 'Thutmose is Pharaoh as long as he lives.' How would you interpret this answer? What should I do next?"

Grandfather reached for his earlobe, circling it with his thumb and index finger, his signature sign of deep thought. After a minute, "You've asked what seems a simple question, but isn't. Because it is not simple, I cannot give a simple answer. First, unpack the assumptions behind the question.

"You asked if Amun intended for Thutmose the Younger to be Pharaoh. It appears as a question about Amun's intents. That is not the case. It is about the god's future knowledge. Examine it: You asked if Amun intended (past tense) for Thutmose the Younger to be Pharaoh (future event). Therefore, the question actually asks 'at a specific time in the past, did you mean for this future to occur?' The essential background: do the gods *know* the future or *create* it? If all gods knew the future, they would not fight among themselves to create the result they preferred. Fate would make fighting useless. Similarly, if any of the gods knew the future, the others would not challenge them. Therefore, the inference is that *no* god knows the future. That implies the gods *create* the future."

Amunemhet recoiled in his seat. Concepts like this had never occurred to him.

Grandfather continued, "Now examine Amun's answer. The first part is 'Thutmose is Pharaoh.' It is an unchangeable fact; you cannot alter its current existence. The key meaning is in the second part: 'for as long as he lives.' This says the gods have not determined how long Thutmose will live. Conversely, when he will die. Some gods want a brief life, others a long one."

Amunemhet nodded. "OK, I can understand that. But it doesn't give me guidance."

Grandfather corrected him, "Actually, it does. Your actual trip's question: 'What should I do?' Remember, gods in heaven cannot mandate the future; they can only desire it. Their human champions must carry out their wishes to create that desired future on earth. So, if the gods are disputing the future, it means their human champions must carry out their will."

Grandfather let that thought germinate, then continued, "How does this apply to you? If a god calls you as their champion, answer the call and obey the god's direction. The god will protect you. If no god calls you, wait for the result–whatever it is–and be ready to take advantage of the opportunity. Do nothing without divine intervention. If you enter a dispute between gods without divine backing, the opposing side's gods will shred you to pieces. You will die a tragic death."

Amunemhet nodded understanding and agreement.

Grandfather concluded, "So, to sum up, I can't answer your question because I would need divine guidance. I have none. I simply hope I have shed a little wisdom on what Amun was telling you."

Amunemhet nodded, "Thank you, Grandfather. You have been a great help."

Amunemhet had no sooner closed the door on his way out than Grandfather sported a huge smile. *That was not a small nudge. That was a large shove. It is only a matter of time before he knocks other players off the board, clearing my path.*

LOUNGE IN THE HOUSE OF AMUNEMHET AND AST

That Evening

On reaching his house, with delight tingling his voice, Amunemhet announced, "Grandfather proclaimed I am acting for the gods in trying to shorten Thutmose's life. It is time to get to work. I need to carry out god's will. I need to determine who's first."

Amunemhet had been so fixated on being a god's champion that he had not considered its ramifications. Now that he had openly stated it, his brain kicked into gear and he suddenly realized the obvious. "Of course, I need to remove the one with the easiest access. Why? The first's death will sound an alert. Everyone's security will tighten."

Ast raised one eyebrow. *What is wrong here? Amunemhet, you did not mention divine guidance shortening Hatshepsut's or Neferure's lives. It sounds like you are only hearing what you want to hear. Is there anything I can do to make you think through this again?* A cold, sinking feeling congealed in her heart. She allowed her head to shake slightly, recognizing the inevitable.

ROYAL CHILDREN'S NURSERY, WASET

December 1484 BC

The Royal Nursery was at the end of one palace wing. Its central corridor ended with an outside access door. Senenmut and Neferure sat on the floor, in the corner opposite the door to the corridor. A window on the far wall allowed sunlight. Two nurses were next to the window, talking.

Without preamble, Senenmut heard obvious danger sounds through the hallway door. In rapid succession, he heard the corridor's outside door slam open, the guard's shout for help, the sound of sandaled feet running, a grunt, and a thud. As a soldier, he did not need to see what had happened; he knew. Someone, more likely a group, had killed the nursery guard.

His military training kicked into gear. His feelings shut down. Feelings slow down or even inhibit action in the heat of battle. As a soldier, he had learned to damp down his feelings below the level of consciousness, so they would not interfere with what he needed his body to do. He would only turn his feelings back on after the action was over. Only then would he have to deal with them.

His senses became hyper-alert. He needed spit-second attention to his surroundings, so he could ask his body for split-second reactions.

There is a mantra in soldiering: your body needs to become a killing machine. It should become an extension of your mind; and separate from it. He had trained his body in the mechanics of motion of multiple different sequences of action, so all his mind had to decide was what sequence to execute, and his body could perform that sequence without further detailed guidance. His mind would not need to give his body movement-by-movement commands.

A leader's mind also needs to become calm, as if in a state of yoga meditation. Alert to everything in the surroundings. Discerning and evaluating everything happening without consciously having to pay attention to any single detail. An officer's every decision and action should be suffused with calm and confidence. Men's lives depend on their leaders mastering these techniques.

Senenmut went into soldier-mode. Their only escape was the window; they would never make it across the room in time.

Jumping to his feet, he spoke calmly, "Tahemet, get behind me. There's danger."

A calm leader instills calm in others, even when events would normally incite panic. Neferure crawled to the corner behind his legs.

His hands went to both inside kilt pockets, extracting his two throwing knives from their scabbards. Holding one hilt against his chest, his right held the other's blade resting on his shoulder, with the hilt behind his body.

The nursery door flew open and a sword, still dripping blood, led the way in, followed by the man carrying it. He took two steps, stopping to survey the room. Pointing his arm at Neferure, he said, "The girl's over . . ."

Senenmut's right hand flew forward. The knife appeared in the center of the intruder's chest. The man was dead before his nose hit the floor. Senenmut unconsciously muttered, "Never stand still in a knife-fight."

Two more men rushed into the room. One went left of his companion's body, the other right. Senenmut switched his second knife to his right hand and wound his arm up. Selecting the larger of the two men, he threw as the man rounded his fallen comrade. This lessened his sideways motion to the flight of the knife. It pierced his lung just to the side of the heart. He gurgled and fell, writhing on the floor with both hands on the hilt, every breath further cutting open his lung.

The last man charged the now unarmed Senenmut, raising his sword to give a downward chop to the head. The intruder expected Senenmut to retreat. However, Senenmut stepped forward, half turning his body. Senenmut's right hip hit the intruder on his left side and Senenmut stuck out his right leg across the intruder's legs. The intruder's momentum made him stumble over Senenmut's leg. Senenmut reached up and grabbed the wrist of the man's sword arm with both hands. He twisted the man's wrist, so the blade pointed down. When the two men fell to the floor, the sword blade hit first, ricocheting out of the intruder's grasp, and bounced several feet away.

The intruder lay sprawled and disoriented for a second. Senenmut was rolling even as his body hit the floor. He reached for the sword before the intruder could react. Grasping the hilt, he swung the blade, slicing where the neck meets the shoulders. The blade sank an inch into the shoulder before hitting the backbone, rupturing it and severing the spinal cord. The intruder's body jerked uncontrollably and went still.

Senenmut got to his feet. Two men were unquestionably down for the count. He moved to check the one with the knife in his chest. A cursory examination confirmed this man was no longer a danger. His breath wheezed and gurgled; blood was surging into his lungs. He would not last long; Senenmut needed to act fast. Kneeling beside the intruder, he lifted the man's chest off the floor. Senenmut's face adopted an angry scowl six inches from the intruder's nose, "Who?"

The intruder gulped for air. "Amu . . . Amu," and he went limp.

A pleading call came from Neferure. She had her eyes screwed shut, reaching out to the air, "Uncle Kyky, hold me, I'm scared."

Senenmut walked to the corner where she was, picked her up in his arms, and hugged her. She clung to his neck.

"It's over. These men cannot hurt you ever again. Keep your eyes closed for a while longer. I need to stay here until your father and mother and the guards arrive. I need to tell them what happened. Do you want to go with one of your nurses or stay with me?"

She immediately answered, "I don't want to go; I'm safe with you. I promise I'll keep my eyes closed."

"All right, let's sit down and wait for Mommy, Daddy and the guards." He sat down and put her into his lap, keeping his arms loose around her so she could feel their comforting enclosure.

Action over, Senenmut allowed himself to recover from soldier-mode. However, it still was not the time to face his feelings about today's fight. He delayed doing that for now.

They did not have to wait long. Within two minutes, additional guards arrived, and spread out to take stations at the door, corridors and window. Thutmose and Hatshepsut arrived three minutes later. On entering the room, Hatshepsut called out to Neferure, "Come here, Honey."

"No, Mommy, I'm safe here in Uncle Kyky's lap; please come here."

Her response startled Hatshepsut, but on second thought, she understood what her daughter was saying. Neferure was not rejecting her; she was affirming Senenmut. She looked around the room at the three bodies on the floor, realized how frightening it would be for Neferure to experience, and understood why a six-year-old would implicitly trust him.

"All right, Honey, I'm coming." She walked over and hugged her daughter. "Let's take Uncle Kyky with us while we go to the Audience Room. Daddy will stay here."

"All right. Uncle Kyky can carry me until we're far away from here."

Senenmut carried her out and around the first bend. One nurse followed. Once they were out of sight of the dead guard in the corridor, he put her on her feet. "Would you like to hold Mommy's and Uncle Kyky's hand the rest of the way?"

"Oh, yes," and she reached up to take one adult's hand in each of hers. They continued to the Audience Chamber. Neferure played with her nurse.

Thutmose joined them in a few minutes. He walked straight to Senenmut, "I talked to one nurse who witnesses what you had done, and from the depths of our hearts, Egypt thanks you."

"Thank you, Your Majesty, but I didn't do anything more than you would have done if you had been there."

Thutmose smiled, "I think not. I am neither skilled nor trained. I would have failed; they would have succeeded. I would be dead. I remember one story my father told me from the battle of Nubia. After the Hebrew archers outclassed the Nubians, my father commented Hebrew bows were the most dangerous weapons he had ever seen. Your father replied, 'Sire, there are no dangerous weapons; only dangerous men.' Thank you for being a dangerous man. Please, always wear those two throwing knives of yours. I don't know how you did it, but I saw the results."

"May I speak, Sire?" Senenmut asked.

"Speak," he responded.

"Sire, we need to react rapidly. This was an inside job. He or they knew where to go. They knew when. They knew there was one guard. That is why there were three attackers.

"Before he died, I asked the lone man left, 'Who?' He tried answering, but only managed, 'Amu' before dying. 'Amu' is not enough to identify the perpetrator. A quarter of the men in Waset have names beginning with 'Amu.' We do not know who is responsible.

"Now ask: why kill Neferure? She is a child. There is only one condition where her loss could adversely affect Egypt. If this is a threat to the women's line of divine succession, there are three divine women at risk: Neferure, Hatshepsut and Ast. An attack on one suggests all three may face danger. Neferure was the first on the attacker's list because he believed she had the weakest defense.

"What preparations do I believe we should make? First, the perpetrator knew where Neferure would be. To counter that threat, we need seven identical nursery rooms spread over several wings of the palace. Each day, Neferure and I will go to one of them, but we will throw chicken knuckles to discover where we go that day. That way no one can plan where to attack because even we will not know where to go until we throw the bones.

"Hatshepsut is the current God's Wife of Amun. We also need the same preparations for her. She needs seven different sleeping chambers.

"We also need to protect Ast.

"Next; we need to keep the perpetrator in the dark. No attacker survived to report how close to succeeding it was. The perpetrator must believe the attack was an abject failure. That requires him to take more time and employ more men. That makes it harder and gives us a better chance of early detection.

"Last, we need Medjay around all three women, not Egyptians. Egyptians can talk or accept bribes.

"And I would like one last detail, sire."

He turned and called to Neferure, who came skipping to him. He kneeled on the floor and said, "I have an idea. You remember the cocoon a caterpillar makes to hide in while she becomes a butterfly? When the caterpillar is in her cocoon, nothing can harm her. What would you think if we made you a bronze cocoon? If anything happened, you could crawl inside and close the door. Then nothing could harm you. We could make a door on top so you could stick your head out to see if everything was safe. Would you like that?"

"Yes, Uncle Kyky; that would be fun."

"We'll practice until you can get in lickety-split. That fast. What do you think?"

"I like the idea." She turned to Thutmose. "Father, could you make a statue of me sticking my head out of my cocoon with Uncle Kyky behind me, keeping me safe?"

"Yes, we'll make the statue." Turning to his counselor, he finished, "Make everything happen. I am putting Senenmut in charge. Give him everything he needs."

Queen Hatshepsut looked back and forth between her husband and Senenmut. Thutmose was a gentle, kind man of barely average intelligence. If he had not been royalty, he could only earn a modest income. Senenmut was brilliant, brave, strong, and vibrantly male–everything women dream of looking for in a man. She looked again at her husband. Although he was a good man, she found him wanting. She looked at Senenmut and gave a gentle sigh. She knew he was beyond her reach.

As Senenmut left the Audience Chamber, he slowly allowed his feelings to catch up with him. His first reaction was relief: he had won. Then his thoughts rebounded to today's results. *Right! I have created my destiny. I am in charge. The world will dance to the tune I have created. I will tell the King's Counselor what to do. I am important. I will decide what the court will do. The court will obey my orders. I am now the royal protector. That is another title! On the statue, yes, she will be in front, but I will be behind her. The world will know my face. Immortalized in stone — forever.*

That night, he rewarded himself for the day's success by getting pleasantly drunk.

Chapter 3

Providence, Rhode Island

Present

Hemenway's proves that you cannot use table size to judge food quality. As the premier seafood restaurant in Providence, the atmosphere was questionable. A garish neon-lit stand-alone bar with a wall-length picture of the river centered on a sailboat just under the ceiling. Despite never having met, David Scortun easily identified Professor Alex P. James, Brown University's eminent social anthropologist. What distinguished him was not his thin frame with an almost military haircut; it was his sun-parched skin, revealing his Egyptologist pedigree.

They had steep menu prices compared with Washington, but David shrugged it off; the Smithsonian was picking up the tab. This was business. David zeroed in on the paella. Done correctly, it was a rare delicacy. Alex settled on the seafood casserole.

After ordering, the two men switched to the meeting substance. David started by detailing the Ephod artifact. He explained he was trying to understand Egypt's evolution as a state, especially its religion. Specifically, how might it interconnect with early Jewish beliefs?

Alex moved his chair back and stroked his chin a few times. "How to begin?" After a few seconds, he decided, "At the beginning, I suppose.

"We need to begin the story before Egypt existed. It does not begin in the Nile valley. Periodic climate change is natural; instability has always been endemic. Toward the end of the Qadan era, say 13,000 to 9,000 BCE, the annual tropical North African summer rain front moved 1000 kilometers north. This lasted until the Faiyum era, or around 6,000 BCE. During

36

this time, the Nile was a raging, uncontrolled river, prone to wild swings in water level and speed. In short, the Nile valley was uninhabitable. Instead, people lived for several hundred miles south of the ocean, all along the Mediterranean coast of Africa, which was then a semi-arid region with lakes and rivers, much like the prairies of America's west. For example, the same genetically identical crocodiles occupied rivers from Egypt to Morocco on the Atlantic. In today's climate, the rivers are so far apart, the migration distance needed would be impossible.

"Before the Qadan, Egyptians were hunter-gatherers. Starting with the Qadan, they shifted to pastoralism and there is evidence for grain use. Archaeologists dispute when it switched from harvesting wild populations to cultivation. Then, the climate of the northern Africa continent changed again. At the Faiyum, the rain front drifted south. The lakes and rivers dried to the desert. Concurrent with returning to desert, the Nile calmed into today's well-controlled river. Over 1500 years, the desert gradually forced the people into the Nile valley. By 4,500 BCE, their migration was complete.

"When the people were pastoralists, they had a common culture and common religious beliefs. Although we suspect there were minor differences between different clans, their attitude was to stress what was common among them. When moving to the Nile, they morphed into agriculturists. Now they 'owned' land. The emphasis flipped to stress differences. Gradually the differences magnified, so, instead of being cousins, they became enemies."

Alex paused, "If this is the people's story, we would expect their religious beliefs to mirror the culture–sameness punctuated with difference. As an example, a common religious belief was that, in the beginning, there was Nun, a vast expanse of a sea in lifeless darkness. To summarize, chaos. Emphasis: sameness. In Lower Egypt's Heliopolis, Atum created himself. Everything else is his emanation. In Upper Egypt's Thebes, the creator was Amun. However, he only emanated other gods. The material world was a creation. Emphasis: difference. Some gods fashioned, others caused. Ptah, the patron god of Memphis, spoke the Word, and the act of speaking was the method of creation.

"Now, you asked how these Egyptian beliefs might correlate to Jewish ones. Let us equate Egyptian beliefs with Judaism. Genesis 1:2 (Revised Standard Version): 'darkness was upon the face of *the deep* and the Spirit of God was moving over the face of *the waters*.' The transliterated word for deep is 'tehom.' The story's key: 'tehom' existed *before* God created the world. However, God created order from chaos. This story part of Genesis mirrors the Egyptian creation story. There remain story descendants today.

For example, in a burial at sea, the words said as the body enters the ocean are 'we consign the body to *the deep*.'

"In the creation story of Memphis, the god Ptah 'spoke' and the act of speaking created the various parts of the cosmos. What is striking is Judaism's likeness. In Genesis, God *spoke* the various parts of the cosmos into being. What could explain this likeness between Egyptian and Hebrew beliefs? When Pharaoh released Joseph from prison and made him second in command, a Hyksos was Pharaoh.

"Traditionally, the pharaoh ruled from Waset, modern Thebes, hundreds of miles to the south. However, the Hyksos never conquered Upper Egypt. Their capital was Memphis, where Ptah was the patron god. When Joseph became vizier and moved his Hebrew clan to Egypt, he settled them in the delta near Memphis. Following this logic, how does the Bible say the act of creation happened? By *speaking* the word, as Ptah did. Coincidence? Since there is no surviving documentary evidence, I do not know. However, it is intriguing. Does that answer your question?

"Yes," replied David. That gives a likely account. I agree with you. We may never know for sure, but it is fascinating."

Just then, the server brought their food.

David suggested, "What say we continue after lunch? The food looks too good to let it get cold."

"Excellent suggestion."

The food proved as advertised; Hemenway's would be a five-star restaurant anywhere. David had come to Providence for the story. He came to Hemenway's for the food. It did not disappoint.

ROYAL CHILDREN'S NURSERY, WASET

December 1484 BC

Tahemet looked up from her doll. "Uncle Kyky, yesterday you used a word I've never heard before. What's a Medjay?"

Senenmut hung his head and took a deep breath. *I can explain it to an adult, but how can I do it for a six-year-old?* After a second, he lifted his head. "Tahemet, that's a good question. However, Medjay has multiple meanings. Originally, Medjay was the name for a Sahara tribe of goat and sheep herders. Because of severe desert heat and water scarcity, they often became mercenaries to make a living. We hired them for jobs where Egyptians may not be reliable, like bodyguards. What made Medjay valuable was they were fiercely loyal. They preferred death before betraying that trust. They were the most reliable bodyguards. However, overtime the tribe shrank, and to-day it no longer exists.

"But the name continued. Other tribes of foreigners proved as good as Medjay, so we hired them, but we also called them by the old tribe's name. Today we call all trustworthy foreign mercenaries Medjay."

"All?"

"Yes. I will hire a group of mercenaries Egyptians call Hapiru. How-ever, that name actually has a different meaning; it refers to any person who sells their labor. However, we call this tribe Haibrw. They call themselves Hebrew. When I was with your grandfather in the Nubian Campaign, I commanded a detachment of Hebrew archers. They proved better than Nubians, and everyone had thought Nubian archers were the best. Not one man flinched in battle; they stood their ground. If they guard you, they will allow no one past them. You can trust them."

"Oh, so I'll be safe?"

"As safe as we can make you."

"Thank you, Uncle Kyky. If you say I'll be safe, I can trust you."

Yes, I understand your simple statement as a sign of complete trust. However, it also feels like you placed the weight of the world on my shoulders. An adult would have said, "Do the best you can," meaning everyone knows I am human, and humans are innately prone to mistakes. Your complete trust means I can never make a mistake–ever. That would betray your trust. Now, my good enough is not good enough. I must do better than my best. I must make you impregnable against any potential attack.

Senenmut sighed, straightening his shoulders. *So be it, Tahemet, I ac-cept. I will not fail you. I will devise a defense against any likely attack.*

HIGH PRIEST'S AUDIENCE CHAMBER, TEMPLE OF AMUN, WASET

December 1484 BC

After finishing his report on the events of the Neferure assassination at-tempt, Khusebek left the High Priest's Council Room. Pawah considered what to do for several hours.

Amunemhet, when you left the Great Ten Council Room, your haughty air suggested that you failed to accept the Council's judgment. Immediately going to the Oracle confirmed it. That was your mistake. You forgot that the Oracle's priest reports to me, and he told me what happened. This suggests you are the perpetrator.

Now, you force my hand. As High Priest of Amun, I need to remain neutral in secular affairs. In the other band, Neferure represents a religious domain. What should I do? What can I do? Before taking any overt action, I need to verify you are the perpetrator. Should I warn Thutmose? No. First, he knows the threat. Second, Thutmose is a secular concern. That is not my responsibility. The women are my concern. Should I tell Thutmose what I know? Not yet. I do not want to accuse a possibly innocent man.

Pawah sent for Ibebi. Twenty minutes later, Ibebi entered the audience chamber.

Pawah started as he had with Khusebek, "I need you to perform a special task. Someone tried to kill Neferure. Thankfully, it was unsuccessful. There are only three divine women in the primary line of succession for God's Wife of Amun. Hatshepsut is an expert in her duties. Khusebek is teaching Neferure. The third woman is Ast, wife of Amunemhet. We have never trained her in the rituals. I need you to take two weeks to refresh yourself so you can teach her how to conduct God's Wife of Amun duties. Remember, the proclaimed purpose is teaching.

"However, teaching is not the primary reason I am sending you. Recently, her husband, Amunemhet, petitioned the Council of Ten to depose Thutmose the Younger and install himself as Pharaoh. The Council rejected his petition, and he did not accept the disappointment well. He went to the Oracle of Amun-Ra and asked the god if he should be Pharaoh. The god replied, 'Thutmose is pharaoh for as long as he lives.' The assassination attempt happened shortly after his return from Siwa. I suspect he may be the attack's perpetrator.

"Therefore, the primary reason I'm sending you is to spy on Amunemhet. To kill someone of noble blood like Pharaoh Thutmose the Younger is a secular affair. That is not our concern. However, Neferure is of divine blood, and her divinity makes it a religious affair. Note everyone visiting Amunemhet's household and record what happens. If he is behind this plot, we will need to take action."

HOUSE OF AMUNEMHET, WASET

December 1484 BC

A servant answered the door and escorted Senenmut and his unit of nine soldiers into the atrium. Waiting there were Amunemhet and Ast.

If a five-foot two man could look down on someone five-eleven, Amunemhet's glare would have done it. Amunemhet began on a sour note, "And to what do we owe your disagreeable presence?"

Senenmut ignored Amunemhet's haughtiness, speaking in a professional, neutral tone, "Your Eminence, recently someone tried to kill Neferure. The Pharaoh believes it may involve a court intrigue from lesser princes. If someone were to kill the three divine women descended from Hatshepsut's mother Ahmose, the title of pharaoh would transfer to a lesser branch of the royal line. That means your wife, Ast, is at significant risk. The Pharaoh will not tolerate threats to the kingdom. Therefore, I have doubled the palace guards. In addition, until he can identify the perpetrators and bring them to justice, we must protect Ast. I have brought two units of Medjay soldiers–eight men and their sergeant. Two men will always escort her, except of course, at bath and bed. Then they will guard her door. I apologize, but the threat's urgent nature means only their sergeant Elpalet speaks or understands Egyptian."

Elpalet bowed to Amunemhet in respect.

Senenmut continued, "We have sent to Inebu-hedj for Medjay who speak Egyptian. I expect them in a few months."

Amunemhet crossed his arms, signaling an objection. "I have no place in my small house for them."

"Pharaoh expected that. He has confiscated the house of your neighbor and given him a new and larger house. The soldiers will garrison next door."

Amunemhet would not accept the soldier's intrusion lightly. "What if I don't want the soldiers?"

"Amunemhet," Senenmut replied, "I am sorry, but you have no choice. The well-being of Egypt is at stake. That makes Ast's safety of critical concern. The Pharaoh will build an addition to your house. It will have seven identical bedrooms. No one–including her–will know where she will sleep that night. The same palace preparations are underway for Hatshepsut and Neferure. It will be six months before we complete the additions to your house and the palace."

Amunemhet's face reddened from restrained anger, but he kept his voice level. "It seems I have no choice."

"You are correct; you have no choice." Senenmut's feelings wanted enjoyment, gloating from outmaneuvering the egotistical Amunemhet, but that would have been personal. He clamped down his emotions and continued with a professional tone. "If you would, please show me the house. Elpalet and I need to know the floor layout and the room interconnections to ensure his men can always go the fastest routes in case of an attack. We will leave the Medjay here with Ast."

Reluctantly, room by room, Amunemhet showed them through the house, but tried to bypass one.

Senenmut commanded, "Stop. What's this room?"

Amunemhet replied, "It's private."

Senenmut continued, "I'm sorry, but when the kingdom is at stake, there is no private."

Amunemhet let out an almost inaudible groan and opened the door.

Inside, on a large table, was a scale model of the private wing of the palace. It had no roof, disclosing every room and corridor.

"What's this?" asked Senenmut.

"I'm learning architectural design. I want to design the house Ast and I will move into before we reach old age. Pharaoh's palace is the perfect model. The kingdom's best architects designed it."

"I see," replied Senenmut.

They continued through the house until winding up in the atrium where they started.

Senenmut closed the conversation. "I apologize again for these actions, but they are necessary. You can work with Elpalet to make the soldiers' presence as discrete as possible, or you can assume a passive resistance. If so, it will merely increase your irritation. With either choice, the soldiers remain. With your permission, I will not take more of your time. If you need me, please work through Elpalet." Senenmut bowed, leaving unaccompanied. Amunemhet refused to give him the courtesy of showing him to the door, even by a servant.

Amunemhet allowed himself a hint of a smile. *Senenmut, you are blind. I outwitted you. You did not even understand what you were looking at. Just keep thinking the assassination was by a faction of the minor princes. Better, you even told me you doubled the guards–that means from one to two. I have four months, perhaps five, before you can complete palace renovations. I have enough information to develop a plan.*

The problem is that I cannot repeat what I have done before. Senenmut, I grant you, you can be a brilliant man. You will devise a defense for every attack I have tried, so that method will be ineffectual. I must invent more deadly methods of attack.

SENENMUT'S ANTECHAMBER

A Few Days Later

Elpalet was standing in Senenmut's small antechamber, giving his daily report. Elpalet said, "It is what you expected, Senenmut. Sometime between yesterday and today, the palace model has disappeared from Amunemhet's house."

When Elpalet had left, Senenmut allowed himself a smile. *Architecture? I am no fool. Someone with an ego like yours does not study menial tasks below their station in life. Menial work is beneath your dignity. If you were truthful, it would have included palace plumbing—and it did not. However, it is ideal for attack planning and approach instruction.*

The former presence, and now disappearance, of that model suggests you are, at least, a perpetrator. Given your ego, if you are, you will not stop. You will try again before palace construction is complete, so the countdown to the next attack has started.

However, I cannot assume—I need enough proof to convince a court. How to get it?

I have one advantage: you are more clever than smart.

Now, I need to list every new weapon or tactic you could use, then devise a defense for each. I must keep one-step ahead, thwarting anything you can invent.

I will become even greater than today. All I have to do is earn it.

He basked in the image of his expected victory.

KHUENRE'S HOUSE, WASET

December 1484 BC

I could always slip a knife into Thutmose's ribs, but they would catch me.

If I want to survive, I must do it through stealth. No one must be able to deduce responsibility.

How? Sickness. It will appear natural.

What sickness? Toxic epidermal necrolysis. It is rare, but I can pay the doctors to alert me when a case happens. Then, I can get skin samples and grow the sickness. Then bide my time until my chance appears. I may wait, but waiting will prove worthwhile. The disease is deadly. Better yet, excruciatingly painful. I will enjoy watching the effects most of all.

Revenge is sweetest when served cold. On a plate of pain with a garnish of suffering.

ROYAL PALACE PRIVATE WING, HATSHEPSUT'S SLEEPING CHAMBERS, WASET

March 1483 BC

The Plan needed a moonless night. Tonight was the last new moon night before the first palace renovations would be complete. The moon would not skirt the sky tonight. However, starlight still brightens the sky, especially when reflected off light-colored desert ground.

Movement attracts the human eye at long distances. Starlight enables detecting movement at a hundred yards, but there is inadequate light to identify what moved. Even if someone saw them, they still could not understand what they saw. Starlight provides illumination for identification for twenty yards only before shadows swallow everything. The men wore black clothing from head to toe to impede night recognition vision. The Plan accounted for limited visibility.

They were hyper-alert, freezing if anyone peered out a window. With no movement, there would be no identifiable threat. No one would sound an alarm. The Plan counted on it.

Seven shadows hugged the sides of the palace's private wing building, embracing the deeper darkness. They walked hunched over so they would not be visible to someone casually looking straight out of their window. They wanted no premature alarm.

Medjay protected the corridors outside room six. That prevented using the corridors.

Medjay patrolled between the buildings, but kept to a rigid schedule. Therefore, also a predictable timetable. The patrol had passed two minutes ago and would not return for another eighteen. It limited the attack's time window, but the Plan accounted for it.

The Plan was simplistic in its approach: enter through a window. They knew which window they sought: Hatshepsut sleeping quarters, the sixth window along this wall. It was in the Plan.

They counted the windows as they ducked under them. Three men ducked under the sixth window and hugged the wall on the far side. The Leader stationed himself directly under it. They were ready.

The sixth room had no lights. There was no visible movement. There was no snoring; no sounds.

On the Leader's hand signal, all slowly drew their swords.

On the next signal, the men rose, converging on the window. Then froze. The window had vertical bronze bars every six inches from top to bottom. A bronze frame mounting the bars surrounded the window. Hunched over, looking down during their approach, they had not noticed them.

The Leader tried yanking on the bars. They refused to budge. Ordering the men to his left and right, the three each grabbed a bar in the center, left and right, and braced a foot on the wall. On the Leader's signal, they pulled. The bars refused to budge.

The Leader rocketed backward, landing flat on the ground. An arrow protruded from between his eyes, transfixing his skull. He was dead before he hit the ground. The arrow had come from inside the room.

A commotion sounded around the corner. They could hear a corridor entrance door at the end of the wing open and slam shut. Six men, two with torches and four with bows, appeared around the side of the building.

Medjay, they instinctively knew. The torchlight brightened them. They bolted.

The Medjay already had their first volley strung in their bows. Taking firing position, they pulled back, aimed and released. Four arrows dropped three intruders. The last escaped before the Medjay could reload.

AMUNEMHET'S RENTED HOUSE

Thirty Minutes Later

The three survivors reported to Amunemhet, "Sire, it was a trap. First, there were vertical bronze bars in rooms five, six and seven. Then, less than thirty seconds after we began the assault, Medjay rounded the corner. Two carried torches for light and four had bows. Their arrows were already on their bowstrings, primed and ready. They expected our attack."

Amunemhet wondered. *The Medjay carried torches already lighted. Arrows already on bowstrings. They must have had advance knowledge. There is a spy! There was no forewarning of the Neferure attack, meaning the spy must be new. The only new person is Ibebi.*

He continued, "Tell me more."

"It was pitch black inside. Seeing was impossible."

Amunemhet interrupted, "But the arrow came from inside the room?"

"Yes, Sire."

"An arrow coming from the room means Hatshepsut was not inside. If Egyptian guards were inside, they would have used swords. Arrows mean bows–and bows imply Medjay. That means Senenmut had doors installed in the sidewalls from room six to rooms five or seven–or both. She must have entered room six and moved to a bordering room. Even if we had broken into room six, Medjay would have thwarted the attack before we could discover her location."

Amunemhet rubbed his hand under his jaw and pondered for a couple of minutes. His eyes narrowed as his emotions swirled down a whirlpool into vitriol. *Ibebi. You want to be a spy. I will show you what happens to spies. And Senenmut. Yes, you are wily; I will grant you that. This round goes to you. Perhaps I should have expected that. You are as brilliant as your reputation suggests. You also have a kingdom's assets behind you, and I do not. However, time is my ally. The next problem will be harder because the new building construction is almost complete. She will have seven identical rooms and even she will not know which room she will be in that night. I have to devise a method to reveal which room she's using. Then I will get her.*

His resolve hardened, Amunemhet's attention returned to the men before him. "They've outsmarted us this time. However, we will win in the end. You have done well. I'll contact you when it is time." Amunemhet counted out their money and thanked them. The men left and a few minutes later, so did Amunemhet.

ANTECHAMBER OF SENENMUT'S PALACE ROOM

Thirty Minutes Later

The scouts reported to Senenmut. "We followed the survivors to a building in the city. They disappeared inside. Five minutes after they left, Amunemhet exited the building. We followed him to his house."

"Thank you, men, you've done well."

After the scouts left, Senenmut mused, gloating. *Amunemhet, I now have evidence linking you to the crime. However, I do not have proof that you are the primary instigator. In case you are not, I cannot act yet. I need to get everyone. I also have none of your men's identities, so they could offer evidence against you. However, at least you are a conspirator.*

I have earned a reward. He reached for his beer jug. Lifting the mug into the air, he congratulated himself: *I won this round, Amunemhet.* The result was a morning hangover.

CHAPTER 4

Providence, Rhode Island

Present

David finally pushed away from the table. "This was incredible, but I just can't eat it all." Looking up, he noticed Alex had put his fork down and was waiting. "Would you like to add the rest in your to-go box?"

"I'm not going to say no to that," Alex smiled. "They give you large portions here, knowing most people can't eat it all. It's another meal, helping justify the bill."

While the server cleared the table and returned with Alex's food container, the two men resumed their discussion. "OK," began Alex, "the key is everything flowing from Egypt's worldview.

"Implicit in Judaism–and Christianity, humanity acts as God's steward. This world is defective. Our purpose is improving it. We will grow individually and corporately, becoming the people God desires. It is a forward-looking worldview. You can think of this world as a school and God wants us to graduate.

"Ancient Egypt's worldview was the opposite. This world was already as good as it gets. However, because the world began as unordered, the natural tendency was reverting to chaos. We must actively preserve its current state. Left unattended, the world becomes defective. It needs continuous maintenance and repair.

"Everything follows from these two perspectives.

"For example, in all major modern religions, hope centers on the future. Religion stresses improvement and growth. Present sacrifice results in a better future life.

"Ancient Egypt believed this life was already as good as possible. Why sacrifice your pleasures? The result? Egypt was a pleasure-seeking society. Enjoy this life."

Alex paused for a full minute, thinking, "Allow me to digress to complete the illustration. In the world's major religions, there are three commonalities.

"The first. In each belief, this life is a trial. An eternal result follows. In Judaism, Christianity, and Islam, this world is for learning and growth. On successfully graduating, you get the reward; you graduate to the place of perfection: heaven. In Hinduism and Buddhism, on successful graduation, you go to nirvana. In the ancient Egyptian understanding, on dying, and after waiting, you return to the place of perfection, achieve resurrection on earth, and live forever.

"The second. What happens if you fail? In Judaism, Christianity and Islam, you go to everlasting hell. In Hinduism and Buddhism, you experience the same result that happens if you flunk a grade in school. You repeat that grade; called reincarnation. In the Egyptian understanding, you cannot transition through the lake of fire and the scales of Maat, and your existence ends.

"The third. Who provides the wisdom, leadership, and guidance in each religion? In Judaism, Christianity and Islam, that is a rabbi, a priest, or an imam. In Hinduism and Buddhism, it is a sage. In the Egyptian religion, it was a priest. Think of them as a doctor or repair man.

"It's the same three basic ideas in all the major religions. Only the implementation details are different."

SENENMUT'S PALACE ROOM, WASET

March 1483 BC

Senenmut was lying on his bed, too excited for sleep, pondering his progress. *Three of Neferure's identical playrooms completed. Today's test worked well. The builders are finishing the first two of Hatshepsut's sleeping chambers. She will use them next week.*

I still cannot believe Neferure cajoled her father into making a black granite block statue for each of the seven nursery rooms. Granite–the hardest rock we can carve. Sent from the southern quarries. It must cost a small fortune. If I struggle to understand how a woman's mind works, I will never fathom a girl's. Thutmose might be a demanding general, but he is so much soft putty in his daughter's hands. Senenmut shook his head.

The immediate issue: I have to assume every defense I have used is now ineffective. Amunemhet will contrive a countermeasure to evade them. I need to continue inventing new ideas–stay ahead of him.

However, I actually need more. What is crucial is to prevent Amunemhet from launching an attack.

How? Could I change the soldiers guarding Ast into jailers imprisoning Amunemhet? That would cut his communication lines, preventing him from leaving the house and his accomplices from entering. I have evidence linking him to the Hatshepsut attack, but only deductions about him being the ring-leader, not proof. I need more.

To find additional evidence, I need research. There is always something in someone's past you can use; I need to find it. Time to wear out a pair of sandals looking for clues. I will start from his recent past: he returned from a diplomatic mission to the Minoans this past year. Then go backward to his birth.

I will start with Marytatum; he has been Djat for twenty years. If anyone knows what skeletons are in Amunemhet's closet, he will.

MARYTATUM'S HOUSE

Two Days Later

Senenmut began, "Grandfather, thank you for agreeing to see me. I need some knowledge about background history that I lack. Amunemhet left for Minoan Crete just before Thutmose the Elder died. I had always thought that a diplomatic post was for five years, yet he stayed in Crete for ten. Why?"

"Good question. You are correct; a diplomatic post is normally for five years. After four, Amunemhet wrote the Pharaoh saying the Minoans asked that he stay for another five, so Thutmose agreed. After ten years, he returned. However, our new ambassador talked to the Minoan government. They stated they made no such request. In fact, they had wanted to get rid of him as soon as possible. They complained about Amunemhet's attitude of superiority. They were also insistent on how much they had hated enduring his constant demands for favors–money and otherwise."

Senenmut's eyebrows pinched together in puzzlement. "That doesn't agree with what he told us."

"Precisely. That possibility occurred to me around six years into his tenure. What was happening? I did some cross checking. Egypt exchanges gifts with her diplomatic counterparts each year, including the Minoans. A portion of our gifts were in gold bullion, since we mine the gold from the old Nubian mines. Each year, the Minoans sent us a letter thanking us for the gifts. The letter detailed the gifts they received. There is one consistency. They reported receiving each gift we sent except for gold. The gold they reported receiving is consistently only three-fourths of what we sent our ambassador to give to them. Odd, isn't it?"

Senenmut evaluated the implications of what he had just learned. "That suggests Amunemhet was skimming gold. At the end of five years, he had not stolen as much as he wanted, so he asked for another five years. Is my summary accurate?

"Precisely."

"But, Grandfather, why didn't you do anything?"

Grandfather just smiled, "Senenmut, you're thinking on a microcosm level. I have been a Djat for twenty years. As Djat, you need to think of the entire government: the macrocosm. Your job is to keep the government running. There is not enough of you to manage details. Amunemhet's example is common. Only one in ten government officials care about what is best for Egypt. The majority go to work every day and put in their time, but never their heart. After all, it is not their money. If their boss does not care, why should they? Therefore, they do not. As Djat, it is hard enough to fix the broken parts of government and keep the wheels turning on the rest. If it works after a fashion, leave it alone. That happened with Amunemhet. He survived the inertia of government."

Senenmut thought for a minute, "That explains why he didn't make an appeal to be Pharaoh during those long years in Crete; he hadn't stolen enough money yet. He filed his appeal only after he returned. That makes sense."

"But Amunemhet didn't take history into account. I sit on the Council of Ten of Upper and Lower Egypt. I ensured the council rejected his petition. The vote was not unanimous. Some opted for the smarter unknown rather than the mentally challenged current Pharaoh."

Senenmut thought that over. "Thank you. I believe I know what I need to do."

Upon Senenmut leaving, Marytatum smiled. *Playing both sides is intriguing. First Amunemhet, now Senenmut. With neither being any the wiser. All I needed to do was to give a little guidance. Another player falls from the board. Things are going nicely. With everything transpiring in the court, it should not be much longer.*

GATE TO AMUN'S TEMPLE, WASET

April 1483 BC

Amunemhet waited for Ibebi to emerge from the temple gate.

"Morning, Ibebi, finished with your priestly duties this early?"

"Amunemhet. Good to see you. I had none this morning. I reviewed what Ast and I would practice; making sure I got every detail correct."

"Good. I had a thought this morning. I believe I have something to show which will interest you. Would you mind taking a detour on the way to my house?"

"If you think I would find it interesting, I am sure I will as well. Please lead on and I will follow."

The two made small talk for the fifteen minutes it took for the two men to walk to Amunemhet's rented building. Its living room prominently displayed the palace model.

On entering the room, the model attracted Ibebi's interest, but not being a regular visitor to the palace, he did not recognize it. "This is exquisite. What is it?"

"It is the private wing of the palace. It is a replica; every inch is eight feet, so the two hundred by two hundred yard palace wing is this six feet by six feet model. Everything is to scale: the rooms, hallways, doors, and windows.

"This is fantastic. I've never been to the palace's private wing, but using this model, I could find my way with no problem."

"That's the whole point. Let me show you." Amunemhet put a wooden block inside a room as a marker. "This is Neferure's original playroom. When the attack on her took place, the attackers came along this corridor to reach her playroom." Amunemhet changed the block to another room. "When the attack on Hatshepsut's sleeping room took place, the attackers went along this route to her window. However, she was not in that room. After they built this model, someone added a door from this room to a side room. Those aren't in this model."

As Amunemhet was pointing out the events, Ibebi's eyebrows narrowed in confusion. "How do you know all this?" Suddenly Ibebi's eyebrows raised in surprise. "Wait, you're telling me you are behind the attacks on the palace? Why are you telling me this?"

Amunemhet's face slowly morphed into a crooked grin. "I meticulously planned the attack on Neferure. Why did it not succeed? The only unplanned factor was Senenmut, who was a last-minute addition. Senenmut being with Neferure was bad luck. I can understand that.

"However, examine what happened next. Senenmut added side doors to Hatshepsut's current sleeping room and bars on all three windows. Senenmut added Medjay. Senenmut's countermeasures have proven how effective? Medjay reacted within thirty seconds of the beginning of the attack on Hatshepsut. Thirty seconds. What meaning do these facts suggest?"

Amunemhet waited five seconds for his words to take effect, continuing, "That means after the first Neferure attack, a spy has fed information to Senenmut. You are my only household change, Ibebi. It means you've been informing Senenmut about my plans."

Ibebi's face morphed in fright and he back two steps away from Amunemhet, "No. No. I have not told Senenmut anything. Pawah asked me to keep a journal of everyone who came to your house. That's all."

"Ibebi, that's enough. You told Senenmut; Pawah told Senenmut; it's all the same." Amunemhet withdrew a dagger from its scabbard at his waist.

Ibebi turned and ran for one of the two doors. On opening it, he found a man with a drawn sword standing there. Ibebi backed away. Turning, he found Amunemhet standing less than two feet from him.

Amunemhet's arm thrust upward.

Ibebi felt the sharp point plunge into his abdomen, up and through his heart. In reflex, he expelled the air in his lungs, slumped on the blade, and was still.

Amunemhet amazed himself. He had never taken someone's life before. He enjoyed it. Was it because he enjoyed exacting revenge for spying or for sheer sadism? He did not know and did not care. He only knew he enjoyed it.

As he was wiping blood from his blade, Amunemhet thought, *Pawah, so you want to play intrigue? I will get you as well. Why not? If I will kill Thutmose, Hatshepsut and Neferure, why not add one more: you? You are a conspirator against me; that makes you my enemy.*

That night Amunemhet directed his men to dump Ibebi's body at the Amun Temple door.

HIGH PRIEST'S AUDIENCE CHAMBER, TEMPLE OF AMUN, WASET

The Following Day

"What?" Despite the question's wording, it was not a question. Pawah had heard correctly; he could not accept that he *had* heard correctly.

His mind reviewed the facts: *Someone dumped Ibebi's body outside the temple gate last night. They murdered him. It could not have been a mistaken identity; he was wearing his priestly robes. It could not have been a robbery; everyone knows priests never carry money. They would have abandoned the body of an unplanned murder. No, someone advertised the murder by dumping the body at our gate. They wanted us to know they had murdered him.*

Pawah's nobility and connections had prevented hindrances from rejecting him becoming a high priest, but his mind had earned the position. *There is only one man whose means, motive and opportunity fit the crime: Amunemhet.*

Pawah's resolve hardened into a tight fist. *Retribution. You forgot, you cold-hearted fiend: no one can become pharaoh if Amun does not approve. I sit on the Council of Great Ten as the conduit for Amun's voice. Ibebi* will *receive his retribution. You will* never *become pharaoh.*

LOUNGE IN THE HOUSE OF AMUNEMHET AND AST, WASET

December 1483 BC

Amunemhet was sitting on his divan, chin on his hand, his eyes unfocused. *Why have my attacks not succeeded? Did the gods not give me their blessing to assassinate the royal family? Was I wrong in interpreting their guidance? Did Grandfather lead me astray?*

Yes, Senenmut's addition upset the first plan. However, Senenmut–as Senenmut–is not important. Some god or gods are using Senenmut to contend against the god or gods backing me. The other gods caused Senenmut to thwart my plans.

His mind settled on what he needed to do. *I need to go back to the Oracle of Amun and corroborate that I am doing what the gods have asked me to do.*

FIVE WEEKS LATER

Tired, bedraggled, filthy, Amunemhet returned. Ast was lying on the divan, feet curled beside her, her nålebinding set down.

He flopped in a chair facing her. "Ast, remember the last time I went to the Oracle? I asked you to remind me that an Oracle never gives you a straight answer. Guess what? Gods never change. I ask one question and the

Oracle gives me an answer I cannot decipher. It sounds like an answer to a question I did not ask. I do not understand what is happening.

"I asked a specific question, 'In trying to remove Thutmose, Hatshepsut and Neferure, am I acting on the bidding of one or more gods?'

"The Oracle replied, 'Attitude cuts both ways. Deprecation rebounds. The bastard will die three deaths. The first should mean thankfulness and contentment. Arrogance means a second of degradation. Extinction is the third.' Whose attitude? It cannot be Amun; gods do not have attitudes. Who is the bastard? Thutmose the Younger had a legitimate birth. What does it mean to die three deaths? If I thought Amun confused me with his first answer, I am perplexed now.

"But the question elicited a backhanded answer. First, by the Oracle not giving a negative answer to my question, I can safely assume I am acting to support one or more gods. Therefore, I need to continue the assassination attempts. Hatshepsut will be my next target. I have carefully designed this next assault to guarantee killing Hatshepsut indirectly, even if we cannot get past the Medjay to kill her directly. Either way, she will be dead."

Amunemhet continued, his tone coldly calculating. "But there is another implication. If I am acting for one faction of the gods, then Senenmut is acting for another. The other gods are enabling him to block me. That makes him my enemy. If he thwarts this assassination attempt, it means I will never succeed while he lives. So, if this next attack doesn't kill Hatshepsut, then I need to eliminate Senenmut before doing anything else."

Ast sat there. Helpless. Amunemhet was descending a staircase of destruction, and she could not see what waited at the bottom. Her fear was that it was a quagmire engulfing them both. She did not know what to say. Or do.

ROYAL PALACE PRIVATE WING, HATSHEPSUT'S SLEEPING CHAMBERS, WASET

May 1482 BCE

Hatshepsut called out, "Surero, could you please come here?"

The door opened, and a head appeared. "Yes, my Lady?"

"Please get a mug of beer and a warm loaf of honey date bread?"

"Yes, my Lady." The head disappeared, and fifteen minutes later, the door opened. Surero brought in a tray holding a cool mug of beer and a warm loaf of bread still steaming from the oven."

Hatshepsut said, "Thank you, Surero, please put the tray on the table. You can retire for the night; I won't need you anymore."

Surero walked along the corridors to his room, muttering, "room 4, room 4." He had to ensure he did not forget.

Once in his room, he took the candelabrum from the windowsill. It contained seven burning candles in a straight line. He checked his papyrus instruction sheet.

Room 1: X_XXXXX

Room 2: XX_XXXX

Room 3: XXX_XXX

Room 4: XXXX_XX

Room 5: XXXXX_X

Room 6: X_XXX_X

Room 7: XX_X_XX

The words "room and 4" were not on the papyrus since Surero could not read. It had pictures of hands holding up fingers.

He identified the number of "X" lit candles matching room 4. Remove candle five. Taking out candle five, he blew it out, replacing it in the candelabrum on the windowsill.

He had done this every night for three weeks, after Hatshepsut dismissed him. Each night, the candle pattern changed to match the room where she was sleeping. He did not know why he was doing it. He did not know for how long. He only knew Amunemhet had paid him six months' salary. At the end of the job, he would get an entire year.

An observer stationed a hundred yards away noted the candelabrum change. He shuffled through the seven sheets of papyrus he carried in his hand and selected the one that matched the candle pattern with the fifth candle quenched. Since he could not read, he never knew the hieroglyphs on the papyrus meant "room 4." He ran for the Amunemhet rented house and delivered the papyrus.

Amunemhet paid him, took the papyrus and went into the living room to the palace model. The assault commander and his team leaders were waiting. Amunemhet pointed out room 4. The Commander and his leaders quickly planned their route.

Amunemhet reminded them. "Remember, men, she won't be in room 4. Bars will cover room 4's window and those on either side. Medjay will be in room 4 and corridor; Hatshepsut in a side room. If you can kill the corridor Medjay, you will have her trapped. She cannot escape out through the bars, just as you cannot get in them. If you can get through the Medjay, bring back her severed head. Every survivor gets a five-time bonus. If you cannot, fight for five minutes, then retreat. Good luck, men."

He watched them as they disappeared down the street to meet their teams.

The attack party assembled and headed east for the foothills. Twenty-three men in one party could not avoid undue attention entering through the palace enclosure's main gate during nighttime hours, even splitting into multiple groups. They circled the enclosure and approached from the compound's backside. Collecting the two ladders they had stashed, one man climbed his ladder and peeked over the wall. No one. He waited until the Medjay patrol passed their location. They had twenty minutes before the Medjay would return.

The men scrambled up, shimmied over the wall, and dropped on the far side. The last man tied a rope on one ladder's top rung and dropped the end down the inside wall. For their escape, one man would climb the rope and pull its ladder up and over-the-top.

The men formed into their attack teams and hugged the building's shadows, approaching room 4 from two directions. Exact timing was critical. The Medjay patrol was a quarter way around the compound. Both teams advanced undetected. As expected, metal bars encased room 4's window and those on both sides, but the second windows on each side of room 4 were open and dark inside.

When everyone reached their assigned position, swords ready, the Commander signaled the attack. Each team's arsonists removed their lamp cover. Holding it at the windowsill, it lit up the room's interior. The sword-fighters clambered through the windows. One room contained a sleeping man; the other a woman. They dispatched the man before he awakened. The woman screamed before they could silence her. The noise alerted the Medjay.

One four-man unit and the leader of each team raced for the corridor, threw the door open and rounded the jam. They hoped to bypass any Medjay guarding room 4's door by entering the side rooms through the side room's doors. Senenmut frustrated their hopes. His renovation removed these doors and walled them in. There was no straight path to Hatshepsut; they would have to fight. However, just like Medjay blocking their path to Hatshepsut, they blocked her escape route.

Four Medjay waited for them–swords out and ready, two facing each team of five. The corridor was only wide enough to allow one man at a time to wield his sword. This forced each team to attack in single file. Five against two.

The second four-member team split in half, two men formed in the corridor facing away from room 4, blocking possible reinforcements. Two men remained outside the building, protecting their escape route.

The last two men of each team were the arsonists. One carried a bucket of bitumen and a cloth paintbrush. The other a sack filled with dry straw. One quickly spread bitumen on the sidewall nearest room 4. The other spread his straw along the wall. Then, he threw anything flammable from the room on top of the straw.

The sword fight began.

Poets and bards tell tales of each side's heroes battling for an hour, but words are not as fast or sharp as swords. Each individual battle rarely lasts longer than a minute. One antagonist will overpower the other with strength, overwhelm him with speed or skill, or take advantage of a fatal error. In three minutes, they had cleared the corridor of Medjay.

The Commander yelled for the arsonists. They spread their bitumen on room 4's corridor walls and dried grass along the wall's base.

However, if the assault team wanted their pay multiplied five times, they needed to eliminate the Medjay in room 4. The first man to try going directly into the room fell back through the doorway, an arrow in his chest. Two more tried leaping sideways through the doorway, only to discover Medjay on either side of the doorway with swords at the ready.

After losing three more men, the Commander stopped the attack. Almost five minutes had elapsed; they could not get to Hatshepsut in time to kill her directly. Time for the indirect method. He gave the signal for the arsonists to light the fire. The arsonists threw one more bundle of straw in room 4's open doorway, torched the straw on the floor and bitumen on the walls, and ran. They waited another half-minute, ensuring no one escaped room 4 until the fire blocked the corridor. The arsonists torched the entrance rooms and everyone went out the windows.

The compound was awake. However, there had not been enough time for the guards to prevent their escape.

The attackers raced for the wall. One man climbed the rope. Reaching the top, he lifted the ladder and lowered it on the inside. The survivors climbed the ladder, clambered over the wall, and dropped on the far side. The Commander went last. He hesitated at the top of the wall. Flames erupted through the building roof thirty feet into the air. He had hoped to hear the screams of the trapped when the flames reached them, but there had not been time. However, he smiled, satisfied with a job well-done, hearing Hatshepsut's screams in his imagination. She was already dead; she just had not taken her last breath. He dropped to the ground, formed up his men, and led them back to Amunemhet's house. He had lost eight men, but the mission was a success.

Amunemhet was content. He was standing on the roof of his rented house, enjoying the flames erupting from the palace complex. He also was listening to Hatshepsut's screams in his imagination.

He did not lose a wink of sleep over the sixteen men who would now sleep forever because of tonight's attack.

PALACE PRIVATE WING

The Following Day

The next day, Surero failed to report for work. Hatshepsut sent a servant to awaken him. However, Surero would never wake again; the servant found him with his throat slit. He could never testify who had hired him to signal which room Hatshepsut was sleeping in.

LOUNGE IN THE HOUSE OF AMUNEMHET AND AST

An informant told Amunemhet that Hatshepsut had appeared in Amun's Temple for the Nehebkau Festival. That surprised and shocked him. When he thought through everything, he realized Senenmut had planned for the one detail he had not considered. Hatshepsut had a second way out of the room through an escape hatch in the roof.

He scowled, fuming. *Senenmut, you are wily; you always block my plans. I can see the unavoidable. A faction of the gods is using you to block my faction's gods. That means I will never get Thutmose and the women until I kill you. So be it; you are next.*

Chapter 5

INTERLUDE

University of Chicago, Chicago, Illinois

Present

Doctor Scortun met Professor Bob Rinter in his office. Bob had the reputation of being the eminent American Egyptologist specializing in its ancient religion. Before shaking hands, Bob asked, "Have you tasted Chicago deep-dish pizza?"

"No, I've never had one."

"Then we're going to Lou Malnati's. It's Chicago's best."

"I thought Uno's was the best."

"Only if you believe their advertisements. Remember, we're going for the food, not the atmosphere."

Once there, Bob told David it would take forty minutes to get their pizza.

That surprised David. "What? Forty minutes? It never takes over ten at home. What gives?"

"What gives is a deep-dish pizza doesn't use tomato sauce–you put on whole tomatoes and bake them down. Believe me, when you taste it, you'll never complain about the wait again."

"You know, maybe that's not bad. It gives us time to discuss what I need to learn. As I understand it, there was no 'one' ancient Egyptian religion. How do I assign investigation teams to provide a report if there is no consistency among competing world-views?"

Bob surprised David. "The answer is both worse and better than you expected. What does that mean? When Egypt's written history began, we have thirty or forty city-states lining the Nile. Each one of them had a different patron city god. The relevant question: How did they coalesce into one kingdom?"

Bob thought about how to continue for a half-minute. "Let me give you an analogy. Think of founding the United States. The individual states began as charters. Each charter had boundaries marked on a map, but there were no border signposts. There were only wide swaths of land separating groups of small villages and towns. Everyone believed they were English-men first and members of the charter second. Overtime, local dialect distinctions emerged. The dialects were mutually understandable, yet readily identifiable. Think of a Boston dialect today. Bostonians delete 'r' where it belongs and insert it where it does not belong. Bob changed to a mock voice, "Time to pa-k the ca-, and go back to the drarwing board." Likewise, in Georgia, the drawl takes three times as long to say something. Returning to the analogy, everyone's dialects were mutually understandable, just painful for listening. As people settled on the vacant land, they bumped into each other. Reality required adjusting maps.

"Now, switch to Egypt. In 6,000 BCE, no one occupied the Nile valley; the raging river making the valley uninhabitable. In 4,500 BCE, everyone did. The old land of lakes had become an uninhabitable desert. 1,500 years equates to the time between the Roman Empire's fall until now. In 6,000 BCE we estimate from twenty to forty individual tribes occupied what is now the western Egyptian and eastern Libyan deserts, concentrated in and separated by their own separate streams and lakes. There were loose southern and northern congregations, united by a common language and culture, but already with different dialects.

"As the climate gradually dried, the individual streams and lakes dried up at different times. As each area became uninhabitable, individual tribes settled the Nile, growing and flourishing. Each brought their own patron deity. Gradually, they expanded their territory and finally bumped into their neighbors.

"Then regions coalesced to become nomes, what we in America would call 'states.' That created a problem: which city god had the highest nome status? Its companion question: what status did the other gods have? They solved that problem by giving every god a distinct job, mimicking human society. The result; the god's hierarchy resembled human society. Over time, however, that idea flipped. They came to believe people's society mimicked that of the gods.'

"This solution resolved a god's status within individual nomes. However, what happened when trying to combine nomes into the two regions of Upper and Lower Egypt? By that time, each region's hierarchy of gods had solidified. Now, status conflicts were irreconcilable. An example is the north's Atum and the south's Amun performed identical roles. Each region believed all other gods were their region's emanation. So, how did the Egyptians resolve the conflict? They never did; they kept both. Therefore, the Egyptian religion is a hodgepodge patchwork quilt slapped together willy-nilly.

"But Egyptian religious beliefs were even more convoluted. The god Heka broke all rules. The name was synonymous with magic itself. Heka meant both the god and the practice of magic. In Spell 261 of the 'Coffin Texts,' Heka had a primordial status. 'I existed before Nun, before the universe and before the other gods came into being.' Heka was the primal force present throughout the universe. However, the texts are very clear. Heka and Maat may have existed before Nun, but they did not create Nun. No stories relate how Nun came to be. In every story, it existed before creation.

"After creation, Heka sustained the world. He provided the power used by other gods to perform their tasks. They defined magic as harnessing the powers of Heka to achieve a goal. He did not create the world; he provided the power used to create it. Heka also provided the power to uphold Maat, the delicate universal balance of order.

"To ancient Egyptians, a world without magic was inconceivable. The gods created the world using magic. Magic continually sustained the world. It healed when one was sick, gave nourishment when one had nothing, and assured one of everlasting life after death. Its power animated the universe. For them, the world was magic's proof of existence.

"The means of harnessing Heka's power was the use of spells, usually comprising two parts: the words to speak and a description of the actions to take. Both gods and mortals used this method.

"Heka was so pervasive that he permeated every aspect of Egyptian life. However, he had no temple, no cult following, and no formal worship.

"So, to summarize, Heka does no work. He simply provides the power that others used to do their work. I know that's confusing, but does it make sense?"

"I think so. I am still wrapping my head around it. I had never heard of Heka."

"That's OK, most people haven't."

The server delivered their pizza. David discovered Bob was right. Malnati's was worth the wait.

SENENMUT'S PALACE ROOM, WASET

March 1481 BC

Ten men kept to the building's shadows. Two carried a ladder. Two men stopped in front of the door leading to the inside corridor. The rest continued down the row of windows. Reaching the seventh window, they spread out. There were no bars on any windows; Senenmut had not expected an attack on him.

Two men climbed the ladder onto the flat roof. Yes, there were escape doors to the roof from rooms 6, 7 and 8. Amunemhet had correctly guessed that was how Hatshepsut had evaded the last attack. They gingerly tried opening them, but they locked on the inside. No matter. If one opened, they could respond before someone could climb through.

Two men each took station on either side of windows 6 and 8. Amunemhet had warned them of this man's skill with throwing knives. Standing before a window would present an inviting target to Senenmut. However, if he tried climbing out the window, he would be off balance, a sitting duck in a sword fight.

There were two assault teams. Two men remained on either side of window 7. They would go in. The second team of two would go through the corridor door. Unless he was a heavy sleeper, they did not expect they would overtake Senenmut before he could awaken. However, Senenmut had only four escape routes. They had blocked all of them.

When the men on the roof gave the "start" signal, the corridor team opened the door and snuck down the corridor. They had practiced their timing to arrive at the count of one-hundred. The men outside duplicated the count. When both reached a hundred, they launched their attacks within a half-second is each other.

The team going in the window encountered a thin mesh of threads, invisible in the room's darkness, strung across the window. The threads pulled ceramic jars off a shelf, shattering on the floor. A thin thread connected the corridor door to another ceramic jar above the door. On swinging open, the jar fell to the floor, shattering.

Had Senenmut been asleep, he was awake now.

As expected, Senenmut was not in room 7. That was no surprise. The team entering the door moved to room 6; the one entering the window moved to room 8.

The shattered jars had another effect. It slowed the attack teams. When they reached the side rooms, they found no one. Under the bed, no one.

They examined the three rooms again–no one. Finally, they exhausted their allotted time; either escape or fight their way out through Medjay.

AMUNEMHET'S RENTED HOUSE

The attack team leader reported no one in the three rooms. Amunemhet's shoulders were a dejected shrug. Senenmut had outwitted him again. Like the women, he must rotate sleeping rooms.

Amunemhet thought, *Senenmut, how could you know? I do not know how you do it, but I need to discover how before I try again.*

SENENMUT'S PALACE ROOM

The attack teams were muscle men of limited intelligence. If they had average reasoning ability, they could have earned a legal income. It is usual for men of limited reasoning to search at eye level or down. Beyond a cursory glance, only a few look up. No one on the attack team noticed the three sleeping chambers for Senenmut had ten-foot-high ceilings, whereas the palace complex had twelve-foot high. Senenmut had used the time the broken jars had delayed the attack teams to climb a rope into a false ceiling, pull the rope up after him, and close the hatch. Amunemhet never gained enough information to detect the deception. He never discovered how Senenmut escaped. He was, and remained, frustrated.

WASET

April 28, 1481 BC

News spreads quickly. Thutmose II had an heir. His concubine Iset had given birth to a boy. They named him Thutmose III.

On hearing the news, Amunemhet realized it was time. They could not name the baby as heir yet; he was too young. However, if Amunemhet let events unfold, they eventually would. If Amun blessed it, he would lose his opportunity to be pharaoh forever.

It was time to act.

APRIL 29, 1481 BC

Clerk's Office of the Great Ten of Upper and Lower Egypt

The day following the birth announcement of Pharaoh Thutmose the Younger's son, Amunemhet filed a petition with the Council of the Great Ten. 'May the Council rule that Amunemhet, being of double divine blood of Neferibity and Ahmose, has primacy of place before the lineage of Thutmose the Elder.'

Although it seemed a straightforward sentence, it threatened to upset Egyptian society. If anything happened to Thutmose the Younger, it would make Egypt leaderless until the Council defined the throne's hierarchy of heritage.

THREE WEEKS LATER

Great Ten Council Room, Waset

Nefer-Weben opened the proceedings.

Pawah's hand went up immediately. "Gentlemen, we've adjudicated an earlier Amunemhet petition. This time, he did not ask Amun. There is no need to rush. I suggest we table this discussion for three to six months for guidance."

The Council approved the proposal. Perhaps it was prudent, but also, no one wanted to adjudicate it.

When all agreed, Pawah allowed himself an inward smile. *All right, you bloodthirsty fiend, now comes your penalty. At the next meeting, Amun will deny your petition. You will* never *become pharaoh. Ibebi, your retribution will come.*

STUDY, HOUSE OF USERHAT, WASET

November 1481 BC

As Nebetka entered the room, his voice, at a quick pace and high pitch, portrayed his excitement, "I've found it; I've found it!"

His two older brothers, Userhat and Meriptah, had been discussing nothing in particular in Userhat's study. Meriptah's voice responded in a dry tone, "You've found the spell to banish flies from the house?"

"I wasn't looking for it. I was looking for the spell to give you laryngitis and relieve our suffering."

Userhat chimed in, "That wouldn't be a spell; that would be a miracle."

Nebetka held up a scroll, from its color and tattered condition, obviously ancient. "I was looking through the Temple Library and found this. It is a spell to cast a wasting disease on someone. It's designed to kill an enemy king or general, but we'll use it on our enemy."

That grabbed Userhat's attention. His face beamed, "Thutmose the Younger?"

"Exactly," confirmed Nebetka.

Mariptah added, "Now you're talking. We have been waiting for this. However, remember that all spells contain a catch. What's the details?"

Nebetka unrolled the scroll and, using his finger to mark the fitting sections of the scroll, summarized the scroll's contents. "Start with one quart of water. Fill it with mashed barley seeds and let the broth seep for eight hours. Strain out the seed residue. Smash thirteen pomegranate seeds one-by-one. Accompany each seed by amputating a wax model of the target. Add a tongue harvested from a freshly killed cobra. Boil the mixture until reduced by half. The spirit of the boiling broth rising to heaven will attract the god's attention. Burn the tongue and seeds in a dried cow dung fire. Say the proper incantations to attend the spirit of the tongue and seeds as they rise to heaven, then douse the fire with the reduced malt. The spell must incubate for six months to become effective. After six months, the victim will decline. Death will come before the end of the ninth month."

Mariptah thought that over. "Something's missing. Where's the catch?"

Nebetka paused. "I saved that. Part of the spell's verbiage is that you have to use the victim's real name. The birth name the gods gave him, not his throne name."

Mariptah groaned, "We'll never know that. Perhaps six people in the world knew that, and five of them are dead."

Nebetka grinned, "And the scroll continues: lacking that, you can use something gathered from the victim's body to burn in the fire."

Userhat caught on, "Like a lock of his hair!"

Mariptah nodded, "Exactly!" He paused. "Remember Hentaneb, the girl who used to live next door? She works at the pharaoh's harem. She can work with the harem women to cut a lock of his hair while he's sleeping off one of his sprees."

Nebetka interjected, "There's one disappointment; the spell specifies that we have to have a persimmon that was picked that day. We'll have to wait until next year's harvest in September."

A wave of Meriptah's hand dismissed that suggestion. "A minor delay. We've been preparing this for a decade. What's a few months more?"

Userhat thought that over for a second, then said, "Gentlemen." He stood up and stretched out his arm with the hand down and chanted, "Pharaoh." The other two men rose. Mariptah put his arm, hand down, into Userhat's fist at the halfway point between Mariptah's elbow and hand, after which Userhat closed his fist on Meriptah's arm. Then Mariptah chanted, "Djat." Nebetka inserted his arm into Mariptah's fist at the halfway point between Nebetka's elbow and hand, with Meriptah's hand closing on it, after which Nebetka closed his fist on Userhat's arm and the triangle was complete. Nebetka chanted, "High Priest." Userhat continued the sequence, "All for one." Mariptah and Nebetka echoed, "One for all." They broke the chain of hands.

Userhat pointed out, "With Thutmose out of the way, there's only Marytatum and Amunemhet ahead of us in the sequence of order for the pharaoh."

Mariptah added, "And, Marytatum is too old for the Council of Great Ten to choose him."

Nebetka finished, "And Amunemhet has enraged the Great Ten with his arrogance."

Userhat inferred, "Meaning, we're next in line. We may have to wait for the spell to work, but all our plans will finally succeed."

The result was in sight, just not yet within reach. A satisfied feeling permeated the room.

CITY RECORDS CLERK'S OFFICE, WASET

June 1480 BC

Senenmut asked, "How far back do the records go?"

"Almost a hundred years–to the time of Pharaoh Ahmose," replied the Curator.

"That's long enough. I need you to gather all the royal line's records for Amenhotep's fourteenth regnal year. How long would it take?"

"I can have them for you tomorrow morning, after breakfast."

"Please do so."

CITY RECORDS CLERK'S OFFICE, WASET

The Following Day

Senenmut was waiting when the Curator arrived.

"Well, you're here early," the Curator observed. "I'm glad I stayed late yesterday to ensure everything was ready."

"And, I thank you."

"I can't understand why thirty-one-year-old records are important, but that's why we keep them." He led Senenmut to a table where he had arranged them.

Senenmut thanked him and began his review. It took two hours to find the document. He had not expected this result. However, this was why you checked everything. Its script was in highly ligatured and cursive Hieratic, which helped ensure it was genuine.

Senenmut asked, "Do you have a papyrus, quill, and ink that I could use? I'd like to make a copy."

On receiving them, he meticulously made a faithful copy, even duplicating the misspelled word. The Curator corroborated the copy matched the original, after which both Senenmut and the Curator signed their names at the bottom. Senenmut thanked him and left.

DJAT'S OFFICE, DJAT

Later that Day

On returning to the palace, Senenmut asked to schedule an appointment with the Djat at his first opportunity.

That night Senenmut rewarded himself. He overindulged. A morning hangover was an acceptable consequence.

DJAT'S COUNCIL ROOM

Two Days Later

Senenmut presented himself before the Djat. "Your eminence, I believe it is critical to locate a certain woman, and if she has died, to locate her oldest daughter. The court doctor during the reign of Pharaoh Amenhotep thirty-one years ago was Pentu. His daughter, Merti, was a midwife. We need to locate and talk with her.

"May I ask the subject of your investigation?"

"She was the midwife at this birth." Senenmut handed him the copy of the document.

The Djat scanned it quickly. Marytatum had not gotten the reputation of the wisest man in Egypt because of an inability to connect dots. Senenmut was right. They needed to find this woman.

"I'll put our men on it."

The document pleased both men. Each for a different reason. Both could see the light at the end of their respective tunnel.

HOUSE OF AMUNEMHET AND AST, WASET

July 1480 BC

The last time Senenmut visited Amunemhet and Ast's house, he was in haste. This time, he examined the house itself. The foyer was the first room on entering. Normally, a small anteroom for cloaks and accessories. This was twenty by thirty-feet. Hooks for thirty guests lined the walls. Each hook had unique identification symbols, so guests could quickly identify their garments. Minoan scenes frescoed the walls. Ships plied the water with flying fish leaping from the ocean.

The Minoan diplomat to Egypt had provided a team of painters as a gift to Egypt. These painters had originally put these scenes on Pharaoh's palace walls. After they had finished, Amunemhet hired them to reproduce the paintings in his house. Amunemhet's statement was obvious: *I* am the *rightful* pharaoh.

The foyer led to a garden with colonnaded walkways on either side of a rectangular pool. A thin bed of papyrus divided the pool. In the first half floated white lotus flowers, the second half blue. Senenmut recognized the imagery. Icon symbols for Egypt comprised blue and white lotus flowers (representing Upper and Lower Egypt) bound by papyrus. The pool proclaimed the owner of this house was the binder for Upper and Lower Egypt. This was pharaoh imagery.

This portion of the house was new, built since his return from Crete, but before the Council denied his petition. The house portrayed Amunemhet proclaiming himself Pharaoh. This display lacked subtlety; it was flagrant, ostentatious snobbery.

The extravagant display of wealth continued throughout the house. New plaster overlaid the older walls. The Minoan artists had painted every wall. Youthful athletes jumped over bulls. Bare-breasted women carried plates of food. Jeweled representations of bull's heads hung on the walls. Ornamental vases of octopus looked out at the observer. The frescoes alone would have taken the Minoan artists six months to complete.

Senenmut wondered: *Minor royalty received an income. However, this was wealth worthy of a pharaoh.*

Continuing throughout the house revealed Amunemhet had rebuilt, refurnished and redecorated all public rooms and all living quarters. Only the servant's sections and kitchens remained in an original shabby condition, sunlight trickling into one storeroom from an unrepaired hole in the roof.

In the back was a flower garden producing cut flowers for decorating guestrooms and family living quarters. Amunemhet himself tended this. One section for chrysanthemums was doing poorly, their leaf edges displaying yellow-brownish wrinkles. He bent down to feel the soil–the gardener had saturated it.

However, the leaves exhibit the symptoms of water-starvation.

Then its significance hit Senenmut: *The chrysanthemums are a masquerade! Amunemhet, I have you by the throat.*

That night, it called for a celebration–with its inevitable morning result.

DJAT'S AUDIENCE CHAMBER, WASET

July 1480 BC

The Djat's messenger told Senenmut to bring Pentu's document, rendering the topic obvious. Senenmut entered the Djat's Audience Chamber and reported. "Sire, you asked for me."

Marytatum motioned to an old woman standing against the wall, leaning on her walking stick. Senenmut gave Pentu's document to Marytatum and stood to the side. Marytatum asked the woman to come and sit on the dais ledge.

Marytatum used a soothing, supporting voice, "Merti, we need some information only you can provide." He handed her the document.

Merti said, "I'm sorry, I can't read. What does this say?"

"It is a newborn baby's certificate of death. Its name was Amunemhet. The reason for death was umbilical cord strangulation. The baby was dead at birth. Your father Pentu signed it."

Merti slumped, her head resting on her breast. She whispered to herself, "Thirty-odd years, thirty-odd years."

Marytatum spoke, "Merti, you are not in any danger. No one will accuse you of anything. We are trying to discover the truth. Can you tell us what happened?"

Merti sat in silence for ten seconds, gathering her courage. She needed to wrestle with old events pushed into her mind's dark recesses, now glaring in the sunlight. She sighed, raised her head and looked–not at what was before her now, but what was before her thirty years ago. "I had two births that day. The first was a commoner, pregnant out of wedlock, disowned, and evicted by her family. Alone, no support, not in good health, she gave birth to a healthy baby boy. However, she tore and bled profusely. I tried, but could not stop it. She died. There was no one who cared. I left the woman's body and took the baby.

"When I got home, a messenger from my father told me to rush to the house of Amunmose and Neferibity. I had nowhere to take the baby, and no time, so I brought it with me. When I arrived, I was too late. The birth had already happened; their baby was already dead. My father had just left. Neferibity was beyond distraught; my father having told her she had lost the baby. What should I do? The commoner's baby needed a home. Why not Neferibity? They would love and care for him. I presented the dead girl's baby to Neferibity, telling her we revived him. I took Neferibity's dead baby with me–no one ever knew. My father died a week later. I never told him about switching babies. I never knew that he had written the death certificate. I did what I thought was best for everyone."

Marytatum said, "Merti, you did the best you could. No one will blame you for that. Egypt wants to thank you; you have helped clear up another problem. Thank you. You may leave."

The old woman rose and slowly left.

Senenmut remained silent throughout the proceedings. However, his mind was in overdrive. He thought, *How to best use this information?*

That night, Senenmut rewarded himself for the day's success. It had been a long, uphill fight, but he felt the satisfied sense of accomplishment. Amunemhet was ready for the 'coup de grâce.' He reached for his jug; the following morning's headache was the unavoidable price he would gladly pay.

PHARAOH'S AUDIENCE CHAMBER, WASET

July, 1480 BC

Pharaoh Thutmose's empty throne sat on the dais. Senenmut stood facing it, while Amunemhet stood a few feet to his side. Directly behind them stood four guards, ensuring any bitterness would not erupt in violence.

The Pharaoh had sent for Amunemhet, but had not stated the reason.

When all were present, the Clerk rang a bell. Pharaoh Thutmose entered, took his seat and began, "Amunemhet, Senenmut, you are here as part of an investigation. The records for the annual diplomatic gifts Egypt sent to the Minoans and what they say they received do not agree."

At those words, Amunemhet's face turned white, but he preserved his composure.

"Senenmut, present the documents."

Senenmut began, "I visited the Hall of Diplomatic Records to examine the reports of Egypt's annual diplomatic gifts. We sent the Minoan gifts to our ambassador, Amunemhet. The Minoans stated what they had received in their annual Letter of Thanks. The Minister of Records and I both corroborated these copies as accurate." Senenmut gave a stack of papyrus documents to the Pharaoh's Clerk. The Clerk offered them to Amunemhet, who raised his hand, declining.

Senenmut continued, "I have summarized just the gold sent to the ambassador and reported as received by the Minoans on this sheet of papyrus. The details suggest one-quarter of the gold sent to Amunemhet did not reach the Minoans." Senenmut offered the sheet to Thutmose, who examined it.

Thutmose took a few minutes. He turned to Amunemhet, "Would you like to see the totals?"

"No, Sire, I trust Senenmut, so I'm sure the totals are accurate. It appears Senenmut is accusing me of stealing the gold. However, the evidence he presents cannot confirm that. For example, a Minoan official could have under-reported the gifts."

Thutmose added, "I agree. This evidence arouses suspicion, but falls short of proof. We need additional evidence."

"Sire, I agree," added Amunemhet.

Thutmose turned to Senenmut. "You suggested you had more information?"

"I did, Sire. I inspected Amunemhet's house as part of my duties to ensure Ast's safety. Since his return from Crete, it has undergone extensive renovations. A preliminary cost estimate suggests it needed over twenty years of his income. This arouses suspicion. I would suggest we need a

thorough examination of his house. A particular spot in his garden is unusual. The chrysanthemums display signs of water starvation despite the soil
being saturated. That suggests gold poisoning. For example, with gold ingots
buried just beneath them. Therefore, I suggest a search party exploration. I
will lead them and show where to dig."

At Senenmut's statement, the blood drained from Amunemhet's face
and his legs almost buckled. He remained impassive at Thutmose's order.

"Senenmut, lead the search party and show them where to dig. Report
to me when you have completed the investigation." He faced the guards.
"Guards, escort Amunemhet and go with the search party."

The six men bowed, turned and left through the exit door, finding the
search party waiting.

Senenmut led them to Amunemhet's flower garden and directed them
to dig among the chrysanthemums. At the first plunge of the shovel, the
sound of a thud revealed a hard object buried beneath. Switching from
shovels to trowels, the party soon uncovered a trove of gold bars. Each bar
bore Pharaoh's official stamp, marked as belonging to the Pharaoh when
processed at the Nubian mines. Each also bore a Minoan gift stamp.

Senenmut left the digging party to uncover more bars and took Amunemhet and the guards back to the Pharaoh's Audience Chamber, where they
reported their return to the Clerk. The Pharaoh appeared five minutes later,
asking Senenmut to make his report.

"Sire. We have uncovered evidence of illegality in Amunemhet's garden. Here is a gold bar we found hidden under his flowers." He handed a
bar to Thutmose. "As you can see, sire, your Nubian mine produced the
bar. It bears your manufacturing stamp. It also bears a stamp labeling it as
a Minoan gift."

Thutmose examined the bar. "Amunemhet, this is clear and convincing evidence of a crime against Egypt. It warrants the death sentence. However, you are divine, so I cannot kill you. I sentence you to house arrest until
further notice. You are to receive no one but your wife and servants. The
work in your garden will continue, and I will issue a final sentence when the
search is complete."

Thutmose addressed the guards. "Escort him to his house. I will reinforce your party and set up procedures. Two of you are to attend him,
including meals, bathing, sleep and sex. Without my permission, he is to see
no one except Ast, his wife and his servants. Carry out your orders."

The four guards surrounded Amunemhet and marched him out of the
Audience Chamber.

LOUNGE IN THE HOUSE OF AMUNEMHET AND AST

Later that Day

Amunemhet sat, scowled and seethed.

They have stolen my money. They have discovered and confiscated my main gold horde. They have confiscated all my valuable ornaments. If it were not for Ast, they would have confiscated my house. I am no longer wealthy.

However, I am not a pauper. They have not discovered my emergency stash.

I am under house arrest–for life.

I have one alternative to escape lifelong humiliation. I must become Pharaoh. Pharaoh is above the law.

I have two alternatives to become Pharaoh. One is legal: to convince the Council to make me the legal successor to Thutmose. That will involve a lengthy wait for Thutmose to die a natural death, but it is legal. The second is illegal: to murder Thutmose. Then I must convince the Council of Ten to declare me the rightful Pharaoh and marry Hatshepsut.

All other possibilities result in never becoming Pharaoh. Then, I would remain a prisoner for life. That is unacceptable!

ROYAL CHILDREN'S NURSERY, WASET

September 1480 BC

Hatshepsut observed her daughter learning Eastern Semitic.

"But it makes no sense," Neferure's frown complained.

Senenmut's eyebrows raised in a question, but his smile suggested otherwise, "Why does it make no sense?"

"That's not how you're supposed to say it."

"But it is how they say it."

"It's backward."

"Yes, it's backward, but that doesn't make it wrong. It just makes it different. Look at an example. In Egyptian we say, 'Gave Hatshepsut Neferure to hug big a.' In Western Semitic they would also say, 'Gave Hatshepsut Neferure to hug big a.' But in Eastern Semitic they would say, 'Hatshepsut gave a big hug to Neferure.' With some exceptions, the individual words the Eastern and Western Semitic languages use are the same. However, the word order changes. That is why Eastern and Western Semitic are different languages. It is difficult for Eastern and Western Semitic peoples to understand each other."

After allowing Neferure to absorb what he'd said, Senenmut continued, "Here is what is happening. In the sentence, 'gave' is the verb, 'Hatshepsut' is the subject and 'hug' is the object. Egyptian is a VSO language–'verb,' then 'subject,' then 'object.' All the countries west of the desert between the Levant and the Tigris-Euphrates speak a VSO language. Not only Egyptian, also Libyan, Nubian, Arabian, Canaanite, and Western Semitic. Everyone to the East and North speaks an SVO language–'subject,' then 'verb,' then 'object.' Not only Eastern Semitic, also Babylonian, Akkadian, Sumerian, Mittanian, and Hittite are SVO languages. So Egyptian is 'Gave Hatshepsut hug,' while Eastern Semitic is 'Hatshepsut gave hug.'

"Now you can understand why I taught you Western Semitic first. All you needed to learn were extra words, not both words and a new sentence structure. Once you've learned the words of Western Semitic, all you need to learn for Eastern Semitic is sentence structure; you don't have to learn extra words."

Neferure put a hand on each of her ears, exclaiming, "I think my head is going to break."

Senenmut held up a hand in mock excitement, "Wait, wait!" Reaching for a strip of cloth he had positioned next to him, he tied it around Neferure's head just above the ears. "OK," he said, "I tied your head together; it cannot break now," and he smiled.

Both Neferure and Hatshepsut broke out laughing.

Senenmut continued, "One last illustration that ends today's lesson. For the direct object, Egyptian says 'Neferure to' while Eastern Semitic says 'to Neferure.' In addition, all word modifiers go from back to front. Therefore, in Eastern Semitic, we call the word order 'pre-position,' or preposition, while in Western Semitic it is called 'post-position,' or postposition Therefore, the Egyptian sentence is 'Gave Hatshepsut Neferure to hug big a' becomes 'Hatshepsut gave a big hug to Neferure.' Now, do you need to have the doll maker make you a new doll with a busted head?"

Neferure giggled in unrestrained mirth.

Senenmut ended, "I'll end today by changing the sentence, 'Senenmut gave a big hug to Neferure,'" and he wrapped his arms around her. She responded by reaching up to hug him around the neck.

Hatshepsut walked over and stated, "Now it's time for 'Hatshepsut gave a big hug to Neferure,'" and she wrapped Neferure in her arms.

Turning to Senenmut, she continued, "Now we need to thank you for all you've done for us," and both women enveloped Senenmut in a hug.

The hug began as a symbol of innocent gratitude. It ended in a significant realization.

Shocking Senenmut.

I am forbidden to touch this woman. However, pressed against him, he became aware she was more than just a Queen, brilliant and aloof. She was all woman–and strongly attracting. He softly wrapped his arms around both Hatshepsut and Neferure and gently returned their hugs.

Hatshepsut felt his arms gently pressing on her back. It forced a realization. *I am falling in love with this man.*

Neferure, the unaware child, was the first to break the hug. Two seconds later, the two adults reluctantly followed her lead, dropping their arms and backing away from each other.

Each noticed the other blushing.

Each realized the innocent act influenced both of them.

Each knew they should never repeat it.

Each hungered for the attraction of physical contact.

GARDEN, HOUSE OF USERHAT, WASET

September 1480 BC

After dinner, Nebetka and his two brothers, Userhat and Meriptah, sat on the ground next to Userhat's back-yard vegetable garden.

Before going to work, the three men had mashed barley grains and left them to seep all-day in a quart of water. Arrayed around them were the spell ingredients. A cage contained a live cobra. A pomegranate harvested that morning. A lock of Thutmose's hair. A small wax human figurine. A knife. A shovel-full of dried cow dung. Last, a small fire.

Nebetka started by drizzling the barley mash through a cloth and into a pot to remove the barley residue, chanting the scroll's ritual words. He placed the pot over a fire until it boiled. One-by-one, he smashed pomegranate seeds and added them. With each seed, he severed a portion of the wax figurine: in order, the left foot, the right foot, the left hand, and the right hand. Next was the left leg at the knee, then the right, the left arm at the elbow, then the right. Finally, he removed the upper legs and arms. When he had smashed the last seed, he beheaded the figurine. Its ritual chant accompanied every action. Finally, he removed the cobra from its cage, killed it, removed its tongue and added it to the broth.

They waited while the aroma, carried by the steam from the pot, wafted aloft to attract the attention of the gods. When half the water had boiled away, they lit the cow dung fire. Its pungent aroma was a stark contrast to the boiling water's clean smell. First, so the gods would know whom to curse, they threw Thutmose's lock of hair onto the fire. They ladled the tongue and seeds from the pot and added them to the fire. When the fire had consumed the tongue and seeds, they poured the remaining mash liquid onto the fire, quenching it.

The ritual was complete. Thutmose was already dead; he just had not drawn his last breath. That would take another six to nine months.

Broad smiles covered all three faces. They had accomplished their goal.

Userhat stood and said, "Gentlemen." He stretched out his arm with the hand down and chanted, "Pharaoh." The other two men rose. Mariptah put his arm, hand down, into Userhat's fist at Mariptah's halfway point between the elbow and hand, after which Userhat closed his fist on it. Then Mariptah chanted, "Djat." Nebetka inserted his arm into Mariptah's fist at the halfway point between his elbow and hand, after which Mariptah closed his fist on Nebetka's arm and Nebetka closed his on Userhat's arm. The triangle was complete. Nebetka chanted, "High Priest." Userhat continued the sequence, "All for one." Mariptah and Nebetka echoed, "One for all." They broke the chain of hands.

Now the long wait while the spell incubated.

COUNCIL ROOM OF THE GREAT TEN OF UPPER AND LOWER EGYPT, WASET

September 1480 BC

The chair Nefer-Weben opened the meeting, the Great Ten of Upper and Lower Egypt sat on the dais; the plaintiff, Amunemhet and his sister-wife Ast, were standing before them, wearing their best white linen, and escorted by four guards.

Amunemhet was under house arrest. However, when the messenger from the Council told Thutmose the Council needed to see Amunemhet in person to adjudicate his appeal, he granted their request.

Nefer-Weben began the proceedings. "The Council has received your appeal. You state that since Amenhotep, no pharaoh has been divine. They were pharaoh because they married a divine woman on the line of Amenhotep and Ahmose-Marytatum. The baby Thutmose does not have divine blood. You ask the title of pharaoh should revert to a divine male in the line of Amenhotep on the death of Pharaoh Thutmose the Younger. Except for the Djat, Merytatum, you claim you are the only divine male remaining in that lineage. Are these statements correct?"

Amunemhet responded, "Yes, your eminence."

"The Djat has relevant evidence. Djat, please show Amunemhet a copy of the original document."

The Djat stood, stepped off the dais and gave the document to Amunemhet, then resumed his seat.

Amunemhet scanned the document with a puzzled look. He needed to reread it. He blurted out, "I don't understand. This is a Death Certificate. It has my name on it, but I'm not dead."

Nefer-Weben gestured for the Djat to explain, "Yes, I agree: you aren't dead. Look at the date."

"It's my birth date."

The Djat continued, "Precisely. I located the midwife for your birth, and she told me what happened. She arrived after the birth was already over. Her father, Pentu, the doctor, performed the delivery. The document states the baby was dead at birth from strangulation of the umbilical cord. She was late because she delivered a healthy baby boy to a destitute woman, who died during delivery. The midwife substituted the healthy commoner baby for the dead, divine blood baby. The mother never knew. The doctor never knew. Therefore, you are correct: you are not dead. However, you are not Amunemhet; the real Amunemhet is dead. You are not of divine blood. There is no royal blood in you. You don't even have noble blood."

Pawah spoke, "Amunemhet, this is the voice of Amun. I sent you on a diplomatic mission to the Minoans to prevent you from becoming pharaoh. It was not time to reveal your identity. Egypt was not ready. Now is the time."

Nefer-Weben ended the proceedings. "You are not Amunemhet; you are a commoner. Commoners may not be pharaoh, even if they marry a divine woman. The Council denies your appeal."

The man called Amunemhet turned sheet-white; Ast collapsed on the floor, weeping.

The Djat spoke once more, "Man formerly called Amunemhet, choose a commoner's name and register it. Until then, everyone will call you by your description: bastard."

The Council rose and left the dais by the side door. They left the former Amunemhet standing, stunned, and speechless, his wife weeping on the floor. After a few minutes, he gathered his composure and reached down to her, "Come, Ast, we have to go home."

After a moment, she lifted her arm for him to help her to her feet. Still too distraught to be steady, she leaned into him for support as they left the Council Chamber, escorted by the guards back to their house.

Clouds of doom surrounded them. Their former life had fled, never to return. The darkness of uncertainty was their only future. An atmosphere of emptiness enveloped them.

HOUSE OF UNNAMED FRIEND, WASET

October 1480 BC

After a month, the Pharaoh referred the former Amunemhet's house arrest decisions to a judge. Since Ast and her husband, newly renamed Masaharta, had received an invitation for dinner before his sentencing, the judge approved their going, provided Masaharta remained under constant guard.

Ast and Masaharta, with his guards, arrived at the house of Ast's friend for dinner.

A servant greeted them at the entrance. He asked Ast to enter and, when Masaharta followed, stopped him with a hand to his chest. "You will not enter this house. My master did not invite you."

"But he did."

"No, he invited Amunemhet. Amunemhet is dead. He does not invite commoners, and your status is below a beggar. At least beggars know their family history. There is no history for you; you are a bastard. You have no father. You have no mother. For Ast's sake, my master has directed the cook to prepare a meal of what the staff eats. It is waiting for you and your guards in the kitchen. Remember; you do not deserve the dinner. For years, you have lorded it over my master–believing you were divine, and that made you a better man than my master. Now we know what you are: pond scum. For all your life, you have given everyone no respect; now and for the rest of your life, you will reap the disrespect you have shown others. For you, disrespect will be worse than death. Your later years will not be worth the former." He closed the door in Masaharta's face.

Followed by the guards, Masaharta moped to the back door. He was not sure the dinner would be worth the humiliation. However, hunger mastered his pride.

He had to admit the lentil and leek soup was delicious. The date bread was excellent. *Their staff is better,* he thought, then corrected himself. *Better than Ast's.* The beer was excellent. He ate. And waited. And waited.

Eventually, a servant arrived to tell him Ast was waiting at the front door. He thanked them and received a glower of silent hatred in return.

On his way to the front door, he wondered, *Disrespect feels like this. Must I endure this wretched life? Is there no future hope?*

He and Ast started home, trailed by the guards, the evening's events roiling in his mind. *Who am I?* Finally, his ego would not accept his former friend's treatment of his commoner status. *No! My divine status did not deserve respect; 'I' deserved respect. 'I' was better. I am still better. I refuse to accept disrespect. I am right; everyone else is wrong. If they cannot accept me for who I am, that is their error, not mine.*

The first cracks had formed in the mortar holding the brick wall of his ego together. No amount of added mortar covering the crack could repair the wall, or prevent the cracks from enlarging.

Outwardly, his ego demanded an even more vigorous defense of his arrogant superiority. Inwardly, he had built his house on shifting sand. Rain washing it away was inevitable. In the core of his being, he knew it, but did not have the moral turpitude to acknowledge or face it. What he did not understand was that the longer he delayed that realization, the more catastrophic would be the inevitable fall.

DOCTOR'S OFFICE, WASET

February 1479 BC

Over four years had passed before the Doctor reported a commoner had contracted the wasting disease. Carrying his bucket of water, Khuenre rushed to the Doctor to ensure he arrived in time to collect pus and skin samples needed for his revenge.

He arrived to find a man lying on a plain wooden examining table, slowly writhing in misery, struggling with his remaining strength to discover any way to maneuver his body to relieve his suffering. There was no way. He wore no clothes–any cloth rubbing on skin caused misery. A quarter of his skin had sloughed off. Pus pockets riddled the exposed flesh, seeping slime. One eyelid was gone, its eye bubbling mucus. Three patches of skin hung loosely.

Any touch caused screams from the pain. Between screams, he could only whimper.

He could no longer drink; sores peppered the inside of his mouth. Any touch of water caused agony. Combined with loss of moisture through oozing pus, he was dying of dehydration faster than the disease.

He slipped into unconsciousness and remained unresponsive to any stimulus not associated with his suffering. He finally passed into delirium.

Khuenre joined the Doctor in the deathwatch. It took four hours. The patient was comatose at the end; he could no longer even whimper. Though Khuenre knew he was alive, he could no longer think of this as a man. In his mind, it was already a corpse, separated from death by a few breaths.

As a soldier, Khuenre understood battlefield death. However, a soldier's death is sudden and short. Even slow bleed-out wounds rarely take more than tens of minutes. This was a death never imagined.

Khuenre waited patiently for the Doctor to pronounce the man dead. He used a spoon to scrape out the pus from each boil and drop the mucus into his water bucket. He cut off the sloughed and dangling shreds of flesh and added them to the mixture. He had his weapon. He had only to feed it, so it remained at full strength until needed.

He made a mental note. Every week he would have to visit the mortician to buy newly harvested human flesh for the pus to eat.

He waited. He was a soldier. Like two swordsmen in battle, he needed to keep his feelings rigidly in check, not allowing them to influence the outcome. The first sword swipes are always tentative, feeling each other out, seeking an advantage or allowing the other to make a mistake. He knew he had victory in his hand; he just needed the opportune moment to strike the death blow.

HOUSE OF MASAHARTA AND AST, WASET

March 1479 BC

Masaharta went to the front window to discover the source of the singing. Five girls were playing jump rope, dancing in and out of the skipping rope. Masaharta leaned out the window to catch the song's words, "Amunemhet was a phony. Amunemhet was a phony."

The words crushed him. *Even children; even children.* The brick wall of his ego shattered and fell into crumbled pieces. He could keep it intact no longer. He did not even know these girls. His old name had become a symbol of ridicule.

He returned to the lounge and slumped in his chair. His hands clasped into a knot and fell to his ankles. His head drooped to a few inches above his waist. The Oracle's meaning was finally clear:

'Attitude cuts both ways.' *That was not Thutmose's attitude; that was mine. My attitude of superiority created resentment in others. Now that their status is higher, their attitude of resentment cuts me.*

'Deprecation rebounds.' *I looked down at them; now, they look down at me.*

'The bastard will die three deaths.' *I am the bastard, not Thutmose.*

'The first death should mean thankfulness and contentment.' *The real Amunemhet died the first death. I inherited his life and should have shown thankfulness and felt contentment. I did not. I was arrogant.*

'Arrogance means a second death of degradation.' *When my life as Amunemhet died, I died a death of degradation.*

'Extinction is the third death.' *That is all that remains. I must die. Forever. Masaharta, not Amunemhet. The Lake of Fire awaits me. I have no divine blood, no noble blood, not even pure commoner blood. I am only dross. There will be no 'refined me,' no 'pure me' to survive on the lake's other side. My third death is extinction. The end.*

What is better? A life of unremitting humiliation followed by extinction, or extinction now? Extinction awaits both choices. There is no hope.

Is enduring unending degradation worth the few years left of my life?

Ast awoke the next morning to discover Masaharta had not joined her in bed. She found his body hanging by the neck from a lounge rafter.

ROYAL PALACE PRIVATE WING, LOUNGE OF PHARAOH, WASET

April 17 1479 BC

The weather was mild. It would remain stable until May, when the warm temperature would slowly climb for summer. Four men, friends from childhood, were relaxing in Thutmose's personal rooms in the palace, drinking beer and reminiscing about boyhood escapades.

Thutmose thought for a moment, and asked the others, "You know what we haven't done in ages?"

The other's heads turned to him.

"It's been ages since we went hunting," he continued, his eyebrows raised. "What do you think if the four of us go up into the mountains to hunt goat? Say, day after tomorrow?"

A chorus of nods gave the answer.

Khuenre piped in, "Can you get us four chariots from the army, one each, and food for lunch from the palace kitchen?"

Thutmose agreed, "I can. Join me for breakfast at first light and we'll leave afterward."

MOUNTAINS EAST OF WASET

April 19

After breakfast two days later, the four friends walked to the chariots, their water skins over their shoulder. When they arrived, five chariots awaited them.

That surprised Khuenre. He asked, "I thought you said the four of us? There's five chariots."

Thutmose jerked his thumb at the two bodyguards following them. "We have to take the Medjay with us. Since someone tried to kill Hatshepsut and Neferure, I have to have a constant bodyguard. They will take the fifth chariot. However, they will not join the hunt. That's for us."

The four strung their water skins on their chariot's railing. No one noticed, but Khuenre hung two skins. They headed for the hills.

After an hour, they were in the foothills. Winter rains had left the hillsides lush with growth, so the female goats had descended from the mountaintops for mating, the males following them down. The flat landscape was easier for their kids to get their legs under them.

The four men stopped their chariots at a clearing, tethering the horses to bushes with room to nibble on grass, and gathered to make plans. Khuenre and the two others would make a wide swing uphill. Thutmose would find a concealed shooting site and remain in the valley. It would take an hour to get uphill of the goat herd. When each was ready, they would signal Thutmose. When all were ready, Thutmose would give the signal to close in and drive the herd into his ambush site. All nodded consent to the plan.

On the pretext he had brought his bow, but left the quiver, Khuenre returned to his chariot. He passed by Thutmose's chariot and, with a quick motion, withdrew an awl and punctured Thutmose's water-skin. It slowly seeped its contents.

An hour later, the three companions were in place uphill, with Thutmose concealed behind a bush. Each herder had a small six-inch wide handheld drum. Even before standing, they slowly beat their drum. They began in sequence with one beat every thirty seconds.

At the first beat, every goat's head came up. Their heads slewed from one drumbeat source to another. They milled about, knowing they needed to do something, but unsure what.

At a double beat, all three beaters stood up, the goats locating each beater in the landscape.

The beaters began plodding downhill.

The goats' apprehension level ratcheted up. Several bleated. One moved downhill straight for Thutmose, the rest following. Suddenly one male realized there might be danger going downhill, turned, and raced for a gap between two beaters.

The two beaters immediately started continuous drumming and ran to close the gap.

The goat, convinced escape in that direction was futile, joined the rest going downhill.

The beaters resumed their methodical walk. They wanted to drive the goats toward Thutmose at a slow pace, not panic them. Thutmose needed a high likelihood shot at a slow-moving animal, not a high-risk one at a galloping goat.

At twenty-five yards' distance, Thutmose popped up from behind his bush, aimed and fired.

The shot hit a large male in the chest. Wounded, he fell. Struggling to his feet, he tried running a few paces, but fell again. He took another few breaths, shuddered and was still.

The rest of the herd panicked, turned, and fled. The men let them go; they had gotten their prize.

Khuenre raised his arms in the air and shouted, "Yes!" followed by the rest, each echoing their exultant "Yes." Khuenre pounded his drum rapidly, the others joining. The celebration in sound continued until the four re-united in hugs. All bore huge smiles.

Thutmose recommended, "Let's eat," which elicited hearty responses. The men chose a small clearing and spread a mat on the ground. They went to their chariots for their baskets of food and skins of water. On trying to remove his water-skin, Thutmose noticed it had no weight. He groaned in disappointment.

"What's wrong?" Khuenre asked.

"My water-skin has a tear. My water's gone." He answered.

"No worry; I brought a spare." Khuenre untied an old skin from his chariot railing. "A word of caution," he said. "This is an old skin, so the water may have an off-taste."

"Thanks," Thutmose gave a heartfelt response to his friend's generous gift.

The four sat to eat.

Thutmose lifted the water-skin, cocked his head back and allowed three quick gulps of water to flow into his throat before his brain registered the water's taste. In reflex, he spewed the remnants out of his mouth, "This isn't an off-taste; it's putrid."

"Here, let me see." Khuenre reached for the skin.

Thutmose passed it to him. Khuenre took a small sip and spat it out. He reached for his own skin and rinsed out his mouth with water from his clean water-skin. "You're right; it's foul. I apologize; I hadn't realized it had grown so bad." He flung the water-skin into the bushes behind them. "Here, I'll share mine. I've got plenty." Khuenre held out his own water-skin toward Thutmose.

"Thanks, Khuenre, you're a genuine friend." Thutmose accepted the offered skin.

The friends enjoyed a hearty meal.

After eating, they tied their kill to Thutmose's chariot–it was his trophy. They raced back to deliver it to the kitchen. That night Thutmose ate fresh goat for supper.

Before following in their chariot, the Medjay recovered the discarded water-skin and gave it to Senenmut, describing the day's events.

Senenmut wondered. *Was anything suspicious? Was it innocent? I need to wait and see.*

STUDY, HOUSE OF KHUENRE

The Next Day

Khuenre left Waset to rejoin his army corps for scheduled training. He wanted to be far away from Waset for the next couple of weeks. Further, he fervently hoped, far away from suspicion.

He basked in the feeling of a long job finally fulfilled. Thutmose was dead; it would just take a few days to complete the process. *Father, you can now rest in peace. You will resurrect to vindication.*

Chapter 6

Lou Malnati's, Chicago, Illinois

Present

There were still two pieces left in the pan, but there was no room left in either man's stomach. Bob Rinter offered to give them to David, but he politely refused. "No thanks, I've eaten enough for lunch and dinner combined, and they're too good to trash. You take them."

"I'll give them to my grandkids. They'll eat anything, but Malnati's is a treat."

David nodded agreement. "Back to business. From my limited understanding, priests made up an undue percent of ancient Egypt's population. Why? What did they do?"

Bob leaned back in his chair. "Before answering, we need to understand a priest's function. Remember, they believed their gods created this world from Nun's disordered chaos. Therefore, this world is not in its natural state. Without continuous maintenance, the cosmos attempts to revert to disorder. Maintaining order was a priest's function. Priests were masters of Heka's power. They guarded against degradation and decay, continuously preserved Maat, and repaired what damage had occurred.

"Why were there so many priests? Ancient Egypt's aristocrats were thinkers. Commoners and slaves were doers. Aristocrats did not get their hands dirty, carving stone blocks for monuments. Aristocrats, with few exceptions, essentially had three alternatives: government, the army, or the priesthood.

"The first branch of priesthood was small; they managed the priestly administration.

"The second branch served the court and government. One department supported daily court functions. This included interpreting the pharaoh's dreams, advising him, and performing rituals and spells to help him perform his duties. A second department used apotropaic spells and protective rites to keep evil forces at bay. A third department countered an enemy's use of black magic.

"A third branch was temple priests, by far the largest by number. There were hundreds of gods. Each needed propitiation in a separate, dedicated temple. Matching that were hundreds of aristocratic second and third sons, each needing a job. These performed the temple rites, rituals, and ceremonies. Spells comprised two parts: words and actions. Each spell required both. They believed the daily washing and clothing of the god's statue mimicked the god doing so in heaven, by receiving some of the god's power. For example, when fruit offered to the god wizened overtime from its water evaporation, they believed the god had consumed the fruit's 'godly essence,' leaving the earthen counterpart of its 'rind.'

"The fourth branch was Doctors. They considered doctors part of the temple staff, in the temple or not. A disease's origin was supernatural; it was chaos trying to reassert itself. Gods gave humanity magic as self-defense. Heka was the god of medicine and magic, and medical professionals considered both equally important. Thus, general practitioner doctors had the title 'Swnw,' while magical practitioners were 'Sau.' Each primarily used their respective areas of expertise. However, there was no sharp dividing line. Both used magic. Doctors worked out of an institution known as the Per-Ankh ("The House of Life"), a part of a temple where they wrote, copied, studied, and discussed medical texts. The medical texts of ancient Egypt contained spells, as well as what we would consider 'practical measures' in treating disease and injury.

"The fifth and last branch were Lector priests. This was the only branch requiring literacy. Their expertise included both white and black magic. They could read the ancient magic books kept in temple and palace libraries. When presented with a need, they would research to discover the correct spell to match that need. They carried out the spell by saying the required words and performing the ritual actions. The Lector priests performed white magic rituals to protect their king. They also cast black magic disaster spells on Egypt's enemies, both human and divine. One prerequisite for a spell's effectiveness was performing all mechanics without error. If you mispronounced a word, the spell would be ineffective.

"Now you can understand the large number of priests."

David nodded. "It sounds like, if anyone could imagine something, they would need a priest to find the spell to do it. And, a government can image an endless number of tasks it wants done."

Bob nodded, "You got it."

ROYAL DOCTOR'S OFFICE, WASET

April 21, 1479 BC

Two days after the hunt, Thutmose ran a high fever.

Pawah immediately assigned a team of Sau Doctors to counter the fever with healing spells. Nebetka led the team and ensured he mispronounced at least one word in each spell.

The next day, Thutmose's body erupted in boils and pustules.

The spells proved ineffective.

Senenmut wondered: *Was the foul water innocent? Well-intended? Malevolent?* Senenmut rebuked himself for not warning the Pharaoh. Would a warning have helped? He did not know.

Senenmut visited the Royal Doctor and bared his soul: Could he have prevented the death? No. If Thutmose had contracted necrolysis, once he had drunk the water, he was dead. There was no cure. No one knew what caused it, but the doctors knew that one person could pass it to another by unsanitary care such as handling the sick person's pustules.

The following day, Thutmose's skin began sloughing off. The Swnw Doctors tried everything within their knowledge—to no avail.

PALACE, WASET

April 24, 1479 BC

Thutmose II died.

STUDY, HOUSE OF USERHAT

That evening

Nebetka entered the door to Userhat's house. His brothers were waiting in the antechamber. He announced, "It's done. He's dead."

His brothers chimed in, "Yes!"

Userhat added, "That only leaves Marytatum and the baby Thutmose III between us and pharaoh."

Nebetka added, "Marytatum is too old."

Mariptah had a sudden thought, "Today, at the staff meeting, the Djat announced that tomorrow he will ask Hapshepsut if she wants him to announce that Thutmose III will be Pharaoh with her as regent."

Userhat stood and replied, "Doesn't matter. The Djat can announce anything he wants, but the Great Ten Council decides succession, not the Djat or Regent. The Djat has one vote; Hatshepsut none."

Userhat stretched out his arm with the hand down and chanted, "Pharaoh." Mariptah put his arm, hand down, into Userhat's fist at the halfway point between Mariptah's elbow and hand, after which Userhat closed his fist on it. Then Mariptah chanted, "Djat." Nebetka inserted his arm into Mariptah's fist at the halfway point between Nebetka's elbow and hand, after which Mariptah closed his hand on Nebetka's arm. Nebetka closed his fist on Userhat's arm and the triangle was complete. Nebetka chanted, "High Priest." Userhat continued the sequence, "All for one." Mariptah and Nebetka echoed, "One for all." They broke the chain of hands.

Userhat concluded, "Tomorrow, we file our appeal to the Great Ten."

Everyone's anticipation excitement went through the roof.

TRIP TO THE EMBALMERS, WASET

April 25, 1479 BC

The Djat and Hatshepsut walked behind the litter bearers carrying the body of Thutmose to the Embalmers. They exchanged no words. The formal atmosphere carried decorum, but without grief. Thutmose had married Hatshepsut to become pharaoh; there was never love between them. He had performed his conjugal duties until she had born him a daughter. The position of God's future Wife of Amun secured, they had not shared a bed since. For them, marriage had been a duty, not a pleasure. For pleasure, he had a harem.

Having delivered the body, the Djat accompanied Hatshepsut back to the palace. "Your Majesty, would you like me to announce your nephew succeeding to Pharaoh with you as regent, or would you prefer something else?"

"Egypt needs a pharaoh. I will be Regent. Please make it happen."

The Djat wondered at her lack of grief, even as a facade, but said nothing?

Hatshepsut immersed herself in her own mind, wondering how to manage her additional responsibilities. She knew the court's duties, intrigue, pomp and ceremony exceeded her preparation. The task before her was daunting.

Senenmut was caring for Neferure in her grief. Neferure was at the "between" age of ten. She knew her father was dying and the doctors could not cure him. She was no longer a small child, so she grasped the idea of his impending death. However, abstract ideas of future possibilities were not yet real. When Hatshepsut told her Thutmose had died, she burst into distraught tears. Grief overwhelmed her, and she could not control it.

ROYAL PALACE HAREM

The Same Day

In Pharaoh's harem, there were no secrets. All the women knew of Thutmose's sudden sickness and death.

Hentaneb felt distressed. Nebetka had lured her into giving him a lock of Pharaoh's hair. Nebetka had paid handsomely for it and her parents needed the money. Now, she wondered if that act had contributed to Pharaoh's death. She bared her soul to the Harem Matron, who reported it, eventually reaching the ears of the Djat the following day.

He contacted Pawah, who ordered an investigation.

ROYAL PALACE, LOUNGE OF THE PHARAOH, WASET

April 1479 BC

Hatshepsut, Senenmut and Neferure were eating lunch. Neferure looked up from her meal. "Mommy, can you eat the King's Bread now?"

"No, Honey, I'm the Regent, not the King. Your little brother is the King, so he gets the King's Bread. However, calling it the King's Bread is not the right name. The real name is the Pharaoh's Bread."

"Why is it called Pharaoh's Bread?"

"I don't know. I probably heard the explanation when I was your age, but I have forgotten. Why don't you ask Uncle Kyky?"

Neferure turned in her seat to face him. "Uncle Kyky, why is it called the Pharaoh's Bread?"

Senenmut sighed. *I get all the simple questions.* "Tahemet, I can tell you the story of the legend, but Khusebek could probably give you a better answer."

"Uncle Kyky, I don't want a better answer later. I want your answer now."

"All right. Many years ago, the Sahara had many lakes. Our people lived in Siwa. Amun's Oracle is still there. We had not invented embalming, so it was not possible to preserve a body after death. However, the gods wanted a pharaoh to continue after death. The only way our people knew to fulfill the god's mandate to preserve the dead body was inside a living one. So the son of each pharaoh ate his dead father's body."

Neferure immediately grimaced. "Ew, that's disgusting."

"Tahemet, I know it sounds odd, but think for a minute. By eating his father, the son took on his father's strength in battle, his bravery, his wisdom, and many other good qualities his father had. Father and son became one. The father gained immortality through his son. The gods commanded this."

"I think I understand, but it's still disgusting."

Senenmut smiled. "It will take time to become comfortable with the idea. Let us continue the story. One pharaoh died in battle many days' journey away, and when his men returned with his body, it was so rotten the son could not eat it. They chopped the pharaoh's body into tiny pieces and buried the pieces in a field. The priests called this 'Pharaoh's Field.' The priests grew wheat in that field. When the priests harvested the grain, they used it to make bread, calling it 'Pharaoh's Bread.' We also call it the 'Bread of Life.' By absorbing the pharaoh's body into the wheat, the son could eat the dead pharaoh's body in its wheat form. The priests turn the spent stalks under every year, so the pharaoh's Ka returns to the field. All the ancient pharaohs remain immortal through the current pharaoh's body. That pharaoh is now your little brother."

"But we don't cut up the pharaohs and plant their bodies in the field anymore, do we?"

"No, we stopped doing that when we learned how to embalm the pharaoh's body. Now his Ka goes directly to Ra."

"All the old pharaohs remain immortal through my little brother?"

"That's right, Tahemet." She lapsed into pensive silence for a couple of minutes. Senenmut waited for her to finish thinking.

"Uncle Kyky, I don't think I can ever think of my little brother as only my little brother again; he has so many pharaohs living inside him."

Senenmut smiled. She experienced the emotional result he wanted. He had not been sure he could do it.

Tahemet had gained an expanded understanding of her young brother. Alongside the unchanging irritation with a toddler's antics would now live a deep respect for the generations of her ancestors who lived on inside him.

Hatshepsut had been following what Senenmut said with rapt attention. She was reliving the story anew. It captivated her how Neferure was so much putty in Senenmut's hands. Senenmut was molding Neferure into a future God's Wife of Amun. He unfailingly did what was best for her.

She also realized her attraction for him had reawakened. She wanted to be putty in his hands herself. However, her status had changed. She was Regent and had genuine power. She wondered: *How can I get him?* Anticipation kindled excitement.

COUNCIL ROOM FOR THE DJAT, WASET

April 1479 BC

When the Djat orders an investigation into Pharaoh's death, it takes precedence. The investigators discovered Nebetka's record for two sign-outs of the death scroll on the morning of the second day. It took an hour to examine. Two hours later, the written report was in Pawah's hand. He delivered it personally to the Djat that afternoon.

Few people need cobras. The Waset marketplace had only two vendors dealing in them. One remembered selling Userhat the cobra.

The following day, Hentaneb, Userhat, Meriptah and Nebetka were standing in front of the Djat. Behind each stood two guards. Pawah sat on the dais beside the Djat.

The Djat spoke, "Hentaneb, tell us what happened with Pharaoh Thutmosc's lock of hair."

"Sire, Nebetka approached me and asked to get a lock of hair from his head after one of his trysts with the harem. He offered me two-month's pay. My parents were in dire monetary straights and needed the money, so I agreed. I didn't see any harm in it."

"Guard," the Djat ordered, "Bring the Cobra Vendor."

After a minute, the vendor stood before the Djat, who inquired, "Have you seen anyone here before?"

Obviously nervous, the man stammered, "Yes, Sire," and he pointed to Userhat, "I sold this man a cobra a little over six months ago."

"Thank you, you may go." The man breathed an enormous sigh of relief. The guard accompanied him from the room.

The Djat waited until the guard returned, then continued, "Pawah, will you please tell me what you discovered in your investigation?"

"We went through the library records, seeking any spell scrolls that anyone had called for and discovered that Nebetka had checked out this scroll." He held it up. "This is its spell . . ." Pawah held up the ancient scroll and read its contents. "Nebetka kept it for a few days. This is when he contacted Hentaneb. Then, a little over six months ago, he checked it out again and kept it for two weeks. This was when Userhat bought the cobra. Why the delay? The second time he checked it out was the time the pomegranates matured. That was the last necessary ingredient. Why the delay between the spell and the death? The spell needed to incubate before becoming effective. All the individual events agree with the spell requirements. All the events lead to a conclusion of malicious intent toward Thutmose."

The Djat continued, "Userhat, Meriptah and Nebetka, what have you to say?"

Userhat replied, "The Great Ten must select a successor for Thutmose. I have already presented my petition for consideration as the next pharaoh."

Pawah broke in, "I understand your motivation. However, you also understand that you failed to ask the temple priests for Amun's guidance. As his representative, I can tell you that Amun has already spoken, and he has denied your application."

Nebetka interjected, "Thutmose died of a disease. We did not cause his disease."

Pawah objected, "Nebetka, you know better than that. The Djat may not know, but you and I do. I will explain it to him." He turned to face the Djat. "Nebetka used a spell to harness Heka to upset the balance of Maat. In addition, he chose Thutmose as its target. Therefore, the gods did not choose 'if' Thutmose would die–the curse did that. They only chose the spell's *manifestation*–the 'how' he would die. Therefore, Nebetka is guilty of premeditated murder. In addition, his two brothers were his accomplices."

Pawah continued, "Hentaneb did not take part in the spell. However, without the lock of Thutmose's hair, the gods would not know whom to curse. What she did was violate a living god's body, the Pharaoh. That crime carries a death sentence."

The Djat closed the proceedings. "With that understanding, it is Egypt's sentence that Userhat, Mariptah, and Nebetka are guilty of premeditated murder. Hentaneb is guilty of a violation of the pharaoh's person. Egypt sentences them to death." He turned his head, "Guards. Bind their hands behind them and carry out the sentence."

OFFICE OF THE WARDEN, WASET PRISON, WASET

April 1479

Senenmut knew of Userhat's, Mariptah's, and Nebetka's execution. They were guilty on the god level. However, gods need human champions to carry out their will on earth. That was Senenmut's goal: to research the human level. He needed confirming evidence the water-skin was the source of the sickness.

He visited the Warden. Did he have a prisoner sentenced to death? Yes, there were three. He took the men's names to the magistrate. He proposed one man would volunteer to drink the water and, if he lived, he would go free. The magistrate asked for the odds. Senenmut replied he did not know, but probably at least three chances in four of death within a week. The magistrate agreed to allow one man to try it.

One man jumped at the chance. *Walk away free? Against certain death? Freedom was worth the risk.* He was sick in three days and dead in five.

Senenmut had his answer. Now, how to use it?

MAGISTRATE'S COURTROOM, WASET

May 1479 BC

When Khuenre returned from his training exercise, two Medjay appeared with a summons to the Magistrate's Chambers. They escorted him to the courtroom. After he entered, another Medjay entered the chamber from each of the three doors. They outnumbered him five to one. Each drew his sword and held it at the ready. Khuenre recognized this was an inquisition, not an investigation–but believed no evidence remained.

Then his heart dropped through the floor when Senenmut entered from the door behind the Magistrate carrying the water-skin he had used to kill Thutmose.

The Magistrate asked two of the Medjay what they had seen. Khuenre did not recognize them because he had not noticed them. Servants were wallpaper; ignorant, unimportant, and ignored. They had not seen him puncture Thutmose's water-skin, but they had noted that it was full before he had recovered his quiver, and was leaking afterwards. They related the events and conversations the four companions had at lunch, noting where the water-skin had landed and had given it to Senenmut.

The Magistrate asked Senenmut for his testimony. Senenmut described the condemned prisoner test; how his death mirrored that of Thutmose.

The Magistrate turned to Khuenre. "You have heard the evidence against you. Have you anything in defense?

"Your honor, I have," Khuenre paused for effect, "The two Medjay admit they did not see what they claim had happened. This is a deduction, not a fact.

"Next, there has been no connection shown between the water-skin and Thutmose becoming ill. That is another deduction, not fact. Remember, I also drank from the skin, and I have not died. Last, Senenmut stated the prisoner died after having drunk from the skin, but he showed no evidence the prisoner had not already contracted the disease before he drank. In short, your honor, all the evidence presented is circumstantial and deduced, not factual. You need facts to convict."

Senenmut spoke, "Your honor, if I could speak?"

The Magistrate nodded, and Senenmut continued, "Your honor, I agree with Khuenre."

Senenmut stunned the Magistrate, the Medjay and even Khuenre.

Senenmut continued, "The facts confirm Khuenre owned the water-skin. He brought it. No one touched it at lunch except Thutmose and Khuenre. Only the Medjay and I handled it afterwards. We could not have infected Thutmose. I propose allowing Khuenre to prove his innocence. Let him drink a long quaff from the water-skin. If he is innocent, and the water did not carry the disease, then he will live. If he is guilty, he will be dead within a week from the same illness that killed Thutmose."

The Magistrate thought through the idea Senenmut proposed for a minute, then spoke, "Senenmut, your logic is flawless." Turning to Khuenre, he continued, "Drink and you may walk out of here a free man. If you are guiltless, Amun will protect you. If you are guilty, you will have earned the death you dealt to Thutmose."

Without warning, Khuenre withdrew the dagger from the scabbard he carried at his waist, spun around, and brandished it at those in the room. The Medjay started forward, but Senenmut gestured for them to halt in place.

"Yes, I killed Thutmose," admitted Khuenre. "His father committed the sin against my father, but the children inherit the sins of the father. Exacting vengeance was my duty. As for you, your honor, I prefer a clean, quick death." With those words, he spun the knife around and plunged it into his heart. He took one breath, dropped to his knees, leaned to one side, and fell to the floor.

Senenmut looked down at the body, bleeding on the floor before the Magistrate attendants carried it away. *Odd,* he thought. *I felt nothing. No satisfaction that Khuenre got what he deserved. Nor for me; I did not fail in my duty to protect Thutmose. There was no way I could have expected this to plan a countermeasure. The only thing I feel is a lingering sadness for Thutmose. He accomplished nothing during his reign. Egypt drifted without a rudder to steer it. What a waste of a life.*

MARYTATUM'S HOUSE, WASET

May 1479 BC

You thought you were playing Senet, and you had landed on Nefer. You believed Amun had given you good luck, so you tossed the knuckles. However, you landed on Water and returned to the House of Life.

Chapter 7

Secretary's Office for the Smithsonian Director

Present

Karen was standing in front of the Smithsonian Director's Secretary, "Nancy, I don't want to tell David. He just got back from his travels after opening Ian Maccleith's Ephod Display to the public and believes all the troubles it's caused are over. He already thinks Ian's tablet has thrown him more curveballs than Dizzy Dean. Now we have to tell him the surprises haven't ended?"

"He needs to know. Is anyone better suited to tell him?"

Karen thought for a few seconds. "Probably not." She breathed a deep breath. "Oh, all right, I'll tell him."

Nancy pressed the intercom button for the Director, "Doctor Scortun, Karen, Lab Tech, needs to see you; have you got a few minutes?"

The intercom answered. "Sure, please send her in."

By the time she reached his desk, David had taken his feet off the desk and back to the floor. "What's up, Karen?"

Karen handed him a CT scan of the Ephod box. "Doctor Scortun, you remember the wooden box Ian's tablet was in?"

David's quizzically raised eyebrow confirmed her question was rhetorical.

"We never finished the box examination. Specifically, we never performed a scan. Well, now we did. You will remember we always questioned why the box was deeper than needed? The scan reveals why. The tablet has a hidden chamber. It contains perhaps thirty parchment sheets."

Both of David's eyebrows raised.

"Each sheet contains writing on both sides."

Now David's head and shoulders slumped as the import of the revelation dropped on him like a two-hundred-pound rock.

Karen concluded, "What do you want me to do?"

David thought for a few minutes, then pressed the intercom button and entered the Lab Manager's number. "George, Karen's in my office. We're talking about the parchment sheets in Ian's box. Have you got a small chamber ready for nitrogen charging? These sheets have not seen oxygen for almost four thousand years. The minute we expose them to air, they will start degrading. We need to take pictures and get them in the chamber as rapidly as possible. Right. Please make it so. Call me when you are ready; I want to be there when we crack the seal on the box. Thanks."

COUNCIL ROOM FOR THE PHARAOH, WASET

May 1479 BC

Late that afternoon, Hatshepsut called for Senenmut to come to her Conference Chamber. When Senenmut arrived, she looked tired and bedraggled–as if she was trying to carry the world on her shoulders. She told him what she had decided. "Senenmut, I've made some preliminary decisions. To begin, I have officially declared my nephew Thutmose III to be Pharaoh. I will assume the duties of Regent until he becomes of age. The affairs of state need significant time. I am also ill prepared for Egyptian politics.

"I will have the Vizier assume the day-to-day political administration. He is capable in the role of carrying out policy. However, he is not a leader, able to set Egypt's goals effectively. Someone must decide those. The Vizier can then direct the government to achieve them. I just do not have the experience to decide.

"I need to protect Egypt's interests. Therefore, I need someone to sift through foreign ambassadors' deceptive and manipulative tactics to discern their actual goals. I need someone who can think. Someone who can judge what facts are important. Someone who solves problems. Someone who can figure out what direction Egypt should take. Someone as my personal adviser. In other words, I need you. Please launch an investigation to find a suitable replacement for your former role as Neferure's tutor."

Senenmut let that simmer in his head for a minute. *Hatshepsut was asking a lot. Probably more than she understood. Did she–could she–understand that?* He thought about that for a few seconds. *In reality, it does not matter if she understands. It is what needs done that matters. Am I ready? Can*

I rise to the task? Even if not ready–or cannot rise to the task–how could I say no? I need to make Egypt successful. Finally, he responded, "Your Majesty, I believe Neferure is ready for an older man. My cousin Senimen is a decade older that I am. He would not have made a good choice three years ago, but Neferure is no longer playing with dolls on the floor. She is ready for a wise man. Excluding military wisdom, he is the one who taught me most of what I know. He has been a Waset government official for twenty-five years, and his record is exemplary. I am Neferure's Uncle Kyky; he would be her Grandfather."

"Senenmut, if you say he would be a good choice, that's enough for me. Please contact him and introduce him to Neferure. His ability to work with her will be key."

"I will visit him tonight after he gets home."

As he left the Council Room, Senenmut thought, *I just realized. This means I have reached the pinnacle! Adviser to the Regent. Adviser to Thutmose III when he becomes Pharaoh. More titles. One of Egypt's most important people. Since Hatshepsut does not know how to govern, I will decide for the empire. That calls for a celebration tonight.*

The morning's hangover was exceptionally severe.

A week later, Neferure had a new tutor.

COUNCIL ROOM FOR THE PHARAOH, WASET

May 1479 BC

In his first meeting with Hatshepsut, Senenmut surprised her with his initial advice, "Your Majesty, the first order of business must be to prepare for imminent war."

"What? Why prepare for war? There have been no war signals."

"Your Majesty, I beg to differ from you. In the last two hundred years, the only newly crowned pharaoh not faced with war was Thutmose the Younger. Why? Because his father had just humiliated the Nubian army, and the generals and troops from that campaign were still in service. Fourteen years have elapsed since then. The generals have retired. Untested troops have replaced the experienced army. Your army is no longer proven and battle-tested.

"We have three to six months to prepare before they will thrust war upon us. It will come in one of two ways: either passive resistance by failure to pay annual tribute, or active invasion. It is unlikely Nubia will rebel; their experience is still too recent. However, I expect either Libya or kingdoms in the Levant. The war will come to you uninvited. You must prepare.

"I know the Military Academy in Inebu-hedj has been experimenting with new weapons, strategy and tactics. In about a month, I will need to visit for one to two weeks, so I will know how to incorporate what they have done into an overall Egyptian strategic plan."

Hatshepsut cocked her head. "Do we have enough trained men to win the war?"

"Your Highness, the number of men almost never decides a war's outcome."

Hatshepsut's head did a double take. "What? That's what everyone says!"

"I understand. However, I wager the men who told you were government officials, not military men. Am I right?"

"Yes, but . . ."

Senenmut raised his hand, interrupting, "They don't know what they're talking about. The three categories most important in warfare are balance, speed, and power, in that order. Balance is the most important; numbers come in a distant fourth, after power."

"I don't understand."

"You should expect that. You are learning something new and out of your expertise. To explain, let me give you an example: two hundred years ago, when the Hyksos conquered Egypt, the Egyptian army outnumbered the Hyksos almost ten to one."

"Then why did the Hyksos win?"

"Let's look at the hierarchy of importance. If numbers counted most, Egypt should have won, but they did not. The Hyksos slaughtered the Egyptians. Why? Numbers are only important when all else is equal. If you have twenty swordsmen with bronze swords and I only have ten, I will lose. Equal power means the side with significantly greater numbers wins. However, the Hyksos and the Egyptians did not have equal power. Power is more important than numbers. The Hyksos had bronze swords and shields. The Egyptians had copper swords and no shields. Bronze is harder than copper. In a one-to-one battle, bronze swords will hit and bend copper ones, so a copper sword will become useless. If a copper sword hits a bronze shield, it will bend. In summary, a Hyksos swordsman's power was three times an Egyptian's.

"Now examine speed. The Hyksos had chariots; the Egyptians did not. The Hyksos could outmaneuver the Egyptians. The Hyksos rode to the Egyptian flank or rear, and the Egyptians could not turn their battle line to respond. The Hyksos poured volley after volley of arrows into the Egyptian infantry, and the Egyptians could not respond. The Hyksos could kill the Egyptians and the Egyptians could not touch them. The Hyksos simply positioned their chariots where the Egyptians did not have archers. The Hyksos had a speed advantage.

"Last, examine balance. The Egyptian tactics used an equally weighted, straight battle line. The Hyksos did not fight that way. Their flank units were stronger. First, their chariot archers decimated the Egyptian flank unit. Then, Hyksos swordsmen attacked, overwhelming the flank unit. What remained fled the battle. The Hyksos wheeled and attacked the next Egyptian line unit. The Egyptians had not trained to wheel their line, so they broke and fled the battle. In summary, the Hyksos routed the Egyptian army. Why? Because the Hyksos attack unbalanced the Egyptian battle line. In short, the Egyptians lost the comparison of balance, speed, and power. The Egyptians lost the comparison on everything except numbers. And numbers are not important in deciding who wins. In summary: first the Egyptians lost their balance, then they lost the battle, then they lost the war."

Hatshepsut nodded. She had always known she was weak in warfare knowledge. Today, she had learned that warfare was not what she had thought. She also guessed the example Senenmut had used was about tactics. He touched on weapons, but only in passing. He did not mention strategy. Its absence suggested strategy was even more obtuse. If that was true, she was not sure she wanted to learn strategy yet.

She felt the emptiness that accompanies the realization that you lack what you need–and did not even know that you did not know.

She signed, shaking her head. Time to take baby steps, learning weapons and tactics before trying an adult's meal of strategy.

COUNCIL ROOM FOR THE PHARAOH, WASET

May 1479 BC

The last of the day's appointments left Pharaoh's Conference Chamber, leaving Hatshepsut and Senenmut. She cocked her head. "Let me ask a question. Pharaohs keep large harems of women and chose with whom to mate. If I were Pharaoh, I should have the same privilege, shouldn't I?"

"I agree. It would be logical," he replied.

"As Regent, I stand in the place of Pharaoh. Therefore, I am entitled to a harem. Come with me." She led him through the maze of corridors to her sleeping chamber.

Closing the door, she turned to face him. "I am twenty-eight years old and have not slept with a man for nine years. I choose you."

She blew out the room's candle. She slipped off her sandals and removed the dress over her head, standing naked before him. The moonlight from the window glistened off the curves of her body.

She moved to stand next to him. Unfastening his shendyt, she needed to lift its front to go over the protrusion from underneath. She allowed it to fall to the floor and pressed her body against his. He was as ready as she was.

He lifted her into his arms and carried her to the shadows of the bed.

The talking stopped.

ROYAL PALACE, LOUNGE OF THE PHARAOH, WASET

June 1479 BC

The royal family returned to the palace after interning Thutmose's mummy in his tomb. "Uncle Kyky," Neferure looked up with furrowed brow, "What will happen to father?"

"Tahemet. That is a question Khusebek should answer."

Khusebek came closer, but Neferure put her hand out, stopping him. "No," Tahemet said firmly. "He answers my questions, but he's dull and boring. I want you to answer."

Senenmut turned, looking at Khusebek, raising eyebrows in a silent question: *What should I do?* Khusebek shrugged a silent reply: *She is the boss.*

"All right. I will do that. However, this is a seeing question. Hearing is not enough to understand. Would you like to visit the jewelers tomorrow so you can understand what I mean?"

"Yes, Kyky. Tomorrow is soon enough."

"And ask your mother if she will come with us. You may also have questions to ask her."

"All right."

THE ROYAL JEWELERS GUILD

The Next Day

Queen Hatshepsut and her daughter could not spontaneously take a trip. Trips required pre-arranging. Scouts cleared the road of potential dangers and anything possibly causing a litter bearer to trip or stumble, rerouting normal traffic. Armed guards preceded and followed them. Everything needed careful choreographing to appear spontaneous.

The next day dawned a gentle day. Cloud wisps floated in the sky; a light breeze stirring the air. The Queen and her daughter each climbed onto their litters; the bearers hoisting them onto their shoulders. Every bearer in a set had identical shoulder height.

The Queen's many litter trips inured her to distractions. However, the trip held Neferure spellbound. Normally remaining in the palace, she had made only a few outside excursions. Unlike an enclosed palanquin, her litter was open on the top and sides, offering an unobstructed view. Senenmut walked beside her, explaining the sights they passed. They completed the quarter-mile trip to the Royal Jewelry Guild too quickly to satisfy her curiosity.

When her bearers lowered her litter to the ground and she swung her legs around to stand, Senenmut stood beside her, introducing her to the Guild Master. "Tahemet, I have asked him to show you how we begin from ore in the ground and end with pure metal. Normally they work in gold, which is common in Egypt. However, silver provides a better demonstration for what you need to see about what happened to your father. I therefore asked them to use silver today. Are we ready?"

She jumped up, "I'm ready." Queen Hatshepsut watched the exchange between the two. The effortless ease Senenmut used as a teacher, guide, guardian and playmate, all wrapped into one, continued to amaze her.

Senenmut led Tahemet to the Royal Jewelry Guild door. There was a bucket of silver ore staged just outside the door to begin the presentation. "Your Majesty," the Guild Master began, "this is how silver looks when dug from the ground."

Tahemet cocked her head and looked at it, then asked, "It looks like a rock. Can I touch it?"

"Yes, Your Majesty, you may."

She giggled, rarely allowed to 'play with dirt.' As she picked up a chunk of ore, it amazed her. "Why, it's just a rock."

"Yes and no, Tahemet," Senenmut replied. "It's a special rock." Senenmut picked up another rock sitting on the ground in his left hand. "This gray rock in my left hand is an ordinary rock, but the one you have contains silver. Can you tell the difference?"

"No, Kyky, they look the same to me–just rocks."

Senenmut put the ordinary rock down and pointed out a white grain running through the silver ore's rock. He took it from her, turned and rotated it so the sun's rays reflected off the streak. "See, Tahemet, if you shine the sun on the streak, it sparkles in pink and green. That means there is silver hiding inside. However, if it shines blue, it is not silver; it is quartz. Only silver shines this color of pink and green."

Tahemet gasped in awe, "Oh! Now I see why you wanted to bring me here. Seeing this makes it come alive. I would not have understood if you just tried to tell me. Can I hold it?"

Senenmut passed the rock to her, and she spent several minutes looking at it from all angles. She also tried examining the ordinary rock, but it did not shine.

Hatshepsut moved to join them. She had never experienced silver in its raw ore state and had never questioned how the jewelers refined it.

When the two had examined the ore, Senenmut led them inside, followed by the Guild Master. He carried the silver rock with him. Just inside the door was a workstation with a stone anvil. Senenmut traced the joint line between the hard outer stone and the softer silver for the two women. "The silver often fills cracks in harder rock. First, the jeweler needs to separate the soft silver from the hard rock." He passed the rock to the man at the anvil table.

The man at the anvil table twisted the rock into place and balanced a small stone on top of the joint line. He then used a large granite stone to hammer the small stone into the joint between the hard outer rock and the soft silver lode line, splitting the two halves of hard stone apart. Senenmut explained what had happened. "The jewelers only need the silver ore. They split the hard rock apart, discarding the plain rock. Then they use a hard granite rock to pulverize the silver into small grains and dust."

Beside the stone anvil was a bowl of silver dust. Senenmut pointed it out and told Neferure the silver ore looked like this after pounding. He asked, "Tahemet, would you like to feel it?"

"Oh, yes," she replied, but when she had dug her fingers into the bowl, she exclaimed, "Uncle Kyky, this looks like dirt, but it feels like rock."

"I know," he answered. "That seems weird, doesn't it?" After which, Hatshepsut felt some between her fingers, just nodding.

Senenmut gestured to the next display. "This is a kiln, made of hardened mud, using charcoal to fuel its fire. He gave a small charcoal piece to Tahemet. She took it and rolled it in her hands, blackening them. She looked down at her fingers, puzzled.

"It's an artificial fuel called charcoal," he explained. "It's specially prepared wood that burns hotter than normal wood. You put the fuel for the fire inside at the bottom," and he pointed out where it went into the kiln. "The ore goes into a ceramic bowl just above the fire. Someone then blows air through one of these tubes to give the fire extra air to melt silver," and he handed her a long ceramic blow tube. She looked through the blowpipe center.

"Next, let's go to two of the kilns that the jewelers are using."

Senenmut asked the first jeweler to pull his pot out of the kiln. It looked like brown sludge with silt floating on top. "Tahemet, the sludge and silt are impurities. We call them dross. The impurities float on top of the silver. The jeweler needs to scrape off and throw away the impurities to leave pure silver." While they watched, the jeweler scraped away the top layer of sludge and dropped it into a bucket. More brown sludge lay underneath. Senenmut continued, "You have to heat the pot many times to remove all impurities. Let's go to the next kiln."

They walked to the second jeweler as he was taking his pot out of the kiln. There were a few particles of brown floating on the top, which he picked off, leaving a perfect liquid silver in the pot. Senenmut told Tahemet, "Lean down and look into the silver surface. What do you see?"

Tahemet gasped, "I see myself in the silver. It is like my bronze mirror, but better. Instead of skin color, it's pure silver."

Senenmut said, "You asked what would happen to your father. This will happen. Your father has lost the dross of his earthen body. His heavenly body is pure silver. He looks like this. Tahemet, when we are in our earthen bodies, the dust of the earth surrounds us. Like the rock encased the silver. Silver is inside, but you only see rock.

"When we die, everyone goes through a lake of fire. Like the jeweler's fire, the lake burns off the impurities, leaving just the precious metal behind to come out the other side. If divine like you and your mother, you will come out like gold. You father is noble so he will look like silver. If an honorable commoner, you will look like bronze. Unworthy commoners are all dross. They burn away. They disappear."

"Will Amunemhet disappear? He's mean and nasty."

"Yes, Amunemhet will burn and disappear–nothing will remain."

"When I die, will the fire hurt me?"

"No, it will feel refreshing. Like you have been carrying a heavy sack that you can finally put down. You can move and breathe freely."

"What about mean and nasty people like Amunemhet? Will they feel pain?"

"I don't know. Since they burn completely away, they cannot tell us if they felt pain or punishment. I only know *we* will not feel pain."

"I guess that's all right." Then she thought a minute, "But that evil Khuenre was a noble; you mean he passed through the lake of fire test?"

"Yes, Tahemet, he did. However, we are getting ahead of ourselves; we will get to Khuenre in a minute. We need to finish the people's different categories. We have covered gold, silver and bronze. However, there is one other category. Your father was not divine, so he was mostly silver. However, he was Pharaoh, so he went to join the gods. Because he joined the gods, they made him into a special combination of silver and gold called electrum or white gold. This is the reason Pharaoh's Chariot uses electrum gilding."

"Oh, I know what that looks like; I've seen father's chariot."

Senenmut continued, "There is a second test your father went through. At the other end of the lake stands Anubis. Beside him is Maat. Your father handed his heart to Anubis, who put it on one side of a balance scale. Maat handed Anubis his ostrich feather of truth and he put it on the other side. The heart must be lighter than the feather to pass the test. That means he was not mean and did not amass a weight of wicked deeds during his life. You do not need to worry about your father; he was a good man and a noble Pharaoh, so we know he passed that test. However, Khuenre was a murderer, so his heart failed the feather test. What happens if you fail the test? Standing next to Osiris is Ammut, the demon. If any heart fails the test, she eats the person, and they are gone forever. So, Khuenre is gone forever."

"But what happened after father passed the feather test?"

"He traveled to Ra, the sun god, and merged with him. Every day, your father and Ra together make the journey across the sky. Now your father brings light and life to Egypt every day."

"Will I ever see father again?"

"Yes, but not for a while. After you and your mother and I all die, we will all go through the lake of fire and feather tests. But we aren't pharaoh, so we will go to Aaru, the Land of Reeds."

"Mommy, when you die, will you wait for me in Aaru?"

"Yes, darling, of course I will."

"Thank you, Mommy." She gave Hatshepsut a hug.

After the two women untangled, Senenmut continued, "I need to finish the story. In the future, we will resurrect into our earthen bodies. Since we will wait in the spirit world, our wait will seem like one day. On resurrection day, you will join your father again and live forever. Remember, he is an important man with an important job. Egypt depends on him. Can you wait one day in eternity to see him again?"

"I want to see him now. But, yes, I can wait for one day in eternity."

"Thank you, Tahemet. Now you know what happened to your father, and now you understand why I needed to show you how our heavenly soul looks."

"Can I look at myself in the silver?"

"For as long as you like."

Hatshepsut smiled.

Chapter 8

Smithsonian Laboratory

Present

Doctor David Scortun watched preparations for the removal of the box's false bottom with mixed emotions. This artifact had provided more twists and turns than his switchback ride up Palomar Mountain as a young adult. Time after time, when he believed they had solved its mysteries, it revealed another puzzle.

One part of him wished Ian had never given him the Ephod, but that was frustration. He reminded himself: frustration was an unavoidable side of archaeology. Frustration was the back of archaeology's coin. The front was exhilaration. Every archaeologist dreams of holding something in their hands that the world has not seen in a thousand years. You could not have one without the other; they were like ham and eggs.

He had to admit, this artifact was his first experience where it came to him. Usually, he traveled on-site to a dig. Was this worth it? He reluctantly admitted it was.

COUNCIL ROOM FOR THE PHARAOH, WASET

July 1479 BC

Senenmut entered Hatshepsut's Council Chamber, having just returned from his trip to the Military Academy. Bowing low, he began, "Your Majesty, I bring you good news and bad news. The bad news is that our Libyan ambassador reports they are massing an army of five thousand. It appears they will mount an invasion of Egypt. The good news: we are ready for them."

The news did not catch Hatshepsut by surprise. She nodded, continuing in a calm voice, asking, "What do we have to meet them?"

"Our Libyan army corps of three thousand."

"Do we know the estimated breakdown of their weapons divisions?"

"Yes, Your Majesty, they will have about one division of a thousand swordsmen, four divisions of a thousand spearmen each, and two hundred fifty archers."

"Our army has trained on the new khopesh sword?"

Yes, Your Majesty. They are ready and hungry for a fight. They want to be first to wield the weapon in battle." Senenmut paused. "You have been studying." It was not a question. "My cousin?"

"Yes, I asked Senimen to give me an introductory lesson in strategy, tactics, and weapons. For example, strategy is used to prepare and move your army to battle, and you use tactics on the battlefield." She raised her eyebrow quizzically. "Good beginner's explanation?"

Senenmut smiled, "Well done. A good one-sentence summary?"

Hatshepsut forced her face to remain impassive. She wanted to return Senenmut's smile, but no, there were other people in the Conference Chamber. She needed to act as if compliments were unnecessary. She had prepared; she was the Queen and Regent.

Senenmut continued, "If you would like, I have arranged for a demonstration of the new sword."

Hatshepsut rose from her throne. "Yes, please, I'd like to see that." She followed Senenmut as he led the way outside the building. Her court attendants and guards trailed. In the square in front of the building were several men waiting. One carried an eight foot spear, another two swords.

Senenmut led the Queen to the swords, took a regular sword and turned to show it to the Queen. "This is our standard sword. The blade emerges from the hilt narrow and thin, grows wider and thicker as it reaches two-thirds length, then narrows rapidly to a point." His finger followed the words, pointing out the section of the blade he was referencing. "It is chiefly a slashing weapon, designed to hit the target at the widest section of the blade. That is the strongest with the most mass. However, the blade has a significant design weakness. Bronze is a relatively weak metal. If the man you are fighting steps closer as you swing the blade, he is inside the power range of the sword. Alternately, if he lifts his shield to parry and your sword hits near the blade's hilt, the blade can bend or break. In battle, broken swords are common. You can use the sword for a thrusting blow. However, it bends when hitting something dense. The sword's power range is two to six feet. Too close and you can't swing the sword; too far and the enemy is beyond reach."

Senenmut returned the standard sword and took the khopesh, turned and held it out in his hands for the Queen to examine. "This is a khopesh." It is actually an old copper design, but Egypt has not used it since we started using bronze. This is the redesigned weapon. The sword has a different shape: semicircular with a flattened tip. "This is a cutting weapon; it has almost no thrusting ability. You can hit the target at any distance and anywhere along the blade, and the blade will preserve maximum strength. The secret: no matter where the blade hits the target, the blade's sides are behind it, supporting the strike point. The sides will not allow the blade to bend. Therefore, this has additional power."

The Queen took the sword and examined it, running her finger along the edge to gauge its sharpness, then handed it back.

Senenmut continued, "There is an additional advantage with this sword. I'll have to use it to enable understanding." He turned and spoke to the spearman. "Spear out."

The spearman lowered his spear and thrust it out at arm's reach. Senenmut walked over to him and explained how he wielded the spear. "This is an eight-foot spear, the standard size for all armies. The spearman holds onto the shaft at the rear two feet, so six feet of shaft and point are in front of his forward hand. Two feet more for the forward hand in front of his body means the point is eight feet in front of his body at maximum extension. That is where we get the term "eight-foot" spear. It's not necessarily the spear's length, but the spear's maximum power range."

Senenmut commanded, "Spear in." The spearman drew back his hands, so he held his arms straight down from his shoulders. The spear-point was now six feet in front of his body.

Senenmut moved to stand five feet in front of the spearman, and commanded, "Spear out–in–out–in." Senenmut was always standing inside the range of the spear tip. "The spear's power range is six to eight feet; outside that range–either farther or closer–and the spear has no power.

"Now image a second rank of spearmen standing three feet behind the first. There is a one-foot gap between the first and second rank's power range. Theoretically, I could stand there all day and neither spearman could touch me."

Senenmut paused for the effect of what he had said to sink in. "Now, the next step."

Senenmut moved in front of the spearman and stood outside the spear's reach. "Spear out." The spearman thrust forward. Senenmut commanded,

"Hold your spear steady; don't let me move it." The spearman braced himself. Senenmut put one finger on the side of the spear and pushed the shaft sideways, despite the best efforts of the spearman. "What's important? The spearman has little resistance against sideways motion.

"OK. Let us summarize. Spears have a power range straight ahead from six to eight feet. Outside that limit, they are ineffective. Most armies use spearmen in three ranks. The first two ranks are spears forward at six to eight feet for the first rank and three to five for the second. The third is reserve. If a man in the first rank falls, the second rank man moves forward to fill the gap, and the third moves to the second. Until something happens, the third rank holds their spears upright. Lowering them would interfere with the first rank."

Senenmut said, "Now that you understand the power range and limits of spearmen, it's time to display the khopesh power." Turning to the spearman, he said, "Ready? I am coming for you. Try stopping me."

Senenmut backed up to a ten-foot distance and took one-step toward the spearman. He held the khopesh blade-side toward the spearman, whose spear shot straight for Senenmut's chest. In two seconds, faster than the spearman could recover, Senenmut flipped his wrist, turning the inside blunt-side toward the spear shaft. Wrapping the spear's shaft inside the curve of the khopesh blade, and pulling the shaft aside, he stepped forward inside the power range of the spear. The spearman dropped the spear in shock and held up his hands in an "I give up" gesture.

Hatshepsut's eyes went wide and her jaw dropped.

Senenmut continued, "The same movement can grab the edge of a swordsman's shield, pulling it aside and giving you a free chop at him. The last advantage is slicing the throat or arm at one to two feet distance from the swordsman. At that distance, you are inside the swinging radius of his straight blade. With its design features, the khopesh has a significant power advantage."

Senenmut thanked the men conducting the demonstration and escorted Hatshepsut and her retinue inside to her Conference Chamber. When she had resumed her throne, she commented, "A convincing demonstration. Despite Libya's numerical advantage, we should have a significant power advantage. What do you calculate our losses to be?"

Senenmut smiled, "Your Majesty, our calculated losses depend on the strategy we decide to use. Have you decided on the strategy for our government?"

Senenmut's statement and question caught her off-guard. Hatshepsut countered, "Now that you've reminded me, I knew that." She let out a long sigh. "This discussion needs advisers. The Djat will represent the govern-ment, the Chief Treasurer for finances, the Chief of Ambassadors for our neighbors, Pawah for Amun, and you for the military. That is six. Let's meet here one hour after the morning meal."

"Yes, Your Majesty," Senenmut answered, "I'll arrange it."

COUNCIL ROOM FOR THE PHARAOH, WASET

July 1479 BC

Five occupied chairs sat in a semi-circle on the room's dais, facing the Pha-raoh's empty throne. The Djat spoke for the government, the Treasurer for finances, the Chief of Ambassadors for international relations, the High Priest for Amun, and Senenmut for the Military. Hatshepsut entered and sat on her throne, nodding for Senenmut to conduct the meeting.

He began, "A quick summary. With Thutmose the Younger's death, our ambassador reports Libya is massing an army estimated at five-thousand. Their goal is invading Egypt and conquering the delta to feed their growing population. Chief Ambassador, is there anything else to add?"

"Only that they intend to attack soon. They have planned this for years. They were waiting for a suitable time. The Pharaoh's death is the trigger for timing. They hope to strike before we can reinforce the Delta Army."

Senenmut started the next discussion topic. "Our troops have trained on the new weapons. We will use our standard three thousand man Delta Army to face them. The Libyans will not disrupt our delta farmers or crops. They are unaware of our new weapons or our new navy."

That shocked Hatshepsut. "Navy? What navy?"

Senenmut handled that question. "I've been coordinating with Ra-mose, the Dean of the Military Academy. I have directed the Djat to build a small fleet of coastal ships for transporting troops and supplies. We cur-rently have five ships available for service. If the army stays within a rea-sonable distance from landing sites along the coasts or rivers, we are no longer dependent on marching to battle or using oxen and carts to supply our troops. That increases both flexibility and mobility."

The reaction was shock. Where did Senenmut get the power to "direct" the Djat? The Djat lowered his head, avoiding eye contact.

The Treasurer asked, "How much governmental and economic disrup-tion will this invasion create?"

Senenmut parried the question. "That's what we have to decide. If the decision is simply to stop them, there will essentially be little extra cost or disruption. We will merely replace supplies and equipment. The country will not realize we have fought a war. However, as an example, if we invade Libya to exact reparations, or other long-term actions, it will create added cost."

The Treasurer would not let his query go unanswered just because his first question was not specific. "All right. Give us the main alternatives you believe we may want to consider and the costs and benefits of each."

Senenmut parried yet again. "I agree. We need to get to that question, but I believe we need to set the stage first." He asked the Treasurer, "If we were to rank our close neighbors in order of tribute, trade, and economic importance to Egypt, how would you rank order Libya, Nubia and the Levant countries?"

"There are vast differences. Nubia is most important, followed by the Levant. However, Levant countries have significant differences. Libya comprises less than five percent of our trade and tribute."

Senenmut summarized, "Therefore, if we wish to make the strongest statement, this means there is less economic risk making that statement with Libya. Is that accurate?"

"I hadn't thought of it in that manner," replied the Treasurer, "but I believe you're right."

Senenmut shifted his gaze to the Chief of Ambassadors. "What risks do we face from our Levant neighbors, and what statement do you want this Libya conflict to give to them?"

It was obvious the Chief of Ambassadors had thought through what Egypt needed. "The aim is winning this war rapidly and decisively. In doing that, we cannot portray any weakness. We do not want anyone else mobilizing to join the Libyans. Therefore, we cannot move troops from our Levant border to reinforce. That would send the message that we are not strong enough for multiple rebels simultaneously. It would encourage Levant kingdoms to form a coalition. Those eastern border troops must remain as a deterrent. Last, the best message would reinforce the idea that, although we do not want war, we will not tolerate rebellion and have the power to defeat multiple threats simultaneously. That would be the message we need to send."

Senenmut summarized what everyone had injected into the discussion. "I'm hearing that we want to send a powerful message without disrupting the economy. Is that correct?"

There were universal nods.

He continued, "Then I believe we need to inflict maximum casualties on Libya. The remaining decision: first, do we want our army killing them on the battlefield? That means incurring significant casualties ourselves. Or second, allow them to flee, but not survive the return to Libya?" That means minimizing our casualties.

Queen Hatshepsut spoke to that question. "I don't want to lose a single soldier more than necessary. Let the Libyans die returning."

Senenmut nodded at what she was saying, "I believe that what we have decided is in Egypt's best interests is also well within our ability. I can now answer everyone's questions. Ramose has formulated plans for defeating Libya, which will accomplish these goals." He explained the campaign details.

Consent was unanimous.

THE ROAD PAST RUWEISAT RIDGE

July 1479 BC

The Egyptians knew the Libyan army was massing.

Armies need to eat and sleep. They cannot march twenty-four hours a day. However, ships can sail around the clock. As long as wind remains favorable, ships always travel faster than marching men. The ships reached Egypt well before the Libyan army, carrying advanced warning. The Libyans were coming.

For the Libyans, speed was crucial. Only the Egyptian Western Corps faced them. That gave them a five-thousand to three-thousand man advantage. If they slowed, then the Egyptians could move their Eastern Corps to reinforce. That would give the Egyptians six-thousand men. The Libyans could not afford to lose their numerical advantage. A normal warfare marching distance is fifteen to twenty-miles a day. The Libyans marched twenty-five.

Unless a commander preserves tight control, marching armies spread out. Trailing units fall further and further behind. However, allowing increasing following distance means increasing the time to close for battle. They could not allow that and forced tight march spacing.

Since an ox pulls a cart for twelve to fourteen miles daily, this created a gap between the forward battle formations and the following baggage train.

No Bedouin with over one brain cell would venture into the Qattara Depression. It represented the desert at its worst. It was marginally possible to walk in it. For a short distance. The Depression's northernmost tip fell short of the Mediterranean by a mile. Halfway from the Depression to the Sea and one hundred miles inside Libya laid a ridge with a nondescript name: Ruweisat Ridge.

Just westward of Ruweisat Ridge and halfway to the sea lay a short ridgeline named Miteinya–even more humble in appearance than Ruweisat. One physical feature defined this spot. Its quarter-mile gap between ridge and sea was the choke point between Libya and Egypt. It was the preferred defensive position, whether for a Libyan army blocking a westward advancing Egyptian army, or an Egyptian blocking an eastward advancing Libyan army. A quarter-mile gap between the ridgeline and the sea did not permit spreading out. In the thousand years of Egyptian history, armies had shed the most blood at Miteinya Ridge.

In waging war, it is often the unnoticed that provides the killing blow. An old warfare tactic is showing an enemy one look and giving him another. The advancing Libyan army gave no notice to four boats slowly sailing west. How could four boats affect their army? They ignored them.

It is impossible to hide a five-thousand man marching army. On the fourth day after the Libyans crossed the border, the Egyptian scouts on Miteinya Ridge spotted the dust cloud created by the advancing Libyan army when still ten-miles away.

The Libyans stopped a mile from Miteinya Ridge. They could not see the Egyptians, but they knew they had to be there. If the Egyptians had not attempted to stop them at the border, then the Ruweisat-Miteinya Ridge complex was the best defensive ground. They would get a good night's sleep, eat a hearty breakfast and be fresh for battle in the morning.

The Libyans were ready.

So was Egypt.

THE ROAD PAST MITEINYA RIDGE

July 1479 BC

After breakfast, the Libyan chariots circled south. They knew they had a disadvantage with twenty-five chariots to the Egyptian's sixty. However, the rewards justified the risk. Could they thread the gap between Ruweisat and Miteinya Ridges and assault an unsuspecting Egyptian rear? Harassing them would create chaos and confusion, possibly creating a rout mentality. That might save a thousand lives and seal victory. However, such was not to be.

Still a half mile away, they spotted Egyptian chariots in the gap. The Libyan chariots returned. The abortive try proved the day's harbinger of fortune.

Field armies of the eighteenth dynasty era called for three standard tactical phases for battle. First was the approach march to the battlefield. Second was the advance to the enemy lines. Last was the charge, launching the battle. On the approach, men marched in column formation, shifting to line abreast for the advance phase. When should they switch? All other things being equal, when reaching a quarter-mile from the battlefield.

Standard tactics for the approach phase called for spearmen to form the first division of men in three ranks of line abreast, followed by swordsmen. When the first rank reached fifty yards of separation, they charged. Spearmen attacking are more effective than spearmen defending.

The Libyans followed standard tactics. Their first line was a division of a thousand spearmen in three ranks of three-hundred-fifty each. The second division was swordsmen, followed by the last three divisions of spearmen. Each rank stretched the entire distance from Miteinya Ridge to the Sea.

The Egyptians did nothing standard. Yes, they were already in line abreast. However, they did not form their line of battle at the midpoint of Miteinya Ridge, where the separation from the sea was shortest, but on the far side, a quarter-mile farther distance. Second, their first rank was not spearmen, but swordsmen. Unusually, they had not drawn their swords. These remained visible in their scabbards, their shields on their backs.

The Libyan General wondered at that, but knowing Egyptians appointed aristocrats as generals rather than proven field soldiers, he believed that worked in Libya's favor. Besides, he had met the Egyptian General, and assessed his counterpart to have questionable mental acumen. He smiled in expectation; he would gladly take the gift of a win. This fight promised to be a waste of good Egyptian infantry.

No sooner had the Libyans switched from approach column to advance line abreast than the Egyptian soldiers removed their shields from their backs and slung them on their left arms. Then they drew their swords–if you could call them swords. They looked like sickles, not swords. Then they began their own advance to battle, mirroring the Libyans.

This confused the Libyan General. He had never seen an opponent mirror his actions. Why do this? He did not understand what was happening. Above all, he did not understand this new Egyptian weapon. What was it? How would they use it? How could his men defend against it?

The two sides approached each other step-by-step. The Libyan General grew more confused as the steps amassed and the distance decreased. At a hundred-fifty yards' separation, he wondered if he should order a premature charge and decided against it. It was too far for the troops to run and still arrive breathing normally.

The hair on the back of his neck rose. He sensed the unexpected was happening, did not know what, and did not know how to adjust.

At one-hundred yards' separation, he sensed he should take the initiative. However, what to do?

At seventy-five yards, he opened his mouth to command the charge anyway and lost control of the battle.

The Egyptian trumpets sounded 'charge.'

The swordsmen lifted their swords in the air, twirled them around in a circle over their heads, and ran screaming at the Libyan lines.

The Libyan drums sounded 'brace for battle.' Their first division spearmen thrust their points out to maximum extension and braced their back foot for the onslaught.

The Egyptians halted at five feet distance from the Libyan spear points.

They took two steps forward, flipping their wrists backward. Hooking the spear shaft of the man before them with their sword, they pulled the spear aside and stepped forward. They were inside the spear's killing range.

Almost to a man, the Libyans froze in amazement, awe, and shock.

No one had seen this.

No one expected this.

No one trained for this.

Before the Libyans could recover and react, the Egyptian swordsmen took one more step forward, grabbed the second rank's spear shaft, thrust it aside, and took another step forward.

They were inside the spearmen's killing range.

The slaughter began. The two front ranks were defenseless, while the third could not lower their spears without impaling their own men. In thirty seconds, every spearman realized it was escape or perish.

They dropped their spears, turned and fled–straight into their own swordsmen's ranks.

There were no gaps. Miteinya Ridge forced the men to be shoulder-to shoulder.

The unarmed spearmen fouled the lanes of their own swordsmen, while the onrushing Egyptians could swing at anyone.

A few Libyan swordsmen killed their own men to free their sword lanes.

Too few, too sparsely spaced, too late.

In isolated spots throughout the Libyan swordsmen's lines, the Egyptian onslaught overwhelmed them. Gaps formed, swelling quickly, until the entire line collapsed.

The remnant bolted, screaming to those behind them to take flight or perish. Libyan lines imploded, streaming from the battlefield.

The Egyptians had inflicted a rout.

The Egyptians halted, allowing the Libyans to flee.

They did not want to follow where they had forced the Libyans to go.

The Libyans lost eight-hundred-fifty men on the battlefield, killed or too seriously wounded to take flight. The Egyptians lost fewer than a hundred.

THE ROAD PAST RUWEISAT RIDGE

July 1479 BC

No Libyan ran less than a quarter-mile. Slowly, the running trickled to a halt.

Before them lay a wasteland.

They remembered the boats sailing west before the battle. That had seemed insignificant.

It was not.

They now understood its implication. The boats had disgorged two hundred soldiers who rounded up the civilians and loaded them on the boats. Then the Egyptians marched west, laying waste to the countryside.

The Libyans had left the civilians untouched. The civilians were gone.

The Libyans had left the houses, barns, and fields untouched. The Egyptians burned everything.

The Libyans had left food in the farmer's granaries and livestock in the fields. The Egyptians burned the granaries and butchered the livestock. Their carcasses had bloated; the meat rotted.

The Libyans had left the wells untouched. The Egyptians fouled every well with rotted livestock carcasses. They poisoned the water.

The Libyans reached on the remnant of their baggage trains bringing food and water. The Egyptians had slaughtered every ox, burned every cart, shattered every water container, and massacred every baggage attendant and guardian

The land between them and home was a barren wasteland.

Nothing remained between them and the Libyan border, over a hundred miles away. There was no food.

Worse, there would be no water.

A hundred-mile desert trek without food is possible. A hundred-mile desert trek without water is not.

Death by thirst under a relentless, unforgiving sun is first slow, then agonizing, and finally tormenting. Its only mitigating symptom is unconsciousness before ultimate death.

A thousand surrendered. The Egyptians marched them to slavery. However, they survived.

The rest believed they could make it home.

Most did not.

Barely seventy-five men had the expertise to find enough drinkable water to survive the journey home. The rest left their bodies littered along the road.

The General survived. He drove his chariot until the horses collapsed. Then he butchered the animals, collected their blood, and drank that until reaching the border.

COUNCIL ROOM OF THE LIBYAN KING

The Following Day

Standing before the Libyan King, the General told the tale of new weapons and new tactics. He had witnessed the battle, but was too distant to observe details. Too distant to analyze what happened. Too distant to permit fixing his battle plan's flaws.

The power of this new Egyptian weapon intensified in retelling. The new tactic's effectiveness escalated as word spread. The horror experienced by the survivors swelled as the Libyan ambassadors notified other kingdoms.

The fact not exaggerated was the paltry number of survivors.

All thoughts of resisting Egypt's hold on their vassals evaporated.

No kingdom challenged Hatshepsut's reign. All countries promptly paid their tribute.

No one wanted to endure the torture inflicted on the Libyans.

TRIP TO THE MITEINYA BATTLEFIELD

July 1479 BC

Queen Hatshepsut had wanted to view the Battle at Miteinya Ridge. The ships sailing from Libya gave warning to the Egyptian General of the advancing army. The General had sent runners up the Nile to the Queen, but word spread slowly in the eighteenth dynasty. She knew the battle would be over days before her arrival, but she still needed to go. More important than her wanting to go was the morale boost it would give to her armies to show she cared for them. Her men were not pieces on a Hounds and Jackals board you could remove when landing on Shen. Each soldier mattered. Senenmut and the Djat accompanied her. She needed them for a follow-up meeting she scheduled with her government officials in Inebu-hedj.

The boat coasted on the Nile's leisurely flow. With the boat going south and the wind going north, there was a soft breeze to keep the passengers comfortable for the seven-day journey. They spent the days lounging on deck, and would have spent the nights had etiquette allowed it. Besides, when they went below-decks in the evening, Queen Hatshepsut and Senenmut had various points of a physical nature to explore.

One morning, they were discussing strategy and tactics over lunch and a beer, and watching the scenery drift by. Queen Hatshepsut was studying so she would not appear ignorant to the Delta General. Senenmut was explaining their battle plans. How strategy and tactics would align to give the best chance for battlefield success. On arrival, they would discover how closely the battle followed the plan.

Senenmut explained how strategy and tactics interlocked to give the Egyptians an advantage. He began, "If we just look at numbers, and ignore everything else, the Libyans have five thousand men to our three thousand. That gives them a five-to-three advantage. Attackers need a two-to-one advantage to give likelihood of victory in the offense in an open field battle. A three to one ratio usually ensures it. So raw numbers give the Libyans a significant, but not assured, likelihood of success.

"However, like the Hyksos, power trumps numbers. Power's first category is training. Ours is a standing army, theirs cobbled together. Therefore, we have the training advantage. However, since we do not know the extent of their training, we cannot include that advantage in this examination. Just realize it exists.

"The next category is power. In power's hierarchy, swordsmen are three, archers are two, and spearmen one. The number of archers on both sides is insignificant. Therefore, we can ignore their power contribution. The

Libyans have one thousand swordsmen while we have two; they have four thousand spearmen and we have one. That equates to them having a power ranking of seven thousand and us seven thousand. Therefore, the two sides have equal power. That implies each side has an equal chance of winning

"Now consider strategy. They are the invaders, so we can choose the battlefield. We chose Miteinya Ridge. The battlefield constricts the armies to one thousand men each at a time. That removes the power for those not actively fighting. We expect the Libyan General to use conventional tactics, which means he will lead with a division of spearmen. We will meet them with swordsmen. That gives us a three thousand to one thousand power advantage on the battlefield, almost guaranteeing us an early advantage.

"That's the strategic power balance. However, there is an added tactical power. Spearmen have a one rating. However, spearmen attacking are more formidable than spearmen defending. When spearmen are charging, you need to adjust their power rating to one and a half. Therefore, you want to deny them the tactical opportunity to begin with a charge. That means beginning the battle with our own charge. That is what I directed our General to do.

"We'll find out when we get there if the Libyans allowed us to fight the battle as we designed it. Questions?"

Hatshepsut swallowed. "I could follow what you said, but I'll have to digest everything before I fully understand. Let us review it tomorrow. I need to understand it."

MITEINYA RIDGE BATTLEFIELD

July 1479 BC

The General was showing the Miteinya battlefield to Queen Hatshepsut, explaining what had transpired.

"General," she stopped him, "before we get to the battle, the strategy I asked for was to inflict maximum enemy casualties with minimum loss. Did this happen?" As she uttered the word 'strategy' the General's eyes slid to Senenmut, but he was not responding to the General's attention.

"Yes, Your Majesty. We lost less than a hundred men killed and wounded. This is an unusually low casualty rate for this scale of battle. We estimate less than a hundred Libyans survived their return trip. Almost a thousand surrendered and we have sent them as slaves to the southern quarries. That is a ninety-eight percent Libyan casualty rate. That is an unmitigated disaster."

She asked, "How about our strategic choice of battlefield?"

At the phrase 'strategic choice of battlefield,' the General's eyes flicked to Senenmut, but his eyes were looking down.

"Your Majesty, it was the best possible location. Once the Libyans invaded, they committed to march to the Nile. Therefore, they had no choice but to accept battle at Miteinya. They tried to flank us, but the Qattara forbids a wide southern flanking movement and we blocked them from going through the Ruweisat gap. That forced them to approach us one division at a time, effectively removing their numerical advantage."

"And the tactic of having first-rank khopesh swordsmen?" The General struggled to keep his composure. What was a woman doing using military terms? She obviously understood what she asked.

"That was pure wisdom. Ramose devised the tactic at the Military Academy and it worked. The Libyans had no answer. All but a few dozen of the casualties we suffered were khopesh swordsmen who hadn't had enough training to perfect their techniques."

"And were we able to deny their spearmen their extra power rating by initiating the charge?"

The General was so shocked that he stopped for five seconds to regain his composure. "Yes, Your Majesty, we successfully opened with the charge. The Libyans had no countermeasure."

The General introduced her to a one-hundred man unit at the fighting's forefront. Queen Hatshepsut gave a small speech thanking them for what they had done for Egypt. She knew that, although she could not talk to everyone, this unit would pass on the news of her coming, and the word would spread. Her army would know that she valued them. And, knowing their government valued them mattered to the men in the front ranks.

As she was speaking, the General marveled at her knowledge. It must be Senenmut's training. However, if the army needed support, having a ruler knowing how armies actually functioned was an advantage. He wholeheartedly approved.

After a couple of hours, she boarded the pharaoh's electrum chariot and Senenmut drove her off to return to her boat on the Nile.

COUNCIL ROOM OF THE PHARAOH, INEBU-HEDJ

July 1479 BC

The boat to Inebu-hedj was a two-day trip. On arriving, she went to her dedicated conference room.

It was unusual for Egypt's top officers–the Pharaoh (Regent), Vizier, and Djat–to be in one place. One successful assassination could wipe out the government. However, she needed these men's advice. Guards allowed no one near this conference room. Also present were the Chief of Ambassadors, the Chief of Treasury, The High Priest of Amun, the Dean of the Military Academy, and her personal adviser, Senenmut. Food and drinks in plenty were on a table, and the guards allowed no one to enter or leave.

The Queen started by asking for the condition of Egypt's lands west of Miteinya. Treasury answered, "Your Majesty, the destruction is total. Every home, barn, granary and field burned, every well poisoned, all cattle and livestock slaughtered. We can reuse the fields; we didn't salt them."

She turned to the Chief of Ambassadors. "The Libyans will pay for replacing every building, restocking every granary, and digging every well. I want the King of Libya's personal livestock confiscated. They will be the first fruits restocking the farmer's herds. In addition, they will pay all costs to house and feed our farmers and families until they harvest next year's crops. If the farmers overestimate their losses–well, the Libyans should have considered that before rebelling. I want to send a warning message: Count the cost of losing before dreaming of the profit from winning. Am I clear?"

"Yes, Your Majesty."

Treasury interjected, "Your Majesty, may I offer suggestions?"

"Of course."

"We should not allow them to use their own resources. They will use the cheapest, inferior wood for rebuilding. We should buy quality wood from either Canaanite or Nubian forests and have the Libyans pay the additional cost. We should not allow them to use their builders. They will provide ill-trained carpenters. We should use our people. That will provide jobs for our workers, build our economy, and increase our tax base."

"Cogently put." She turned to the Chief of Ambassadors. "Please tell the Libyans of our requirements."

"Yes, Your Majesty."

"Next. Which vassal must we prepare to fight next? When?

At that, multiple heads jerked toward Senenmut. They knew this woman. What she had just spoken revealed a depth of military knowledge depth and wisdom never displayed before. The question was not "if." She must have recently learned what she had never understood.

This shocked Ramose. His response was a small smile. Senenmut had learned how to teach his military knowledge. It was time to direct the discussion to the kingdom's future risk. "Your Majesty, this victory was overwhelming and devastating to Libya. Couple that with the khopesh, and no subject Kingdom will risk rebellion soon. They need to increase their abilities, produce thousands of khopesh swords, train their army, and develop countermeasures for our tactics. That will take ten years. They cannot effectively disguise their actions. We can watch their progress. By that time, with continuing support of the academy and the army, we will develop new weapons, strategy and tactics. The kingdom has a ten-year respite."

Hatshepsut nodded. Without having to fund exorbitant military expenditures, Egypt now could concentrate on improving its economy. She realized with pleasure that history would remember her reign for its prosperity.

Chapter 9

Smithsonian Laboratory

Present

The technician adjusted the high-intensity lamp to provide the optimum light angle. He donned a surgical gown, gloves, and a mouth mask to prevent breathing on the specimen. He mounted the microscope enlargers over his eyes.

Had David not known this was not an operating room, and the patient was a wooden box, he would not have detected the difference.

Until the technician picked up a Dremel vibrator-saw.

Hardened tree resin sealed the box. They needed to cut it loose.

The technician's hands must be surgeon-steady. Like surgeons, any mistake would cause irrevocable damage. Freeing the lid would require at least three passes. The saw threw dust up for a vacuum to siphon it. If it fell into the chamber, it could contaminate the contents.

The technician was on his fifth pass before David heard a quiet whoosh. The sound told him the chamber's air had partially oxidized its parchment, creating a slight vacuum. Fresh air rushed in to equalize pressure.

The Dremel resumed its muted whine, cutting the four remaining tabs holding the lid. With a soft swoosh like a head dropping on a pillow, the lid landed on the inside parchment sheets.

The technician switched off the Dremel.

David moved in close. The technician reached for two suction cups. Attaching them to the lid, he applied a vacuum. After lifting the lid, David was looking at parchment unseen for three-thousand, five-hundred years.

The photographer and his apprentice moved in. One-by-one, the photographer captured both sides of every sheet. The apprentice replaced the sheets in the box and rushed it to the inert chamber.

David had visually scanned every sheet. He could not read a single one.

ROYAL PALACE, WASET

April 1478 BC

There are secrets in court; but, despite the best efforts at suppression, the vast majority are ill kept. With the Pharaoh's family, suppression of secrets is nonexistent.

There was no way to hide the evening–and all-night–meetings. They were not discussing battlefield tactics. The exchange between Hatshepsut and Senenmut was not a melding of ideas; the melding was three feet lower.

Fooling an experienced midwife is impossible. A pregnant woman's complexion displays the sex of the child. Sex hormones travel through the umbilical cord. Mother and child exchange them. As a female child's body produces estrogen, this raises the overall estrogen level in the mother. Thus, mothers with female babies have smoother skin, giving her a vibrant, radiant, beautiful complexion. Women are never more beautiful than when pregnant with female babies. With male babies, the male child's testosterone lowers the mother's estrogen-testosterone balance, giving her a rougher, mottled complexion. Any experienced midwife can read the mother's skin for the child's sex.

Hatshepsut's midwife revealed her child was a boy.

Six months into the pregnancy, everyone could read the signs of the increasingly extended belly.

Hatshepsut gave birth ten months after the affair began. Hatshepsut named him Sefuamun–meaning 'mysterious sword.'

COUNCIL ROOM OF THE DJAT, WASET

November 1474 BC

At last. Amun is calling, and I am the last divine man standing. Is this my time?

Merytatum, the man everyone called 'Grandfather,' called a meeting between the new Djat, the Chief Treasurer, the General of the Armies, the Amun High Priest and himself. When the five gathered, he began, "Gentlemen, I'm worried. With Hatshepsut declaring herself Regent, we are in a phase that has never happened in Egypt's long history."

The General of the Armies responded, "I don't understand; we've had Queens as regent before."

Grandfather answered, "Yes, but they've always been the mother. Hatshepsut is not his mother; she is his aunt. Egypt has never had an aunt Regent."

The General smirked, "We couldn't make his mother a regent. It was what was between her legs that attracted Pharaoh Thutmose, not what was between her ears. That chamber's empty."

Hands over their mouths muffled the snickers.

The Djat wondered what others thought. However, he directed the question to Merytatum. "What would you propose as an alternative?"

"I'm not proposing; I'm trying to ask the right questions. I do not presume to have the right answers. But I am confident that, between us acting together, we can arrive at the right answer."

That elicited a few sighs of relief. Several had wondered if Merytatum was trying to ramrod his viewpoint down their throats.

His last statement prompted a question from the Djat: "Why us? Isn't this a Council of Ten question?"

Merytatum answered that one, "Yes, I agree. The Council must make the final decision. However, twenty-one men cannot effectively evaluate all alternatives. I propose we do the thinking, search through all the facts, and propose one or two final recommendations for the Council."

That produced a chorus of nods. Although some might not be fully on board, no one opposed the idea.

Merytatum looked around the group, evaluating agreement, and then took a long breath. The breath signaled the group to continue.

Merytatum was careful not to say this group comprised the Council's core. If they agreed, the Council would rubber stamp their recommendation.

Merytatum started, "The first question should be to check if Amun has given any divine guidance." Turning to Pawah, the High Priest, he asked, "Have you had any sign from Amun which path he wants us to take?"

Pawah shook his head. "None."

Merytatum summarized the unspoken result. "Then Amun wants us to use our best judgment. Lacking divine guidance, the second alternative is a choice agreeing with precedents the gods have previously blessed. Only if we cannot find a suitable historical alternative, should we consider

Hatshepsut to be regent. That is why I am concerned. Not that Hatshepsut is incapable. She is actually perhaps the most capable Queen in history. However, the gods have never blessed that choice in a thousand years. Why should we believe they will bless it this time?"

When the group examined how Merytatum presented his logic, no one wanted to challenge it. It made perfect sense. There were general nods of agreement.

It was what Marytatum was not saying that was crucial. He was carefully laying his groundwork, getting the group's agreement: the god's wishes came first, and then the welfare of Egypt. The logic was unselfish. By agreeing to this premise, he was also preventing anyone promoting selfish interests. The group would immediately oppose any such suggestion.

Merytatum began, "The first alternative is choosing a group of three to be a Regency Council. We have chosen Regency Councils in the past. The problem is twofold. First, all three must be capable leaders. Second: the Council must endure for the twenty years before Pharaoh becomes of age. Invariably, capable men, even acting in Egypt's best interests, disagree, and the group loses cohesion. When you have uncertain weight on multiple options, strong opinions, and critical risks to Egypt, it leads to strong emotional disagreements. I'm concerned any group of three would not last the time Pharaoh Thutmose needs."

There were nods of agreement. Merytatum evaluated the group's opinion. "Then let's discard that alternative."

He continued, "The next alternative is choosing one man as Regent. For argument's sake, let us say we propose the Djat. He is already third as head of government. Hatshepsut could remain Queen and God's Wife of Amun. And, Egypt wouldn't run risking the god's becoming angry because she seized the role of regent."

As everyone mulled over the alternative, the head nods grew stronger. However, Pawah suggested, "Merytatum, why don't you propose yourself? You were Djat until last year. That is over twenty years through three different pharaohs. You would make a great Regent."

"Perhaps," Merytatum replied, "but if I were the candidate, it should probably be in another role. Think, if anything happened to the young Thutmose–Amun forbid," He raised his hand, stressing the point. "Who would be first in succession priority? I am the last divine man remaining in the Ahmose Royal line. Therefore, I would theoretically be first in line of succession. If I were the interim solution, instead of Regent, I should be Pharaoh. Yes, I would have to marry Hatshepsut, and as a widow, she is available. However, I have drawbacks. I am fifty years old. Yes, I am in good health, but how many years would I have left? I would probably have ten years. However, Egypt needs fifteen to twenty years. If I died, Egypt would face the same choice of appointing a Regent. Would we want to do that?"

As the discussion developed, the Djat spoke, "Grandfather, ten exceptional years with you as Pharaoh would compensate for ten average years of anyone else's Regency. Everyone knows you. Everyone trusts you. The country's leadership transition would be smooth." He surveyed his colleagues. "I propose we recommend to the Great Ten that we make Merytatum Pharaoh and appoint Thutmose III to be his successor." He waited a few seconds for the first shock to wear off, then continued, "I call for a vote: everyone in favor, raise their hand."

Two hands went up immediately, slowly followed by two more. Finally, only Merytatum's hand was not in the air. He looked around at the others, sighed, and raised his hand. "All right, I accept–but on one condition. Amun has not spoken. Let us not take immediate action. Abrupt changes are dangerous for the country–many will think we were not wise. Let us wait for Amun to signal his acceptance or rejection. If something untoward happens in the next few months, we can announce that Amun wants us to make a change and we are merely complying with his direction. Egypt's people would readily accept that."

The nods signaled the group agreed, and the Djat summarized, "The next time the Council meets, we will propose this as the will of Egypt. Until then, we wait for Amun to act."

The men rose and started for the door, Merytatum shaking each man's hand as he left.

I am now Pharaoh in all but name. Yes, I must wait for something to happen–good or bad. Either will suffice. Something always does. It can be anything, and the Council can interpret it as Amun's will. Therefore, instead of usurping the throne, people will view me as the man the gods chose to rescue Egypt.

THERA EXPLOSION–PHASE II, SANTORINI ISLAND

February 1473 BC

Fifteen years had elapsed since the population fled. When no disaster occurred, many wondered if returning was safe. To a casual observer, the volcano seemed dormant. The only visible danger signs were sulfur vents, and the enlarged central mound broaching the bay's surface. However, the few electing to land immediately experienced the constant ground's rumbling. It shook your bones, rattling a warning: Leave immediately.

The rising lava first filled the old hollow tubes from the last volcanic explosion. Once filled, these forced the dome to continue growing vertically, with hot lava flowing from the top cascading down the dome's sides into the water. This created a lava platform supporting an even higher dome.

Magma, rising from the depths, slowly forced the old layers apart. The dome's central core protruding into the bay was new lava–and impervious. As the central mound expanded, the rising lava in the central core forced the older walls outward, slowly rupturing the ancient tubes, pulverizing these outer edges. As the old walls fissured, they allowed seawater to seep into the mound. However, the cracks only allowed the older outer shell to split. The water seeping in converted to steam as it reached rocks containing new lava. The mound's edges trapped the steam inside, forbidding any pathway for pressure release. Rock lay on the inside. Rock lay above. Rock lay below. Lava blocked those directions. The pressure of the surrounding water resisted any outward release. The water continued absorbing steam until becoming saturated. Then, the steam's pressure level grew–and grew–and grew.

Eventually, the outer dome layers failed, allowing tons of water to hit the torrid lava just inside. The deluge flashed to steam. The water outside and the rock above could no longer contain the pressure. Thera's outer dome exploded.

However, the central dome was still too strong. The force only pulverized the dome's older edges. Not a deep, full-throated roar. It was a hiccup's promise. However, a hiccup of such force it buried Thera's houses in ash within two feet of their rooftops, preserving their pristine condition for future archaeologists.

This was Thera's second eruption phase.

Enough volcanic powder spewed into the air for the prevailing southerly wind to float the powder to the Egyptian delta. It produced a thin haze blanketing the delta. The pumice powder proved only a nuisance, but its unusual nature convinced many it was a divine message.

The explosion's effect sealed shut the vent holes for the magma below. Now there was no path for releasing the lava force pushing toward the surface. Pressure intensified rapidly. The time remaining for reckoning was short.

When gods call, the message rockets through the land. Waset lay five hundred miles south of the Nile, emptying into the Mediterranean, but the message reached the city by runners in six days.

Was the pumice powder a divine message? The problem was how to translate the god-speak message into man-speak meaning. What did the gods want? How did they want humankind to react?

COUNCIL ROOM OF THE GREAT TEN, INEBU-HEDJ

February 1473 BC

Thera's thin dust cloud covered the delta. Gazing at the cloud-obscured sun without damaging one's eyes was abnormal. It must mean that the gods were sending a critical message.

Men appointed vizier must be nobles, but earn appointment by wisdom, mental ability and performance. The Vizier sent runners to the men of the Great Ten of Lower Egypt. The Great Ten of the North would converge at Inebu-hedj in three days. They would sail south to Waset to join the Great Ten of Upper Egypt. He knew the Djat was already sending for them. With the dust cloud cutting wind-speed in half, it would take the men of Lower Egypt two weeks to arrive. That was acceptable, because the distances the men of Upper Egypt must travel were commensurately greater.

Nefer-Weben called the meeting of the Great Ten of Upper and Lower Egypt to order and turned the meeting over to the Djat, who explained the earlier meeting. In the kingdom's history, all female regents had been queen mothers, never queen aunts. Without precedent, Hatshepsut's regency approval might be ill-advised. They reviewed alternatives to present recommendations to the Council. Finally, they waited for the god's message.

The revelation elicited questions, but the Council accepted it.

The Djat summarized the alternatives discussed. They had not rejected Hatshepsut as regent, but without a sign from the gods, they also had not approved her. They rejected various regency alternatives as unstable. Finally, they settled on an older interim pharaoh as the best choice. Marytatum had been reticent, but they twisted his arm. He had accepted becoming interim pharaoh only after receiving god's guidance.

These revelations allayed the Council's concerns. There was no collusion.

The Djat continued, "With the dust hovering over Lower Egypt, waiting for a sign from the gods was prescient. They have given us their message. They have rejected Hatshepsut's becoming regent. I therefore recommend consideration of an older interim pharaoh, and propose Marytatum as that man. Until Thutmose becomes of age, we should select a regent only if he does not survive."

The discussion was long and heated. During it all, Marytatum sat quietly. He had carefully laid the groundwork, and the unavoidable occurred. At the end, there were twenty yes-vote arms in the air. Marytatum had only to raise his own to make the vote unanimous.

Hatshepsut was understandably distraught, but not at the Council. Given the circumstances, they had performed their duty.

You could not fight the gods. You could not demand they reveal their reasoning. It was enough they had spoken, even if you could not understand why they had not spoken earlier. At least the result preserved Thutmose becoming pharaoh when he became of age. She could accept that.

THERA-PHASE III, SANTORINI ISLAND

May 1473 BC

Three months elapsed.

The lava lake lying several thousands of feet under the mountain spread outward for miles in all directions. With new lava surging relentlessly from the depths, pressure on the harbor's lava mound intensified. Pressure relief from below was impossible.

The last explosion had pulverized and ejected the mound's outer walls. The replacement was new lava. Thick, hard, strong. The outer walls refused to budge. With tons of harbor water pressed from the sides, there was no relief of pressure from the side.

The only avenue was up.

In a full-throated roar, Thera exploded, emptying into the air. This was Thera's phase III.

Pumice rocketed into the sky, piercing the stratosphere. A hundred-twenty miles away, pumice buried eastern Crete in three feet of ash. A boat landed on a pumice island between Santorini and Egypt, its sailors leaving the boat and walking on the island. The cloud obscured the sun in Inebu-hedj. For three days, the inhabitants could not see their hand in front of their face. The airborne pumice required breathing through a cloth. Most delta cattle perished; their pumice-coated lungs blocked breathing.

Thera had one last eruption phase remaining.

COUNCIL ROOM OF THE PHARAOH, WASET

May 1473 BC

Egypt once again called the Great Ten of Upper and Lower Egypt to Waset.

Pawah would not wait. He read the sky for the god's frustration and wrath. He needed no augury. There was no alternative.

He entered the palace and asked the guards to fetch the Queen. He sat and waited in her Council Room. At her entrance, he stood for her to take her chair.

"Your Majesty. The Council of the Great Ten of Upper and Lower Egypt has made a grievous error. We have misread the god's message. The gods have rejected Marytatum as pharaoh. You are their choice."

Hatshepsut's face, normally calm, registered shock. "Me?"

"Yes, Your Majesty. You must claim your right as God's Wife of Amun. You must be Pharaoh."

"But . . ."

"Your Majesty, there is no 'but.'"

"There has never been a time in Egypt's history with two pharaohs."

"I understand–and so do the gods. That's precisely why there is an ash cloud covering Egypt."

He waited for a response.

She had none. She could not accept it, nor could she reject it.

"Your Majesty, I will release the announcement."

In short order, the ash cloud scattered, never to reappear.

The gods had spoken, and finally Egypt understood their will.

Hatshepsut's reign of twenty years was peaceful.

Egypt was prosperous.

However, Thera had one more eruption phase remaining.

One person took advantage of Hatshepsut's ascension to Pharaoh–Senenmut. He now regarded himself as Egypt's second-in-command, ahead of even the Vizier and Djat. He often told them what they needed to do–and used his influence with Hatshepsut to enforce it. Year-by-year, his behavior grew more arrogant, but no one disputed his demands. As long as Hatshepsut was Pharaoh, Senenmut's wishes were sacrosanct. He ruled Egypt by fiat.

However, if anything happened to Hatshepsut . . . .

COUNCIL ROOM OF THE PHARAOH, WASET

January 16, 1458 BC

The Kingdom had braced for the news for two years, and the eventual occurred. The announcement was somber: Pharaoh Hatshepsut had died. All Egypt mourned.

Thutmose III had become Pharaoh at two, but his role had been General of the Army. Hatshepsut had governed the empire. Thutmose formerly assumed all Pharaoh's duties.

His first act was to call Senenmut to his Council Room.

With Hatshepsut's declining health, Senenmut's alcohol consumption had grown progressively worse. Four-fifths of his caloric intake was now liquid. Pharaoh's guards arrived at his house before breakfast the following morning. They brought him as-is, clothes disheveled, smelling worse, his senses not recovered from the prior night's consumption.

Senenmut kept upright as he marched into the Council Room, halting before Pharaoh Thutmose.

Thutmose made it fifteen-seconds short. "Senenmut, despite your successes, the Kingdom will no longer indulge your arrogant, superior behavior. I therefore relieve you of all court duties. I strip you of all titles and banish you from the court. You will return to the Academy for whatever duties they assign. That is all."

Senenmut stumbled as he about-faced, but caught himself. He marched out, face hard and back stiffened.

When he had left the Council Room, Pharaoh turned to his Counselor, "I want all records of his existence erased."

The guards marched Senenmut straight to the river piers and put him on a boat to Inebu-hedj and the Academy. A servant had fetched his clothes and belongings and delivered them to the pier. Thutmose chartered a boat with Senenmut and his guards as the only passengers.

When the ship docked in Inebu-hedj, the guards sent a runner to report their arrival to the Academy. An Academy guide came to the dock to escort them, leading them to the Dean's office. Ramose was waiting.

Senenmut marched stiff-backed into the office, followed by the guards. One guard handed a scroll to Ramose, who thanked him.

After reading the scroll, Ramose addressed the guards. "Thank you for bringing Senenmut. You may return to the boat." The two guards bowed and left."

After they had left, Ramose continued, "Relax, son, have a seat."

Senenmut sat, his back no longer ramrod stiff, but remaining straight.

"Son, I'm sorry I'm not prepared, but we got no warning of your arrival. Inebu-hedj received word of Hatshepsut's death the day before yesterday by runner. I am sorry for your loss; You loved her dearly. I remember how I felt when your mother died.

"The scroll says Pharaoh has stripped you of your rank, titles, everything, and directs me to assign you to whatever suitable duties are available. I am sorry, but I have none. You would be a distraction; I simply cannot use you. I will put you up in one of the guest quarters tonight. Tomorrow I will book a passage for you to Iuny. Our old house is still there, vacant, ready. Your old Waset friends will only be twelve miles away. I'll arrange for our old bakery to make you food daily." He called for his clerk to take Senenmut and his belongings to the guest quarters.

Ramose tried visiting Senenmut after the day's work was complete. Senenmut had passed out.

A year later, Senenmut stopped picking up food at the bakery. A missed day, or even three, was usual, but when he had not come for a week, the baker stopped by his house after the day's work. There was no answer to his knock on the front door. On opening it, a foul smell assaulted him. Senenmut's partially decayed body lay on the floor.

No one remained in Iuny who wanted to claim the body.

The town undertaker worked for the embalmers. He rolled Senenmut's body into a blanket and buried it in an unmarked grave. There was no one to commemorate his passing.

Senenmut's deeds evaporated from Egyptian memory, his name erased.

He never existed.

Egypt consigned him to oblivion.

BOOK 2

Yahmose

Time steps back fourteen years to when Sefuamun/Yahmose had just turned seven. Senenmut takes him to the Military Academy to begin his training.

Chapter 10

Office of the Director, Smithsonian Museum

Present

It had taken a month, but finally David held the first page's English translation in his hands. The translator had faced a snag. She had translated the
cuneiform into its equivalent syllables. However, she was an expert in the
ancient Western Semitic language. Her remaining sheets were in ancient
Egyptian. She had to send them to an Egyptian scholar for translation into
English. They would not be ready for another three weeks. David shrugged
his shoulders. The sheets had rested for three-thousand, five hundred years.
Three weeks more were insignificant.

He asked Nancy to hold all calls for a half-hour and settled back to
read–his feet on his desk. The first page contained an explanation from the
Translator: she remarked that seemingly only a few pages remained from
a longer account. Each individual page started and stopped with an event.

Her first page notes read, "This is Abraham's record of his meeting
with the Servant Council." Its account began:

. . . relax; this is not an examination. For a thousand years we have asked
this question of every candidate, and from their wisdom and insight, we
have improved what the Ancients bequeathed to us. We also know that you
are still young and have not achieved full wisdom or ability. What we want
to know is any insight you may have about The-Divine. Who He is. What
He wants of us. How we can grow. How we can become better stewards.' I
took my seat and began, 'Arwain, gentlemen of the Council, thank you. I am
still just a young man and, although I have thought about The-Divine since

I arrived, I am not wise enough that you should give much credence to my tentative ideas. However, you need what little I can offer to help the Servants bring this world closer to what The-Divine wants. The record concluded in mid-sentence shortly after the Council testimony ended.

The central topic linking all pages was religious. The last entry was the episode about his son Isaac's sacrifice. It ended with Abraham's comments. "I had sworn to Yahweh that I would remain faithful–no matter what He asked of me. I would have sacrificed Isaac, but Yahweh prevented it by providing a ram. Why did He test me? To verify that I would fulfill my oath and remain faithful? No, God already knew. My continued growth required *my* knowing. God remained faithful because I was faithful. I verify this is my testimony."

The Translator included a note: Another hand wrote the name Abraham. It was undoubtedly Abraham's signature.

David put the translation down. This blew his mind. This document was genuine! The Biblical account also mirrored it. This story had remained accurate for a thousand years–until codified around 450 BCE in Babylon.

He needed to confirm the document's date by sacrificing a sliver of one sheet for carbon 14 testing. However, there was no doubt Abraham dictated and signed it. He realized that Professor Clifford Geartz's comments were prescient; when this news broke on the world, it would create the havoc of a nuclear bomb on the archaeological landscape.

RAMOSE'S HOUSE, INEBU-HEDJ

May 1471 BC

Senenmut, holding Sefuamun's hand, entered the Dean's office at the Military Academy.

Ramose sat at his table, reading the unavoidable paperwork involved with planning next year's classes. His skin revealed a man who had spent most of his life outdoors. He was almost sixty, with light brown hair. Few Egyptians did not have black hair. No Egyptian had blue eyes. He looked up from his papyrus. "Son!" He jumped up, rounded the desk, and the two men exchanged a hearty bear hug.

After a few seconds, Senenmut stepped back to arm's length, still holding his father's shoulders. "You're looking fit."

"I'm not bad for an old man of fifty-seven. I've got three more good years before I live on borrowed time." He switched the subject. "And who's this young man?"

Senenmut dropped one hand from his father's shoulder, spun sideways, and gestured to Sefuamun, "Father, I'd like you to meet your grandson."

Sefuamun bowed and said, "It is an honor to meet you, sire."

Ramose replied, "None of that. When you are in class, you must call me 'Dean.' That is necessary for decorum and proper military discipline. However, here at my house, I am just 'Grandfather.' Understand?"

"Yes, sir."

Ramose smiled, "Do to mean 'Yes, Grandfather?'"

After a few seconds, a smile crept onto Sefuamun's face. "Yes, Grandfather."

The trio only spent two happy days together. Senenmut needed to return to Waset. Hatshepsut and he were planning an ambassadorial trip to Punt, the land to Nubia's south.

The following morning, as breakfast was nearing an end, Grandfather returned the last piece of bread from his plate to the platter, stretched, and yawned. Sefuamun had finished. Ramose pushed his plate to the middle of the table and turned to his grandson. "It's time for us to begin. I need to start by finding out how much your father has already taught you. We'll begin by asking: What is your name?"

"Sefuamun."

"No, I mean your real name."

"Sefuamun."

"All right, let's switch subjects. What is God's name?"

"Which god?"

"Yahweh."

"I don't know of any god called Yahweh."

Ramose hung his head, whispering, "Just what I was afraid of. He wants acceptance too much."

Looking up, he saw Sefuamun's face, a quizzical look on it. "Sorry, I was just talking to myself."

"Father has a saying about talking to yourself."

"Let me guess? Does it start out: It's all right to talk to yourself?"

"Yes, then it continues. It's all right to answer yourself."

Ramose added, "It's all right to have a full-fledged conversation with yourself."

Sefuamun finished, "But, if you ask yourself: 'Huh, what did you say?' You've got a real problem."

Both laughed.

Ramose asked, "Do you know where your father got that saying?"

Sefuamun caught on quick. "You?"

Ramose replied by nodding a 'yes.'

Sefuamun asked, "Why were you talking to yourself?"

"Your father."

"My father?"

"Yes. He almost surrenders his Hebrew heritage because he wants to blend in. He wants acclaim. Did he tell you he isn't Egyptian?"

"What?"

"Yes, we are not Egyptian. We have adopted Egyptian names, so we can do our jobs effectively, but we aren't Egyptian."

"But, I'm Egyptian, aren't I?"

"No, Sefuamun, you aren't. You are half-Egyptian from your mother. However, a man gets his lineage from his father, not his mother. Therefore, you aren't Egyptian."

"Then who am I."

"You are a Hebrew."

"Oh, I've heard that word, only it's pronounced 'hapiru.'"

"No, that isn't the same word. In Egyptian, 'hapiru' is someone who sells labor, like a day laborer. Another example is a carpenter you hire to work in your house. You pay work supervisors wages, so they aren't hapiru.

"We are Hebrews. The Egyptians spell that as 'Haibrw.' Yes, I know; that is not how you pronounce it, but that is how they say it. When you learn to read and write, you find Egyptians do not always write the word as they pronounce it. Only cuneiform does that. I can say hieroglyphics is better now. Old Egyptian did not write any vowels. Now, they at least write some of them. Who knows how the writing will change in the next hundred years?

"But we've drifted off the subject. Hebrew has only one God–capital G.' The Egyptians have many gods–small 'g.' God's name is 'Yahweh,' and that translates as 'He is.' Yahweh created the world."

"But Egyptians say Atum created the world."

"I know, but even their creation story is inconsistent. It goes: 'Before the world came into being, there was nothing but an infinite expanse of lifeless water, complete darkness, and utter chaos, called Nun. Atum created himself out of Nun by uttering his own name.' Now, can you tell me what is inconsistent?"

"No, Grandfather, have I failed school already?"

"No, Sefuamun, you are a young boy, and we haven't taught you how to reason as an adult. Do not worry, we will teach you. Let me show you the inconsistent part: Atum created himself. Yet, before Atum, Nun was already there. Who created Nun?"

"Oh, I think I understand. Matter cannot create itself, so there must have been a god before Atum. However, in the story there was no god before Atum. That doesn't make sense."

"That's right. Now remember, we may know that their creation story is illogical, but we can never tell them because it angers them. We may ask questions about the inconsistencies, but never tell them they are wrong. Remember, Egyptians force their people to believe. We must allow people to believe what they want to believe, even if it is wrong. Yahweh never forces us to believe. We may believe or not at our choice. We call that 'faith.'

"Back to our original question. Why did I ask for your real name? It takes some explaining. In the Atum creation story, Atum created by speaking. The Egyptians believe in magic, which works by the power of speaking, just like Atum. Atum used 'white' magic, but spellbinders can also use 'black' magic. For their spells, they need to know your real name, your birth name. A pseudonym or nickname will not work. Your mother's throne name is Hatshepsut, but that is not her real name. In Egypt, only a few people can know your real name, so no spellbinder can cast a spell on you. For example, I do not know Hatshepsut's real name, and I never will. So, what is your real name?"

"From your question, my real name isn't Sefuamun, but I don't know what it is."

"It's Yahmose."

"That's a weird name."

"It may sound weird, but isn't. You are half-Hebrew and half-Egyptian. 'Yah' is from 'Yahweh.' 'Mose' is Egyptian for 'son of.' You are half-Hebrew and half-Egyptian, so your name is half-each as well. Your name means 'son of Yahweh.'"

Yahmose suddenly realized the world was more complicated than he had realized.

"Then you have a real name? What is your name?"

"Mine is 'Yahshua.'"

"What does that mean?"

"It means 'cry to Yahweh' or 'call on Yahweh.'"

"But that means I'm one of the few to know your real name?"

"No, Yahmose, black magic isn't real. It is a fake belief, but you cannot tell an Egyptian that, because they believe in it. Again, you can ask questions, which will reveal the inconsistency if they want to examine the problem, but you can never bluntly tell them. They must discover the truth themselves. You must allow them to believe what they want to believe. We can never force the truth on them."

"All right. I understand that. However, you said that we were not Egyptian; we are Hebrew. That means that Hebrew people are not from Egypt. Where are we from?"

Grandfather breathed out a long sigh. "What you are asking is actually two questions. The first: Where do we come from? Originally, our people came from the land between the two seas–the Black Sea and the Caspian Sea. We were sheep and goat herders. The Yamnaya, a horse-riding people, forced us south. We settled at Hebron in the Levant. Hebron is our home.

"Your second question: How did we come to live in Egypt? Two hundred years ago, his jealous brothers sold Joseph, one of our ancestors, into slavery in Egypt. When the Hyksos founded the fifteenth dynasty, Pharaoh Salitis freed him and made him vizier. During a famine, Joseph brought his entire clan to Egypt. We have been here since then. Joseph's Egyptian name was Zaphnath-Paaneah; you can look him up in the court annals.

"Now, I have one very important fact to teach you. Egypt reserves the Military Academy for aristocratic sons. Only on rare occasions has Egypt allowed commoners or foreigners admittance. I am the only non-aristocratic teacher we have ever had. Your father is the only commoner student. As your father's son, you are a half-breed. Therefore, you are going to experience insults. Many of the students will look down upon you, tease you, and taunt you. What can you do? We will start with what you cannot do. You are too old and too big for your mommy's lap. You must learn a fact to become a man: When facing adversity, you have to 'man up.' Never retaliate; never complain. I know you will have times where it will seem impossible. Just endure it. I will protect you from it getting out of hand. You may have heard the saying, 'If at first you don't succeed, try harder.' That does not work. It is a false belief. What is true is, 'If at first you don't succeed, work smarter.' We get our compensation by working harder and becoming smarter. Brains always win.

"Enough for now. I've got work to do."

"Thank you, Grandfather."

That night, lying on his mattress, Yahmose went over his day's experience since arriving.

I am confused. All my life, I have believed in the Egyptian gods. Now Ramose is telling me that is wrong. Logically, I can see that, but that is tough to swallow. My head may say Yahweh is God, but my feelings will not agree. I want to accept both, but I cannot. I feel divided in two and I do not know what to do.

However, he made one decision; he could love Ramose.

Senenmut may be my father, but he does not act like a father. He is distant, aloof. He devotes his attention more to himself than my brother Thutmose and I. Not that father is harsh; he just does not seem concerned about me. He does not care. I am an inconvenience.

I am a token to add to his collection, like all his titles. My existence checks a box on his required list of titles. He is a fake father. He does not want to spend the time to be a real one.

Ramose, however, is a real father, not just a grandfather. He cares; he gives his time and attention. When I grow up and become a father, I want to be like Ramose.

Ramose's House, Inebu-Hedj

May 1471 BC

Grandfather entered the room and saw Yahmose lighting a candle. "What are you doing?" he bellowed.

Yahmose jumped, then answered, "I'm lighting a candle to Amun."

"Put that out. There'll be no candles to Amun in my house."

Yahmose blew out the candle. "Grandfather, I don't understand. Father lights one every morning."

Ramose forced himself to calm down. Yahmose did not understand what he was doing. His voice returned to a normal tone. "I understand. Your father wants acceptance so much that he has almost given up his heritage. He is more Egyptian than Hebrew. Always remember this: we are Hebrews. Egypt is not our home. Here we are sojourners, strangers in a strange land. Hebron in the Levant is our actual home. Until we return home, we will never fully "fit in." What does that mean? I need to explain so you can understand. However, we must explain in two sessions: first the Hebrew and then the Egyptian stories. Only when you understand both, can you compare them. We will discuss the Hebrew story first. Let me think how best to set the stories in context. Let us go outside; I usually go to the garden when I need to think.

Grandfather and Yahmose sat cross-legged, side-by-side on the bench in the roof's shade, enjoying the smell of the flowers in the garden. A worm emerged from the ground. A bird landed, ate it, and flew away.

Grandfather asked, "Did you see the bird eat the worm?"

Yahmose nodded without speaking.

Grandfather continued, "Think of the difference between a bird and a worm. Which is more intelligent?"

"The bird."

"Good answer. Why are birds more intelligent?"

Yahmose thought for a minute. "Because worms don't have eyes. They only feel. However, birds must fly. So a bird needs eyes to see worms?"

"Again, an excellent answer. Now, are worms or flowers more intelligent?"

"I would guess worms. Worms have to move while flowers just sit?"

"Exactly right. So what is common to these facts? Intelligence." Grandfather ensured Yahmose had grasped what he was saying. Continuing, he said. "Now, think of our cook making a stew for dinner. We have watched her. How does she begin?"

"She starts with a fat and flour and mixes them in the cauldron's bottom."

"Then?" asked Ramose.

"She adds. First, she softens and browns pieces of onion. Then she adds garlic and other spices. Then she pours in water and at the last she puts in the meat and cooks the stew.

"Does she ever put the meat in the cauldron first?"

Yahmose thought for a minute. "No, I've never seen her do that. Why?"

"Think for a minute. If you added the meat first, and then tried mixing the fat and the flour, would that work?"

"No, both fat and flour would stick in the meat, not each other."

"Exactly right. This is the first lesson: When you need something complex, begin doing the simple. Then build step-by-step to the complex."

Yahmose smiled and nodded. "Yes, Grandfather, I understand."

Grandfather smiled to approve Yahmose for successfully thinking through the problem. "Now, let's transfer the same lesson to God. If God wanted to make a world, would he start with the most complex creations?"

"No, He would start simple and build to complex."

"That's right. Let us examine four categories: people, animals, plants and the ground. Place them in order from simple to complex."

Yahmose needed only a few seconds to think. "The dirt in the ground just sits there. The plants eat the dirt to grow. The animals eat the plants. Humans eat both plants and animals."

Grandfather clapped his hands, "Yahmose, you're right."

Yahmose beamed.

Grandfather continued, "Let's start at the beginning of the Hebrew creation story. We exist in a world of matter; Yahweh exists in a different world–a world of spirit. Time began when God *created* the matter world.

The spirit world is older. Because they are different, Yahweh put a boundary between the two worlds; a gap. Spirit can cross the gap to matter. Matter cannot cross to spirit.

Now, let us look at how Yahweh created this world. First, He only created three times. First, he *created* matter. From matter He *made* the ground, the water, the air, the sun, moon, and stars, the plants, and finally the fish and animals that do not have red blood. Next, He *created* animals that have red blood. Finally, He *created* us. Can you guess what the difference is between the three creations?

Yahmose thought for a minute, and admitted, "No, Grandfather, I can't. What changed?"

Grandfather explained, "This is a hard question, so I didn't expect you could guess. The first creation was matter and everything that only needs matter to live. The ground, the air, the stars are just matter. Then He added life. Life needs matter. Plants are alive, but they are just matter. Fish are alive, and they have bodies, but they are just matter. However, birds have red blood. Yes, they have bodies, but they are more than bodies. Let's pause before getting to the answer." After the pause, Grandfather asked, "What is God made of?"

Yahmose answered, "That's easy. God is spirit."

Grandfather cocked his head, "Does God have a body made of matter?"

"No, He doesn't have a body. He lives in a spirit world, so he must be all spirit."

"And for animals with red blood, God puts spirit into the animal. That is the difference. There is some of God's spirit in animals with red blood; but there is no spirit in animals like fish. They have no red blood. Fish and worms may have partial-life, but they do not have spirit, so they do not have complete-life."

Yahmose's eyebrows rose and his eyes got bigger. He had just learned something he did not expect.

Grandfather asked, "Can you now explain why we can eat a fish whole, but before we eat an animal that has red blood, we must drain the blood into the ground?"

Yahmose thought for a minute, and exclaimed, "We're not allowed to eat red blood. That means we may not eat spirit. After the animal dies, its spirit must return to God. Is that right?"

"Yes, Yahmose, that is exactly right. However, there is another difference between humans and animals. Do you know what that is?"

"I know that one. Only humans have a soul like God."

"Correct. That separates us from the animals. Animals have red blood, but they don't have a soul."

Grandfather let the importance of what Yahmose had learned sink in. After a minute, he continued, "Now, Yahmose, can you tell me why the words we say in a Hebrew worship service are important? The words: 'You shall love the LORD your God with all your heart, and with all your soul, and with all your might.' What do the words 'heart, soul and might' have to do with God's three creations?"

Yahmose thought about that for a couple of minutes; his head lowered in concentration. Grandfather allowed him the silence to think.

Finally, Yahmose's head popped up. "Oh, I know. The 'might' is our muscles, which is matter. The 'heart' is our blood, which is spirit. The 'soul' is soul. It means we love God with all of our being. All three parts. We hold nothing back."

"Exactly right." Grandfather took a deep breath. "There's a fourth category of creation. However, I will ask another question first. Do we worship the pharaoh?"

"No. He is a man just like us. He doesn't deserve worship."

"Exactly right. We respect him, but we don't worship him." Grandfather paused, "What is the difference between Egypt's gods and us?"

"I don't know."

"They have the same three parts as us. They have a body's matter, blood's spirit, and soul. The one difference is they do not age, so they can be immortal. You can think of them as a higher class of humans.

"Now the question: since they are like us, should we worship them or respect them?"

For Yahmose, the logic was straightforward: "We should respect them, but never worship them."

"Yahmose, this is the most important fact to learn: We worship the Lord, and the Lord alone. Worshipping a god is turning your back on the Lord. It's unforgivable."

That sunk into Yahmose's consciousness like a lead weight. 'I will worship the Lord, and the Lord alone. Worshipping a god is turning my back to the Lord. It's unforgivable.'

Ramose finished, "Now you know why we don't light candles for Amun. It's worship."

"And we only worship Yahweh," finished Yahmose.

Ramose's face beamed with his pleasure. Yahmose returned it, and they shared a hug.

RAMOSE'S HOUSE, INEBU-HEDJ

May 1471 BC

Yahmose chose a divan because it was more comfortable; Grandfather sat in a chair. "We talked about creation yesterday, but we looked at it from a Hebrew perspective.

"However, since we live in Egypt, we need to understand what they believe. There are four major Egyptian creation stories. They are alike in some respects, different in others. Let us start with the Atum story of creation. It goes: 'Before the world came into being, there was nothing but an infinite expanse of lifeless water, complete darkness, and utter chaos, called Nun. Atum created himself out of Nun by uttering his own name.' I need to show you how that story is right and wrong.

"Let's start at the beginning. In both Egyptian and Hebrew creation stories, we live in a matter world.

"However, in the Hebrew Story, Yahweh exists in a different world–a world of spirit. Time began when God *created* the matter world. The spirit world is older. Because they are different, Yahweh put a boundary between them; a gap. Spirit can cross to matter, but not matter to spirit. Once Yahweh *created* matter, he *made* everything in the world. He *fashioned* the matter to the world we see today.

"Now examine the Atum story. In the beginning was Nun, the infinite expanse of lifeless water, complete darkness, and utter chaos. This was the created matter world before Yahweh began fashioning. So, according to the Hebrew perspective, the Egyptian story got the Nun part right. However, in the Egyptian story, Atum created himself. That part is wrong, because Atum is part matter and matter cannot create itself. Therefore, the Egyptians got part of their story right and part wrong.

"Why is it wrong? The Egyptians do not understand that spirit differs from matter. They try forcing all creation into the matter world. That is wrong. Matter is not like that.

"What's wrong with their gods? They are part matter, not all spirit. They are of this world, so they cannot be fully spirit, like Yahweh. Let us use an analogy: the students in the Military Academy must respect me as the Dean. I am superior in rank to them. As superior beings to us, we must also respect the gods. However, the students do not worship me; and we do not worship gods. We only worship Yahweh. The result: we do not worship Egyptian gods; we only respect them. Does that make sense?"

"Yes, I understand, Grandfather."

"Thank you, Yahmose. We are halfway through the lesson. You need to understand what Yahweh wants of us and how that differs from the Egyptian idea. Question: what is 'Maat?'"

Yahmose answered, "Maat means 'order' or 'balance.' A god's job is to keep order or proper balance in the cosmos. The Pharaoh's job is to preserve order in Egypt."

"That is correct. The Egyptians assume this world is already perfect–as good as it can get. In their view, humanity's job is preserving that perfection and fixing it when broken.

Yahmose nodded his head. Then he asked, "Is that what Yahweh wants?"

"No, Grandson. That is not what Yahweh wants. He did not give us a perfect world."

Ramose paused. "When someone acts for their master, and does what their master desires, what do you call him?"

Yahmose did not understand; his face made that obvious.

Grandfather filled in. "You call him a steward. God wants us to grow. Think of this world as a school. God gave us a world with flaws so we would have a challenge. God wants us to learn how to make this world a better place. Now, do you understand the difference between what the Egyptian world asks and what Yahweh wants from us?"

"Yes, Grandfather. I am not ready. I've got growing to do."

Ramose smiled, "We all do, Yahmose, we all do."

That night, lying on his mattress, Yahmose wondered: *Is there anything that Grandfather does not know? I am not Egyptian; I am a Hebrew. I am convinced that Yahweh is real and the Egyptian gods are not 'God' like Yahweh. When I grow up, I want to be like Grandfather.*

That resolution instigated another. *If I am going to be like Grandfather, I need to learn everything. Like he does.*

He thought about that for a few minutes. *I wonder how he knows so much? I know; he reads. Behind his desk is that big bookshelf with a hundred papyrus scrolls. I need to learn how to read; then I will know everything also!*

That thought put a smile of anticipation on his face. *Tomorrow, I will ask him to teach me how to read.*

His mind made up, he turned over and fell asleep.

INEBU-HEDJ, RAMOSE'S HOUSE

May, 1471 BC

When Ramose returned from work one night, he took Yahmose into his office. Wooden shelves stretched the length of the wall behind his table. Half of the shelving was wooden cubicle niches containing papyrus scrolls. There were also flat shelves stacked to overflowing with papyrus sheets, figurines, a Senet board, and a Hounds and Jackals board. On the bottom shelf was a wooden box about sixteen by eighteen inches by three and a half inches deep. Ramose removed the box and put it on the table, then removed the lid. He signaled for Yahmose to look.

Inside was a fourteen by sixteen inch hardened clay tablet resting on white linen. Arrayed along the top in a straight line were eleven signet ring impressions. Yahmose could recognize the patterns from ones he had seen before, but could not read them. He could only recognize that they were two alphabets, because he had seen enough writing to know the last was Egyptian hieroglyphics.

"What is it, Grandfather?"

"It's a record of our clan lineage. It goes back almost three-hundred years. The first two are from our clan founder, Abraham. Each impression goes from father to son, in an unbroken line. My name is next to last in the row. Your father is the last. When you reach adulthood, you will enter your ring, and when you have a son, he will enter his."

"Wow!"

Grandfather stood, looking at Yahmose, who was inhaling the sight of the tablet, bug-eyed, lost in wonder. After a few minutes, he motioned for Yahmose to back up, replaced the top, and carefully turned the box over. He removed a lower lid off the bottom. Inside was a stack of vellum sheets, scraped so thin that, when you held a sheet up to sunlight from the window, you could see the light shining through it. Grandfather removed them and placed them on the table. Yahmose recognized the top sheet's writing as cuneiform.

"What does it say, Grandfather?"

"A scribe wrote this for Abraham himself before he died. It's his record of important life events. His signature, written by his own hand, is on a sheet further down the stack. I would like to read you his story. Please have a seat. This takes a while."

Yahmose jumped on a chair, and Grandfather read. Event by event, Abraham's life unfolded, while Yahmose sat enthralled. Twenty-eight villagers attacked Abraham and his father, but they remained faithful and defeated them. The Regional Council did not select him for Stonehenge priesthood. But, because he remained faithful, the Regional Director appointed him. The trip to Stonehenge. The real meaning of ephod. The trip to the spirit world. Inventing the chariot and compound bow. Council success and rejection. Through it all, Abraham remained faithful. Serving at Hebron. The trip to Egypt. The Border Official taking Sarrai for Pharaoh's harem. The Servant slaughter. Because Abraham had remained faithful, he and he alone survived. God's revelations to him. The battle at Laish that prevented the Sumerian army from using the bitumen they had stolen. The test of Abraham being willing to sacrifice Isaac. There was no need for God to test Abraham; God already knew. He did it so Abraham would know. Through it all, Abraham had remained faithful, and God had blessed him. His last sentence: I got nothing I had longed for, everything I had hoped for. God has blessed me.

Through it all, Yahmose sat unmoving, his rapt attention engulfing the story like the sea swallows a river flowing into it. When Grandfather had read the last of Abraham's sheets and replaced it on the stack, Yahmose commented, "That sounds real, but it also sounds too good to be real."

Grandfather pointed to what looked like a plaster painting in a wood frame. On closer examination, tesserae composed a mosaic of a chariot. However, a weird chariot. Its wheels were tiny and had four spokes. "I wondered about the story's truthfulness myself, so I contacted our ambassador to Mitanni and asked if he could verify the story." Grandfather went to the shelves and searched. On finding the papyrus he wanted, he held it up. "Here is his reply. Kikkuli was in their royal records. He and his two unnamed companions invented both the chariot and compound bow. Kikkuli had a war memorial picture containing his chariot carved into a hill's granite side near Washukkari. The ambassador had this tesserae mosaic copy of it made for me. Incidentally, since he was the King's nephew, Kikkuli survived the Servant slaughter." Grandfather paused while Yahmose gawked at the mosaic. After a few minutes, he pointed to a vase on a table. "I also contacted our ambassador to the Mycenaeans, who visited Pylos. There is a family of chariot makers, but they have no record or memory of Klymenos. But the family had a satellite business making copies of this vase; it's that popular." Yahmose noted that its small wheels and four spokes duplicated the mosaic."

Grandfather and Yahmose resumed their seats, and Grandfather continued, "I went to the Hall of Records and examined the annals of Pharaoh Imyremeshaw. It records a great cattle die-off and an earthquake leveling four towns with seventeen-thousand lost. Of course, there was no record of giving gold to Abraham and shoving him out of Egypt. Last, there was a great battle in 1742 BC between Babylon and its tribute states. Babylon barely won because the Elamite army did not make it to the battlefield. They lacked bitumen to waterproof their ghoofas, and didn't arrive on time."

"Wow," was all Yahmose could say.

"Now," continued Grandfather. There are other stories for other days. Today's last lesson is learning what God is trying to teach us from Abraham's story. Can you guess?"

Yahmose thought about it for a minute. "Can you help me, Grandfather?"

"The key to Abraham's story is, no matter what happens, always remain faithful. If you are faithful, God will be faithful and bless you. You need to make this part of your very soul. You may not get what you want, but He will give you what you need."

"Yes, Grandfather."

That night, before he drifted off to sleep, Yahmose reviewed the day's events in his mind. *I have learned so much, and I have hardly started. The world makes sense in the Yahweh story, and it does not in the Egyptian story. The Egyptian story is wrong.* Then he remembered Nun. *No, not completely wrong, only partly wrong. However, partly wrong in a god-story is all-wrong.*

I can trust Grandfather. I need to believe in Yahweh. I need to do what Yahweh wants of me. Grandfather calls it duty. Just as a soldier's duty is to guard his country, worshipping Yahweh is my duty. I just do not know how God wants me to do it. What is my duty?

Grandfather tells me that, when I am ready, God will show me. But I don't want to wait; I want to know now.

But Grandfather tells me I'm not ready now; I have growing and learning to do first. All right, I can understand that. But when will He tell me? I guess not until I need it. When will I need it?

Whenever that is, whatever it is, I will have to learn to trust him to show me. And, if I am faithful, Yahweh will bless me.

RAMOSE'S HOUSE, INEBU-HEDJ

September 1469 BC

Yahmose returned from the day's training and flopped on a chair, dejection in his posture, scowl on his face, and heartbreak in his voice. "I'm a failure. My first real battle, someone's going to kill me."

Ramose put down the scroll he was studying. "Sounds like today's training didn't go according to your expectations."

"We started quarterstaff training today. I had five different bouts with five different opponents. They slaughtered me–all five times." His voice came close to quavering.

"Good. Your instructor did exactly what I asked him to do."

Yahmose's jaw actually dropped, his mouth opened, utter shock on his face. "What?"

"Of course. You are one of the five smallest boys in your class. You have not started growing yet. I expect that, in your first round of bouts this week, you will lose twenty-two of the twenty-four. No student yet knows how to use the quarterstaff effectively. In the hands of someone with no understanding or training, it is merely a big stick, useful for stirring the fire and not much else. However, in the hands of a trained soldier, it is a lethal weapon. In the first round, the winners will be the bigger, more muscular boys who depend on strength and power alone. However, after training, they will continue to depend on muscle and, in the last round, they will lose twenty bouts."

Yahmose closed his mouth, but he remained speechless. He could not believe what he had just heard, but Ramose had stated it calmly as a fact–so he could not discount it.

Ramose let him have fifteen seconds, then suggested, "Let's go out to the garden and show what I mean."

The two walked out to the back. Waiting there were two quarterstaffs and protective gear. That opened Yahmose's eyes. *Ramose planned this. He knew what would happen in our training today. This means he has an important lesson he wants me to learn. Yahmose went into full-attention student mode. Whenever Ramose did the training himself, it was important, and it always meant that he did not trust his instructors to give the best level of training. It means I am getting something the rest of the class is missing.*

Both donned their protective gear.

Ramose held his quarterstaff horizontally with both hands in the center. "Yahmose, I want you to swing a roundhouse blow and hit me in the chest with all of your strength."

Holding the end of his staff, Yahmose twirled it behind him, and swung it in a horizontal arc as hard as he could at Ramose. Ramose turned his staff vertically and halted Yahmose's swing with a parry ninety degrees to the swing direction.

"Try it again." Ramose commanded.

The same result.

"Let's sit down and discuss what happened and why."

They took off their headgear and sat on the bench. Ramose began, "When you are new to a weapon, and don't know how to use it properly, you always try to depend on power. Let us say that, with your body size and strength, you can swing the staff with seventy-five pounds of force. To stop that blow completely, as I did, I needed to generate at least seventy-five pounds of resistance force. A bigger boy may generate a hundred pounds of force in his blow, but you can only generate seventy-five pounds to stop it. Therefore, by using sheer force and power alone, he can beat you. That happened today. Since you are all new to the quarterstaff, the bigger boys win the first round.

"However, once you learn to use the weapon, power is the least important factor. More important than power is speed. A soldier, depending on strength alone, will always lose to a faster opponent. It takes a long time to execute a roundhouse blow. If you are faster, you can see it coming, react faster and deflect the blow. Then, also because you are faster, you can strike the return blow more quickly than they can parry it. You are smaller and faster than the big boys. Because you are faster, you can win. You will only lose when you make a mistake.

"More important than sheer speed is quickness. In man-to-man combat, we call it finesse. It knocks your opponent off-balance. To sum up, finesse trumps speed, and speed trumps power.

"This first week, you are not ready to learn speed and finesse; your first task is becoming familiar with the weapon. Therefore, this week you will depend on power alone. Starting next week, your instructors will begin introducing the techniques of speed and finesse. You will spend three months on the quarterstaff, then four months learning the sword. The sword uses the same three general categories of power, speed and finesse, but each individual weapon's techniques are different. You need to build these into your muscle-memory so that you can do them without thinking.

"Now, ask why we teach you the quarterstaff first. Since an officer's primary weapon is the sword, you will never fight with the staff again, so why learn it?" Ramose did not pause. "What is a shepherd's crook?" He did not let Yahmose think. "A quarterstaff with a hook on the end. What is a spear?" This time, he paused and motioned for Yahmose to answer.

Yahmose had all the lead-in he needed. "A quarterstaff with a point on the end?"

"Exactly. Even if you are a spearman and the point of your spear sticks to the backbone of the enemy, and comes off your spear, you still have your quarterstaff. In the future, your sergeants will train your spearmen in quarterstaff fighting, but you need to know how well they are doing and be able to make up the difference if they are weak trainers."

Now everything made sense to Yahmose. There was a method to the madness of training with the quarterstaff.

Ramose allowed Yahmose a minute to assimilate what he had just learned, and continued, "Put your headgear back on. It's time for phase two."

When they had assumed the same relative positions as before, Ramose commanded, "Give me another roundhouse blow; the same as before."

Yahmose grabbed the end of his quarterstaff, swung the end behind him, and power-housed the swing at Ramose's chest. However, this time, Ramose did not halt the swing at a ninety-degree angle. He held his staff steady, canting it down at a forty-five degree angle to the blow. Yahmose's staff hit and slid down Ramose's staff and the impetus made Yahmose's blow slam into the ground. Ramose swung the back end of his staff around and gently hit Yahmose on the arm.

Yahmose's jaw dropped in amazement.

Ramose explained, "You invested so much power in your swing that you lost control when I parried your blow. By canting my staff and not stopping the blow abruptly, I did not need as much force to parry your blow. Now your seventy-five pounds of strength is enough to beat your opponent's one hundred pounds. Remember, power takes time to set up and generate. My speed beat your power. Now the last demonstration. Give me another roundhouse blow with everything you've got."

This time, Ramose lifted his staff so Yahmose's blow hit the end of Ramose's staff, but Ramose had only one hand in the middle of his staff. Ramose used his hand as a fulcrum. Yahmose's blow swung the other end of Ramose's staff around the fulcrum and Ramose's staff hit Yahmose in the head, bowling him over and dropping him to the ground."

Rattled and disoriented, Yahmose asked, "What happened?"

"All the force of your blow merely swung my staff around my hand and the back end of my staff hit you in the head with the same amount of force you put into the blow. I used almost no force to hold my fulcrum hand in place. In effect, you hit yourself with the blow you had intended for me. The lesson? Finesse always trumps speed."

"Wow. I need to learn how to do that!" With renewed determination, Yahmose expected the result, "Then nobody can beat me."

Ramose smiled, "That's right. Finesse beats speed and speed beats power. On the battlefield, once you have learned the techniques, brains always beat brawn. You just have to put in the time and effort to learn the techniques.

"Grandfather, I was wrong. I can do this; I just have to put in the work to learn it."

Ramose had achieved the effect he had intended. Yahmose was no longer despondent. The quarterstaff revelation invigorated him. He now looked forward to tomorrow's bouts, confident of eventual success. Yahmose had the brains, ability, and desire to become an outstanding officer. He just needed the time and training to learn.

He felt rejuvenated.

VIZIER'S COUNCIL BUILDING, INEBU-HEDJ

April 1468 BC

Ten-year-old boys do not walk into the Vizier's building to see him. The guard stopped the boy at the door. "I can't allow you in."

"But I need to see the Vizier. It's important."

"The Vizier does not see young boys. Please ask your father to seek an audience."

"I can't. My mother is leading the Egyptian delegation to Punt and my father is with her."

The Vizier does not have guards lacking thinking ability. Pharaoh Hatshepsut was leading the delegation to Punt. Father and mother? A commoner boy would not have the intelligence or bravery to seek an audience with the Vizier. This must not be an ordinary boy. "Who are your father and mother?"

"My father is Senenmut and my mother is Pharaoh Hatshepsut."

That news caught the guard's attention. "I see. Of course you can't ask them, because they aren't here. Tell you what, come with me to the clerk's office to see the Viziers meeting schedule. We will know if he has an opening today, or we will need to schedule you later. All right?"

The boy smiled. That was all he wanted. "All right."

The guard led the boy to the clerk's office, who listened to his report. Turning to the boy, he asked, "If I'm going to put you on the Vizier's appointment list, I need to know who you are. I have to record everyone's name in the meeting records."

"My name is Sefuamun."

The clerk did not suffer from a case of 'The-Dumbs.' *Oh, my god. The Royal Family.* He temporized, "Tell you what. The Vizier has meetings scheduled the whole day, but let's see if he can squeeze you in."

The clerk returned in five minutes. "The Vizier gives his apologies that he has a full meeting schedule. However, if you're willing, he would like to invite you to have lunch with him and you can conduct your business then."

"That will be fine. Please thank him and say that I accept."

When lunchtime came, the Vizier went to see the clerk. Sefuamun sat in a corner chair, waiting. "Sefuamun, I've heard a lot about you, but I haven't had the pleasure of meeting you. If you will come with me to my chamber, they have just delivered lunch. The bread is warm, and the beer is cool."

In the Vizier's chambers, he grabbed some garlic bread and topped it with sliced onion and leek. He motioned for Sefuamun to pick what he liked and sat in his chair."

"Thank you, but I don't want to waste your time. I can eat after we conduct business."

That shocked the Vizier. *This boy appears only ten years old, yet he thinks, talks and acts like an adult. His Academy training has been effective. He has earned his reputation.* He put his sandwich down. "I thank you. I also agree. What brings you to see me?"

"I need you to arrange a meeting for me with the Council of the Great Ten the next time they meet in Inebu-hedj."

That perked up the Vizier's ears. "You realize I can't just put you on the schedule without knowing the decision they must make. The council members like to study the pros and cons of an argument to prepare for the meeting. What's this about?"

Sefuamun told him.

"You're correct. It is important and needs a council decision. I trust, for something of this importance, you have evidence to support your claim?"

Sefuamun told him.

"You're right, that will work. Now, does your father or grandfather know what you're doing?"

"No, sir. When they find out, they will castigate me. They try to act like ordinary Egyptian commoners when they are not. Yes, they want to show they have earned what they have accomplished, but the abuse they have endured is unethical. I am only trying to right the wrong. If I can do that, it's worth the punishment."

"Sefuamun, I believe you are correct. The Council will meet here in six weeks; I will ensure you have an audience. Just realize that you will have to bring your evidence."

"I understand."

COUNCIL CHAMBER OF THE GREAT TEN OF UPPER AND LOWER EGYPT, INEBU-HEDJ

June 1468 BC

The twenty-one members of the Council sat on their dais. Sefuamun was standing on the floor before the chair, with a large wooden box held in his arms. The clerk brought a small table, set it next to Sefuamun and stepped back, and Sefuamun placed the box on the table. The chair motioned for the Vizier to open the proceedings.

"Sefuamun, please tell the Council the story you related to me."

"Yes, Sir," Sefuamun bowed to the Council, and began. "The story happened at the end of the Twelfth Dynasty. The Pharaoh was Amenemhat III. He had no male heir, so he adopted the army general as his son, and the two ruled jointly for a few years. There are three lists of pharaohs recording dates and names from this time. One of them lists Amenemhat IV as his son, the other two as his adopted son. However, Amenemhat IV died before the Pharaoh. Therefore, Amenemhat III next declared his eldest daughter, Neferuptah, to be his heir.

"Amenemhat III wanted to exploit the copper mines in the southern Sinai, so he made a treaty with the Bedouin tribe who controlled that region. As part of the pact, Amenemhat's second daughter married the son of the Bedouin chieftain, a man named Ghassan Fathi. They had a son.

"Before Amenemhat III died, his eldest daughter also died. This left the kingdom to his second daughter, Sobekneferu. She was the last pharaoh of the Twelfth Dynasty. When she died after reigning six years, their son became Pharaoh Sebekhotep I, the founder of the Thirteenth Dynasty. Even though he was of divine blood from his mother, Sebekhotep's father was not a commoner, or he could not become pharaoh. His father had noble blood, just not Egyptian noble blood."

Nefer-Weben interrupted, "Yes, yes, that's all old knowledge. What's today's connection?"

"You see," answered Sefuamun, "I belong to a tribe called Israel. Ramose is the tribal chief and of noble blood. Senenmut is a prince. As his son, I also have noble blood from my father. However, Egypt allows its people to ridicule Ramose and Senenmut for being commoners. Egypt is committing an affront to Egypt's gods, who selected Senenmut to be Hatshepsut's consort."

Pawah asked, "You are of noble blood from your father and of divine blood from your mother? You realize that places you ahead of Thutmose III in the line of succession?"

"Yes, but Thutmose is already Pharaoh, and I don't want to be. I claim my father's heritage, not my mother's."

Nefer-Weben broke in, "What you want is irrelevant. The gods make the rules; we don't."

The Vizier interrupted, "May I suggest the Council may be acting prematurely. I believe we need to verify Sefuamun's claim. He brought a box containing a clay tablet he calls an Ephod, which contains a list of his genealogy going back to its founder." He turned his attention to his clerk. "Please open the box and read its contents?"

"Yes, Sire," replied the clerk. He lifted the lid and described what he saw. "It's a clay tablet resting on a folded white garment. The tablet is about fourteen by sixteen inches and almost two inches thick. It contains a row of signet ring impressions. The first are in cuneiform, the last in Egyptian hieroglyphics. The inscriptions: 'Havram, Abraham, Isaac, Jacob, Israel" and he continued until he had read the eleven impressions, "and ends with Senenmut." Then he continued his evaluation. "This boy could not have forged the tablet. He isn't old enough to be a scribe."

The clerk continued, "However, there's more. He turned the box upside down and removed the bottom lid. Removing several parchment sheets, he held them up. This is Abraham's account of founding the Israelite religion. It begins three-hundred years ago. It tells the story of how he invented the chariot. His partner was Kikkuli, a Hurrian. The Hyksos conquered Egypt using Hurrian chariots and founded the fifteenth dynasty. Also, remember that Egypt broke the secret of the Servant religion. We thought all Servants perished. The sole survivor was Abraham. I have checked this account against our records. These confirm Sefuamun's testimony. The tablet is genuine; and Sefuamun, his father and grandfather, are nobility."

The Vizier took charge, "Sefuamun, thank you for coming. The Council will need to discuss what you have presented. You may leave now. Please take the Ephod with you."

Sefuamun nodded, bowed to the Council, took the box and left.

Council meetings were usually sedate, with measured arguments and calm bearing. To say that Sefuamun's testimony and evidence was upsetting was a gross understatement. A category seven earthquake shook the Council. Heated debate divided its members; there was no consensus how to interpret this evidence. No agreement on how to continue. Had they misread the god's will again? Yes, the ash cloud had receded after Hatshepsut became Pharaoh. However, had they also chosen the wrong successor when proclaiming Thutmose III Pharaoh?

The following day, the Council met again. The members had time to digest the prior day's events. Though no longer heated, the disputes continued.

At last, they compromised. They elected to recognize Ramose, Senenmut, and Sefuamun as nobility. In addition, they assigned Pawah to seek guidance from Amun about the will of the gods for the line of succession. No one was comfortable with the status quo, but there was no consensus on how to continue. They would wait for a sign.

Yahmose took his punishment with his head up; knowing he had done the right thing. Maybe not the best way; but he was too young to know the best way. But the right thing. And the result was worth it.

MILITARY ACADEMY, LIBRARY INEBU-HEDJ

October 1465 BC

Sefuamun was alone, sitting in a chair in the military academy's library, when a sound disturbed him. He looked up from the treatise he was studying. "Pawah, you're a long way from Waset. Another meeting of the Great Ten?"

"No, Sefuamun, I came to see you."

"Me?"

"Yes, it's time to begin your religious training."

"What? Not Khusebek?"

"No. He's satisfactory for Neferure and Thutmose, but you are more intellectually gifted and need sophisticated training."

"I don't need training. I'm not becoming pharaoh."

"I beg to differ. The Council has not chosen you. However, if Thutmose dies, you are next in succession. We must plan for that possibility. We can't leave Egypt unprepared."

"I understand. I am faithful. Therefore, it is my duty to take the training."

Pawah chose a chair and sat beside Sefuamun. "Let's start by determining how much you know already. Can you tell me what you have learned about our creation stories?"

"There are four primary creation stories. They come from the cities of Lunu and Khemenu in the delta, Inebu-hedj, here where the Nile empties into the delta, and Waset in Upper Egypt. Although these different accounts do not agree in all details, they are similar. I will give you my understanding of a conflation of the four accounts.

"Before the world came into being, there was nothing but an infinite expanse of lifeless water, complete darkness, and utter chaos, called Nun. It was lifeless, black, chaos.

"Atum created himself out of Nun by uttering his own name. He created two offspring: Shu, representing dry air, and Tefnut, representing moist air. They separated the sky from the waters. The Ogdoad represented the innate qualities of the primeval waters. These eventually converged, resulting in a great upheaval, producing the primal pyramid-shaped mound. It emerged from Nun first. Thus, everything came from chaos. All this happened before time began.

"From the primal mound emerged the sun in a distant period known as Zep Tepi or 'the first occasion.' There are differing versions of the sun's emergence, either directly from the mound or from a lotus flower growing from the mound. However, in reality, everything is a manifestation of Atum.

"At first, the gods lived on earth and set up kingdoms. When the gods left the earth to live in the heavenly world, the pharaohs inherited the right to rule. The earth is a sacred landscape, a reflection of the heavenly world of the gods. Lacking successful preservation of order, this world's tendency is to degrade to the disorder of the Nun. Pharaoh's responsibility is to preserve Maat, or balance, in Egypt. "

Pawah nodded. "Although I might differ in some minor details, that's a good representation of the four stories. Looks like you've made at least a good beginning."

"Thank you, Pawah. If I may, I have some questions. I know I am still a youth and expect that has much to do with my current limited knowledge and understanding. If I could give you some of my questions, it might help you direct my training. Would you mind?"

"It's a good idea."

"Let me begin with a thought experiment. Imagine five pillars standing in a row. If I do nothing, they will continue to stand forever. However, if I push on the pillar at one end, it will fall toward the next, and so on, until all have fallen. I call this sequence the "Law of Cause and Effect." If I start from the fifth pillar, the ultimate effect, nothing happens without a preceding cause. Does that make sense?"

"It's logical."

If the Law is true, how can a god create himself? That violates the Law."

"The Law only applies to humans. It doesn't apply to gods."

"But, if one god can self-create, why has there only been one self-creation?"

"Because there is only one god. Everything is a manifestation of Atum."

"So there is nothing but Atum?"

"Precisely."

"If everything is a manifestation of Atum, you're saying the Law both applies and does not apply to Atum."

"That is correct."

"That makes no sense."

"Gods don't have to make sense."

"But if I'm Atum, why don't I make sense to myself? That does not seem logical. All right, let me ask another way. In all four major creation stories, Nun was there at the beginning, right?"

"That's correct."

"But, in Spell 261 of the '*Coffin Texts*,' the god Heka had a primordial status. It states, 'I existed before Nun, before the universe and before the other gods came into being.' The god Maat also existed before Nun. Therefore, if Nun was not before Heka, that implies that Nun came into being. How was Nun created?"

"You are getting ahead of yourself. Before Nun, time hadn't started, so asking a time question before time began is irrelevant."

"All right, let me approach my question from a different angle. Why do humans sacrifice to the gods when, in reality, they are only offering sacrifices to themselves? Why offer sacrifices at all? What is the point? Above all, why are some sacrifices accepted and others rejected? If we are Atum, we already know which sacrifices we will accept or reject. "

"Sefuamun, we'll answer these. However, one step at a time. At your level of training, these questions will not make sense. You need to learn more than I can teach you in this brief session before it will make sense."

"All right. I'll wait for that. Allow me to switch to another category of question. First, gods are immortal and immutable. Unchanging. Seth killed his brother, Osiris. If gods are immortal, was Osiris a god? Second, originally the gods lived on the earth with the god Re being the first pharaoh. He ruled for thousands of years. The story says that he grew old and senile, and that other gods and humans made fun of him and plotted behind his back. After taking vengeance, he grew weary of this earth and left for heaven, with the rest of the gods going with him. If Re could grow old and senile, was he a god?"

Pawah gave a barely audible sigh. "Again, we'll examine these later."

Sefuamun broke in, "I have one last category of question. When we return, we come back to Egypt to our bodies and they rejuvenate. Right?"

"Right."

"Let's say there are a billion of us that return. However, Egypt is the same as now, and the land can only grow food to feed ten million. How will we eat?"

Pawah's head physically recoiled, and after a few seconds, he apologized, "I'm sorry, but I don't remember that answer to that question. I will have to go back to the texts and look up the answer. The next time I came back, I will let you know."

"Thank you Pawah, I can wait,"

Pawah stood to end the session. "You have grounding to learn before we can leap ahead. I believe I know enough about your religious knowledge to put a training program together that I can tailor to your needs. I think that is enough for now. I will see you the next time I come to Inebu-hedj, probably in six months. Thank you, Sefuamun."

"Thank you, Pawah. I hope I haven't been too overbearing in asking for understanding."

"No, Sefuamun, it's natural in your state of growth."

Yahmose was content. He had renewed confirmation of Ramose's teaching. *Grandfather is always right. Brains always win. I never attacked Pawah or his beliefs. What did I do? I simply held my religious quarterstaff at the fulcrum point and allowed my staff to swing around from Pawah's blow and strike him in the back of his head. He is now off-balance and, for him, there can be no recovery.*

On leaving the library, Pawah thought, *No one has asked these questions before. I may not know the answers today, but I have six months to find them. There must be answers. I need to dig deep into our religious library. The answers must be there.*

Pawah had booked passage on one of the rare boats that sailed both day and night. That enabled the transit in half the time and resulted in a cheaper fare. However, the night's helmsman grew tired, misjudging the current while transiting a rocky passage. The current grabbed the boat's bow, spinning it sideways. That dropped the sail's air, causing the helmsman to lose control as the current propelled the boat onto a rock, piercing the hull. The boat capsized and sank with all aboard.

Sefuamun's questions remained unanswered.

MILITARY ACADEMY, INEBU-HEDJ

April 1463 BC

Thutmose and Sefuamun were working on a homework assignment in writing cuneiform.

Thutmose passed his clay tablet to Sefuamun and asked. "Have I gotten the right answers?"

Sefuamun pointed to a particular sign. "No, no, Thutmose, you can't do that. It's the wrong sign."

"But that's the sign for 'tum,' isn't it?" Thutmose asked.

"Yes, but there are ten different signs for the syllable 'tum.' You used *a* sign for 'tum,' but an incorrect one. The sign has to match the context where you use it. For example, a religious context uses a different sign than a secular. Here's another mistake." He pointed to a different sign.

"But that's the sign for 'du,' isn't it?" Thutmose asked.

"Remember, when writing in cuneiform, the answer is usually yes and no. Yes, it is the sign for 'du.' However, the sign for 'du' can have seven different contexts, each with a different meaning. Just having that sign by itself, you do not know what it means. The way you wrote, it could also mean 'leg' or 'to bring.' You add a determinative to specify its meaning. This sentence use is 'to stand,' therefore, you add a 'nu' to the sign. Yes, we do not pronounce the 'nu' when read. It's only there to determine which context to use."

Thutmose was shaking his head slowly back and forth.

"Now, the last problem: Write the Akkadian word 'shalamu.' It means peace or greeting. You wrote it as 'shal-a-mu.' The syllables are wrong. You pronounce the Akkadian word as 'sha-la-mu.' The syllables you used give the correct spelling for the word, but not the correct pronunciation."

Thutmose blurted out, "I'll never understand cuneiform's logic."

"That's because there's no systematic logic. Cuneiform is a hodge-podge of different rules pieced together over a thousand years for different languages and purposes. No one piece considered the logic of the entire system."

"I agree. A dysfunctional committee of morons designed it."

The two brothers thought for a moment, then broke out laughing. Finally, Thutmose looked at his brother. "I've reached one conclusion."

"What's that?"

"When I finish this class, I'm never going to touch a stylus again. That's what scribes are for."

MAY 1463 BC—MILITARY ACADEMY, INEBU-HEDJ

Thutmose read the two-question homework assignment; then read it again.

1. Under what conditions should you use an echelon formation

2. What are its advantages and disadvantages

"Sefuamun," whispered Thutmose, "What's an echelon?"

"It is a formation you use when you're in the approach-march phase of combat. You know the enemy is there; but not where. It is a cross between a column and a line abreast. You slant your men behind the point man either left or right. For example, if you think the enemy is in front or on the left, the men behind the lead would slant left. This looks like '/'.

"Why use it? You know you are going to have to adjust to a line abreast, but do not know how. If the enemy appears in front, you swing the rear forward. Conversely, if they appear to the left, then you swing the front side left. Either way, you swing facing the enemy in half the time. The problem is that, if you guess wrong, and the enemy comes from the right and ahead of you, you're in the worst possible formation."

"Now I remember. Ramose covered it in class." He paused and changed the subject. "Brother, I don't mind being the Army Commander. I can lead the men. I need you for my General. I need you to be my Ramose on the battlefield."

"You don't have to worry. I'll always be there for you; it is my duty."

Chapter 11

Office of the Director, Smithsonian Museum

Present

Isaac's entry followed that of Abraham. It contained only a few sentences: Esau's signet ring should have been here. However, Esau sold his birthright. So, our lineage continues with me. After my father almost sacrificed me, I remained with the tents, never venturing outside the compound. Yahweh never contacted me, therefore, I have nothing to record."

This entry shocked David. He had not even considered the question of why Abraham's line of Ephod's inheritance shifted from the oldest to the youngest son. That violated precedent. Now it made perfect sense.

MILITARY ACADEMY, INEBU-HEDJ

September 1461 BC

Pharaoh Thutmose called the meeting to order and then turned it over to Ramose. Present were the three senior staff of the Academy, Sefuamun, and the generals of the Levant and Libyan Armies.

Ramose faced Thutmose, "Your Majesty." Turning to Sefuamun, "my lord." Then he faced the group. "Gentlemen." He began, "Why this meeting? I have spoken with the Djat. He reports that Pharaoh Hatshepsut is not in good health. Her doctors give her two more years to live, but not over five.

When she dies, we expect one or more subject kingdoms to rebel. We have two to five years to prepare."

Ramose paused a few seconds to let everyone absorb the news.

Then he resumed, "For this meeting, I propose we discuss reconnaissance. Why? The side winning the reconnaissance battle usually chooses the battlefield. The side choosing the battlefield increases his side's power and reduces his enemy's. Now, a question: how do we usually conduct reconnaissance?"

"Two ways," the Levant General replied, "by sending out foot patrols and by depending on local informants."

"How reliable are informants?"

"Pffft," the General replied. "Half the time, they'll tell you to go the wrong direction. After all, they don't exactly love you–they have to pay our tribute."

"My point. You can't fully trust the information and, by the time you can corroborate it, too much time has passed to use it effectively."

Head bobs confirmed everyone agree with the assessment.

Ramose continued, "How effective is foot patrol reconnaissance?"

The General handled that also, "When you finally reach the spot your patrol detected the enemy, they have moved on."

Ramose summarized, "The conclusion: our scouting isn't effective."

Nods of agreement.

Ramose continued, "Let us review the background. A normal marching army, depending on food carried by ox-wagons, travels fourteen miles daily. A lightly loaded scout patrol travels twenty-five to thirty miles. That is fifteen miles out to scout and eight back to report. When the army reaches the area where the scouts saw the enemy on the prior day, the enemy is now a day's march away. Therefore, the problem is that we do not receive information on the enemy's location in time to use it effectively.

"First, my background. As you know, my clan is not Egyptian. We arrived during the first Hyksos pharaoh's reign. Originally, we belonged to the Kura-Araxes culture, shepherds living in the fertile grasslands around the Caspian Sea's north shores. A culture called the Yamnaya invaded, riding a large horse breed and traveling at a speed we could not match on foot. They forced us to move south, eventually reaching the southern Levant and Egypt.

"What does that have to do with reconnaissance? Lack of communication speed is our problem's root cause. A horse can travel at the speed we require. However, we cannot use the breed of horses we currently use for our chariots. They are too small to sustain carrying a rider for a long time or distance. The Yamnaya example offers a solution. A Yamnaya horse and rider can maintain a travel distance of fifty miles daily. That is twice the best a man can do on foot. I propose adding a new branch to the infantry. Beside swordsmen, spearmen, and archers, I recommend adding cavalry. The cavalry's job is reconnaissance. That is all they do.

"Imagine three teams of four horsemen each. The front team's station is twenty to twenty-five miles in the proposed line of advance. A left team is fifteen to twenty miles to the left. A right team is fifteen to twenty miles to the right. No opposing army can approach from either the front or sides without detection. We will know exactly where every enemy unit is within a forty-mile swath in front of us. Two men of each team remain in front. The other two shuttle back and forth daily. These report what is there and carry back the army movement plans for the next day. That gives our commanders daily update reports. The cavalry becomes the army's eyes and ears."

The head nods of approval grew more vigorous.

Ramose let the connotations of what he had said sink in, then continued, "Now that we know what our end-result looks like, how do we get there? I propose sending a delegation to the Yamnaya. We want to purchase seventy-five of their horse breed. Fifteen for each of our three standing armies: Levant, Nile, and Nubian. The rest are breeding stock. We also need to hire ten to twelve horsemanship trainers–and their families–for ten years to train the horses and riders. It will take a year to put everything in place and another year to train our own men. Then we integrate the teams into their respective armies and ready ourselves for the expected war."

There was no disagreement. The meeting continued for another two hours, discussing the plan's minor details.

At the meeting's conclusion, Sefuamun stood to gather the group's attention. "Gentlemen. I know I am now too young at seventeen; however, by the time we can implement the plan, I will have graduated from the Academy. I would like to volunteer for the post of Commanding Officer of the Levant Cavalry. They will probably have the first city to rebel and the army's Commanding General will need someone who can think as he does, so he gets the intelligence he needs.

The Levant General replied, "If you successfully pass the training, you'll be my Reconnaissance Commander."

Sefuamun's face remained impassive, but his mind smiled. *I will pass the training. Brains always win. I will put in the needed training. I will ask what extra I can learn to beat everyone else. There are always extras, nuances that the trainer does not teach everyone. I want to learn everything he knows– I want to learn it all!*

In two years, the army had integrated the cavalry. In eight consecutive war games, multiple units tried to infiltrate, outflank, or outmaneuver the Levant army. Each proved unsuccessful. Sefuamun's units were flawlessly efficient. All maneuvers were in the southern desert. No one wanted to reveal that cavalry existed. Why ruin the surprise?

MILITARY ACADEMY, INEBU-HEDJ

May 1458 BC

Pharaoh Thutmose called the meeting to order and then turned it over to Ramose. Present were the three senior staff of the Academy, Sefuamun, the Levant Army General, the new High Priest of Amun, Khusebek, the Vizier, the Ambassador and the Treasury.

Ramose began. "Gentlemen, what we expected has occurred. Most Canaanite cities have reneged on paying annual tribute. They are in revolt. Thankfully, our Levant Egyptian garrison cities remain faithful. However, our garrison troops render their city's actual motivation debatable. Informants report Megiddo leads the uprising. However, the ringleader is Kadesh on the Orantes. It also appears a behind-the-scenes instigator is the Mitanni Kingdom. Eventually, we will need to deal with all of them. However, the immediate threat is Megiddo."

Ramose surveyed the room; there were no questioning faces, no scowls of dissent. He continued, "Our immediate goal is developing our plans. However, I would suggest our eventual goal has two sides. The first is dealing with this revolt. I would suggest, however, the long-term goal is removing their underlying motivation to revolt. For now, let us address this revolt. What should we do?"

The Levant Army General immediately replied, "Let's destroy Megiddo. Kill every man, woman and child. Wipe Megiddo off the map. That teaches what happens when anyone defies us."

Ramose faced the General, remaining silent, gathering their full attention, raising tension in the room, finally asking, "What's Egypt's population?"

"I don't know," replied the General.

"A little under two-million. And Southern Canaan?"

The answer was silence.

"About six hundred thousand. Northern Canaan?"

The silence augmented the General's flabbergasted expression.

"One million, eight-hundred thousand. Add Algeria at a half-million and Nubia at three-quarters of a million, and what results?" Ramose did not wait for an answer. "Enough motivation and numbers to kill every Egyptian man, woman and child and wipe Egypt off the face of the map. Now, do you want to create that strong a motivation in our subject kingdoms?"

The General backed off, "I may have been a bit too hasty,"

Ramose handled the General's put-down gently. "Possibly. Let us change perspectives. Examine our ancient history. Today, there are forty-two sepats and nomes. We could call them "states." Why so many?"

After the General's gaffe, no one wanted to pick up the gauntlet.

"Because, originally, each was a separate kingdom. Over time, these coalesced into the first dynasty's upper and lower kingdoms, which were constantly at war. Narmer, the first dynasty pharaoh, originally united them. We nickname him "the skull crusher" because he united them by force. Repeatedly, however, whenever central power weakened, the kingdoms split.

"Why this ancient history? Because we now think of ourselves as Egyptians, not as upper or lower kingdom Egyptians. It is in our best interest having a united Egypt.

"Now, examine today. Egypt is the empire's ruler and the others are subject kingdoms. Do they think of themselves as Egyptian? No. We have not made it in their best interest to be Egyptian. Nor have we granted them the benefit of being Egyptian. Forcing them to be Egyptian, as Narmer forced the sepats, is only a first step. We have to treat them as Egyptians, so they think of themselves as Egyptian. Until we do, we will continue having revolts with every new pharaoh.

"Let me give you two mental images to illustrate my point. Imagine balancing a large bolder on top of Khufu's pyramid. It will not move. However, any wind gust disturbs its balance, and it rolls down. When the wind blows, it takes a substantial amount of energy to keep it balanced. That is today. We are the pyramid, the subject kingdoms are the boulder. The slightest push incites rebellion. It takes a great effort to re-balance them. Next image. Put the rock into a valley bottom. It takes a great effort to push it uphill because the rock wants to roll down the valley. That is what we want from them; the desire to remain in the valley. But if we want them to be loyal, we have to give them the motivation to be loyal."

"That's all well and good," said the Ambassador, meaning it was not well and good at all. "How do we do that?"

Ramose smiled. "That is why Thutmose called this meeting. Individually, I suggest we take a month to consider how to change their motivation, and meet again. Why a month? Because we have not decided how to address this revolt. Ideally, we should respond immediately, since it would send the strongest message. However, we are not prepared today and will not be until next year. Why? Examine:

1. If we do nothing, the kingdoms will remain in revolt, so this forces us to assume the offensive.

2. Informants tell us they have fifteen-thousand men. That is the bad news. However, they must defend multiple important cities, so they must split their forces. That is the good news. We can destroy each unit piecemeal.

3. Megiddo is the southern Levant's coalition linchpin, so we need to defeat that city. Doing it first will put a dagger into their coalition's heart.

4. To conquer Megiddo, we will need ten-thousand men. Those men are not in today's army. Theoretically, we have nine-thousand in our three standing armies. However, we cannot use the Nubian or Libyan armies. That would invite others to join the revolt.

5. To call up and train the men will take six to eight months. That puts us into next year's planting cycle.

"Here is what I propose as a start for discussion. This year, we assemble and train our forces. We send the men home for the barley planting cycle, mandating an increased barley planting, and reducing the wheat volume. After the men harvest the barley, we give them two weeks to assemble. The boys will need to harvest next year's wheat.

"This timeline means the army leaves Tjaru in mid-March. Anticipating this, we are already increasing our Levant garrison forces and augmenting their food stockpiles. We will increase the wagon auxiliaries to provide the needed support. For example, I expect we will need one wagon carrying just spare chariot wheels. This timeline puts us at Megiddo in mid-April. The early rains will have ended, priming the ground for campaigning."

The Levant General asked, "What deception or surprise tactics can we use?"

"None," replied Ramose. "The interconnectedness of our Levant garrison cities and theirs means secrecy is not possible. What we intend doing will be obvious. However, on the approach march, we will walk our cavalry horses until reaching the jump-off point. We do not want to give them advance knowledge. Note, however, we have another advantage."

"And that is?" asked the General.

Ramose assumed a crooked smile. "They are further north, so their harvest cycle is almost one month after ours. This means our army begins the march from Tjaru when their barley harvest cycle begins. We will force them to recall their men when they should be harvesting. Battle will begin during their wheat harvest. Their men will leave their fields knowing they will have a poor harvest. I'm afraid our pity will be in short supply."

The meeting's other men gained renewed understanding for the detailed planning needed for a military campaign. Everything increasing the chance of success needed incorporating. The plan needed to be seamless and interconnected.

The meeting ended to reconvene in a month.

MILITARY ACADEMY, INEBU-HEDJ

June 1458 BCE

Pharaoh Thutmose called the meeting to order, turning it over to Ramose.

Ramose began, "Gentlemen. We need our subject kingdoms as allies instead of enemies. This meeting's goal is determining incentives. I suggest we adopt a two-pronged approach. I would like Treasury to begin."

Treasury stood. "Thank you, Ramose. Let me begin by defining what money is."

Thutmose objected, "What do you mean? We don't need a definition. It's the silver and gold you have."

"Your Majesty, that's mistaken. Allow me to explain. Before using silver and gold balls as money, we bartered in the marketplace. You exchanged what you had for what you wanted to buy. How did that work? Both sides agreed on the worth of what each had. For example, assume twenty fish are worth a pig, and three pigs are worth a cow.

"Now, for the first example, a fisher arrives with sixty fish, a pig farmer with three pigs, and a cattle herder with a cow. You are the king and have one-hundred eighty silver balls, wanting to exchange your silver for food at a palace banquet. The price is one silver ball for each fish, so you give the fisher sixty silver balls. Since a pig is worth twenty fish, each pig is worth twenty silver balls. You pay the pig farmer sixty silver balls for his three pigs. Similarly, you pay sixty silver balls to the cattle herder. Does this make sense? Yes. Each seller at the market had an equivalent amount of goods. Therefore, each received the same number of silver balls.

"The second example is similar. As before, when arriving at the market, there are sixty fish, three pigs, and a cow. You are still the king, but now you have twice the number of silver balls: three-hundred and sixty. You want to buy the same items. However, the cost has doubled, so you need to give the fisher two silver balls apiece. You have the silver balls to exchange, so you agree and give him one-hundred twenty silver balls. Similarly, for the pig farmer and cattle herder.

"Now the question. In the second example, since the king paid twice the number of silver balls, did the cost of fish, pigs and cows double? The answer is surprising–no. The cost was the same. All the silver balls the king had. In reality, the silver balls were a barter, not money. The real money at the marketplace was not the silver balls, but the fish, pigs and cattle the balls bought. The difference is each ball is *worth* half as much. We call that inflation.

"What does this mean? Remember, the real wealth is the goods exchanged, not the money. There are only two ways to increase a kingdom's real wealth. First, producing more goods and services with the same amount of labor. An example is a farmer planting additional available acreage. As a one-man labor force, he will bring more grain to the market. The second is reducing the cost of moving goods to the market. Often, transport costs make up most of the price.

For example: If the buyer went to the shore to buy the fish off the boat, the price might be two fish per silver ball. Why? The fisher has no cost for transporting them to the market.

"How can we use this knowledge? First, we can select the best and brightest men, train them in how to invent, and subsidize their research. They will invent improved tools and techniques. An example is using nets instead of a fishing line to increase the amount of fish a single man can catch. An improved technique would speed the cleaning method for fishing nets to reduce the time it takes for upkeep. A greater percent of time will be actually fishing.

How does that affect our subject kingdoms? Invite the best and brightest vassal citizens for the same classes as ours, and distribute the news of everyone's inventions throughout the empire. We can increase the rate inventions happen. It benefits everyone.

Second, improve transport. It is cheaper transporting goods by ship rather than by wagon, so we could build harbor piers up and down the Levant coast and rivers. We could also build improved surface roads that reduce the time for travel and the upkeep of the wagons. Last, we can institute a "rent-a-wagon" service so, instead of paying the cost of renting an entire wagon, people can "share" the rent, reducing their individual costs."

Treasury nodded to Ramose, and sat down, signaling his presentation was complete.

Ramose motioned for the Ambassador to begin.

The Ambassador said, "I have much the same recommendation. I propose we select six boys from each major subject kingdom. One must be the king's son, and one from each of five prominent families. Bring them to Egypt for the same training in government and administration given to our sons. Egypt will bear the training cost. We indoctrinate them with Egyptian ideas and values. They return home at nineteen. When they assume leadership from their fathers, they will be knowledgeable and better able to administer their city. An added benefit is that they will already have a pro-Egyptian bias. Several generations will convince the city that being part of Egypt's empire is in their best interest. In time, perhaps, we can make their country a new Egyptian nome with full rights and benefits. In addition, should revolt happen, the boys will be virtual hostages."

The Ambassador nodded to Ramose, signaling he had finished, and resumed his seat.

Ramose asked, "Does anyone have more ideas to offer?" There were no hands raised. "Sire, do these recommendations meet your approval?"

Thutmose said, "This is exactly what we need. Thank you for your ideas."

Ramose added, "I propose we assign two committees. Treasury leads one; the Ambassador leads the other. Each works out idea implementation details. Each committee reports findings and recommendations in three months."

Head nods showed approval. They determined committee assignments and adjourned.

Chapter 12

INTERLUDE

Office of the Director, Smithsonian Museum

Present

The last entry of the translator included a preface: This section of the last page explains why this line of succession transfers to Joseph.

This is Rueben's entry. My brothers and I grew jealous of Father's favor toward Joseph. We first plotted to kill him, but sold him into slavery to a band of Midianites. We broke our faithfulness with Yahweh. Joseph alone kept his faith. My brothers and I are unworthy of inheriting Abraham's line. Therefore, I transfer Abraham's inheritance rights to Joseph and his progeny.

It happened again. The oldest had not inherited. It explained why Joseph's name was on the Ephod.

Would this recur? He would probably never know.

Well, to misquote Paul Harvey, "I must wait for the hieroglyphic translation to discover 'the rest of the story.'"

TJARU, EGYPT–ON THE EGYPTIAN BORDER

March 18, 1457 BC

Tjaru was the Levant Army's home base and traditional launch point for Egyptian armies heading east. It lay on the coast road at the Nile delta's easternmost branch. Normally home to three thousand soldiers and families, seven thousand added men bivouacked in tents outside its gates, swelling the city by a hundred acres.

The army rose and ate at first light, when the upper atmosphere glimmered.

They had allowed an hour to form a marching order. They took longer. The first time always needs adjustment.

The infantry formed three columns of four abreast, the chariots on either side, the wagons following. Even with three columns, the army and wagon train stretched over nine miles.

March-April was ideal campaigning weather. The coast road was a moderate seventy-five degrees temperature. From Tjaru to Gaza was a hundred fifty miles, a ten-day trip. They marched fifteen miles daily, because watering stations spaced every fifteen miles. Even with positions for two-hundred fifty horses and oxen, watering took an hour and over a thousand twenty-six gallon amphorae. However, daily watering was essential. A man could carry two water skins, lasting three to four days. A horse could not survive longer than two days. Depending on temperature and toil, each needed five to ten gallons daily. It is a saying that an army marches on its stomach. Often forgotten: humans are not the only stomachs needing fed.

What is not in army records is the dust clouds an army raises. Thutmose's chariot was just behind the vanguard. He enjoyed the fresh air. Sefuamun walked with the wagon train, behind the infantry and auxiliaries. To an unaware observer, they appeared to be spare chariot horses. They did not look like cavalry, using ropes to bridle their horses. Thirteen hundred sets of chariot and wagon wheels in front of you raise a dust cloud, even on hard-packed dirt.

Inside the cloud, you could not see the sun. The cavalry lived in the cloud. Dust coated Sefuamun's nostrils, tickling his nose, reducing the effective diameter of his nasal passages. He had to force air in and out to breathe. It requiring recurrent blowing to clear accumulation. The fine mist clouded his eyes, resulting in inadvertent tears to flush it frequently. It was hot with the dust reflecting everyone's body heat back down. The dust glommed onto Sefuamun's sweat, creating a thin layer of slime on his skin. He needed to drink extra water to replace what he had lost.

The dust cloud gave life to one of his Academy classes: there is a difference between regular soldiers and their officer. They would both suffer the same discomforts, but the soldiers could bitch about it. Their officer had to suffer in silence.

Their first stop was Gaza, an Egyptian garrison city in the southern Levant. The army halted on the twenty-eighth for a day, giving men and animals a rest. The trip to the next garrison city of Yehem was a hundred-thirty miles, but they would average only eleven miles daily. With plentiful springs from winter rains, that reduced stress on the animals. However, Canaan was now enemy territory, increasing stress for the men. No one trusted their intelligence, suggesting all enemy forces massed to the north. They knew Megiddo's armies received daily updates on their location and marching direction. They did not know what ambushes or other tactics they might spring.

On April 8, the army reached Yehem without incident. On the ninth, Sefuamun sent out three scout teams of five cavalry each. The night was a new moon; no moonlight for enemy sentries. However, the patrol could see campfires and enemy concentrations from a distance. Perfect night for reconnaissance.

There were three routes through the Carmel mountain range to the Jezreel valley and the city of Megiddo. The easiest, widest, and most trav-eled was the coast road past Djefti, over twenty-miles away. The mountain pass at Dothan to the southeast debouched into the Jezreel valley over thirty miles from Megiddo. However, intelligence suggested the enemy positioned their blocking force at Taanach, five miles southeast of Megiddo. The third route was a mere trail through a mountain pass from Aruna, ending at the Qina Brook. It entailed the most risk. Sefuamun led his third team through the pass.

Before saddling, Sefuamun addressed his team. "Our total distance out and back is thirty-two miles. It will be a long night, and we will not return until after daylight. It has been a couple of weeks since we have ridden the horses, so we will take it easy at first to allow them to get comfortable. When we reach the pass, we dismount and walk the horses, reducing our noise signature.

"Remember, we are reconnaissance. Our mission is discovering the enemy's location and intent. If possible, we do not want the enemy to realize we have been there, because that might cause them to alter what they are doing before our army arrives. Two of us will dismount before reaching the pass and sneak through on foot, with the others following. We do not want horse snorts to alert the enemy.

"On the return trip, we alternate walking and trotting, saving a gallop for escaping danger. We do not want any horse injured from night galloping. Questions?"

No one raised a hand. That satisfied Sefuamun. He knew several men would feel jittery. However, there is a world of difference between a reprimand for minor training mistakes and serious blunders with lives on the line. In a first battle, danger wrenches your stomach and your brain refuses to think. Most men survive their first battle because of good training; their bodies know what to do without thinking.

The reminder helped reduce the strain.

The team of five headed out. No one spoke; each carried his own inner demons. "Am I good enough?" Each tried silencing their stomach, concentrating on the mission. However, stomachs do not listen to wishes; they listen to feelings. Each man needed to make peace with his own stomach.

A small brook ran beside the village of Aruna. The brook explained the town's location. The townsfolk built a makeshift dam using rocks removed from their farms. It created a small lake for washing clothes. The lake lifted a thin mist into the night air, swallowing sounds of their passing.

They swung wide around Aruna, taking no chances. That is caution's definition.

Aruna marked the edge of land suitable for farming. From there, the land slowly rose to meet the mountains. Even in the dark, the pass road was easily discernible. Many feet over many decades had pounded it flat, giving off a soft sheen, distinct from the mottled ground beside it. The sound of horse hooves would echo from the road. The ground beside it muffled sounds. They traveled beside the road.

A soft black, twinkling shine marked the pass beginning. They halted a quarter-mile before entering. Sefuamun and his Assistant Team Leader dismounted. One moved left of the road by twenty yards, the other right. Alternating turns, they fast-walked forward, hunching over to make a smaller focus, leapfrogging forward. One moved, the other watched. If spotted, a sentry could detect movement, but it would be too far to identify what they had seen. The sentry would move to try getting a better view. There was no movement. No one was there.

A smart enemy commander would have stationed sentries at the pass entry. There were no sentries; their commander was not smart.

Sefuamun motioned for the Assistant Team Leader to join him. They held a hasty conference. This road did not go through a wadi. That would have meant water rushing off a mountain and sculpting vertical walls on each side. Here, the water flowed gently. That left sloped hills on either side, easily traversable by foot. They would use the hill slopes as their pathway.

Having decided, they split, each going five yards uphill on their side. They continued leapfrogging forward, alternating being a sentry and hunched forward, fast walking. The road itself was hard, but grass grew on the slopes. It kept its twilight dew. After a hundred yards, their feet were so drenched that they kept slipping in their sandals, threatening to make them fall. They removed their sandals, tying them around their necks.

A cautious enemy commander would have placed frequent barriers throughout the pass, slowing the advance of an enemy. There were no barriers; their commander was not cautious.

Finally, the two men reached the far end. The dark shape in the passage center suggested a barrier. Two men stood beside it. One leaned on it, probably lost in thought. The second was eating a meal. Behind the barrier were three tents surrounding the campfire, now burned down to embers.

They snuck closer. The "barrier" in the middle of the pass was two upended wagons.

There was one darker form a hundred yards beyond the camp, attracting Sefuamun's attention. Its location was striking. It was obviously a signal fire, ready to give Megiddo an advance attack warning.

The camp was asleep, oblivious to their presence.

Sefuamun smiled inwardly. Mission accomplished.

Sefuamun and his Assistant Team Leader snuck back out, met the team a quarter-mile back, mounted up, and headed back.

Sefuamun basked in that satisfied feeling which accompanies success. *My first actual mission and we have the intelligence the army needs! Now to get it back.*

YEHEM, CANAAN

April 10, 1457 BC

Sefuamun awoke with a start, then realized he was still sitting in a chair with someone shaking his shoulder. "Sire, the last reconnaissance team has arrived and the War Council is about to begin. Here's a mug of beer to refresh you."

"Thank you." He shook his body, vanishing its residual cobwebs of sleep. Taking the mug of beer, he drained the cup in two long drafts. It went down cool and settled in his stomach, changing to a warm and comforting mellowness. He was now awake.

"That was good. It warmed the belly and awoke the mind. Thank you again."

"You're welcome, sire."

The War Council began within the half hour with Pharaoh Thutmose presiding. Attending were the Levant General, who doubled as the Center Wing General, the Commanding Generals of the Left and Right Infantry Wings, the Commanding General of Chariots, and the Commander of Archers. Present to give their reports were the Team Leaders of the three Reconnaissance Teams.

Thutmose asked the reconnaissance Left Team Leader to give his report.

He stood and stepped forward. "Your Majesty, the Kadesh army is astride the coast road at the southern edge of the Djefti pass. They have spread their seven thousand infantry into three unequal wings. The center contains half their force. They total two thousand swordsmen, the balance spearmen, with two hundred archers. They number about seven to eight hundred chariots. From their dress, they are northern Canaanites from multiple different cities." He resumed his seat.

Thutmose thanked the Left Team Leader and asked for the Right Team Lead, who stepped forward.

"Your Majesty, the army is not at the mountain road exit onto the Jezreel plain. They have arrayed outside the city of Taanach, more than halfway to Megiddo. Six thousand infantry spread roughly into three equal-strength sections, totaling fifteen hundred swordsmen, the balance spearmen, with two hundred fifty archers. They number six hundred chariots. From dress and armament, the center section is from Megiddo. The left and right make up a different city hodgepodge." He stepped back.

Thutmose spoke, "And the Front Team."

Sefuamun stood and spoke, "Your Majesty, the Aruna Pass is undefended. There is a blocking force of thirty to forty-five men at the far end of the pass. They intend fighting a delaying action behind two overturned wagons. They have a signal fire prepared to alert Megiddo of a threat.

Thutmose said, "Left and Right Team Leaders, thank you. The two men left the room.

Thutmose addressed the assembly. "You've heard the reports. I want recommendations. What should we do? Above all, I want to hear options, and I want to hear the logic behind your recommendations." Thutmose began with the Levant General, "Levant."

The Levant Commanding General stood. "We have the force to defeat the Kadesh army on the coast road. We know Kadesh is the ringleader behind this revolt. I recommend we start by destroying their army. Then we march on Megiddo, defeat their army and wipe out the city. Raze it to the ground. Do to them what we did to the Libyans twenty years ago. That will send a message about resisting us."

Thutmose paused before replying, "Right."

The Commanding General resumed his seat, while Right stood, "Majesty, I agree with the Levant."

Thutmose spoke, "Thank you. Now, Left Wing."

Left Wing stood. "I'm afraid that I will have to disagree with my counterparts. We outnumber the Kadesh army, but not decidedly. Therefore, we will suffer significant casualties. After those losses, we will have the same strength differential facing the Megiddo army. I recommend we defeat the Megiddo army first. We will suffer fewer casualties and have a stronger army facing Kadesh. After defeating both armies, we capture Megiddo."

"Sefuamun, I want to hear your thoughts," Thutmose continued.

Sefuamun stood, "Your Majesty, I agree in principle with Left Wing. However, I suggest a unique method. Yes, we should fight the Megiddo army first, but not in Taanach. They chose that battlefield for a reason; they will occupy the better ground and we will be at a relative disadvantage. In addition, by the time we could close for battle, they would know we were coming. The Kadesh force would probably arrive about the same time we would, and maybe a half-day before. We would face a joint force who would outnumber us in both infantry and chariots.

"I recommend we go through the Aruna Pass. We can sweep the defenders aside and chose the battlefield before either the Taanach or Djefti armies could respond."

The Levant General jumped out of his seat. "No," he shouted. "If they bottle us up in the Aruna Pass, they could surround us on both ends and destroy us piecemeal. Aruna Pass is a death trap waiting to swallow us."

Sefuamun silently stood there, arms crossed, staring at the Levant General. After five seconds, Pharaoh Thutmose also crossed his arms. Both silently stared.

After the Levant General's tirade, there was dead silence in the room. In his command, he countenanced no dissent, demanding unquestioning obedience to his every decision. He did not know how to respond to silence. Finally, he realized he had broached proper decorum. "Your Majesty, Sire, I was out of line. I apologize." He sat.

Sefuamun was conciliatory. "I agree you should recognize this possibility, but I can assure you, it can't happen. Allow me to explain. When our forces leave Yehem, Left Wing's command will begin by marching straight towards Djefti and the coast road. Right Wing will begin by marching straight towards Dothan and the Mountain Road. Any spy will observe for an hour or two, then speed on ahead to report to their enemy command to ready themselves, that we are coming their way. Both Djefti and Taanach will lock in place, preparing for battle. After two hours, Center will begin marching straight for Aruna. After their two-hour march, Left and Right wing will swing their columns and march to Aruna from an angle. Meanwhile, the cavalry canters to Aruna and surrounds the town. If no one escapes Aruna to inform the enemy, how can an enemy force block us as we traverse the pass?"

There were understanding nods. Sefuamun's plan made perfect sense. No one ventured to challenge it.

Sefuamun resumed, "It's ten miles to Aruna. That is an easy day-march. We begin mid-morning. The following morning, the main column begins the march through the pass. At its narrowest point, the pass is only ten-yards wide, so we will need to march the infantry in rows of four abreast with the chariots proceeding single file. That makes the column six miles long for a pass of six miles long. The column head will emerge as the tail enters, so the entire operation takes six or seven hours.

"Meanwhile, the cavalry and a twenty-man unit of elite swordsmen go through the pass starting at midnight, so we will be at the other end just before sunrise. Before dawn, when the sky just lightens, the cavalry charges through their camp and executes everyone–no quarter. Three cavalry dismantle their signal fire, so Megiddo will have no warning. The swordsmen upend the wagons and push them aside. Now the pass is clear.

"What will our first units through the pass do? They push on to Megiddo and seize a battleground before the city to give us a tactical advantage.

"What will Megiddo do? Without a signal fire warning, they will not discover our pouring through the pass for several hours. When they realize their plight, they will send a courier to Taanach. Taanach is five miles away. By the time the courier arrives, it will be mid-day. It will take an hour to collect the men and another half-day to arrive at Megiddo. By the time Taanach can react, we will have seized the battlefield. Their Taanach army must fast-march to defend Megiddo. Their column will arrive at days-end about the same time our last men emerge from the pass. The march will stress the Taanach army. A fatigued army is a losing army. They must recuperate overnight. Call it even. Neither side could begin the battle that late in the day. By the following morning, our army will be fully on the field on the ground we have chosen. We will outnumber Megiddo. They cannot dislodge us and will be in the defense.

"What about the Djefti force? Again, the courier cannot arrive before mid-afternoon. However, the distance is greater, so they cannot arrive at Megiddo before mid-afternoon the next day. By that time, the battle will be over."

Sefuamun turned from Thutmose to the Levant General, "Now you understand why they cannot trap us in the Aruna pass?"

"Yes, I see. You are correct. It appears you've thought of everything."

Sefuamun closed, "Those are my recommendations."

Thutmose needed no further time. "I swear, as Ra loves me, as my father Amun favors me, as my nostrils are rejuvenated with life and satisfaction, I shall proceed upon this Aruna road! Let him who wishes follow me! Behold, these enemies whom Ra abominates will never say that I have set out on another road because I am afraid of them."

After Sefuamun's presentation and Thutmose's pronouncement, the generals bowed to his decision.

Sefuamun was content. *I was right–and I could convince everyone I was right. Ramose was correct in his teaching. Right beats numbers. Right beats superior rank. Right beats years of experience. However, right requires brains.*

I put in the time. I put in the effort. I put in the work. It paid off. I put us in the best position to win.

Thutmose used the following day to perform detailed preparation, planning to march to Aruna the following day.

ARUNA PASS

April 13, 1457 BC

The cavalry arrived at their jump-off point when first-light was an hour away. The moon was halfway to the first quarter, and even in the late-night sky, its feeble moonlight was useless. They had walked their horses through the pass, stopping just over two hundred yards–and two turns of the path–before the exit. To make less noise, they went single file beside the road in the soft dirt. Just behind them was the twenty-man unit of elite swordsmen to push aside the wagon barrier. The passage was uneventful.

They had made one change since the War Council. A cavalry team leader asked what action to take if the enemy refused to emerge from their tents. The enemy's disadvantage was bowmen picking them off as they emerged. However, it was suicide for anyone going in. He suggested setting their tents on fire. That would burn them out. Sefuamun liked the idea. *A logical solution.* Without giving it much thought, Sefuamun approved it.

Sefuamun had selected each of his men. An archer or an infantryman needs few skilled movements, so they could depend on training for their first battle. Not so a cavalryman. The cavalry provided the speed for the army's rapid reaction. They needed to react in seconds to changing battlefield conditions. Therefore, they needed to be thinkers. However, thinker's stomachs have just as hard a knot going into their first combat as a foot soldier. Some shook their bodies to full alert; a few more took a second deep gulp; most tried convincing their stomach everything would be fine.

Most boxers preparing to enter a ring experience stomach jitters. Stomachs obey emotions. The boxer cannot tell their stomach to calm down; that is a thought. The thought concentrates attention on the jitters, making them seem even worse. It takes the first blow to stop the stomach. It makes no difference who strikes the blow. The first blow commands full attention; shifting awareness and concentration to the fight. The boxer loses all awareness that his stomach demands attention. With that, jitters melt away.

The same is true for the cavalry.

At the first tinge of light in the sky, twenty minutes before sunrise, Sefuamun gave the "mount-up" hand signal. Once the waiting is over and the commander gives the signal to begin the sequence for battle, subsequent events must be continuous. No pauses. Pauses allow losing concentration on the mission, invariably causing someone's stomach tension to lose their breakfast. That creates a chain-reaction.

Sefuamun gave the light-torches signal. Three infantrymen were waiting. Each carrier lit their torch from the hooded lamp the last man in line carried, and handed them to their cavalry counterpart.

Sefuamun dropped his arm.

Charge.

Fifteen horses leaped forward at full gallop, while twenty infantry vainly tried keeping pace.

Horses at full gallop at night race at twenty-five miles-an-hour, faster in daytime. The horses charged three abreast and broke into the encampment in under seventeen seconds. The two men on duty heard the sounds of horse hooves on the road, but took too long to understand what they had heard and call the alarm.

One sentry reached for his shofar to sound the alert, but the mouthpiece did not reach his lips before the arrow hit his chest.

The second sentry grabbed his torch, racing for the signal pyre thirty-yards away.

Horses are faster.

Sefuamun evaluated the attack's inevitable success, turned his horse and pointed at the two men designated to gallop back to report the pass was clear. "Go," he shouted. They took off at a full gallop. Thutmose began his passage at daybreak twenty minutes later.

The three teams assigned to the tents encircled the tent openings. They pin-cushioned the first few men appearing. As soon as men stopped emerging, torches lit the canvas, erupting in flames. The flames forced out the tent's inhabitants, but the cavalry could not give quarter. They could not dismount to guard prisoners, and the infantry had not arrived.

Tent flames leaped into the sky. Only then did Sefuamun realize its result.

The pass exit to Megiddo was line-of-sight. If he could see Megiddo, they could see him. The tent-fires were visible at Megiddo. Yes, he had prevented the enemy from lighting their signal fire, but the flaming tents were an unintended substitute.

He castigated himself. *I deserve to have the General kick me in the butt so hard his toes will penetrate to the point they tickle my tonsils.*

I assumed. I failed to follow through with an analysis of the recommendation to torch the tents. I failed to follow through with the logical consequences.

I know better. Every detail has significance. I just caused us to lose the element of surprise. Megiddo now has enough warning to seize the high ground before we can get there.

He hung his head. *I must learn from this. I must never make that mistake again.*

Enough. Mind on the mission. We still have a battle to finish.

He forced his mind and his feelings on the current moment's needs.

Less than a minute later, the infantry rounded the last bend, huffing and puffing. They upended the two wagons, pushing them to the side. The pass was clear.

The infantry could hold the pass exit. Sefuamun left one team with them to shuttle reports and instructions.

He sent three men to straddle the road from Megiddo to the coast to interdict any chariot send to alert the Kadesh army. That chariot never made it to Djefti.

He sent three more men to intercept the chariot going to Taanach. However, it was already too late. With the torching of the tents, Megiddo had immediately sent a chariot to alert the Taanach army to fall back to Megiddo. That chariot left Megiddo within minutes and the cavalry team sent to intercept arrived too late.

Megiddo to Taanach is just over five miles.

The message to Thutmose would not reach him to begin his march through the Aruna Pass for another ten minutes, and the pass was six miles long.

The vanguard of the Taanach army arrived at Megiddo an hour after Thutmose emerged from the pass, and the rear of the Egyptian column was hours behind.

The Egyptians had lost the right to choose the battlefield.

Sefuamun took the remaining cavalry to the Qina brook to secure that position for Thutmose's arrival later that day. They dismounted during darkness, and Sefuamun forbid mounting their horses after daybreak.

Megiddo remained ignorant of the cavalry.

On the battlefield, ignorance often proves fatal.

THE BATTLE OF MEGIDDO

April 13, 1457 BC

Megiddo was the city that no army wanted to assault; the one most immune. It sat on top of a circular tor whose sides grew steeper as they rose. Its slope was uniformly smooth. For a thousand years, the city's inhabitants had sculpted it.

No cover. No concealment. More armies had broken their teeth by assaulting Megiddo than anywhere in the southern Levant. The road was so steep oxen could not pull a fully loaded cart. A sharp left preceded the gate; there was no straight path in.

The Canaanite word for hill or mountain is "har." The tor Megiddo occupied was "Har Megiddo." Because of its different grammatical construction, that translated into the Greek as "Har Magedon" and then English as "Armageddon."

The Carmel Mountain range runs southeast from the point where it pokes into the Mediterranean Sea. Megiddo's tor, separated from the range on the north side, sat twenty miles from the Mediterranean. Just to Megiddo's southeast sat a mile-and-a-half long, flat-topped spur a quarter-mile north of and paralleling the main Carmel Mountain ridgeline. A shallow valley about two hundred yards wide and fifty feet lower than the spur-top separated the main ridgeline from the spur, with the Qina brook flowing through the valley. Megiddo's tor reached a hundred feet higher than the spur. The spur's north side dropped off into the Jezreel Valley. Megiddo's spur was not straight; it had the shape of a bow firing southwest. From its northwest endpoint, it gently curved south, then back east.

Thutmose reached the Qina brook to see the Taanach army arriving, setting up battle lines on the spur-top opposite the valley. The Egyptians had lost the element of surprise, and with it, the ability to set the battlefield. He accepted the unavoidable. Thutmose called for a War Council with his commanders just after the evening meal and got some rest himself. He directed his commanders to align their forces to mirror the enemy's placement and allowed his army to get some rest and recuperate from the long night and day's march through the pass. They would join battle tomorrow.

The Egyptian army formed in the upland valley. The Megiddo army occupied the spur's top, fifty feet above the Egyptians.

No army wants to attack uphill. However, that was the price for burning the tents.

Sefuamun walked the valley, inspecting, studying the enemy battle line, evaluating strengths and weaknesses. He would leave no stone unturned. He had promised himself: never again fail to follow the details. Sefuamun's mind ticked through his military training. A tactical rule of thumb for armies is that it takes a two-to-one numerical advantage to achieve victory in an attack on a plain with level ground; a three-to-one guarantees it. However, that applies to a flat landscape–this was not. Attacking uphill, he needed a three-to-one advantage. The Egyptians did not have a three-to-one numerical advantage.

Sefuamun needed to develop a scheme where the Egyptians could achieve a three-to-one power advantage, even if they could not get a three-to-one numerical advantage. To do that, he needed to identify all the opportunities where the two armies were not equal. His ace in the hole: given otherwise equal power, brains always beat brawn. He needed to outsmart the Megiddo army. How could he increase his power ratio to achieve a three-to-one advantage? The key: most of an attacker's casualties occur during the battle's first phase, a defender's during the last. How could he use this true-ism to his advantage?

The Egyptians had ten thousand men to the enemy's six. Their one thousand chariots to the enemy six hundred. The Megiddo army set up in the standard three-wing battle line on top of the spur. Its center comprised half their infantry, the two wings of one-quarter each. They divided their archers equally into two sections, one-half between the right and center wings, the other between the center and left. The weaponry for the center was uniform; however, the weaponry for the two outside wings was a hodgepodge. All swordsmen with shields were in the center wing. All chariots aligned in the center, spaced almost wheel-to-wheel, in front of the infantry's center wing. The King's chariot was gold-plated, positioned dead center, ostentatiously advertising importance and impervious power. For Sefuamun, the consummate tactical key was the King's chariot location.

Sefuamun now had all he needed. From their alignment of forces, he knew how Megiddo intended to fight the battle. It remained for him to determine how the Egyptians could use Megiddo's tactics against them.

What should he recommend this evening? His mind reviewed each side's advantages and disadvantages.

The Megiddo chariot alignment provided the key for the enemy plans. Egypt's cavalry was the one unknown Megiddo could not include in their planning because they did not know of its existence. It needed to be the key to achieving a three-to-one power advantage. Egypt's cavalry needed to provide the key for a decisive win.

At the War Council, Thutmose opened the meeting and asked for recommendations. Predictably, the Levant General spoke before anyone could get a word in edge wise. "Do you see how he positions his chariots in front of his infantry? That blithering idiot does not know what he is doing. What does he think he has: Hittite chariots? Egyptian chariots are maneuver weapons, not blunt force assault weapons."

"I agree," added Right Wing, "He's just wasted his infantry's strength. They cannot fight from between chariots; it breaks up their lines. They can't support each other."

The Yehem Detachment Commander spoke up, "I believe I can give everyone some background information, which will explain what Niqmepa, the Megiddo King, is doing."

Everyone fell silent, Thutmose motioning for him to continue.

"First, Niqmepa's history. Southern Canaan has been peaceful for over fifteen years. Megiddo has not fought a battle in twenty–when he was a small boy. He has had no warfare training or experience and his army has no battle-hardened veterans. The last time there was a war, his father was King. Their coalition of city-states fought the Hittites. The Hittites used their heavy war chariots to charge into the city-state infantry formations and bowl them over. The coalition almost lost. He has heard his father tell the tales of that battle.

"Next, Niqmepa the man. Niqmepa does not understand the tactical strengths and weaknesses Megiddo and the Hittites each had. He is egotistical to a fault. He is not dumb, just ignorant. I believe he wants to lead a chariot charge to mirror what the Hittites did. He wants to be the hero of the battle and earn fame and glory. And, no, he doesn't understand that Egyptian chariots are too light to use like the Hittite ones."

Thutmose looked around the group. "All right, we understand the enemy we're facing. How can we take advantage of his weaknesses? What should we do?"

The Levant General immediately spoke. "He wants a fight. We give it to him. If he is dumb enough to have his chariots in front of his infantry, we begin on the defense, with our archers interspersed with our center's second rank. He wants a chariot charge, so we let him charge. When their chariots get to shooting range, the front rank kneels and the archers shoot over their heads into the chariots. We kill at least one of every chariot horse-pair. That immobilizes their chariots. A sitting chariot is a dead chariot. That will put the fear of god into their following infantry. We turn their fear into terror by charging and demolishing them."

Thutmose looked around the group. No one else moved to take up the gauntlet. "Sefuamun?" he signaled.

"Sire, I agree in principle with what Center has offered, but I believe a slightly different approach might offer added advantages. First, I have noticed some additional clues.

"First, yes, King Niqmepa has set up in the standard three-wing placement of infantry. However, he's center-heavy with half his infantry. Why? The first clue, as the Levant General reported, he has massed his chariots in the center, in front of the infantry. Yes, that implies that he intends to begin the battle on the offense, but not with a chariot charge. Look at the second clue. He is setting his archers between the wings. That implies he will begin with archers firing to soften our resistance. Then, they retreat behind infantry lines. Only then will he use a chariot attack as his base tactic.

"Next. Why has he stationed half his infantry behind the chariots? He has used a center-heavy disposition because a thousand-man, three-deep line at standard sword distance, gives him roughly the same formation width as his six hundred chariots. The logic shows he intends for his infantry to follow his chariot charge and mop up survivors.

"What about the role of his left and right wings? The center has the bulk of the swordsmen and their weaponry is uniform. All of their swordsmen with shields are in the center wing. The side wing's armament is a mixed bag. That shows their standing army's men are in the center with only ill-trained auxiliaries on the two wings. Their wing's role is defensive only–to prevent a flanking attack. Is there confirmation for this? The dress, like the armament, is a mixed bag. Everything implies that their well-equipped and trained men are in the center where he needs his strength in a tough contest.

"I believe those are the rules for the battle he's planning. He has organized for two enemy center wings going head-to-head in a brawl. He also has an advantage by attacking downhill. If we play by his rules, he could win.

"My next point: How can we prevent him from doing what he wants to do? First, we do not fight by his rules. We make up our own rules, and force him to fight by our rules, using our tactics, our speed and our timing.

"To begin with; how do we stop him from carrying out his intentions? Simplifying his plan, he is only using one simple tactic: a chariot charge into our infantry lines. How to counter that? As Center recommended, threatening to shoot their horses, stopping the chariots. However, I do not recommend we conceal our archers in the second rank of the infantry. That invites him to charge and we will sustain significant casualties in the battle. Instead, we line archers in front of the infantry. Now, even an inexperienced commander can tell that a chariot charge would be suicide. Even better, his chariots now block his infantry behind them. He now has no effective alternate plan. What will he do? I suggest we force him to do nothing. That will minimize our casualties.

"Finally, I suggest we should force Megiddo to fight by our rules. Ask: what rules do we want to set for the battle? What do we want to do? Before deciding, ask three questions. Is it necessary to fight his whole battle line? Why fight strength-on-strength? That increases our risk. Why not use our strength to take advantage of his weakness?" Sefuamun continued to outline the battle plan he had developed during his earlier surveying.

They adopted his recommendations.

Tomorrow they would join battle.

Only they could not.

There are two planting seasons in the Levant, called 'the early' and 'the late.' They mirror the prevailing climate. The early rains begin in mid-November. They are consistent; you can count on them. This planting provides the produce for the King's tax. The spring rains are inconsistent. The following day, it rained. On the fourteenth, both sides remained in their tents. Rain only soaked the sentries.

On the fifteenth, the ground was waterlogged. Chariots could hit soggy sections of ground and their one-inch wide wheels would sink into the muck and mire the chariot. Neither side wanted to launch the battle.

They waited for the ground to harden.

By nightfall on the fifteenth, both sides were itching for battle. Both sides were ready. Both sides were confident.

So are both boxers in a contest.

A boxer needs to use three types of maneuvers. The first is stepping forward to deliver blows. The second is stepping back to avoid them. Last, maneuver side-to-side, seeking an advantage.

Chariots need a quarter-mile or more of maneuvering room for maximum effectiveness. The Megiddo upland valley was less than three hundred yards wide, and the opposing sides were less than that. There was no maneuvering room; no room to step back.

At nightfall on the fifteenth, everyone knew the Megiddo King was planning a chariot brawl for the following day. His only options were to stand in place or step forward–he had essentially removed his ability to step backward or sideways.

At daybreak on the sixteenth, the Megiddo infantry wings remained one-quarter, one-half and one-quarter in numbers of men. Their army had three ranks deep across their entire line.

Not the Egyptians. Yes, the Egyptians had three thousand men in their center wing, three-ranks deep, mirroring the three thousand in Megiddo's center wing. However, that left seven thousand more men in the Egyptian army.

When the Megiddo battle lines looked out, they discovered the Egyptian left and right wings each had four-ranks of six hundred men each.

The Egyptian's four-deep ranks did not bother King Niqmepa. The battlefield was a fixed width–it could only be as wide as the spur. Therefore, only the front line was actually fighting. The back lines were merely reinforcements. If your front line held, it did not matter how many men they had behind them.

The remaining Egyptian infantry lined up behind the wing's gaps. These were obviously reinforcements.

Fifteen men walking their horses were behind the Egyptian left wing. No one in the Megiddo army had seen this before.

Not the King.

Not the officers.

Not the men.

No one understood its meaning.

However, what shocked King Niqmepa was that daybreak revealed the Egyptian chariots positioned behind their infantry. Not in front. In addition, Egypt's archers stood in front of their infantry. Archers in front meant that he could not use a chariot charge to begin his attack. The archers would shoot his chariot's horses, stopping the chariots, clogging the battlefield.

It suddenly dawned on King Niqmepa this battle would not progress as he had planned. However, he did not know what to expect.

No idea what to do.

Therefore, he did nothing.

The men of the Megiddo army read the position of the Egyptian chariots as foreboding and ominous.

Doing nothing is invariably worse than doing the wrong thing. His men correctly understood the omen to say the King did not know what to do. They also did not know. However, they knew that the battle they had planned would not happen. With no further orders or instruction, that meant . . . .

They were on their own.

In the front lines, indecision begets apprehension. Apprehension leads to anxiety. Anxiety results in dread. Dread looks for a reason to become terror.

Never having had military training, and this being his first battle, King Niqmepa did not understand how men react when facing battle.

His failure primed his men for panic.

He did not understand that, or take any steps to mitigate it.

As he was contemplating what he could do, the Egyptian trumpets sounded, "Forward, march." Drums pounded out the marching beat. The men on the Megiddo lines heard the drum beat–a resounding 'tomm' and ten thousand Egyptian feet stomped their left foot forward. Another drum beat 'tomm' and ten thousand right feet stomped forward. 'Tomm'–left–'tomm'–right–'tomm'–left–'tomm'–right.

The Egyptian lines advanced to the sound of the drums, one-step–and a heartbeat–at a time. Their heartbeats adjusted to the rhythm. 'Tomm'–heartbeat–right–heartbeat–'tomm'–heartbeat–left–heartbeat. The incessant rhythm congealed their senses–their attention focused to the beat of the drums. Their individual identity dissolved into a corporate union. They were an army.

It is always easier on the nerves when your side is advancing. You are doing something.

Standing and waiting is harder on the stomach. Your stomach has nothing to do but twist and harden. You wonder if this morning's breakfast will be your last.

The two lines closed to one hundred yards, just past effective compound bow distance, and the trumpets sounded again; this time a trumpet call no Megiddo soldier had heard. However, the Egyptians understood the call–they had created it for this battle. The Egyptian center and right wings halted in place. Not the left wing.

The Megiddo army did not understand that only auxiliaries comprised the Egyptian center and right wings. The Egyptian left wing was the Levant Army–trained veterans. The drumbeat commanded "advance." The center and right wings remained in place. At fifty yards, trumpets blasted "Charge." The left wing lifted their swords on high, yelled a battle cry, and charged. They slammed into the front lines of Megiddo's right wing infantry auxiliaries.

The "charge" command was also the signal for two other maneuvers. First, the men leading horses jumped on their backs and withdrew bows from leather covers. They galloped their steeds left, around the edge of their left wing, and behind the Megiddo right wing. They fired volley after volley into the side and back of the Megiddo infantry. Simultaneously, the left fifty men of the Egyptian left wing swung around to attack the unprotected edge of Megiddo's right wing.

Sefuamun's job was to command. He had horse-archers for shooting; his weapon was his brain.

He evaluated the battle's progression, looking for unexploited advantages. The Megiddo right wing had five hundred men in their front rank. The Egyptians had six hundred in their left wing's front line. Just over a one-to-one numerical advantage. However, Egypt's veterans were fighting Megiddo's auxiliaries, giving the Egyptians better than a two-to-one advantage. Yes, the front line men swinging around to attack from the side would also become effective–but the maneuver would take time. That meant a longer battle with higher casualties. The cavalry arrows into the enemy's rear rank would not affect the front. Front ranks would not even know what was happening behind them. However, arrows had made the rear ranks skittish.

Sefuamun looked more comprehensively. The rear ranks were wavering, shifting back and forth, looking at their comrades to judge their uneasiness. His military training kicked in. *These are the symptoms for a panic mentality just before a rout begins. The rear ranks only need a prod to push their fright into terror, and that will start it. And . . . I know how to prod.*

He wheeled his horse to the edge of the enemy's rear rank. Giving his horse two heels in his rib cage to nudge him to a fast walk, he aimed his horse down the Megiddo rear rank. He knew the horse would refuse to rush directly over the men in the rear rank; he only guided the horse to put a shoulder into them, tumbling them. By the time any one man fell, the horse would move on.

It worked. The Megiddo men fell haphazardly. Most careened into someone else, toppling both, some into the front ranks. The front rank men did not know what was happening behind them. The clamor of the front rank battle, the screams of the pin-cushioned last rank, and now their men falling topsy-turvy, pushed men over the edge. Dropping their weapons, they yelled for everyone to run for their lives. A few more panicked, prompting still more to join, until the trickle of men deserting the field became a rivulet, which swelled to a torrent, and grew to a flood. The Megiddo right wing fled down the spur and up the tor to Megiddo city.

When the flight began, Sefuamun guided his horse out of the lanes of the panicked Megiddo infantry. He let them go–his job was done. No sense in becoming an inadvertent casualty. Sefuamun was not interested in glory–let the infantry get the accolades for that. He reviewed the events in his mind. *My fingerprints are all over this battle. We fought the battle I designed. The rout began because of my evaluation of the enemy's weakness during the battle.*

Both brains and bravery. He enjoyed the self-satisfaction of knowing he had helped to swing the tide to victory–even if no one else noticed.

King Niqmepa first wondered what was happening when the advancing Egyptian center halted in place, but the clamor prompted him to look right, to see his infantry wing evaporating before his eyes. The Egyptian left, having killed or forced the remaining Megiddo right wing off the field, swung their battle line to assault his center wing from the side. The impossible was happening before his eyes. What remained would not be a battle, but a slaughter. He did not know how to react. No idea how to prevent it.

The King abandoned the battlefield, deserting his men, rather than be victim to the slaughter. He raced his chariot forward, down the field between the lines of opposing infantry, out the side, down the spur and up the tor to Megiddo. He was almost too late. When the last of the Megiddo right wing had run to shelter inside the city walls, the city closed and barred the gates. Several hundred more men clamored up the hill, desperate for admittance. The residents refused to risk opening their gates. They threw down ropes and hauled the survivors up. After the men, the last lifted was the King's chariot.

The remaining Megiddo army either fled down the rear slopes to the Jezreel Valley or surrendered.

The Egyptians had lost fewer than two hundred killed and wounded. Megiddo left five times that on the battlefield. Over four thousand fled. The rest surrendered. The Egyptian victory was complete and humiliating.

The Egyptian chariots should have chased down Megiddo's fleeing infantry. That would have prevented their escape.

However, the Egyptians did not pursue.

The tales of the battle with the Nubians at Kerma were still resonating in the army. Thutmose I had allowed the Nubians to escape the battlefield and then prevented his army from pillaging the city. Everyone knew the infantry received a paltry wage; they gained wealth only from pillaging. Then Thutmose I compounded the issue by not compensating for losing pillaging.

The Egyptian army had heard those tales. When the Megiddo army fled the field, the Egyptian army did not chase. Instead, they ran to the Megiddo army's tents and ransacked them, rummaging for valuables.

It was two hours before Egypt's officers could regain control over their army. Too late to pursue.

The Levant General approached Thutmose after the active fighting died down. "Pharaoh, I am glad I accepted Sefuamun volunteering for my Cavalry Commander. We lost less than two hundred killed and wounded. If we had fought the battle I had planned, our losses would have been over a thousand. He sees clues right before my eyes that I had not, and evaluates their meaning, accounting for every detail. Please let me make a recommendation. When Ramose retires, choose Sefuamun to run the Academy. That is where he can do Egypt the most good."

When news of the devastating defeat reached the Kadesh army, prudence dictated they return home. They knew Egypt would inevitably respond to their rebellion; they just did not know how or when.

THE BATTLE MEGIDDO—AFTERMATH

April 17, 1457 BC

The next morning, a thousand men of the Megiddo army awoke to question their fate. They had surrendered. What lay before them? Execution? Slavery? Yes, the Egyptians had fed them dinner last night. However, they believed their delayed fate resulted from them being insignificant, merely conscripted peasant farmers and day laborers. The Egyptians had important things to finish first. Their outcome could wait. However, they knew the Egyptians would not delay long.

In that, they were correct.

After breakfast, Egyptian soldiers gathered them into the field on the south end of the spur. The soldiers carried out six tables, and scribes sat behind them. An Egyptian officer stood in a chariot bed. He announced, "Men of the Megiddo army. Egypt knows it was not your decision to take up arms. The King and his council were responsible. Therefore, Egypt has no hostility toward you. Egypt will forgive and send home anyone willing to swear never to bear arms against Egypt again. Those consenting, please line up at the tables. We will take your names for the record and send you home. Those not consenting remain here."

All but thirty men went to the tables. They gave their names, and the scribes recorded them. They swore by the god of their choice they would never bear arms against Egypt again. After which, a soldier gave each five silver shekel balls, a skin of water and a skin of meal, and sent them home.

The officer on the chariot asked the thirty men to gather round. He sat down on the chariot bed and asked if they had questions.

"Absolutely," asked one. "I can understand why you're forgiving them. I do not understand giving each man a month's wages. Last, what happens to us?"

"We will forgive you and send you home with a skin of water and a skin of meal. You also answered your King's call. You served faithfully. You are valuable.

"Why do this? What is different? Allow me to give you some history. A thousand years ago, the people of Egypt did not think of themselves as Egyptians. They were members of their nomes–their individual states–who banded together for mutual benefit. Today they think of themselves as Egyptians first and as members of their nomes second.

"Today, the people of Megiddo think of themselves as people of Megiddo first and, if at all, as Egyptians second. We want to have you think of yourselves as Egyptians who live in Megiddo.

"Egypt's last few monarchs did not devote the attention to your needs that they should. For example, your roads are in terrible shape. We need to rebuild them so your commerce will perform more efficiently. If we treat you as well as we treat ourselves, perhaps in a hundred years, your descendants will think of themselves as Egyptians. However, that will not happen unless we begin today by treating everyone as Egyptians.

"You men are loyal men to Megiddo. That is not wrong. However, it will be harder to win your loyalty. The others do not have as intense a loyalty. Therefore, when we hire a labor force to rebuild your roads, we will hire them first. That is why we are gathering their names. After forgiving their fighting against us, and paying them for their lost labor, they will probably be faithful workers. Their children may think of themselves as Egyptians first and men of Megiddo second.

"You have proven yourselves trustworthy. We hope we can convince you to trust us also, but we first have to earn that trust. Does that make sense?"

Jaws dropped at this revelation.

The Egyptian officer's mission succeeded. Megiddo's men may not have left wanting to be Egyptians. Even being friendly to Egyptians. However, as they hoisted their water and meal skins for their trek home, at least they no longer regarded Egyptians as enemies.

The Egyptian army surrounded the base of the Megiddo tor. Over the next three months, they built a siege wall encircling the base, with ramparts for archers. No sooner had they completed the wall than they dug a moat and diverted the Qina brook to fill it. Since few people knew how to swim, that quenched any hope of escape.

After an eight-month siege, the city surrendered. Egypt forgave everyone. The Megiddo blood lost was to their city's wallet, not their soldier's veins. Hatshepsut's words had become a mantra, "I want to send a simple message to our empire: count the cost of losing before dreaming of the profit from winning."

Egypt took the city leader's sons to Egypt for instruction on leadership, city administration and general education. However, they gave no one military training; they concealed their advanced military knowledge.

The students returned home when they were nineteen. Megiddo was better for its next generation of trained leadership.

Chapter 13

Office of the Director, Smithsonian Museum

Present

David had one rare day when Nancy, his secretary, was on vacation. He went to the mailroom. There was a brown eight-and-a-half by eleven folder resting in his assigned slot. On reaching his desk, he grabbed his paper opener and made quick work of opening it. It was from the translator for the lone hieroglyphic sheet in the Ephod. He walked through the door, flipped the wall hanger to 'Do Not Disturb,' and closed the door. Taking his seat, he leaned back in his chair and put his feet on the desk. The translation read:

Record of Zaphenath-paneah, also known as Joseph

My brothers sold me into slavery. The wife of my owner accused me of sexual assault. I was in prison in Avaris, awaiting trial. When I interpreted the dreams of the butler and baker, the butler told Pharaoh Salitis. I interpreted his dreams and became vizier for twenty years. I built granaries throughout Egypt during the good years for the predicted bad ones. In the good years, I imported weapons of bronze with chariots and horses. When the terrible years struck, Pharaoh fed Egypt. I moved Abraham's clan to Egypt. The family of the old Pharaoh rose against Pharaoh Salitis. Although they heavily outnumbered Pharaoh, the enemy had old weapons of copper. Pharaoh Salitis conquered them and moved the capital to Memphis. Pharaoh Semqen of Thebes was our vassal. I imported many ships and much timber, gold, lapis lazuli, silver, turquoise, bronze, oil, incense, and honey. Egypt was prosperous.

When Seuserenre Khayan became Pharaoh, Neferhotep III of Thebes rebelled. Pharaoh Khayan conquered the Upper Kingdom, uniting all Egypt from Kerma in Nubia to the Sea. Egyptian sway reached from Libya to Kadesh on the Orantes. Our diplomats stretched from Bagdad to Hattushe of the Hittites and Knossos on Crete.

As a slave and a prisoner, was Yahweh punishing me? No. I had to suffer so Yahweh could make me strong. Despite being afflicted, I remained faithful. I became wise. Then God gave me twenty good years for the few I had suffered. God used me to bring forth His will.

I am now an old man and can say, "God has blessed me."

David put down the translation. Like the first two, this had the 'ring' of being genuine. It loosely dovetailed with the Biblical account, adding a few details formerly unknown. It also confirmed the latest archaeology, which had not yet gathered sufficient support from fieldwork.

What can I do? The controversy when we release this data will be tumultuous. When this information blows conflicting archaeologist's inaccurate historical accounts out of the water, my face will be the bulls-eye of a dozen archaeologist's dartboards.

MILITARY ACADEMY, INEBU-HEDJ

March 1456 BC

The Commemoration Ceremony was simple and short. The same white linens wrapped Ramose's body as if embalmed, but they had laid him on a simple wooden plank. Since he had died yesterday, and they had anointed him in preserving oils, the decay had not begun. A mildly scented perfume masked any odor.

Thutmose gave a brief speech, extolling Ramose's virtues. His genius had manifested itself in new weapons and tactics. His meticulous campaign preparations had foreseen and accounted for every contingency their forces had encountered. Every campaign ran smoothly. He had detected every strategy and tactic their enemies could attempt, determined countermeasures, and devised troop training. His battlefield acumen had saved thousands of Egyptian lives and ensured overwhelming victory in every battle fought during his Academy tenure.

Four men carried the body to the Academy entrance. A hole beside the gate waited for him. They placed his body at the bottom and covered it with dirt. They left, some staying longer to say goodbye. A plain stone marker rested on the gravesite.

A stonemason waited until the last had left and then engraved Ramose's name on the stone. That was all Ramose wanted: a simple marker. No statues. No adornments. No aggrandizements. He had said, "If you need to ask what it means, it has no meaning. If it has meaning, you don't need to ask."

As Thutmose and Sefuamun walked back to the visitor rooms where they were staying the night, Thutmose said, "I can't imagine how calm you are. I remember two years ago when we lost mother. It devastated me. Then, a year later, we lost Senenmut. He was the only father I had ever known, even with the little attention that he actually gave to us. I was young when my father died; I do not remember him. Now Grandfather. You and I are all that's left."

Sefuamun nodded. "We still have them in our memories. All the good times. Sitting in her lap. Her singing to us. Grandfather was the caring father Senenmut never was. It was just that Grandfather could not treat you the same as me, because it would have violated 'protocol.' I can understand that, although we both really needed a loving father more than an emotionless protocol. I guess it helped toughen us up, though." Sefuamun laughed, "Speaking of Grandfather, remember him toughening us up with his aphorisms, preparing us to be men and soldiers."

Thutmose joined in the laughter. "It is not what your mind wants; it is what your body needs. Remember that long march into the desert? A day and a half out. Then back. One water skin. We watched him pour out unconsumed water from his skin first. Then we watched him inspect each man. We had to stretch drinking so we would have a little extra to pour out."

Sefuamun added, "Remember the six 'P's?' Proper prior preparation prevents poor performance."

"You must inspect what you expect."

"An animal can't become a carnivore until it's smarter than the herbivore it's hunting."

"It's the sergeant who's responsible for the men's inspection failures. He prepared them."

Thutmose's eyes looked out to the horizon, but his mind saw only the past. "He only allowed good men to attend the Academy. He only graduated great officers."

Sefuamun added, "He always ate what we ate. He only slept as much as we slept. That's what kept us going. If that old buzzard could do it, we could as well. He started with boys and ended up developing men."

Thutmose nodded. "He taught us to believe in ourselves and never quit. We could always do more than we believed possible."

The two men fell silent, returning to the visitor's quarters, lost in memories.

When the two sank into anteroom chairs, Thutmose's mind switched from reminiscing about the past to thinking about the future. He took one look at his brother beside him, still in memory-land, and reached a decision. He called Sefuamun out of his past, "Brother, I need you to take over the Academy in Grandfather's place."

That shocked Sefuamun back to reality. "Run the Academy? I just turned twenty-two. I've only been a man for three years."

"Really? I am just twenty-five. I should not have needed to be Pharaoh for another fifteen. Enough. We are where we are. Egypt needs us–both of us. Yes, they need me as Pharaoh, but you are the most qualified man in Egypt to take over the Academy. I need you. No, Egypt needs you. Remember what Grandfather always said, 'You have to man-up when the occasion happens.' Will you man-up?"

Sefuamun's mind came down to reality. He told himself, no self-aggrandizement and no false modesty. His emotions wanted to swirl wildly between elation and dread, but he clamped them down. *Only what is real. Concentrate on the mission.* He commanded himself to calm down. He asked himself, *Can I?* He suddenly realized Yahweh had prepared him for this role. His gaze shifted to his brother. "Yes, my Pharaoh, I accept. For Egypt, I will do this. For you, I will do this. I will not fail."

Thutmose knew that, when he said that he would not fail Egypt, if required, he might have to move heaven and earth–but failure was not an option.

MILITARY ACADEMY, INEBU-HEDJ

May 1456 BC

Two months later, after he had assured the Academy had returned to normal, Sefuamun called a planning meeting with his three senior instructors. "Gentlemen, Pharaoh Thutmose wants Egypt to conquer Kadesh. For at least the next two or three years, our army has enough to do to ensure the southern Levant remains loyal. Most cities have not voluntarily sent their sons to Egypt for schooling. They need, shall I say, the encouragement that an army at their city gate provides. Therefore, we have the time we will need to perform our task.

"I propose a preliminary timeline for our discussions:

- We use years one and two to design and test new and innovative weapons, tactics, and military techniques
- Use years three and four to build and stage what we need
- Use year five to train the army

   Then . . .

- We go to war

   "First, let me lay out some preliminary goals.

1. Devise something they have never seen and for which they have no existing countermeasure.
2. Increase the implementation speed for what they have seen. The aim is to render countermeasures ineffective. Before they complete their countermeasures, our implementation will be a fait accompli.
3. Whatever we do, it must cause overwhelming victory.

   "Last, let me propose what we can't do. We can never fight a set-piece battle with our vassal kingdoms again."

That was a gauntlet they could not refuse. "Why not?"

"Because, collectively, they outnumber us. We will win the first battle, and probably the second. However, by the third, casualties will deplete our army so severely that we will lose. The first time we lose, our empire will fall apart. Remember, it is our empire–therefore, we have to win every time. They are the rebels. They only need to win once."

Reluctant head nods followed.

Sefuamun continued, "So, we cannot afford to beat Kadesh on an open battlefield, depending on sheer numbers. Our brains must beat them. Questions?"

There were none.

General Satiyet, a retired army veteran, pointed out: "Sounds like you want a miracle."

Sefuamun smiled, "General, I agree with you; it sounds that way. However, take a second look at what your question implies: you are looking at the problem and thinking about why we *cannot* do it. Instead, let us reverse our mind-set. Ask yourself. To make the result happen, what are the individual tasks we need to accomplish? Only then should we ask how to accomplish each individual one. Only when we evaluate everything can we ask whether the complete mission is possible."

The General calmed down. "I agree; at least I think I agree. Continue. When we finish, I'll decide if I still agree."

Head nods from the group showed consensus. Even if not in full agreement, at least they would try.

Sefuamun began, "To begin with, we cannot fight Kadesh on an open plain; we need to besiege the city."

Predictably, General Satiyet was the first to object. "Won't work. People have tried to lay siege to Kadesh for hundreds of years. No one has been successful. The city lies on a loop in the Orontes River. The river occupies three of the city's sides. They bypass land sieges by bringing in food by an armored boat."

"General," Sefuamun gently chided, "You're still thinking negatively: why it can't be done? We need to reverse our thinking."

The General paused, realizing. "You're right. It's just how I'm used to thinking."

"Of course; it's natural. You will begin thinking positively. It just takes a while." Sefuamun continued, addressing the group, "The General is right in one aspect. This siege has two distinct parts: a land siege and a river siege. We'll need both."

By now, no one ventured, saying, "How?" aloud. However, their faces portrayed the question.

Sefuamun said, "Let's break this down into two parts. First is the land siege. Question: what did we do at Megiddo?"

"We built a wooden barricade around the city."

"And how long did it take us?"

"Three and a half months."

"Right. We need to complete it in three weeks. Less, if possible."

"Why?"

"Because," said Sefuamun, if we take months, they will have time to plan and coordinate an attack with their entire coalition to force us into a set-piece battle. So, the progress must be so rapid that, by the time they realize their danger, they can't recover."

"I understand the logic, but how?"

"That is what we have to invent. We built Megiddo's wall log by log, starting in one place and slowly progressing around the city. That won't work again; it's too slow. To speed up building the wall, we'll need exact information of the city and river dimensions. We need to be prepared before we get there.

The General pointed out, "For a minute, assume we can do it. The river still looms before us."

Sefuamun smiled, "Think: the definition of a wall is simply a type of barricade. What is a river barricade? How about a row of boats tied together, stretching from one side to the other?"

That raised the other three men's eyebrows and dropped their jaws.

The General did not become a general by not having two brain cells to rub together; he caught on quickly. "And the river wall doesn't go in until the land wall is complete. That way, they'll continue counting on boat resupply until too late."

"Exactly," agreed Sefuamun. "Last, we must time our Kadesh arrival for one month before barley harvest begins, so we destroy it. We force Kadesh to depend on last year's harvest."

The General cocked his head and paused, thinking. "Ideas are good. However, normally problems surface in the implementation. Where do we build the siege wall? How long does it have to be? If we don't know this and a dozen other details before we arrive, we can't build the wall rapidly."

"Exactly," added Sefuamun. "That's why I said that we needed information. I propose we invent a new team I will call 'Military Intelligence.' Here's my proposal." He removed the cover from a table that had caught no one's attention. It supported a three-foot by five-foot flat board. On one long side's center, where the observer would stand, a three-inch long peg sat an inch from the edge. Fifty-one other pegs were sitting on holes along an arc stretching from the left nearside edge across-the-board to the middle on the far side and back to the nearside at the right side. A number labeled each peg-hole. All pegs were black except the two center ones, colored white. The table sat on three hinged legs. On the table top center were two long grooves. One ran parallel to the long side; another to the short. In each grove, a round metal ball rested.

"What's this?" they collectively asked.

Sefuamun admitted, "It's my invention. An improved surveying tool. It maps the exact dimensions of city walls, a river's width, whatever you need. It is simple to use. Unfold the legs and place the balls in their slot. Level the table by adjusting the legs until both balls remain in their slot's center. Align the two white pegs to look at the center of what you want to measure. The viewing peg is on your side.

"Let's say you want to measure the city's width. Stand far enough away from the city gate until you can get the entire city between any two outer black pegs. Use twine to measure the distance from the city gate to the board center. Record the twine distance and line-of-sight peg numbers from the city wall on your left to your right. Perform these measurements around the city. What is the result? You have surveyed the exact measurements of the city.

"Now, how do we use these? We repeat these readings at a site in the desert. From these line-of-sight readings, we can use stakes to create a full-scale replica of the city and river. We'll know exactly where everything is." Sefuamun paused for effect. He finished, "That's what I call military intelligence."

The General was just as quick on the uptake. "With this knowledge, we can't lose. That's not intelligence; that's brilliance."

SOUTHERN CANAAN

October 1456 BC

The First Three Years

After the Battle of Megiddo, Thutmose conducted annual campaigns with a truncated army in southern Canaan. There was no opposition; after Megiddo, no one wanted to tackle the Egyptian army. It was primarily a show of force with two primary motives:

1. To implant the realization that Egypt was a permanent presence in Canaanite psychology.

2. To enforce the policy that each city must send its sons to Egypt for training. Often, each city king dragged his feet. It required Thutmose and the army appearing at their city gate.

Actually, Egypt's government contrived campaigns to get Pharaoh out of their way. Hatshepsut and Senenmut had assembled a core of administrators that were effective, not just noble's second sons who needed something to do. Egypt ran better with Thutmose as an absent figurehead.

Actually, Thutmose enjoyed it. He could not think of anything else he wanted to do.

One activity *was* visible. Egypt was building and filling grain silos. The year of the Kadesh battle would yield a meager harvest since the army would leave before they could take part. Added to that was Egypt's intent to destroy the Kadesh harvest. That meant Egypt would need grain to feed both populations. Egypt could not conceal this effort's magnitude.

Northern Canaan knew something was stirring. They simply did not know what, when, or who was the target.

Ignorance creates unease on the right hand and tension on the left.

THE SECOND THREE YEARS

Models improve planning. They enable detecting details, which, relying on imagination alone, remain invisible. When staking a city model and its surrounding river in full scale, it was obvious the river's width curving around Kadesh narrowed. That implied the current was faster, meaning the river's backside was too unstable to offload cargo. A faster current explained why there was no backside gate through the shorter ten-foot high walls. The city's front had twenty-foot high walls.

This information revealed the city's critical weakness. It also meant a starvation siege was not the optimum method to subdue the city. To reduce casualties and time, it was better combining the advantages of starvation and attack.

EGYPT WAS READY

Before the army's departure, disappointment marred the ending scene at the Academy.

"No, brother," repeated Thutmose, "You can't come with us."

"But look what we've done in the last five years. I want to share in the victory."

"No, brother, not what we've done. It is what you have done. For Egypt to be victorious, even though I am Pharaoh, I will not be the most important person. You will. I did not conjure the new military inventions for this campaign; you did. I did not develop the tactics to use them; you did. I did not train our army to master their use; you did. With Ramose and now you, the Academy has given Egypt its most successful period in over a thousand years. Every battle has been a lopsided victory. Egypt has not missed a beat.

"Remember what Ramose taught us: when the general does not have the assets he needs and still wins, he goes down in history. When the general has everything he needs, the Pharaoh goes down in history. Both Ramose and you have given Egypt what we needed for overwhelming, decisive victory time after time. Remember, the rest of Northern Canaan and Mitanni are still ahead of us. I cannot afford to lose you. Egypt cannot afford to lose you.

"Let me put it this way: you built this army; I'm only going to lead it. I may be Pharaoh, but you are more important to Egypt's victory than I am. If they kill me, Egypt will go on. I am replaceable. We cannot afford to lose you. You are not replaceable."

Sefuamun hung his head. He did not want to admit it, but perhaps Thutmose was right. If he were in Thutmose's shoes, would he allow himself to go? If he followed his lifelong resolve of faithfulness to duty, he needed to swallow his desires and put Egypt first. "My Pharaoh, your wish is my command. May success follow you into battle–and may the return be glorious."

By now, Kadesh was a long-tailed cat in a room of rocking chairs filled with women nålebinding and socializing. The cat was afraid to move and afraid to sit still.

ON THE EGYPTIAN BORDER, TJARU

January 15th, 1450 BC

From Tjaru to Kadesh on the Orantes is a forty-five-day march. The barley harvest would not begin in northern Canaan until the beginning of April. However, Egypt did not want to interrupt the barley and wheat harvest. She wanted to destroy it. They needed to cut down the stalks before the grains matured. Four wagons carried loads of scythes and sickles. Destroying Kadesh's harvest would send a psychological blow. Unless Kadesh could break a siege, they would starve.

Eight thousand infantry and six hundred chariots left Tjaru in mid-January. Egypt had not fielded that large an army since Megiddo. Concealing more than a thousand chariots and wagons was impossible. Since it was still in the rainy season, there would be at least one rain before they reached Kadesh, so tarpaulins covered all the wagon's contents. Kadesh would not know what was under the tarps, but, whatever it was, they knew it was not gift-wrapped.

Within two weeks, all of northern Canaan knew the Egyptians were coming. The Egyptians had pacified Southern Canaan, and a simple show of force would not need that many men and chariots. The question was, where were they heading? Kadesh was the ringleader of the seven rebellious northern cities. Would the Egyptians begin with the weakest, gradually honing its army's skills? Alternately, start at Kadesh, cutting the head off the snake, allowing the body to die of fright?

FEBRUARY 1ST—KADESH KING'S COUNCIL ROOM

Aqhat, King of Kadesh, called his War Council. Present were Paebel, his son and Army General, and a representative of the six other coalition cities. Keret, Aqhat's eleven-year-old grandson, was also listening in the corner. Aqhat considered it good training.

Paebel delivered the intelligence they had gathered. "There is good and bad news. The upside is our coalition has a chariot advantage, with seven hundred to their six hundred. We have equivalent numbers in infantry, eight to our seven thousand. On numbers alone, an open field battle would cause a draw. That would force them to withdraw. However, there are other factors. They train as a cohesive army, whereas our cities have not. Therefore, they could still win. In three battles, they win one; two would draw. We want better odds. Therefore, defense is our preferred option, which mitigates their training advantage. They are the invaders; they must assume the offense.

"If we rule out an open field battle, our chariot advantage is worthless. Chariots are maneuver weapons. Putting chariots in a static battle robs them of power. Therefore, if the Egyptians commit to a city assault, that city disperses their chariots between us.

"If we deny an open field fight, that either forces a fortified city attack or a siege. A fortified city attack needs a three-to-one advantage, with four-to-one guaranteeing victory. Kadesh has three-thousand, five-hundred men under arms. The Egyptians have significantly less than a three-to-one advantage. Those odds favor us. That leaves a siege. In over a thousand years, we have withstood over a dozen sieges. Boat resupply has always rendered a land siege ineffective.

"Their Levant Army is only three-thousand men. That means they are augmenting their army with five-thousand farmers. Yes, we know they have been stockpiling grain, so they can last for this year with a reduced harvest. However, the farmers will need to go home for next year's harvest, so we will force them to lift their siege before then.

"So, to summarize, we can outlast a siege. That's my recommendation."

Aqhat thanked Paebel, "An authoritative summary. The Orantes will protect us and provide the means to feed us. It is impossible to conquer Kadesh by siege. Let them come. We will outlast them. Thank you, gentlemen."

MARCH 1ST—KADESH KING'S COUNCIL ROOM

Aqhat, King of Kadesh, called his War Council. Present were Paebel, his son and Army General, and a representative of the six other coalition cities. Keret listened in the corner.

Paebel delivered his updated intelligence. "There is little change. The Egyptian march is slow, methodical, and standard. We have confirmed that their direction of advance is Kadesh, so we sent our chariots to our allies.

Their advance guard arrived three days ago, a day or two before expected. They have sent out their cavalry scouts throughout the countryside for fifty miles around.

"The bulk of their army unexpectedly halted fifteen miles away. They had wagons loaded with scythes and sickles. They are systematically cutting all the grain stalks at ground level. There will be no harvest this year. We probably have mere weeks before they finish destroying our crops and arrive at our gates."

Aqhat grimaced. "I had not expected them to destroy the harvest. We have almost six months of grain in our granaries at normal use, perhaps seven if we tighten our belts." He looked around at his allies. "Can we buy enough grain from you to supply our needs until next year's harvest? We'll pick up the grain at your city gates, transport it in our wagons, and ship it down the Orantes in our boats."

One-by-one each agreed to sell their harvest excess to Kadesh.

Aqhat thanked them. "With your help, Kadesh and our league will survive. It is impossible to conquer Kadesh by siege. Let them come. We will outlast them. Thank you, gentlemen."

MARCH 15TH—KADESH KING'S COUNCIL ROOM

Aqhat, King of Kadesh, called his War Council. Present were Paebel, his son and Army General, and a representative of the six other coalition cities. Keret listened in the corner.

Paebel started his report, "This may be the last we'll gather here; the Egyptians are closing in and we expect them to destroy the last grain fields within a week. Their army advance will close off our land access. That will restrict us to our armored boats, the ones with bronze-veneered walls, protecting passengers from arrows and fire."

One of the allied city's representatives asked, "I understand the boats are impervious, but can't the enemy army block you launching and recovering them?"

Paebel responded, "Essentially, no, they cannot. We have six different armored boats. The armor is detachable, and transport wagons can launch and recover them anywhere along the river. Even the boat crew does not know where to land until they see the wagons. The enemy cannot guard the whole Orantes River; that would disperse their men. We could wipe out individual detachments one at a time. That is why we have withstood every siege. The Orantes resupplies us."

The representative responded, "Brilliant."

Aqhat summarized, "With your help, Kadesh and our league will survive. As you can see, it is impossible to conquer Kadesh by siege. Let them come. We will outlast them. Thank you, gentlemen."

MATCH 18TH—KADESH KING'S COUNCIL ROOM–DAY 1

Just after dawn, Aqhat and Paebel, with Keret beside them standing on a stool, were looking out from the city wall parapet, watching the Egyptian army march in and place their forces. Their units formed one-hundred seventy-five yards away from the city walls, much farther than the city's self-bow range of a hundred twenty-five yards.

Keret, looking down, pointed and asked his father, "What's that?"

Paebel looked. It was twine staked at the city gate. From there, it stretched along the road's edge for two-hundred yards, ending at another stake in the field. He looked along the wall to either side. There were additional stakes at the city wall by the river on both sides. Both had twine straight out to stakes by the river. Someone had placed them overnight.

As he was looking, an Egyptian unfolded a three-legged table atop the center roadway stake and fiddled with a wooden tabletop. Then he sighted along pins fixed on top of the table. As he took sightings, he directed a team of men to pound other stakes in the ground.

Paebel pointed this out to Aqhat. After a minute, Aqhat understood what was happening. "This is what you do when surveying your land for boundary stones," he told his son. "They have stealthily surveyed us, likely planning to build something–probably a siege-wall. No matter, even knowing exactly where to build, remember they took three months to build the Megiddo siege-wall. One log at a time. We have time to evaluate what they are doing and develop a plan to thwart it. Kadesh will survive. It is impossible to conquer Kadesh by siege."

The two men continued watching for another fifteen minutes, assumed they had seen everything important, and left. Keret stayed to watch. After completing their survey, an Egyptian tied a twine ball to a stake at the river on one side of the city and unrolled it. He went just around the stake at the road and ended at the river on the other side. The twine unrolled within a hand-width of the river stake at the far side. Keret wondered. *How did they do that? That twine was a half-mile long, yet they were accurate to within a hand-width.* That fascinated him. Then he looked closer. Every five feet, the twine changed color from white to red and back. *Why?*

The Egyptians pounded wall-stakes at every color change, stabilizing the twine so it could not move. They finished just before dusk. Day one.

MARCH 19TH—KADESH CITY WALLS–DAY 2

The following morning at dawn, the Egyptians were back at it. Twenty-five teams of men took identical lengths of twine with knots in the middle. One team member placed one end of his twine at a wall-stake on one end of a color change while a second put his end on the other side's wall-stake. A third man pulled the knot out toward Kadesh until the twine was taut. A fourth drove a stake in the ground at the knot. The team repeated this on the other side. The two stakes had color-coding to match that section's wall-twine color. Red stakes for red sections of wall-twine, white for white. The teams finished by noon.

Aqhat and Paebel stopped by to view the progress, but not seeing teams sinking siege-wall logs in the ground, they lost interest and left. Keret watched all-day, trying to understand what was happening.

No sooner had the last team marked his stakes than wagons arrived. Teams of men directed the wagons where to go. All "white" teams drove their wagons beyond the wall-twine, then straight toward the city, centered over the white stakes. The "red" teams drove inside the wall-twine, then out from the city, centered over the red stakes. The drivers halted each team when the horse yoke was exactly over their far side stake. Each wagon aligned perpendicular to the wall-twine.

No sooner had each wagon stopped than a team pushed a five foot wide wall-section off the wagon. The team offloaded within a hand-width of the twine. Then the teams placed their section of parapet walkway and bracing pole on the city's far side of the twine.

After off-loading, the wagons reformed on the road and left for Egypt.

MARCH 20TH—KADESH CITY WALLS–DAY 3

The next day, the Egyptian army dug a half-mile long trench for the wall two feet deep. Each team sergeant had a T-bar for measurement. He laid his T atop the trench with the measuring length dropped into the trench. If the top crossbar did not reach the ground, the hole was not deep enough. If the measuring length did not reach the bottom, the team shoveled dirt back into the hole. By noon, the entire trench-line was two feet deep.

Aqhat and Paebel stopped by to view the progress in midmorning, but not seeing teams sinking siege-wall logs in the ground, they lost interest and left. Keret watched all-day.

At noon, teams erected each wall-section, first dropping the base into the trench and then pushing it erect. Once they erected two adjoining sections, a man climbed a ladder and dropped a bronze oblong ring over the two adjacent sections of bronze side-posts. This locked the two sections together.

Every wall-section backside had a bronze mounting post on its far side, shaped in a "U." Each section also had its long, wooden bracing pole with a hole drilled through both ends. The team lifted the pole into place with its end between the wall's "U" bracket sides. A team member inserted a one-inch thick bronze pin through the "U" bracket and mounting post, locking the post to the wall. They dropped the post's other end to the ground. The team placed a second 'U' bracket on the ground with its mounting arms up, and adjusted it so the ground end of the support post fit at the hole in the bracket. Another one-inch pin inserted through the "U" bracket and the hole in the post's ground and locked the post. Finally, the team hammered pins through the bracket's bottom into the ground, locking the wall-section to the ground. That section of wall was now impervious to battering rams.

MARCH 21ST—KADESH CITY WALLS–DAY 4

Aqhat and Paebel stopped by to view the progress, but could not develop a plan to impede the Egyptian's progress. After watching for a half hour, Aqhat said, "I didn't believe they could do this, but it doesn't matter. It is only a siege-wall. We have endured these before. They cannot block the river. That is impossible. Kadesh will survive. It is impossible to conquer Kadesh by siege."

His grandfather's comments initially shocked Keret, but he still had faith that his grandfather knew what he was doing. He watched all-day, trying to understand what was happening.

The last task on each siege-wall section was to mount the parapet walkway to the wall sections.

MARCH 22ND—KADESH CITY WALLS–DAY 5

By nightfall, the entire siege-wall was complete.

MARCH 23ND—KADESH CITY WALLS–DAY 6

Morning brought another surprise. The Egyptian siege-wall was one-hundred seventy-five yards from the city wall. They had not considered the importance of that distance.

Paebel brought the news to his father. "Father, I made a mistake. We sent all of our chariots to our ally's cities. The chariots took all of our composite bows with them. We only have standard self-bows left. They don't have the range to reach the Egyptian siege-wall."

"Why don't we have composite bows for everyone?"

"Because we can buy four self-bows for each composite bow. I was saving the city money. I have never faced a siege-wall before and I didn't think to have extra composite bows available in case of emergency."

"That's all right. Even if the maximum range of a composite bow is two-hundred twenty-five yards, the maximum accuracy range is only one-hundred twenty-five yards. The siege-wall is well beyond that."

Although any one Egyptian archer's probability of hitting a man-sized target at a hundred seventy-five yards was only one-in-three, with three archers simultaneously firing on the same target, the odds of a hit rose to fifty-fifty. In a half hour, with three Egyptian archers on the siege-wall firing on one sentry on the city wall, the Egyptians forced the soldiers on the city walls to take shelter. Kadesh could mount lookouts to see what the Egyptians were doing, but anyone standing on the city wall was a dead man.

That astonished Aqhat. "I thought that was impossible. However, that is all right. The enemy of wood is fire. Tonight, we will have a dozen archers firing flaming arrows at the siege-wall. We will burn it down. We will break this siege yet. It is impossible to lay siege to our city successfully." Keret was in the room, listening.

MARCH 24TH—DAY 7, AFTER DARK

That night, twenty-five archers crept out of the city gate, hugging the city wall. They had explicit orders. When the torchbearer lit their arrow, run zigzag, never over ten strides before changing direction and speed. That way, the Egyptian archers could not get a bead on them.

Within two minutes, twenty-five archers raced to get within firing range of the siege-wall. Egyptian arrows dropped some, but the line continued approaching the wall. Finally, seventeen loosed their arrows. Every arrow they fired hit the wall, immediately going out in a burst of steam.

When the surviving archers returned to the Kadesh city gate, thirteen bodies littered the field outside the gate, both wounded and dead. The Egyptians sent out men with stretchers, led by torches, picked them up, and carried them to the city gate. After they had deposited the dead and wounded at the city gate, they left.

The next morning, Paebel brought one of the night watchman to the King. He gave his report, "At first light, the Egyptians began hauling up blankets which had hung on the wall during the night. They had water-soaked each blanket. Its water extinguished every arrow. However, blankets do not have the strength to hang their own weight plus their water. Egyptians had sewn each blanket to a tarpaulin. The tarpaulins wouldn't absorb any water, but its strength held the blanket and the blanket's water."

Paebel told the King, "The flaming arrows couldn't penetrate to the siege-wall; so the tactic of setting the wall ablaze won't work."

Aqhat shook his head. "I thought that was impossible. However, that is all right. We still have the Orantes. We will break this siege yet. It is impossible to successfully siege our city."

Keret sat in the back corner, listening. He began to doubt.

MARCH 25TH—KADESH CITY WALLS-DAY 8

Dawn brought another surprise. Paebel and Keret reported the news to Aqhat. "The Egyptians are erecting archery towers across the river on the city's backside. There were three, each thirty yards long, twenty feet high, spaced along the wall. They are just over a hundred twenty-five feet away, beyond our bow range. However, at twenty-five feet high, they can fire down on our sentries on the wall. We'll have to pull our men back and use observers instead."

Aqhat pondered the news for a minute. "That makes no sense. Why waste personnel when it will not serve a purpose? There is a river between us. They cannot affect us. No matter. It does not change the siege. Taking the city by siege is impossible. We will outlast them."

Keret was not so sure. In his experience, adults did not waste time doing something for nothing. The Egyptians must consider it important. Why? How dangerous could it be?

MARCH 26TH—KADESH CITY WALLS-DAY 9

Dawn brought another omen of disaster. Ten feet upriver from the siege-wall, on each side of the Orantes, a team of men offloaded a ten-foot long, six-inch diameter post and then dug postholes six-feet deep. More wagons offloaded halves of a boat, carried them to the riverside, and tied the halves together. When assembled one-by-one, they floated them. They tied the first to the post on its side of the river, then others prow-to-prow, eventually forming a line of boats stretching across the Orantes. A second rope also connected two adjoining boats. That line connected the rear of the boat nearest to the shoreline with the prow of its companion toward the river's center. An archer and a swordsman crewed each boat. When assembled, the line of boats formed a riverine siege-wall, blocking Orantes' boat travel.

Aqhat, with Paebel and Keret standing beside him, looked out from the city wall. Aqhat shook his head. "I thought this was impossible."

Keret offered, "Grandfather, perhaps 'impossible' doesn't mean what you thought it meant."

"No, Keret. In the centuries Kadesh has stood here, no one has done this. I did not consider this possible, so we have not developed a counter-measure. We have to break this riverine siege-wall. If we can't, the city could fall."

MARCH 27TH—KADESH CITY WALLS–DAY 10

At dawn, three bronze-plate armored boats, each manned by twenty Kadesh archers and swordsmen, slowly floated downstream toward the riverine siege-wall. However, with a current speed of one and a half miles-an-hour, Egyptian sentries spotted them long before their boats reached the wall. Egyptian archers on both sides of the river fired. The arrows could not penetrate the boat's bronze side armor, but the archers adjusted their fire to drop arrows over the side and into the men massed in the boat's center. They killed or wounded half the Kadesh crews before their boats reached the Egyptian wall of boats.

By that time, a hundred additional Egyptian swordsmen lined the riverine siege-wall boats. The Egyptian soldiers heavily outnumbered the Kadesh warriors. The resulting fight was short and certain.

The Egyptians pushed the three Kadesh boats with their lifeless cargo to the center of the river, loaded them with dry straw, and set them ablaze. They used long poles to keep the burning boats ten feet away from theirs. They removed the prow-to-prow ropes joining the Egyptian's four center boats, allowing the Egyptian boats to drift downriver and behind the boat beside it, creating a lane wide enough for the Kadesh boats to go through the gap. Then they pulled the Egyptian boats back together, rejoining the riverine siege-wall's two sides.

The three Kadesh boats slowly drifted downstream. Eventually, fire ate through each boat's sidewall, allowing river-water to stream through, filling the boat, and sinking it. The Orantes left no monument to mark its graves.

MARCH 28TH—KADESH CITY WALLS–DAY 11

The following day, three boats, already aflame, appeared around the bend upriver from Kadesh. Beginning with the two center boats, each Egyptian boat crew lifted their prow-to-prow rope. The current pulled the center boat downstream until each stern-to-prow rope allowed the Egyptian's river-center boat to drift behind the shore-side boat. This slowly formed a long boat column on each side of the river, leaving the center of the river clear for the fireboats to drift harmlessly by. Then the crews pulled on the stern-to-prow ropes to pull the boats alongside and replace the prow-to-prow ropes. This reformed the riverine siege-wall.

Aqhat and Paebel had exhausted their alternatives. Both sides hunkered down for a long siege.

THE MIDNIGHT WATCH, DAY FORTY-TWO

A month passed without the Egyptians taking any observable action. However, they were cataloging the actions of each pair of wall-guard watches on the backside of Kadesh.

The midnight watch is the least desired duty, and sergeants normally assign their worst men to this watch. Therefore, the night-watch duty is also the least diligent. The Kadesh ten-foot back-wall's nightly watches never varied. Unvarying routine leads to boredom, causing inattention, resulting in lethargic complacency.

Nothing ever happened; nothing would.

Except it did.

The third-shift sergeant of the guard always made his round at the same time every night. His two wall sentries came to count on it, eating an extended lunch together in the guardhouse instead of on the wall.

Spring rains are common, but intermittent. The Egyptians waited until it rained. As soon as the night watchmen disappeared for lunch, the soldiers began. This was the most-practiced maneuver of the entire operation. The soldiers had trained nine times until they could do it in their sleep. The practice paid handsome dividends. They constructed a floating walkway across the Orantes, one mini-boat at a time, despite the three-mile current, and completed it in forty minutes. The first eight men across carried ladders, and climbed the wall. Swords drawn, they waited just outside the guard shack door for the sentries to emerge. When the sentries exited, the Egyptians greeted them with sword points. They became docile. The Egyptians blindfolded, gagged and truss-tied the sentries. They accomplished everything in complete silence.

A hand signal triggered six more ladders against the wall and, within an hour, there were a thousand Egyptian soldiers within the city walls. Six teams of fifty penetrated the city streets for a hundred yards, and halted. Their job was just to be there, and, by that, prevent the backside's inhabitants from coming out of their houses.

FIRST LIGHT, DAY FORTY-THREE

At first light, twenty minutes before dawn, Egyptian soldiers at the siege-wall lowered ladders. Three-thousand formed parade ranks in front of the siege-wall, being careful to ensure their front rank was not within bow range of the Kadesh wall. Between every company of fifty stood a crew carrying a twenty-five foot ladder.

The Commanding General of the Levant Army advanced to fifty yards of the Kadesh wall, stopped and yelled to the sentries, "Call the King. I will wait."

Soldiers had alerted Aqhat and Paebel, who were dressing. It took only five minutes for them to reach the wall, sword belts around their waists. Keret trailed behind them.

The Egyptian General spoke, "King, you may not be aware, but Kadesh has already fallen. There are a thousand Egyptian soldiers already within your backside walls, with two thousand more waiting on a signal to climb their ladders. Our archers can clear your ramparts and you cannot stop our frontal assault. However, there is no need to shed blood needlessly. Let your people live. We ask for your surrender."

"What are your terms?"

"Egypt will forgive everyone; there will be no recriminations. Egypt will feed your citizens until next year's harvest. Kadesh will become a garrison city with a cohort of three-hundred. Tribute will resume. Egypt will guarantee that we will spend three-fourths of the tribute collected here at Kadesh. This is what we have already done in the southern Levant. We will hire local men to build better roads, ferries, and docks. Ask Megiddo's King how we have improved their economy. Trading costs will go down and trade increase, bringing more wealth into your city. Ask Megiddo, they will verify what happened after they surrendered. The last requirement will be to take your grandson Keret and five other boys aged six to twelve from prominent families. We will train them in Egypt in diplomacy, administration and planning. When they return at nineteen, they will improve your government." He allowed the King to absorb the ramifications of what he had said, finally finishing. "What is your answer?"

"A minute to confer with my son."

Aqhat turned to Paebel. "I don't want Keret going to Egypt."

Keret broke in, "But, Grandfather, I need to go to Egypt."

Both men gawked, looking down at Keret, who continued, "Don't you understand? The Egyptians are not any smarter than we are, but they have planned better and executed those plans better. I need to go to Egypt to learn how they do it. Then, ten years after I return, we'll be as good as they are, maybe better." He looked at his father. "It's necessary. Otherwise, Kadesh may fall again."

Despite his best efforts to stop it, a tear rolled down Paebel's cheek as he hugged his son. "Keret, you're right. It is best for Kadesh. Your mother and I will miss you terribly, but we will look forward to your return."

Aqhat leaned over the parapet. "Kadesh has one stipulation–that Keret attends your Military Academy.

That stymied the general. He was not expecting that reply. He turned to Thutmose, standing on the siege-wall. Thutmose nodded. The general turned back to Aqhat. "Agreed."

Aqhat said, "We accept your terms."

Thutmose greeted the General as he returned, climbing the ladder over the siege-wall. "Not one man, General. We didn't lose a single man! Only four wounded. In a month and a half. Sefuamun is a genius."

NORTHERN CANAAN

1450–48 BC

The Egyptians spent the next few years consolidating their hold over northern Canaan. City-by-city, the Egyptians visited and subdued the seven city-states of the northern coalition. The first was Byblos on the Mediterranean Sea, which required building a small fleet of fifty ships to interdict harbor traffic and halt commerce.

Egypt continued its policy of exacting pain from the wallet and not blood from the veins of its conquered rebellious vassals.

MITANNI

January 1447 BC

Mitanni was the unheralded instigator, mastermind, and funder of the original Megiddo revolt at Hatshepsut's death.

Mitanni is a plains kingdom. The rolling grasslands of southeastern Turkey provide plentiful pastureland for grazing, but it does not suit the land for farming. The soil is too thin to support continuing disturbance of the fertile topsoil. Without a large farming population to provide infantry, Mitanni depended on her horses and chariots to provide its power base. It had a large chariot army, outnumbering Egypt almost two to one, but it did not have the population base to field a significant infantry. With hundreds of miles distance to isolate it from its more populated neighbors, its cities had no walls suitable for defense against infantry assault.

Chariots can defeat opposing armies, but they cannot hold territory. Only sandals on the ground can do that, and the name for sandals is infantry.

Egypt's chariots could negate the Mitanni advantage in chariot numbers and defend its infantry, and Egypt's infantry could conquer the land of Mitanni.

Mitanni's army was one-dimensional. One-dimensional armies seldom prevail against multi-dimensional ones.

Thutmose I had invaded Mitanni during his realm, and left a stele marking the place where his army crossed the Euphrates. Sefuamun had the records and had a matching stele carved. Thutmose III's army would erect it alongside his grandfather's stele.

That plan delighted his brother.

The Egyptians used the same boat-bridge concept they had used at Kadesh, only with larger boats, so they could support a chariot and its horses. Crossing the Euphrates, they left a small detachment to disassemble and guard the bridge, and it was time for pillage and plunder.

Before climbing on his chariot to cross the boat-bridge, Thutmose hugged his brother. "You have what you wanted," he said. "You've seen our victory stele erected beside our Grandfather's. Now I have to leave you; Egypt has work to do. Remember what our mother said, 'I want to send a simple message to all of our empire: count the cost of losing before dreaming of the profit from winning.' It's time for Mitanni to face the cost of losing."

Through a tearful face, Sefuamun choked out the words, "Stay safe, brother, we need you back."

Thutmose's chariot was the first to cross the boat-bridge. Sefuamun watched him as he disappeared into the distance.

The same wagons that carried the army's food into Mitanni carried out vast quantities of gold, silver, bronze, lapis lazuli, and steatite.

They took no sons of city kings back to Egypt. This campaign's goal was to defeat and humiliate, and not to incorporate into the Egyptian empire.

The conquest was triumphant.

When the General does not have all he needs for the battle, yet wins, his name goes down in history. When the General has all he needs for the battle, the pharaoh's name goes down in history. Ramose and Sefuamun had ensured Egypt had everything it needed to win decisively. Under Thutmose III, Egypt reached its empire's greatest extent.

Chapter 14

Manheim, Pennsylvania

Present

David thought, *I'm glad I can read a map. Manheim isn't exactly a "blink and you'll miss it" town, but it's a far cry from Washington. Where are we going? Kountry Kitchen, 944 Lebanon Road, route 72, on the left.* On seeing it: *Well, cars fill all the front spaces–that is always a good sign. However, there are spaces on the side.* He turned in.

Before opening the car door, he reached into his suit pocket for the introductory information paper the Smithsonian had given him. *OK. I am looking for Doctor Brian Woods, Contributing Editor of "Archeology and the Bible," a fundamentalist magazine. What did they tell me about him? Oh, here it is.* Excellent archaeologist. Expert on pottery analysis. He evaluates the science of an artifact flawlessly, but may misjudge its meaning to fit his beliefs. For example, He maintains dates of Jericho's fall 150 years after Kathleen Kenyan's radiocarbon dating. Why do we recommend him? Because his magazine gets a review-copy of all recently released field reports. He keeps up with the latest data. *OK, I will believe his facts, but not put too much faith in his evaluation.*

When he entered the building, an elderly man waved to him from a back table. David did not have to guess it was Brian. They were the only two over fifty and wearing suit jackets.

Once they had shaken hands, and David had taken his seat, Brian began. "Welcome to Manheim. This is not Washington, so we don't have any five-star restaurants, but I hope you'll find that the Kountry Kitchen offers good, down-home food like grandma used to make. It also offers good Greek food. The spanakopita is good.

"Great, thank you, I'll try it."

After ordering, David started, "I am particularly interested in a Hebrew four-room versus the Canaanite three-room house, and the use of a household cistern water supply. Can you tell me about them?"

"Let me start with a Canaanite three-room house," began Brian. "Let's say the house is thirty feet wide and fifty feet long. It is two stories high. The entrance is on the first floor in the middle of the short, thirty-foot wall. As you come in, there are pillars or walls from the front to the back dividing the bottom floor into three sections. The left, middle and right side rooms are ten feet wide and fifty feet long, all with dirt floors. The household cooking pit for the fire is in the middle room, about two-thirds of the way back. The upstairs are the living quarters. There might be stairs to the roof, often with a grass floor, where you would often sleep in the summer.

"Now shift to a Hebrew house. The second story and roof were the same. However, the ground floor was different. There would be the same three ten-foot wide room dividers as you came into the house, but instead of going all the way to the back wall, they would stop after thirty-five to forty feet. At that point, an inside wall would go from side-to-side with a door in the middle, making a fourth room on the ground floor backside. Hence the names three-room and four-room house. Three-room houses were only Canaanite and four-rooms were only Hebrew-Israelite.

"Now, for the second part of your question, the cisterns. This is more complicated. The Levant used cisterns for over a thousand years before the Hebrew exodus in the 1200s BCE. However, they had been non-hydrolic, meaning they had hard, rigid walls. Therefore, they were in something like rock. You could not put them directly in dirt, because, as they filled and emptied, the dirt walls would not provide even support pressure. The walls would crack and leak. In the late thirteenth century BC, they invented the hydrolic lime-plastered cistern for dirt. It had flexible walls, using pozzolanic agents including animal fat and hair for a stiff, but flexible additive. The Egyptians and Canaanites primarily used horsehair for their stiffener, while the Hebrews used goat or sheep.

"Why is this important? Because the Canaanites already located their houses and farms on the brooks and streams when the Hebrews arrived. There was no water supply for an additional population. However, by using cisterns to collect rainwater from the roof, a house could collect enough water in the rainy season to last through the summer, so the Hebrews did not depend on the brooks and streams. Last item. Besides not depleting their water supplies, the additional animals on the market lowered the meat price. The local population welcomed the Hebrews."

David thought for a minute, then replied, "Thank you. I hadn't thought through the consequences of the Hebrew addition to market values. They did not compete with the Canaanites for water resources, and lowered the price the Canaanites had to pay for their food. Question: where is the oldest four-room house discovered?"

"The oldest is in southern Jordan in the tribal area of Reuben, but it isn't Hebrew."

David's eyebrow raised. "How can you say that?"

"Because it is carbon dated from 1415 BCE to 1425 BCE. Since the Hebrews wouldn't arrive in Canaan until the 1200s, it couldn't be a Hebrew house."

Right? That sounds like Brian is bending his evaluation of the facts to fit his beliefs. "Were there any other differences in population density?"

"Well, other than in this one house in Jordan, there were no four-room houses before 1200 BCE yet discovered in the southern kingdom area. And in 1200 BCE, all the new settlements were in the northern kingdom."

David's other eyebrow went up. "All? What could explain that data?"

"If the southern tribes all remained pastoralists, they would leave essentially no archaeological record. Only the northern tribes switched to become agriculturists."

"So, the facts suggest two dissimilar Israelite populations. Why would there be two different populations entering Canaan if they were a unified population leaving Egypt?"

"When they arrived in Canaan, Joshua cast lots–see Joshua 18:10–for allocation of land. God assigned the pastoralists to the south and the agriculturists to the north."

Right? That sounds like Brian is stretching the facts to fit his predetermined results again. In twelve throws of the dice, all pastoralists went south, and all agriculturalists went north? The odds of that happening are less than three in ten thousand. That would be divine intervention.

David continued, "OK, what does the Bible say? In Exodus, chapter 12, in the story of the Passover, it records that the Israelites put blood on the doorposts and lintel of their 'house.' There is no mention of what to do with tents. That only fits one population–the northern kingdom. That suggests the northern tribes had already switched to an agricultural lifestyle before leaving Egypt. No mention of the southern tribes. Can you explain that?"

Brian shrugged, but said nothing.

"OK, let me ask a related question. You are the pottery expert, so I hope you can help fill in my knowledge gap. I believe that Canaanite pottery

was distinctively different from Hebrew/Israelite in artistry, style, and painting and glazing techniques. Therefore, it is readily distinguishable. What
was the northern Hebrew pottery like compared to the Canaanites?"

"Drastically different. So different a half-dozen sherds from two
or three unique examples of tableware is enough to differentiate them
conclusively."

"What about the Jordan house–what ceramic-ware remains were there?"

"I don't have enough data to know for certain. Incidental remarks
show it was brown ware similar to Hebrew use. However, they have not
released the field reports on the ceramic artifacts, so I cannot say with any
certainty. I just know it wasn't a Hebrew house."

"What about Egypt? Are there any remains of the Hebrew houses of
the Bible?"

"Essentially, no. Remember, the Hebrews lived in the delta. The Nile
inundated the delta annually, leaving a thin deposit layer to enrich the soil
every year. Those annual deposits have accumulated to where the level containing the Biblical period is twenty to twenty-two feet down. Couple this
with the fact that someone owns every square foot of today's land. To do any
extensive archaeological excavation is prohibitively expensive. We have to
know exactly where to look. With the Hebrews, we do not. It is all we can do
to locate the more important ancient Egyptian sites.

"However, archaeologists have located a waddle and daub four-room
house outside Thebes, preliminarily dated to the late thirteenth century
BCE. That shows Hebrews there. However, the team has not released its
field report, including radiocarbon dating, so I don't know more about it."

David continued, "The eminent archeologist Kathleen Kenyon exca-
vated Jericho. Her radiocarbon dating placed the destruction layer in the
late 1400s BCE. Her field report also states that, although no one rebuilt the
walls, settlers constructed a surface-layer of houses at the top of the mound
and settled there for at least a hundred years. She identified these as Israelite.
How do you explain that?"

"I don't. She made a mistake; the houses were not Israelite."

"Why do you say that?"

"Because the Israelites hadn't arrived yet."

*Right. You are telling me that a four-room house in Egypt is Hebrew,
but a four-room house in Canaan is not. Yet no one but the Israelites built
four-room houses.* "Change of subject: the battles recorded in the Bible when
the Israelites entered Canaan. All but the last couple of battles occurred in
the southern kingdom area. There were none in the mid to far north. That
shows that, at the time they fought these battles, the northern Canaanites
welcomed the incoming Israelites, but there was animosity in the south.

Why did they not welcome the southern Israelites? Why did they have to go to war? After all, unlike the Israelites with two distinct populations of pastoralists and agriculturists, the Canaanites were one continuous population. Why would the north and south treat the new arrivals differently? In addition, the southern Israelites brought sheep to market, but the northern were agriculturalists. Their added produce on the northern market would have lowered the price the northern Canaanites would receive for their crops. That would have created animosity to the northern Israelites, but not to the southern. It would seem the southern Canaanites would welcome the cheaper meat supply, but they were the ones with the animosity.

"Let me put forward a hypothesis. Might the southern Israelites have been there so long that an antipathy built up against them to where the Canaanites rejected them, perhaps persecuted them? Otherwise, there would have been no need for a battle. Remember, the southern Israelites were not competing for land; they were still pastoralists. When their northern cousins arrived, the southern ones appealed to them for help. Old family ties–even perhaps tenuous, were enough to entice the northern tribes to join them in battle. Does this make sense?"

"No sense at all. All the tribes arrived together in the 1200's BCE."

"All right. Last question. In First Kings 6:1 (RSV), it says: In the four hundred and eightieth year after the people of Israel came out of the land of Egypt, in the fourth year of Solomon's reign over Israel, in the month of Ziv, which is the second month, he built the house of the LORD. Solomon's fourth regnal year was 967 BCE. That means that the Bible states that the exodus occurred in 1447 BCE. If the exodus occurred in the 1200s BCE, how do you explain that?

Brian's response was abrupt. "I don't. It's wrong."

Brian's response took David aback, but, taking a breath, he forced himself to calm down. "All right. In what way is it wrong?"

"It doesn't give the right answer, so it's wrong."

"So you're saying the Bible is wrong?"

That stopped Brian in his tracks. "Of course not. The Bible is inerrant. Something else is wrong; I just can't account for it."

David could not help it. He shook his head, stopping after having barely started. *Brian, you are trying to use a sledgehammer to pound the facts into your belief system's mental model. Cut to the chase. There is too much data showing that one exodus from Egypt in the 1200s does not account for all the facts. Yes, the evidence is overwhelming for an exodus in the 1200s. However, you refuse to examine any facts not fitting your belief system.*

I did not even ask my last question, because I cannot trust you to give me an unbiased answer. The two exodus miracle accounts in the books of Exodus and Psalm 78 do not agree. For example, Psalm 78 does not include the dark- ness miracle. Does that mean that the 1400's BCE exodus included a miracle of darkness, but the 1200's account did not? How can I learn something new when you refuse to examine the facts?

Just then, the food arrived. David apologized, saying he was not feeling well, and asked for a to-go box. He hopped in his car and started home. His mind kept going over the meeting. *Brian, when you twist the facts, or even just your evaluation of the facts, it is lying. When you lie, then no one can trust you. You have betrayed the facts for the cause of your beliefs. You are no longer an archaeologist. Disreputable archaeologists who misrepresent or only use selected facts have caused gullible people to doubt all archaeologist's results. It's no wonder you aren't a professor at a reputable university. No one should hire you.*

The same works for Christians. If you have to lie to fit the facts into your belief system, then no one can trust you as a Christian either. God is a God of truth. He is big enough and patient enough to allow us to know him through the truth. The truth is usually more complicated than a first impres- sion. However, the truth remains the truth. We do not decide what facts are the truth and reject all others not in compliance. Therefore, we cannot trust your Christianity any more that we can your archaeology.

Therefore, Brian, you lose on both counts. I must evaluate the facts, be- cause I cannot trust your judgement.

As he was cogitating, he noticed a sign for a rest stop. He pulled over to eat his lunch. The spanakopita at the Kountry Kitchen was good. He could stomach the food. He could not stomach the company.

COUNCIL ROOM OF THE GREAT TEN OF UPPER AND LOWER EGYPT, INEBU-HEDJ

March 1447 BC

Nefer-Weben called the meeting to order and motioned for the Vizier to take control. "Gentlemen, the more events unfold in our empire, the more convinced I am that we have made a grave mistake. We have misread the will of the gods.

"Allow me to refresh you on the sequence of succession for pharaoh:

- First, a doubly divine blood man, married to the God's Wife of Amun
- Second, a doubly divine blood man, married to a divine wife
- Third, a divine man married to the God's Wife of Amun

- Fourth, a divine man married to a divine wife

- Fifth, a noble blood man married to the God's Wife of Amun

- Sixth, a noble blood man married to a divine wife

- Seventh, lacking an available divine wife, a noble blood man married to a noble blood woman

"What did we do? When Hatshepsut proclaimed Thutmose III Pharaoh with herself as Regent, we questioned our wisdom allowing this, since an aunt regent had never happened in Egypt's long history. The result? We voted for Marytatum as pharaoh. We misread the will of the gods and they sent the Disaster of Darkness upon us. Hatshepsut exercised her right as God's Wife of Amun to reclaim the right to pharaoh and we had twenty years of prosperity and peace.

"Thutmose was fifth in the line of succession, so we did not question allowing him to continue as Pharaoh. That was when we failed. You should ask what went wrong. Nothing went wrong. Instead, it is what did not go right. What happened? We did not look to fail; we completely failed to look.

"First, allow me to summarize the prime points of Ramose's career:

- First, because of his brilliance and military wisdom, Pharaoh Thutmose gave him command of the military academy

- Second, he planned, executed and then commanded at the Battle of Kerma

- Third, he re-invented the khopesh sword and the tactics to use it

- Fourth, he devised the tactics used to rout the Libyans at the Battle of Miteinya Ridge

- Last, he discerned the need for cavalry and created it in time for the Battle at Megiddo

"Gentlemen, we deluded ourselves. We assumed that Ramose was of commoner blood. We could not see the facts in front of our faces. The gods do not grant his level of intelligence and wisdom to commoners. Yes, he was not of Egyptian noble blood, but we failed to ask if he was of noble blood from another country. We even overlooked what should have been a dead giveaway: his name. His local city official allowed him to have a noble's name.

"To summarize, we failed in our duty.

"When did we go wrong? Sefuamun was born within the first year of declaring Thutmose III Pharaoh. Then, the Disaster of Darkness in the Nile delta happened. By that time, we already had all the evidence and signs from the gods that we needed, and we did not even look at them. Thutmose is noble; but Sefuamun is divine. Therefore, Thutmose was fifth in line of succession, whereas Sefuamun was third. Sefuamun had priority.

"Now look at today's evidence. First, Thutmose III. He is of average intelligence. That results from too much commoner blood in the harem. His redeeming character is that he knows it and follows the guidance of his advisers. Therefore, he is an adequate pharaoh.

"Now, Sefuamun. Look at the evidence:

- At Megiddo, he invented new tactics for the cavalry
- At Megiddo, his personal bravery swung the tide of battle
- At Megiddo, he instigated the siege wall and moat
- For Kadesh, he invented the segmented siege walls, siege boats, and archer towers
- For Kadesh, he invented the tactic to force their surrender without losing a single man
- For Byblos, he invented the boat siege to close its harbor
- For Mitanni, he invented the chariot bridge and the tactics to subdue them

"To summarize, Sefuamun is as brilliant in devising tactical and engineering solutions for our army's success as Ramose was in devising weapons. He is also a strong and brave leader. Exactly what the empire needs for a pharaoh.

"Now, for my closing argument. The gods are patient and gracious, but they expect us to use our wisdom and evaluate the facts before us. We failed when we approved Marytatum, and they punished us with the Disaster of Darkness. I have no wish for the gods to repeat that punishment–or worse. We had all the evidence we needed. What should we have done? What should we do now?"

The Djat pointed out, "But Sefuamun has already told the Council he doesn't want to be pharaoh."

The Vizier replied, "I agree, and we told him that what he wanted didn't matter; it was what the gods wanted."

The Djat grimaced. The Vizier was correct.

One member spoke up, "What do we do if he refuses to serve?"

The Vizier handled that objection. "That won't happen. Examine his character. He has always answered the call and risen to the occasion on every instance Egypt needed him. His motivation, like that of Ramose, is duty first. Regardless of his personal feelings, he will serve, because that's who he is."

Discussion continued for well over an hour. The arguments were contentious and heated. Two-thirds were leaning toward proclaiming Sefuamun as Pharaoh, one-third for keeping Thutmose.

Finally, Khusebek proposed. "Gentlemen, we did not get here overnight. Therefore, I also do not believe we need a solution overnight. The gods know we are reexamining the evidence. They will be patient. I propose we table this decision until the next meeting in three months. I will ask Amun for guidance, and we will have time for a sign from him."

Lacking a clear consensus, they accepted this suggestion. The meeting adjourned. All left with the weight of the decision dragging on their shoulders. However, that was what the Council was for: to make the hard decisions. This was the hardest in many decades.

IN A HEBREW TENT IN THE DELTA PASTURELANDS WEST OF TJARU, EGYPT

April 1447 BCE

News of a possible change of pharaoh does not remain secret. Within days, it reached the Military Academy. After reflecting on its ramifications, Yahmose called a meeting of all Israelite Tribal Leaders.

One week later, Yahmose addressed the leaders of the twelve tribes of Israel, "Men, we are facing a condition that has not occurred in two-hundred years. We are Hebrews, sojourners in a foreign land. Egypt is not our actual home; Hebron in the Levant is. Until now, Egypt has welcomed us. That will change in two weeks."

Heads jerked to attention; backs straightened. At first merely curious, everyone went to hyper-alert. The tribal leader of Reuben spoke. "Why? What's changed?"

"The Great Ten held their quarterly meeting two weeks ago. They are considering replacing Pharaoh Thutmose with me."

Issachar chimed in, "That sounds like great news to me. You would make a great pharaoh."

Yahmose shook his head. "No, that is a disaster. I cannot and will not be pharaoh."

Simeon spoke, "First, I must agree with Issachar. You would make a great pharaoh. Why would you refuse? Every time Egypt has depended on you, you have said yes. You have led us in battle. You have always put Egypt first and yourself second. If Egypt says they need you and asks you to be pharaoh, why would this be any different?"

"Because I would have to conduct the daily worship ceremonies to the Egyptian gods. I cannot do that."

Zebulun objected, "That sounds like a small compromise."

"Because it isn't a small compromise; it is the most important fact in the world. The Egyptian gods are gods *of* this world. They are not the *Creator* of the world; they are not the Lord. I must respect them as gods, but never will I revere them as God. I worship Yahweh and Yahweh alone. I cannot conduct worship ceremonies to the gods of Egypt. It would mean surrendering who I am; my very soul. Above all else, I am faithful. Yes, I am faithful to Egypt, but I am faithful to the Lord first. If being faithful to Egypt conflicts with being faithful to the Lord, then my faith to the Lord comes first."

Naphtali questioned, "All right, I respect that. However, why should your personal decision make a difference to us? Why should it affect the Hebrew people?"

"Because Thutmose is Pharaoh. Thutmose is not an evil man, but he is petulant. With him, you are completely for him or you are completely against him. There can be no middle ground. By deciding I cannot do this, in his eyes, he will believe that I am rejecting Egypt. Therefore, I have no choice; I must leave. Thus, that decision affects you. I stand in the line and lineage of Abraham. If Thutmose believes I will not put Egypt first, it means he will believe all Hebrews will not. That means we must all leave. It is time for us to go home."

Benjamin shook his head. "I can't believe that. It makes no sense."

"By definition, emotions do not depend on logic. I am Thutmose's brother. I am telling you that is how he will feel, what he will think, and how he will react. You can believe or not. What you believe will not affect what he will do. For example, I can tell you that, at the least, no Hebrew will remain in the army. He will replace all archers."

Gad objected, "He can't do that. It will take years to train new archers."

"But that is what he will do." Yahmose paused, surveying the group. "Gentlemen, it is time to decide. When the local officials discover news of our preparations to leave, they will send runners to Thutmose in Waset. Normal runners take nine days for the trip, but I expect these to run around-the-clock. That will take only six days, twelve for the round-trip. That means that I must leave for Hebron in ten days. With the flocks and herds of everyone who elects to go with me. We will be gone for two days before orders on what to do will arrive from Waset. Those that remain are at the mercy of Thutmose–and I tell you now: there will be no mercy. What is your decision?"

The discussion was long and contentious. One-third of the tribes– Reuben, Simeon, Judah and Dan–would leave and the remaining two-thirds would remain in Egypt.

On reflection, Yahmose thought that ironic. Two-thirds of the Egyptian Council wanted him to be pharaoh, but only one-third of the Tribes would leave with him.

THERA–PHASE IV, SANTORINI ISLAND

April 1447 BC

Twenty-six years had passed. Thera had exhausted its magma in the great eruption in 1473. There was no longer pressure from below supporting the empty cone in the middle of Santorini's bay.

The sea is relentless.

It never rests.

It never surrenders.

It girdles the hardest of seashore rocks, eventually toppling them.

It dissolves the most resistant of surfaces with its mildly caustic chemicals, softening the surface layers, slowly seeping deeper and deeper.

Eventually, the sea always wins.

Thera finally lost its battle with the ocean. The volcano's softened underpinning could no longer support the weight above it, and the tall cone cratered almost a thousand feet down into its now-empty magma chamber. The sea rushed into the bay to fill the void. However, the sea has no intelligence. Water continues to rush in until the void overfills. In Thera's case, there was a temporary mountain of water, its peak reaching over eight hundred feet. After a moment's pause, the mountain of water spewed outward in all directions, the wave slowly losing height with distance.

When the tidal wave reached eastern Crete, it was sixty feet high. Most of the Minoan population lived on the Northeast side of the island. Most near the shore. They had no warning. The tidal wave scoured the coastline. Nothing remained. The Minoan civilization never recovered, finally collapsing from Mycenaean conquest.

The wall of water continued, heading south and east.

SINAI DESERT–BY PIHAHIROTH

April 1447 BC

The flight of the tribes faced no problems for the first three days of their Canaan journey. Although the border guards looked at them askance, they had no orders to stop them, and the tribes were breaking no laws. They left peacefully.

Fifty archers led the march, followed by the families with their wagons, donkeys, flocks and herds. Last was the force of two hundred archers. The greater danger would be behind them, not in front.

They had just passed the small hamlet of Pihahiroth when dust clouds a half-mile wide appeared on the horizon behind them. Yahmose did not need to see the cause of the dust cloud. That size could only be the Levant Army's chariots. The timing was favorable. They had just reached a small finger of a hillock, flat-topped and just over twenty-five feet high, rising from an inland range of hills and protruding toward the sea. It left a gap between the sea and hill a hundred-fifty yards wide. Here the road turned inland from the shore, climbed the hill, and continued to the next watering station by the wells eight miles beyond.

Yahmose took quick stock of the terrain. This was the best defensive position he had seen. He could have wished for a thirty-foot hill, but twenty-five would do. No infantry wants to assault uphill against a hail of arrows. Even chariots would have to slow their charge, which risks having the horses shot. Even better, the hundred-fifty yard wide piece of shoreline would be a death trap. On the seaward side, they could not be out-flanked. Yes, this was good terrain.

Yahmose sent a runner to have the forward archers return. The column would pick up the pace for the rest of the day. Yahmose carefully aligned the bowmen along the top of the hill in five-yard increments. They formed a battle line on the hill-front almost a half-mile across, waiting.

The dust cloud gradually grew closer until they could identify individual chariots. Yahmose did not need to count them; they had brought all six hundred of the Levant Army. The chariots stopped three hundred yards away–beyond the effective range of their longbows.

A man dismounted and approached to fifty yards from the hill. There was no sword in his scabbard. His hands were in the air, obviously wanting to negotiate. As he got closer, Yahmose recognized the Commanding

General of the Levant Army. Yahmose ordered a no-fire signal sent down the line.

The General looked over the archers, and recognizing Yahmose, called out. "Sefuamun, I have an order signed by Thutmose himself." He held a short-scroll aloft and unrolled it. 'Bring every Hebrew back alive or leave their carcass to be picked to their bones by the birds and crumble into dust.' I do not wish to kill you. You are an honorable man and your death would be a significant loss to Egypt and the army."

Yahmose merely stood there. Unmoving. Silent.

After a moment, the General called out, "I will give you time to consider your alternatives. It will be dusk before the infantry arrives. We will not start combat until morning. I will set my tent on this spot. You have until morning to reconsider and return with your people. You have my word no harm or recriminations will happen to anyone choosing to return to Egypt."

Yahmose merely stood there.

"As you wish, Sefuamun," and the General about faced, returned to his lines, and gave orders for his men to dismount, remove the chariot harnesses, and care for the horses.

The General returned with a crew who erected his tent where he was standing.

The two sides settled in for a long wait.

An hour before dusk, the infantry and wagon trains arrived and set up camp.

The Israelites remained at their stations, ate and slept in place on the open ground.

Both sides set watches, but both knew it was only a precaution. Neither side wanted to break the interim truce.

As first light tickled the darkness in the sky over the horizon, Yahmose awoke, a complete thought flooding his mind. It had an intense, overwhelming power, yet pervaded with a calm, benevolent peace. He had to put the thought into his own words, "Fear not, stand firm, and see my salvation, which I will work for you today. For the Egyptians whom you see today, you shall never see again. I will fight for you, and you have only to be still." This mirrored the type of message from God that Abraham had recorded in his memoirs in the Ephod container. Yahmose knew, with a quality of surety he had never experienced, that this was directly from Yahweh himself. A peace beyond understanding, a peace he had never experienced before, settled over him.

At first light, just before daybreak, the Egyptian camp came alive. Their men began a cold breakfast. There was no wood for campfires.

The Israelite archers carried three types of skins. Each man ate cheese curdled from his goat's milk skin, used some of the milk whey to wet grains from his grain-skin, and drank water from the third.

As his men stood up from breakfast, Yahmose went down the line, giving the same order. "Unstring your bows. Simply stand in place. Today, the Lord will fight for us. We only have to be still." Over-and-over, he received the same incredulous stares voicelessly asking the same unbelieving question, "Are you crazy?" Over-and-over, he gave the same answer, "No, I'm not crazy. The Lord will fight for us today. He will win the victory. We have only to stand and watch. Just remain faithful."

However, from Yahmose fighting with his men in other battles, he had earned their trust. His men were soldiers, and soldiers obey orders, even when the orders make no sense. They unstrung their bows.

An hour after daybreak, both sides had settled into their battle formations. The Egyptian chariots in the lead, infantry in company order behind them.

Yahmose stood five yards in front of his line of men, waiting.

When everyone was ready, the General exited his tent and walked ten paces forward. "Sefuamun, you have heard the orders Thutmose has given. What is your decision, to return and live, or utterly perish, you and your men?"

Yahmose merely stood there. Unmoving. Silent.

After a moment, the General shouted, "You decision be upon your own head." He turned and gave the order to his attendants, who were waiting at the tent stakes. "Strike the tent."

It took but moments to remove it.

The General wheeled about to face the Hebrews, drew his sword from its scabbard, and lifted it.

Before he could shout, "Charge," a loud noise like water pouring through rapids sounded to his left. An overpowering urge forced everyone's heads to turn toward the sea.

The sea was not there.

The beach was dry for a quarter mile. Looking further, the sea was retreating from the beach at a speed a fast horse could not match. For perhaps a half-minute, it receded. The incoming and outgoing waters merged into a towering wall eighty feet high.

For a moment, the two incoming and outgoing waters paused. Breathlessly.

Then, with a tumult deafening in the ears, the wall of water roared toward the beach, screaming.

The Egyptians turned to flee. They were too late. When the wall hit the beach, it was only twenty feet high, but it swept everything before it.

The water passed by only a few feet from where the Hebrew archers were standing. No one's sandals got wet.

What had been the Egyptian Levant Army disappeared. The wave ripped chariots into kindling, depositing everything two miles inland. It tore every horse from its harness, its body dumped amid the wreckage. There were warrior corpses helter-skelter. It left nothing alive.

No one discovered where the bodies came to rest. No one found them. Birds picked their bones. The wind and sand crumbled the bones into dust.

Nothing remained but distant memories.

The wave scoured the beach clean. Flat. Pristine. As if humanity had never existed. Not so much as a rut from a chariot or wagon wheel remained. Not so much as a sandal print marred primeval sand.

It struck Yahmose. Ever since Ramose had introduced him to Yahweh, he had thought of reality as two universes: this material universe and the spiritual one of God. However, that was not reality. Yes, there was the separate and spiritual world of God, and God was present throughout it. However, this world was not just a material world. As God was present throughout the spiritual world, He was also present throughout this world. God was the God of this world as much as He was of the spiritual world. There was no iota in this world where God was not. When Yahmose had prayed to God; when he had called on God, he had not prayed or called to a distant God in another universe. God was already here. God penetrated this world, suffusing it. When Yahmose walked, God was there beside him, walking with him. Yahmose was never alone.

As that thought settled into his being, that peace beyond understanding again permeated his entire being. God was in charge. All was well.

Yahmose allowed his men five minutes to absorb the sight and shock, and commanded, "Form march."

Their brains still befuddled, the men's bodies performed the mechanics of mindless motion. It was hours before the inevitable military bantering allowed the men's consciousness to return to normal.

They had experienced the incredible. It took days to believe the miraculous.

Several days later, Yahmose composed a song they later used in their worship services to commemorate and celebrate their deliverance. They intended this song for use by their children's children. As a memorial, less they forget this event.

I will sing unto the LORD, for he has triumphed gloriously; the horse and his rider he has thrown into the sea.

The LORD is my strength and my song, and he has become my salvation.

This is my God, and I will praise him, my father's God, and I will exalt him.

The LORD is a man of war; the LORD is his name.

Pharaoh's chariots and his host he cast into the sea.

The floods covered them.

Thy right hand, O LORD, glorious in power; thy right hand, O LORD, shatters the enemy.

In the greatness of thy majesty thou overthrow thy adversaries.

Thou send forth thy fury, it consumes thy enemy like stubble.

At the blast of thy nostrils the waters piled up, the floods stood up in a heap; the deeps congealed in the heart of the sea.

The sea covered them; they sank as lead in the mighty waters.

Who is like thee, O LORD? Who is like thee, majestic in holiness, terrible in glorious deeds, doing wonders?

Thou didst stretch out thy right hand, and the earth swallowed them.

Thou hast led in thy steadfast love the people whom thou hast redeemed; thou hast guided them by thy strength to thy holy abode.'

They were pastoralists; their ancestral homelands welcomed them. Dan settled to the west of Jerusalem with Judah south of them and Simeon around Beer Sheba on the west of the Dead Sea. Ruben settled to the south of Ammon on the east side.

A TENT IN THE PASTURELANDS OUTSIDE HEBRON, CANAAN

June 1439 BC

Yahmose was breaking down his tent as Alue wandered by.

Alue asked, but it was not a question. He simply could not believe it. "You're going to return?"

Yahmose continued with his task, not even looking up. "I told you I have to."

"I know, I know, but I still can't believe you're doing this. That prophecy happened three hundred years ago. And it's so vague that you can't be sure you are interpreting it correctly."

"God gave the prophecy to Abraham. It was a promise. He said, 'Go from your kindred and your father's land to the land that I have prepared for you. And, I will make of you a great nation. I will bless you and make your name great, so you will be a blessing. I will bless those who bless you, and him who curses you I will curse; and by you, all the families of the earth shall bless themselves.' God did not promise to give this land to a portion of Abraham's progeny. God did not promise to make only some of Abraham's descendants into a great nation. God's promise applied to everyone. Our brothers and sisters remain in Egypt; Egypt is not their home. They are sojourners. If I do not go back and remind them of who they are, they will abandon their roots and become Egyptians. They will turn their backs on God, and God will withdraw His blessing from them. God does not give promises lightly; and, when He does, He keeps them. I stand in the line and lineage of Abraham. It is my duty; I must return."

"But you detoured to Hebron, just to return to Egypt? Why didn't you just stay there?"

"Because I did not really detour. Bringing our people back to Hebron was necessary. Now, returning is necessary. With God, sometimes a detour is the shortest journey."

"But if you return, you'll be enslaved like they've done to those who remained."

Yahmose stood, still holding a tent pole in his hand, looking at his friend. "No, slavery is not the correct translation from Egyptian to Hebrew. They still buy our meat and wool. They have not taken our sheep and goats. They have not taken our weapons. Therefore, we are not slaves. The proper term is corvée labor. It is a tax of labor instead of money. What they have done is double the labor tax. It is now six years of a man's life instead of three. Our men have gone to Saqqara to build a temple complex for their crocodile god, Sobek. That is not slavery."

"They will force you to serve on their labor gangs."

"Yes, that's right."

"They will never allow you to come back to Hebron."

"Yes, that's right. For me, it is a one-way trip. Hebron will again be a dream, but never a home." He paused, his eyes looking inward more than at Alue. "God grants everyone skills and abilities. He granted intelligence and wisdom to my grandfather, Ramose. Ramose served God and Egypt, and Egypt rewarded his service. They commemorate him with a stone memorial at the entrance to the academy. My father spent his talents on his own advantage. As much as he benefited Egypt, he treated others as pawns to manipulate to his own profit. Today, Egypt has erased his accomplishments from memory. No one knows where his body lies. No one cares.

"Like my grandfather, God has granted me intelligence and wisdom. Like him, I choose to serve to God's greater glory. I choose to leave the world a better place for my having lived. There will be no stone memorial for me, but I do not need it. God will remember me for being faithful, even if my descendants may not.

"This is the task God has given me. It is my duty. I may wish that God had chosen someone else, but He has not. He created me for this. This is who I am. I may not get everything that I want in life, but God will give me what I need. He has given my life meaning. He will be with me every step of the way; He will share my life. He is a true Father. He has shared my joy with me; He will share my hardship.

"Because of what I do today, someday, one of my descendants will bring our people out of Egypt. There will be a second exodus. God promised us this land. He will remain faithful.

"He did not promise freedom from hardship. I am going to face my share of that hardship. All He asks is faithfulness. For me, and my house, we will follow the Lord. It is my duty to God. I will believe. I will remain faithful."

An hour later, Alue watched as Yahmose, his family, and his flocks and herds disappeared over the horizon on their return to Egypt.

He shook his head in disbelief; he could not have done what he just witnessed.

www.ingramcontent.com/pod-product-compliance
Lightning Source LLC
Chambersburg PA
CBHW070222030726
47505CB00006B/1789